Stealing His Heart

Historical Western Romance

Nancy Lynn White

Copyright © 2023 Nancy Lynn White

All rights reserved.

Dedication

To the cherished memories of my late parents, Don and Kathleen Grist, I earnestly aspire to have brought you a sense of pride. Additionally, I extend my heartfelt regards to my sister, Linda, my daughter, Mindy, and my niece, Diane.

Acknowledgment

I want to say thank you for two of the best critique partners I have ever had.

Kelley Amrein and Elyse Garrett

Contents

Dedication i
Acknowledgment ii
Chapter One 1
   1844, The Columbus Female Benevolent Society, Columbus, Ohio 1
Chapter Two 33
   December 9, 1859, Broke 33
   December 17, 1859, The Bible Goes to Jail 39
   December 19, 1859, Chicago, Pinkerton National Detective Agency 40
   December 21, 1859, Split Profits with Victims 49
Chapter Three 55
   December 21, 1859, Go West 55
   December 23, 1859, Manna from Heaven 63
   December 26, 1859, Pony Express is Hiring 76
   December 28, 1859, The Adoptees Arrive 76
Chapter Four 82
   January 2, 1860, The Jeweler 82
   January 6, 1860, Prepared For the Oregon Trail 87
   January 15, 1860, Columbus, Ohio, Digging Up Dirt 95

Chapter Five ... 102
January 27, 1860, Philipp Hangs ... 102
January 27, 1860, Cincinnati, Ohio, The Truth Hurts ... 124

Chapter Six ... 131
January 28, 1860, Rescued ... 131
January 28, 1860, An Answered Prayer ... 138

Chapter Seven ... 150
January 29, 1860, Who's the Adult Here? ... 150

Chapter Eight ... 170
February 3, 1860, A Meeting of the Minds ... 170
February 15, 1860, The villain Frets ... 179

Chapter Nine ... 195
March 9, 1860, The Big Sandy, Nebraska ... 195
March 15, 1860, Hire a Detective ... 219

Chapter Ten ... 226
March 15, 1860, Innocent? ... 226
April 4, 1860, Carrie Darns a Sock ... 228
April 4, 1860, Zeke in & JT and Billy Out ... 234

Chapter Eleven ... 253
April 7, 1860, Where Did Billy Go? ... 253
April 15, 1860, Philipp's Guilty ... 262

Chapter Twelve ... 289
April 20, 1860, Carrie Resigns ... 289

April 20-21, 1860, Baptismal of Sorts 296
April 21, 1860, Hangover 302

Chapter Thirteen 319
May 1, 1860, The Muddle 319
May 10, 1860, St. Joseph Rebound 326

Chapter Fourteen 339
May 15, 1860, Mrs. Lipton's Letter 339
May 15, 1860, Assaulted 342

Chapter Fifteen 362
May 16, 1860, The Morning After 362
May 17, 1860, JT Proposes 377

Chapter Sixteen 389
May 20, 1860, The Unnoticed Clue 389

Chapter Seventeen 419
May 20, 1860, Will I Go To Prison? 419
May 20, 1860, Bushwhacked 421

Chapter Eighteen 445
May 21, 1860, Hank's Letter to Leticia 445
June 18, 1860, Billy's Adoption 455
June 25, 1860, Drunk 462
June 26, 1860, The Adopted California Children 472

Chapter Nineteen 478
July 1, 1860, War and Slavery 478

July 1, 1860, Billy Kidnapped 482
Chapter Twenty 513
   August 20, 1860, New Orleans, Louisiana 513
Chapter Twenty-One 549
   October 26, 1860, Waiting in Texas 549
   November 15, 1860, At Last 552
Chapter Twenty-Two 572
   November 17, 1860, Wedding Day 572
   December 20, 1860, San Francisco At Last 581

Chapter One

1844, The Columbus Female Benevolent Society, Columbus, Ohio

Five-year-old Carrie writhed and thrashed, bowing her back and viciously flaying as her Mama pushed her into the outstretched arms of a stranger. They were new to this country. Everyone was a stranger and Carrie recognized no one. When her mother kissed Carrie on her hands and said, "I'm sorry, my baby," her heart lurched. She couldn't understand what was happening, but it felt like a goodbye. A voice in her head was telling her to hold on to Mama, to not let go. And so, she floundered in the stranger's arms, desperately trying to get away as an uncontrollable trembling took hold of her shaky limbs. She gasped for air as her sobs became too heavy for her tiny body to bear. Then she let out a loud scream and grabbed a lock of her mother's hair in her fist.

"No, Mama, I'll be good." She sobbed, holding on to her mama's hair tightly.

Untangling Carrie's fingers, mama tucked a Bible under her arm, tears streaming down her face, her voice unsteady and trembling she said, "Baby, take care of this. You must never lose it. This will protect you."

Carrie let the Bible slide to the ground, her mind going haywire from all the thoughts racing, wondering what was happening, wondering what would happen next. The strange woman holding her prisoner picked up the fallen bible from the floor with one hand while the other held her tightly, keeping her locked in. Mama glanced over toward Papa in the wagon and then back at Carrie, wiping the tears from her face.

For a split second, Carrie thought she might do something. She might take Carrie and run away, that she might protect her but the small flicker of rebellion that had appeared on her face left as quickly as it came as her father growled.

"Come, voman. Schnell!"

There were days when Carrie knew she had to stay away from her father. Today was one of those days. There was no love lost on his face, no remorse. His face was a shadow of nothing but anger. Anger of being made to wait. Anger as her mother dared to defy him for a few more seconds with Carrie.

She turned towards Carrie as she cradled her soft face, their noses only inches apart. She stroked her cheek fondly, her face a picture of absolute misery as she said, "Carrie, keep this with you." She tapped the Bible with work-worn knuckles.

"Don't lose it." she murmured through choked tears. Carrie looked up and saw her Mama's eyes drop away, as more tears fell from her eyes, dripping all over her clothes and the floor. She took out a pale pink handkerchief which had flowers embroidered on the corner from her sleeve and wiped away her tears.

"Be good for Mama," she said as she placed a fist over her heart, indicating herself, "and grow strong." She pushed Carrie's chestnut hair away which had been plastered to her forehead due to the heat and her constant flailing as she kissed her forehead.

"I'm sorry mein baby, it was not by my hand, I never wanted this. Try to forgive me if you can." She said, her voice filled with sorrow as she turned away and walked towards the Conestoga wagon where her husband had been waiting for her impatiently.

"Dumme Frau!" Her angry husband barked. She hurriedly climbed into the wagon and took a seat beside her husband who whipped the horses into action.

Confused and scared, Carrie began screaming, "Mama, Stop!"

No amount of wriggling or thrashing, however was resulting in freedom, and so she resorted to biting the woman. She sunk her teeth into the woman's hand who let out a small shriek and dropped Carrie. Her feet hit the ground; however, she was free but was still unable to run after her Mama.

The woman shook her hand as she complained, "Ouch, that hurts." Using her free hand, she grabbed Carrie, tightly holding her.

Carrie had no idea what the woman was saying or what anyone else said. She stood on the threshold of the orphanage sobbing. She couldn't understand why her mother was doing this to her. Her father had never liked her, but she thought that meant he wouldn't speak to her or love her as he loved her brother. She did not think it would mean that he would abandon her at an orphanage. After all, whoever heard of an orphan whose parents were still alive? How could they leave their only daughter here all alone? Why wouldn't they let her go with them? Did they not love her?

She reached out toward the wagon's retreating silhouette with a free hand as it headed into the setting sun, hoping they would come back not bothering to wipe away the never-ending tears.

Carrie screamed as loudly as she could. Her little brother's face appeared between the canvas flaps at the back of the wagon. He waved at her sadly, and she could tell he was crying, and scared. She felt a pang in her heart. Part of her wanted to hold her brother and comfort him, the other part was angry. What right did he have to cry? He was not the one being abandoned.

Neither her mama nor her father looked back. They would be out of sight if this woman didn't release her soon. The woman transferred Carrie's care to an older girl.

"As long as I live, I'll never understand people like them." The woman shook her head and pulled Carrie's attention from the retreating wagon to the older girl standing next to her.

She tucked Carrie's Bible under Ruth's arm. "Ruth, this is Carrie; she's from Germany and doesn't speak English yet. I would like you to be her buddy since you speak German. Please ensure she gets something to eat and show her around the place until the headmistress assigns a bed and a job." Then she bent down, using her apron to wipe the tears from Carrie's face. "Ruth, please tell her what I'm saying."

"Yes, 'em."

"You'll be all right here, sweetheart. It won't take any time at all to fit in with us. We'll take a little getting used to, that's all. Don't fret; Ruth will watch after you." She soothed Carrie with a friendly pat on the shoulder and hurried off.

Carrie cowered at the stranger; she seemed to be a young girl, only a little older than Carrie, but what had happened to her skin? It resembled the Swiss chocolate Mama would buy if she'd been especially good. She wondered if she had licked her if Ruth would taste sweet, but she didn't dare.

Switching to German, Ruth said, "Come away now, child," tugging Carrie's hand. "There's no use crying over those no-account low lives calling themselves your ma and pa. They done gone off and left you here. Whatever you was before, you a Buckeye now."

Ruth tugged Carrie further into the building. She turned for one last look, but they were gone. She whimpered but let Ruth drag her along. Then, with a sweep of her head, she absorbed her surroundings. The worn plank floors thudded below her feet as she walked. Carrie looked down at her feet. The brown floor may have lacked varnish, but it sure did stand up for inspection, clean as anything despite feet dragging through it nearly all the time.

She looked at the walls next to her which gleamed as white as lightning striking at midnight, whiter than the first snow. She couldn't help but wonder how much effort it must take to keep the walls so white. 'They must whitewash them every morning.' She thought to herself. The nearest wall craved to be touched. Carrie ran a hand along the wall as she and Ruth progressed.

"All us'n here wish someone would come for us, but it never happens. You best set your mind on it; we your family now." Ruth draped an arm around Carrie's shoulder. "We ain't so bad."

Ruth's words bounced around inside her head as if hollow. Fear swelled in her throat until it threatened to burst from her like a blood-curdling scream. It can't be true. They could not have possibly left me here to rot. They have to come back for me. What will happen to me if they don't?

Ruth cut into Carrie's musing, "You not lucky at all, girl, you done got here on a Monday. Wild greens and beans tonight, and I guarantee you will hate them later if you don't like them now." The older girl scanned her briefly and noticed her hand on the wall. "Girl, you better not let the headmistress catch you messing with those walls."

Carrie snatched her hand back and broke into tears.

Ruth shushed her and patted her back while she said, "I'm sorry I didn't mean to scare you. It's just that the headmistress is real picky about those walls."

Carrie continued to sob. It was like a dam had erupted within her and the tears refused to stop spilling out.

Ruth gathered Carrie into a hug. Then, dragging her to the floor, she pulled Carrie into her lap and gently wiped away the tears with her threadbare skirt. Ruth rocked back and forth while singing a hymn to calm Carrie. Carrie soon stopped crying and tucked a weary head under Ruth's chin while sucking her thumb, trying to muster up the courage to hope that this was a dream, that her mama would be back.

Ruth could tell the girl was beginning to get lost in her thoughts again and so she asked her a question to break her chain of thought and distract her.

"Why do you have gray hair when the rest is dark brown?"

"Mama says it's a birthmark." Replied Carrie.

"Wow, it's been there since you were born? What will they think of next? I've got a birthmark, too. Master branded me when I was born. I'll show it to you later because it's hidden when I'm dressed but don't ever ask me about it again. Hear?"

Carrie nodded in fear.

Ruth's tone switched back to friendly after the stern warning, "The mistress always tells us cleanliness is next to godliness.' Whenever a mark appears on one of them walls, we must whitewash them again. Best you keep your hands to yourself and not create more work, or you won't find many friends around here."

Ruth placed a hand around Carrie's upper arm. Her middle finger and thumb almost met. "You kinda skinny. When the mistress asks what you're good at, better say kitchen work, or she'll have you working in the garden all day in the sun or doing laundry until your arms have gone numb and fallen plumb off. That's where I work. You don't want to go there. If you end up in the kitchen, I sure enough hope you learn to bake a decent loaf of bread. Half the time, it doesn't rise, and we gotta eat it anyways. Don't nothing go to waste around here. My drawers have so many patches on 'em I done forgot what color they used to was."

Mama said she asked too many questions. So, Carried decided it was better to not ask Ruth any questions. Carrie didn't want to make Ruth mad. Carrie and her family had gotten kicked off the boat prematurely because of her sickly brother, Eduard. That's when papa became mean to mama and herself because women were useless, he said. I think mama worked hard because she was busy all day. And I'm not sick. He wanted boys to work the land with him when they finally reached their farm yet all mama could give him was a daughter and a sickly son.

Ruth swung their joined hands back and forth as they walked. "At least you're a white girl. Mistress starts all us darky girls with emptying and cleaning the chamber pots." Ruth nodded her head. "Maybe you is lucky after all."

Carrie peeked upward into Ruth's smiling face and thought, she sure didn't feel lucky. If this was luck, Carrie hoped to be unlucky from now on. She had fallen into a dark hole in the ground, tumbling head over tail end, reaching for something to latch onto, and failing. Her screams fell on deaf ears. Something twisted and fell flat inside her. Something heavy. Nothing in life will ever be the same again. The trembling returned. The only lifeline in sight was Ruth.

Carrie squeezed the girl's hand, knowing she was the only person she knew.

"Girl! I ain't goin' nowhere. Let up on squeezing my hand like you're drowning." Ruth looked Carrie over. Her face softened as she asked, "Don't you talk none?"

No one had ever asked Carrie to speak before. Ever since she could remember, it had been Carrie's job to stay quiet and invisible. She had to pretend she didn't exist or her papa would lose his temper. But while on shipboard, she listened while others learned the language of their new home. Carrie vowed that she'd learn whatever Ruth taught her. She wouldn't annoy her by asking too many questions and hoped that being a girl didn't matter because Ruth was a girl herself. She might as well start now.

"What's a buckeye and a darky?"

"You're in Ohio. The state tree is the buckeye. So, you're a Buckeye. And a darky is poor, abused people with dark skin like mine.

"How do you know to speak German here?" asked Carried timidly.

"I don't speak it anymore since I ran away north, but the headmistress caught me saying it to myself. So, now she makes me help the German-speaking children." Replied Ruth ruefully.

"Do you taste like chocolate?"

"No one's ever asked me that. I don't know." She held an arm out toward Carrie. "Have a lick and see."

Carrie stuck out her tongue and licked Ruth's forearm. "No, you taste just like me."

She threw both her arms around Ruth's waist as she grabbed onto her and said, "I'm scared. Will you be my friend?"

Ruth hugged her back and that was answer enough for Carrie.

November 23, 1859, Thanksgiving Eve

When she awoke on her birthday, the one the orphanage assigned to her, not like she remembered the one she had when she had still been with her parents, Carrie thought, "Thank you, Lord. I've never been happier in my life."

She sat up and stretched, gathering her long chestnut hair in both arms up off her neck, tying them up in a bun. Greeting herself, she said, "Good morning, Mrs. Wagner," and then bounded out of bed. She loved the sound of her new name.

"Carrie! Carrie Wagner! You best open that door before I get there." Ruth's passionate cries from the street pulled Carrie away from her holiday preparations in the kitchen. Then, wiping her delicate hands on a towel, she pulled the heavy wooden door open to one of the coldest autumn winds in recent history and found her best friend rushing up the walkway to her German Village neighborhood cottage.

Carrie called back, "You sound like a circus barker. Since when do you run down the street caterwauling my name? What's all the excitement about?"

As was their childhood habit, Carrie and Ruth kissed each other's cheeks as they greeted one another. Then, breathless, Ruth staggered past her into the house in a blur of green and red material. While she shrugged out of her coat, Carrie closed the door behind her friend. "Come into the kitchen. I'm making dressing for the orphanage's thanksgiving dinner."

But Ruth didn't follow her into the kitchen. Carrie went back to the front door to find her friend in tears. "What's the matter, Ruth?"

Ruth and Carrie walked into the kitchen together, where Ruth hugged her tightly, declaring, "Remember, I love you."

"I love you, too. What's the commotion about?"

Still gasping for air, Ruth rubbed Carrie's warm, soft hand with her other hand. It seemed like she had run miles to come see Carrie. Carrie frowned as she watched Ruth try to either catch her breath or gather the courage to say what she had to say. Either way, it was worrying Carrie who asked, "What on earth is the matter?"

Ruth looked at her sadly as she bit her lip and lowered her voice to break the horrible news, "Brace yourself, Carrie. I've got bad news. I'm sorry to say Mr. Wagner's bank got robbed, and no one can find him. The Sheriff says one theory is the thieves forced Philipp to bring the money to them."

Carrie pulled her hand from Ruth's and slid into a dining chair with a hand over her mouth. Did she hear Ruth correctly? Her heart raced, and something squeezed her innards. At only twenty-one, she can't lose her soul mate. She placed her palm on her abdomen to soothe the agitation until she found out what she needed to know. "Has Philipp been harmed?"

Her eyes locked onto Ruth's face searching for the truth.

Carrie chewed on a fingernail while wondering if her curse had returned. Stop. It's way too early to be thinking like that. She must remain hopeful.

When Carrie first introduced Philipp to Ruth, her best friend immediately disliked her betrothed, claiming he was hiding something or didn't have true intentions towards Carrie. Ruth launched a campaign to change her mind about marrying the man. But Philipp Wagner had already claimed Carrie's heart and no amount of convincing from Ruth could change her mind.

They seldom disagreed, but the subject of her marriage usually clenched Ruth's jaw. Despite being married to him, Ruth still had no space for Phillip in her heart which is why it was both foolish and easier to believe that Ruth was perhaps playing a sick joke on her.

"Stop with your foolishness! These jokes about Philipp are as old as last week's bread." Carrie said.

Ruth wrung her hands, her expression stung as she replied indignantly, "He's your husband now. I wouldn't josh you about this."

"Tell me then, is Philipp all right or not?" Her voice quivered and sounded a bit too loud, even to herself. She jumped out of her chair and paced.

"I'm not sure of Philipp's condition. The Sheriff just said he was missing and to tell you he's coming to call on you in a few minutes. When he gets here, you can ask him all your questions." Ruth pulled up one of the dining chairs next to her and collapsed into it.

Lord, you granted me a miracle. Please keep him safe. Stop; way too early to be thinking like that. Try to remain hopeful. A flush climbed up her neck to her face. She pulled the tortoiseshell pins out of her thick chestnut hair, sending it down her back and allowing her scalp to breathe. "Were the tellers working at the time? Did they notice anything?"

"Oh, I forgot that part. Earl Butler said Philipp came out of his office just after noon, with a money belt bulging under his shirt, then left the bank."

Mulling that over for a second, Carrie said, "Maybe he was forced to take the money to the thieves. My Philip wouldn't rob his bank." Carrie and Ruth jumped when they heard a heavy knock at the front door.

Ruth ushered the sheriff in and guided him to another dining chair at the table.

Eager for more details, Carrie poured a cup of coffee for the Sheriff without asking if he wanted one. "Please, Sheriff Huffman, tell me what's happened so far." Little beads of sweat broke out on her upper lip, and she slipped her arm through Ruth's for courage.

After hunkering down into his curly lamb coat, he wrapped his white fingertips around the steaming cup as worry lines streaked across his forehead, plainly visible after he removed his hat. "Mrs. Wagner, I would typically ask to speak to you alone, but the two of you always come as a set. I am sorry I had to come since the wedding happened only two weeks ago. But, unfortunately, bank robbery trumps the honeymoon.

Please don't tell me he's dead. Give me hope. She prayed he had come as a friend instead of the law.

With a formal tone of voice, the Sheriff launched into the story. "Mr. Wagner robbed the bank of $18,000 and left a little after noon with a money belt strapped to his waist. Maybe some criminal gang threatened to hurt you to force him to rob his bank, or Philipp robbed his bank."

Carrie gasped. Ruth grabbed her hand in both of hers. "But is he all right?" All her happiness lies in Philipp's hands.

Carrie noticed the shadow of the lawman's two-day beard as he rubbed his rough hand on his chin. After clearing his throat, he continued, "As far as I know, he's finer than frog hair, but a preponderance of evidence says he's a thief."

Carrie's head jerked back.

"Witnesses report him consorting with unsavory characters and neglecting you."

Shocked, Carrie said, "Neglecting me? Who in the world told you such a lie?" It's true, but repeating gossip spoken against her husband before proof doesn't interest her much. She won't have people denigrate him.

The sheriff said, "It's common knowledge around town. So why would you lie for him?"

Carrie chewed on her lip but eventually said, "Because he's my husband, and I'm the suspected neglected one. I'm not being neglected. Where's your proof?"

The sheriff shook his head. "I have legal permission to ask you personal questions, like do you know how he spends his leisure time?"

Tears rolled down her cheeks. Her heart was breaking. Ruth rose beside her, and Carrie rested her head against her midsection. "Philipp's guilt can't be true. Not Philipp." Carrie needed to declare ignorance and seek her bed. Bile rose in her throat. She had thought her fairytale marriage impervious to assault and rubbed her forehead in disbelief. *Philipp was my one true love.* This couldn't be!

"Mrs. Wagner. Your husband has committed a serious crime. It is my responsibility to investigate. I realize you need time to allow all this to sink in, but I need facts to solve this crime immediately. So please put your breaking heart aside until this interview is over." His tone sounded like the president briefing the troops on bad news.

Something in the pit of her stomach warned her of more to come. Oh, Lord, what could it be? Then, raising her tone to meet his, she asked, "What information do you require?" My truth was Philipp Wagner. No matter what gibberish the Sheriff shoveled at her in her home, only Philipp and she knew the strength of their love. Philipp would never rob his bank. People depended on him.

Ruth spoke up, "Why are you upsetting her like this?"

The sheriff's eyes bore into Ruth. "Well, Ruth, because Philipp stole the townsfolk's money and ran off with his unsavory cronies, I'm paid to find him and bring the money back."

Ruth's harrumph got Carrie's attention because, usually, that was a bad sign. "Ruth, please, he's only doing his job. It's not his fault my constitution isn't as strong as yours." Ruth squeezed her hand for a moment.

Carrie thought about Philipp's supposed cronies and who they could be. She came up blank. He's never introduced her to anyone. Thanks to the sheriff, she knew where her husband had been every night until dawn, with his cronies. She only laid eyes on him when he crawled into bed every morning just before sunrise, bringing the unpleasant odors of stale perfume and cigar smoke. He never cared to be intimate and only stayed until he had bathed and had breakfast.

Then he'd run off to the office, and she wouldn't see him again until noon when she delivered his lunch. He'd kiss her cheek, and she wouldn't see him again until dawn. Strange behavior, but who was she to question her husband's comings and goings? She thought her husband was kind, and he merely allowed time for her to adjust to marriage. But she acknowledged how villainous somebody could interpret his daily routine. She would have happily continued in blind ignorance. Philipp wouldn't leave her and run off.

The sheriff broke into her thoughts. "When did you see him last?"

Carrie dragged in a shaky breath. "I took his lunch to him at noon. He thanked me, kissed my cheek, and I left. We didn't discuss the bank robbery."

"Can you think of anything that could help me find him?"

Goodness gracious, if he wasn't at the bank, she couldn't find him herself if she wanted to. Should she confess she only sees him from predawn to post-breakfast? How could that possibly help in the investigation? Far too embarrassing to admit. Even Ruth wasn't privy to that information. This was one situation where her invisibility as an orphan came in handy.

Carrie dropped her eyes to her lap. "I can't think of where he would be. Do other wives track where their husbands are every minute of the day?" She would never question Philipp after making her the happiest woman on earth. "What's being done to find him?"

She searched her pockets for a handkerchief, pausing only to wipe the tears away with the back of her hand.

"Wade, at the train station, witnessed Mr. Wagner board the southbound train to Cincinnati at 1 p.m. He's left my jurisdiction. I notified the Sheriff in Cincinnati to be on the lookout, and our City Council wants to hire a Pinkerton agent to track him down and retrieve the money." The Sheriff offered his handkerchief.

"Thank you." Carrie held the handkerchief to her face while her shoulders shook and her throat closed on a choke. After a moment, "Then he's gone without me. Why would Philipp do this to her? Snapping out of a trance, she asked, "They won't hurt him, will they?"

The sheriff's eyes cut to her, "Carrie, he's a fugitive from the law. When they close in on him, if he tries to run or shoots at them, their job requires them to return fire and apprehend the fugitive, if possible, or bring him back dead, if necessary." He dropped his palm on the table, causing Carrie to tremble. "You need to understand how serious this is. Philipp Wagner is not the stars in your eyes kind of man."

What did he mean by that? She felt cold like someone had left the door open during a blizzard. She crossed her arms and gently rocked back and forth. Has Philipp abandoned her as her mother did? Time seemed to stop. Why would Philipp do this to her? Was she his one good deed before embarking on a life of crime? Was he saving her from obscurity?

"You don't think criminals forced him to do it?"

"I originally thought that a possibility because of the presence of the unsavory people he was dealing with, but I would not put my money on it. I'm still tracking all of them down. No one divulged anything about him being coerced so far."

The weight of her husband's sins hung from her heart, and she'd heard enough about her hero turned criminal for one day. Love and marriage—too ideal to be true, after all. History repeated itself. That stake her mother drove through her heart eons ago, which felt like yesterday, remained raw and angry. Philipp knew of her heartbreak and fear of betrayal, but had he callously tossed her fears aside, leaving her heart torn asunder? If so, this devastation's similarity to the abandonment by her mother finally finished her heart off. Perhaps Philipp was flesh, bone, and human, not the hero on the white steed as she dreamt. No, no, she must talk to him and hear the truth.

"Sheriff, I know nothing about the bank robbery. Therefore, I'm of little help to you. Philipp never mentioned a desire to commit financial suicide to me. If you don't mind, I would like to excuse myself to grieve and attend to my broken heart. Thank you for the information."

Ruth asked, "Is that everything, Sheriff?"

"Yeah, I guess that covers it for now. I'll keep you posted. Take care of each other. Good night." He grabbed his hat, and Ruth walked him out.

As soon as the door closed, Carrie dashed to the kitchen cabinet to retrieve the brandy, and she poured a finger's worth into a small utilitarian glass, unaware of the insult to the brandy.

Ruth joined her. "That's the first time I saw you take brandy between your monthlies." She poured a finger's worth for herself.

Curling a lip at Ruth's admonition, Carrie replied, "Jesus drank wine every day."

"I don't blame you for resorting to liquor. You've had quite the shock, but remember, you aren't Jesus, and this isn't wine," Ruth said as she slipped into her big sister role. "I know what you're thinking, but this is *not* your fault." Her free arm wrapped around Carrie's waist.

Carrie shook her head at Ruth's denial. "You forget, this is my second shot through the heart. Too young for brandy the first time." She watched out the north window of her kitchen. Due to the pastureland next to her cottage, she watched as the sheriff returned to his office. He walked like the king of his destiny, head up and back straight. Men were born lucky that way, but that doesn't stop her from starching her spine. *Where do I go to learn how to act like a man?*

"Oh, Ruth, you know where the blame lies. I'm cursed, unloved, and destined for spinsterhood. I had hoped and prayed to find love someday and thought it finally happened, but I should've known better. He made me forget the curse for a little while." Turning away from the window, she faced her friend. "You warned me, and I ignored you. My apologies."

The more practical of the duo grunted, "Nonsense." She knocked the cork back into the brandy bottle with her palm and shoved it back on the shelf.

Philipp noticed her, and he asked her out to dinner. The day she married him, he gave her the most precious gift she'd ever received, an identity, Mrs. Philipp Wagner, the banker's wife. At church, she got down on her knees and thanked the Lord for the gift of love and marriage for so long that her knees snapped when she walked home.

What evil lurked inside her to deserve abandonment by the people she loved? How can I trust anyone again? If the Sheriff is right, nothing but ashes remain. She placed her head on Ruth's shoulder and hugged her, whispering, "I love you."

Ruth soothed Carrie's back in lazy circles with her palm and whispered into her ear, "Don't you worry, I ain't ever leaving you."

"The same is true for me." Yes, she would rely on Ruth until her dying day. Her kind endearment reminded Carrie of when she was six and Ruth rescued her from the burning orphanage. Someone tried to pull Ruth out of the flames, but she kicked him and said, "Carrie's my only friend. If she burns, I burn too." She's more of a sister than a friend and, thankfully, not cursed.

Tonight, in her prayers, she must ask the Lord for a miracle intervention on Philipp's behalf.

<u>Matthew 16:9</u> *Do you still not understand? Don't you remember the five loaves for the five thousand, and how many basketfuls you gathered?*

Thanksgiving, 1859

On Thanksgiving morning, two children from the orphanage would drop by to pick up the turkey dressing Carrie had prepared yesterday as they did every thanksgiving. The children loved her turkey dressing and requested it every year since she became the head cook. She'd been out of the orphanage for five years but still contributed to the Thanksgiving and Christmas dinners. It was a minor task with a huge reward, and she really did not mind putting in the work for the children, after all, she had been one of them herself, and making dozens of children happy pleased her down to her toes.

Then, a little after 7:00 a.m., she heard the little darlings tapping at her door; she could gather from the squeaking outside they were excited. Someday she wanted a posse of children for herself. Maybe she's lost that dream, too now.

Opening the door with a big smile, she greeted them, "Good morning, Rose, and Tammy. How are you on this fine day?"

Both the children rushed in, leaving the cart that they had hauled with them outside. The autumn chill blew in with the children, and she hurried to close the door behind them. "We're fine, Carrie. Oh boy, that dressing sure smells good," Tammy quipped.

"For goodness' sake, come on, and I'll give you a taste if you don't tell. We don't want the other children to be cross with me, do we?"

Carrie led them to the kitchen. She bent to kiss each child on the forehead and fetched a couple of spoons. Pulling back the empty flour sack covering one pan, she scooped a healthy portion and gave it to Rose, and the same for Tammy. Then, she reshaped the remaining dressing in the pan. "Now, tell the cook to only bake it for twenty-five minutes, give or take."

They "mmmed" in unison, feeling the dressing at the back of their tongues; they were in rapt. Then Tammy asked, "Will you be here next year to make the turkey dressing? The headmistress told us you may not be because of all the trouble with your husband."

Rose had to squeeze in her opinion as well. "I don't like your husband because he's a bad man and ruined everything for us. I hope you stay Carrie."

God bless little children and their penchant for speaking their minds. "You two shouldn't be worried about that yet. It only just happened. No one knows the future. Carrie knelt before Rose, caressed her cheek, and said, "Sweetie, I married my husband because I loved him. Besides, it's not nice to say bad things about a woman's husband to her face. You'll understand that one day. Now, let's get these pans loaded into the wagon." She shrugged into her coat before grabbing some pans.

Rose twisted the toes of one foot into the floor. "I'm sorry, Carrie."

Looking down at Rose's misty eyes, she decided that wouldn't do for a holiday. "Thank you, Rose; remember, 'life is a struggle, but every lesson learned is God's way of helping you grow stronger.'" She laid the pans aside and hugged her. "Bless you, little one."

On the second trip out to the cart, two of Carrie's neighbors waited beside it. The anger evident on their faces nearly drove her back into the house.

Mrs. Blanchard attempted to speak, but Carrie raised a finger to her lips. "Shh, please wait until the children leave." Holding eye contact with the woman, she sent the children back to fetch the remaining pans. With all the turkey dressing tucked in the cart, she kissed their foreheads again, despite her frosty lips, and wished them a Happy Thanksgiving. Off they went trotting down the path happily, waving to her. Like a mother hen, she watched the children until they were safely out of earshot.

Reluctant to hear Mrs. Blanchard's rant about her husband, she greeted her like her mercantile days. "Now, Mrs. Blanchard, how may I help you?"

The woman wagged a finger in Carrie's face and spat words on the verge of exploding. "You can help me by getting my money back. We saved in your husband's bank to buy our place. Then he stole it from us. You must know something about this. A man spends half his time with his wife." Her lip curled, and her eyes darkened.

Mr. Pollard said, minus the wagging finger, "She's right Mrs. Wagner; we find it impossible that you don't know something about that bank robbery. Please help us."

By this time, the winter wind caused her knees to shake, and she crossed her arms to keep warm, but she wouldn't invite them into her home. Not when they talk about her husband like this and accuse her of lying when she had not done anything.

"Don't you think I would've helped you by now if I knew anything? All I can say is what little I know." She paced back and forth. Generating some heat, she hoped. "I'm just as shocked as anybody else in this town. My husband stole money, ran off, and abandoned me without so much as a pat on the head. Not even a note. He told me nothing and left me penniless. I'm in the same position you are, maybe worse." Finally, she stopped in front of Mrs. Blanchard and looked her in the eye. "He set me up for the vultures to pick over." Oh, dear, how did that slip out? One more thing to ask forgiveness for in my prayers tonight.

Mrs. Blanchard huffed, probably stifling her temper at being compared to a vulture.

Mr. Pollard said, "I'm sorry we bothered you, Mrs. Wagner." He took Mrs. Blanchard's elbow as they turned to leave.

However, Mrs. Blanchard still had something stuck in her craw. "Did you hear? The City Council hired a Pinkerton agent to find your husband and our money."

The statement sucked her breath away at first. "The sheriff said it was a possibility. So, they decided. I hope you get your money back."

"I don't believe a word flying out of your lying mouth. The two of you plotted this as payback for the town who never adopted you, didn't you? That innocent-looking face doesn't fool me one tiny bit."

Caught by surprise, she couldn't reply. But Mr. Pollard's capability to speak didn't fail him. "Mrs. Blanchard, there's no need to add to her suffering."

"The hell with her suffering, she's making all of us suffer. I am telling you she is in on it." The old crane shook a fist at her violently.

The pleasures of home and hearth called out to her, and she dashed for the door as her chilled-to-the-bone legs would allow. She told her neighbors more than she should. She didn't react well when poked with a stick. An orphan learns to stand up for herself early, but that information will take on a life of its own by tomorrow. She'd gifted the town with a lot of ammunition to torture her with now that her invisibility had returned. It wouldn't surprise her to read about it in tomorrow's newspaper. Being cursed was worse than being an orphan, even if one led to another.

Proverbs 16:29 *The violent entice their neighbor and lead them down a path that is not good.*

Chapter Two

December 9, 1859, Broke

After her fight with Mrs. Blanchard, the details of their fight spread like wildfire and the details would soon became a game of Chinese whisper. Soon, the local newspaper released an article detailing the incident adding further fuel to the fire. The entirety of the town became adamant about her guilt. They were convinced that she was involved in the bank robbery because of that darn newspaper article.

She became a social pariah. People refused to meet her eyes and when they did, she found nothing but hatred and loathing within them. The sheriff came for a follow up and it was then that he suggested that she lay low for a while and restrict her movements around town which Carrie agreed to do.

However, reality soon began to dawn; the mortgage was due. Groceries needed purchasing, and wood for the fireplace and stove lay absent leaving the oven stone cold. After searching every nook and cranny of the house from top to bottom, she realized bitterly that Philipp had not left a single dollar behind on her behalf. She would now have to resort to using her personal savings, which luckily Phillip knew nothing about.

A wife's property becomes her husband's when they marry, but Carrie had been sewing money into her corset since she started working at the mercantile. No matter how many people used banks, Carrie could never make peace with the idea of someone else having control over her money. The bank robbery proved why she avoided banks. Orphans make the best hiders. When you grow up with hundreds of kids, you learn to protect what is yours, you have to be clever to hide something from the other orphans. All those years of concealing her belongings and getting away with it seemed to have culminated in this moment.

Philipp did not love her; this she knew now. However, what she failed to understand was, if he planned on running away and partaking in such vile crimes, why would he involve her? What purpose did she serve in his criminal plans? Why would he need to be married for two weeks before turning to crime? He had showered her with gifts and professed his love, only to smear her new name all over town.

<u>Philippians 4:6</u> *Be anxious for nothing, but in everything by prayer and supplication, with thanksgiving, let your requests be made known to God.*

December 16, 1859, Pinkerton Agent Murdered

Three weeks after his last visit, the sheriff knocked on Carrie's door again. She no longer greeted visitors with a smile. "Afternoon, Sheriff, come in." Directing him to the parlor, she chose the settee, and he went straight towards the fireplace and stood before the roaring fire. She can't blame him; the temperature outside is cold enough to snap clothes off the line.

He removed his hat and fiddled with the brim. "I'm sorry to tell you this, but the news has worsened. Yesterday, Mr. Wagner shot and killed a Pinkerton agent in a Cincinnati hotel room."

Carrie gasped. Her mouth dropped, and her eyes widened at the outlandish accusation. Murder? It can't be true! He was a thief yes but why on earth would he do such an awful thing? It made no sense.

The sheriff shifted noticeably and said, "There was a woman in the room, but she escaped before the authorities arrived."

Carrie staggered a little. A woman? Maybe he suffered an injury and needed a nurse. Her heart was in her mouth and she felt breathless.

"The other hotel guests kept Mr. Wagner from escaping until the sheriff arrived. They arrested him for murder and will bring him back to Columbus."

An cry of despair fell from Carrie's lips, "What woman, who was she? Are you sure she was with my Phillip?"

Carrie's head felt heavy, it felt like the weight of the world had been dropped upon her and all she wanted to do was close her ears and stop listening to this. She couldn't believe it. theft? Murder? And now an affair? She couldn't bear listening to the constant bombardment on her fairy tale marriage, on the wonderful man who had saved her from a dreary future and given her a new identity, a home, and so much love.

"Nobody knew who she was," the sheriff confessed. He couldn't help but pity Carrie. It was obvious that this young girl's entire world had been upended and her life would surely get harder from here once the townspeople were made aware of the latest update.

Giving the sheriff the side eye, she wrung her hands together as tears streamed down her face, she asked, "Are you sure about this? I didn't think Philipp capable of murder."

"He confessed." Murmured the sheriff softly.

Carrie's eyes blinked rapidly. Finally, she turned away and shielded her face.

"He's coming in on the train tomorrow, and I don't want to see you anywhere near the train station or the jail. Some yahoo will probably take it upon himself to seek revenge and they might harm you too."

Pulling herself together, she said, "I appreciate your concern for my safety, but I need to ask him what happened and why he did it. My husband owes me an explanation. It's the least he can do for me."

Sheriff Huffman shook his head. "Philipp Wagner owes you much more than that. You're a good woman and deserved better." He settled his hat on his head and headed to the door, "Good Evening, Mrs. Wagner," and let himself out and closed the door behind himself.

Two days later, one of Sheriff Huffman's deputies dropped by to deliver a note. This time, she poured a finger's worth of brandy before reading the news. It seemed that each time the sheriff visited, he brought upon nothing but bad news. She curled up in the comfortable leather chair in the parlor, removed the note from the envelope, and read:

Mrs. Wagner,

Again, I must apologize. Your husband has asked me to relay this information to you. He requests that you not visit him in jail or try to contact him.

He's not speaking with anyone.

Sheriff Huffman

So, this was it? This was all the explanation her cowardly husband was willing to give her? This was how knight in shining armor would treat her?

The last part of her that had some hope he might love her now shattered into a thousand pieces and she could feel her heart bleed. This was all the proof she needed, and it had been cowardly confessed in two sentences without an endearment.

He didn't love her one bit; she had merely been a pawn in his game.

She crumpled the note in her fist and tossed it into the fire. Then the tears came rolling down her cheeks.

A loving husband would want to spend his remaining time with his true love. That, coupled with the fact that they never consummated their marriage, proved there was another motive for him marrying her, but what? She thought he was giving her time to adjust to marriage. But that note helped her to rebuild the surrounding fortifications around her broken heart.

Please, Lord, help me conquer the rage that consumes my soul.

Ephesians 4:31-32 *Let all bitterness, wrath, anger, clamor, and evil speaking be put away from you, with all malice. And be kind to one another, tenderhearted, forgiving one another, even as God in Christ forgave you.*

December 17, 1859, The Bible Goes to Jail

Bright and early the following day, Carrie took her family Bible to the sheriff's office. The jail and the sheriff's office abutted, divided only by a heavy wooden door reinforced with metal strips, so there would be no danger of intruding on Philipp's need for privacy. The Bible was her mother's. She had given to her on the day she abandoned Carrie at the orphanage, insisting that she keep it close to her heart. She prayed he would find comfort in its pages. The Bible, printed in German, could easily be read by her husband, who was a first-generation German immigrant to America.

It also proved her German heritage as well. She never opened it because she didn't speak German.

She knew Phillip wouldn't see her and she did not even need to ask when she saw the sheriff's face droop with pity. She squared her shoulders; she would not have anyone's pity. She gave the bible to the sheriff and asked him if he could give it to Phillip. The sheriff took the bible and promised to give it to him.

Philipp confessed to the murder, negating the need for a trial, but he remained silent on the location of the bank loot and the identity of his cronies. A judge sentenced him to hang in front of the courthouse the next time the hangman's rotation brought him to Columbus.

So much for fairy tales and true love. She swore to herself that If ever another suitor dogs her tracks again, which she knew they certainly would not, she'll ask Ruth to shoot him.

Proverbs 19:17 *He who has pity on the poor lends to the* LORD, *And He will pay back what he has given.*

December 19, 1859, Chicago, Pinkerton National Detective Agency

On his last day as a Pinkerton Detective, JT Grant stood on the railroad platform waiting for the southbound train reading the newspaper when his eyes caught a story headline. "Rumored Co-conspirator in Pinkerton Agent's Murder Remains Unnamed During Trial."

"Dagnabit!" He folded the paper and stuck it under his arm. "Not again. This time I'm finding who did it." Then, lifting his satchel, he turned toward the street to hail a cab. Allowing the murderer of a loved one to escape justice without lifting a finger will never happen again on his watch, this he was sure of. The faces of those four butchers who had murdered his father had haunted his dreams for ten years. He'd recognize any of those bastards if he ever saw them again without a moment's hesitation.

Fifteen minutes later, JT found himself on the losing end of an argument with his former boss.

"No, JT, and that's my final word on the subject." Allan Pinkerton, Captain of the Pinkerton National Detective Agency, followed that statement with a solid thud of his fist to the desk. "Your letter of resignation has been accepted and filed. Go to that Texas ranch you and your brothers have worked on to pay off.

You've been talking my ear off about it for the last five years. Get out of my office. I have work to do."

JT Grant may be the quintessential Pinkerton agent. At medium height, a working man with good looks and a natural-born ability to blend in, no one ever suspects he's an undercover agent.

"Captain." JT meant to put up a fight if he had to. "Resignation or no resignation. If a woman contributed to Hank's murder, I'm tracking her down."

JT hung his wet overcoat on a hook on the wall outside the captain's office, slumped into one of the much-abused leather office chairs opposite Pinkerton's desk, and dropped his satchel to the floor.

Pinkerton rose to throw another log into the firebox. The Washington Street office faced north and lacked coziness because of the breath of St. Nick himself seeping in from every windowpane. Outside, the weather painted the Chicago cityscape to match a Currier and Ives winter engraving.

"You know darn well I don't send you out on cases involving women anymore." Turning from the hearth, he fixed JT with a knowing look. "You tarnished poor innocent Miss Carter's reputation so badly with your insistence of her guilt that I had to find the woman a suitable gentleman in Chicago to court her. Cost me $500. You remember that don't you?" snarled Pinkerton.

"I was still green then." JT shifted uncomfortably in his seat. "And you know, Captain, just because a woman cleans herself up more than once a week, wears calico, and attends church regularly doesn't mean she's a candidate for sainthood. Not in my book." JT shoved his fingers through wavy black hair, pushing it away from his face.

"Yes, I'm very familiar with that book of yours. Harris will follow up in Columbus." Pinkerton said.

"All due respect to Harris, but he wasn't Hank's best friend," JT said. "If the law couldn't find evidence of her involvement, we must investigate and find the missing proof ourselves." JT pulled his gloves off and slapped them against his thigh for emphasis.

"Like you, I thought the evidence about the mysterious woman would come forth at the trial, but not so." Pinkerton smoothed his waxed mustache. "Maybe she doesn't exist. But, the fact remains, you're not the only agent employed here." He waved a dismissal. "Harris can handle the job. Get on with your life. For God's sake, I can't believe you returned from the train station." Pinkerton licked his thumb and began sorting through the documents on the desk.

Not willing to be discharged out of hand, JT pushed the point. "Hank wasn't your standard Pinkerton agent.

He saved my life more than once.

A man couldn't have asked for a better friend.

Someone shot him in the back of the head.

He didn't have a chance in hell.

He's the reason I worked here.

He recommended me to you." Pinkerton did not glance up or stop sorting papers. Instead, JT slapped the Stetson he'd been holding onto the stack of papers in front of the captain. "Look at me, sir!"

Pinkerton leaned back in his chair with folded hands in his lap. The captain's eyes locked onto JT's. "The only reason being a Pinkerton suited you was because you wanted to track down that little heartbreaker that ran off with your money years ago, don't try to kid yourself that there was any reason but that."

JT leaned forward with elbows on his knees and hands clasped as he locked his jaw before responding, "My past is my business. Except for the Carter case, I've been the best agent next to Hank for the last five years. I'm a professional. I get the job done; you already know that."

Pinkerton arched a brow.

JT took a cleansing breath. "I took my best friend's wife and children back home to her parents after Hank's funeral two months ago. All the way to Virginia. I promised Clara I would find the murderers." He paused as the grief-stricken vision of Clara Lipton returned to haunt him. She was the lucky one. Society allowed the wife public displays of mourning.

"She knows we've done our best, boy."

"I don't make idle promises! It's the last thing she deserves. I promise you I will find out if a woman colluded in Hank's murder, and if she did I will track her down to the ends of this earth and bring her to justice. If she was involved, she must hang as well, not just the bastard who pulled the trigger." JT growled.

Pinkerton reached for a cigar and lit it. He sighed deeply. "You'll go even if I send someone else, won't you?"

"Darn right, I will."

"What about the commitment to your brothers?" He rolled the cigar between his fingers. The cold draft caused the cigar smoke to waft toward the open office door. "Darn draft!" The captain reached into the bottom drawer of his desk and retrieved a bottle of fine Kentucky Bourbon. He poured two fingers for himself. "I'd offer you a drink, but I know you abstain. God only knows why."

JT shook his head and promptly steered the conversation back to business. "Captain, my brothers will understand because I haven't told them I'm coming home yet. I won't be leaving unfinished business behind me here. Especially business involving Hank Lipton. My conscience would simply not allow me to do so."

"All right, JT. It's quite apparent that you'll sit there like Santa Anna at the Alamo until I surrender. The job's yours. All we've got are rumors of a female accomplice. The wife is the assumed accomplice. Here's the file on her." Pinkerton pulled the file from a drawer in his desk and thrust the folder toward JT.

JT flipped through the few pages inside. "There's not much in here."

He knew he would have investigated the case independently, but having the captain back him up gave him more clout, not to mention the available resources if needed.

The captain tugged at his shirt collar. "She may not be guilty, JT. Search for evidence of another woman as well because the woman who escaped his hotel room could be different from his lawfully wedded wife."

With his face buried in the folder the captain handed him, he said, "You surprise me, captain. A fine upstanding citizen like Philipp Wagner, the bank manager, with a new bride, suspected of keeping time with another woman?" JT asked while shaking his head in feigned astonishment. "You have your wish. There are two ladies to investigate. By the time I'm done, I'll know more about Philipp Wagner and his new bride than their mommas."

"Throw yourself out of here and save me the trouble. I'm feeling sorry for the poor girl already." Pinkerton smashed the cigar out against the sole of his shoe.

"Yeah? If you're inclined to sympathize with women in the future, it would be wiser to remember Clara Lipton and her two fatherless children in Virginia. They are the ones who deserve your sympathy." JT slapped his gloves against the edge of Pinkerton's desk. "That will keep everything in perspective for you."

"She's an alleged suspect until we have proof otherwise, JT. They're innocent until proven guilty. Since this is your last job, I have one remaining piece of advice for you." Pinkerton leaned forward, causing the armrests to slam into the wooden desk with a sharp thud. He placed an elbow in the center of his desk and pointed at JT.

"You're one of the best dang Pinkerton men I've seen in ten years, but, son, the world isn't always black or white. Sometimes things are not as they seem. You make darn sure you have solid evidence before you arrest a woman. I know how determined you get, and I don't want it coming back to bite you in your judgmental ass or reflecting poorly on this company or tarnishing another poor girl's reputation who may very well not have had anything to do with the matter."

He extended a hand, and JT shook it before grabbing his hat and satchel.

"Thank you, Sir, but don't worry about me. I plan on being the one doing the biting." He replied with a crooked smile.

With that, he turned and headed back to the train station, this time with Columbus, Ohio, as his destination.

At the station, he caught the eastbound to Columbus. He'd arrive in Columbus within a few days. Say your prayers, girl. JT Grant is on your trail now.

December 21, 1859, Split Profits with Victims

There was a knock-on Carrie's door. Good Lord, who could it possibly be? Perhaps the townspeople had finally come to stake her for husbands' crimes, she thought ruefully.

It was the sheriff.

He tipped his hat, "Good evening, Carrie,"

"Please come in before you freeze." Replied Carrie as she begrudgingly invited him in. What on earth could this man want now? Or rather what else had Phillip done.

Carrie's mouth went dry at the thought of more bad news. She tried to convince herself that perhaps it was good news, perhaps Phillip was innocent. Just that idea seemed so comical, Carrie almost snorted as she chided herself, 'Sure, and maybe miracles grow in furrows.'

"Would you like some tea, sheriff?" she asked mutely.

"No, thank you. I'm not staying long enough for that. I'm afraid I come bearing more bad news for you, Mrs. Wagner." He replied apologetically.

He did not have to tell her though. He had come by so often the past few weeks that she had figured out when he twirled the rim of his hat through his fingers, it was a giveaway of his stress.

He sniffed the aroma in the air. "Wait, is that the smell of spiced tea?"

"Yes, I steep dried orange rind leftover from summer to enjoy it in winter. I'll get you a cup." The pot sat on the back of the stove to keep it hot, so she returned swiftly and set the teacup on the table next to his seat.

"Thank you, Mrs. Wagner. I love spiced tea." He said as he took a sip.

Tapping her fingers on the arm of her chair, she waited for the bad news while he continued to sip.

"Delicious. I shouldn't be surprised. I've heard about your good cooking at the orphanage. Anyone who has tasted your food never stops raving about it but you're too young to cook this well."

"I've worked in the orphanage kitchen since I was five. After that, I had to pass muster or face the firing squad. And I'm twenty-one now, not so young." She replied quietly.

He gulped another swallow of tea. "This sure beats my mother's recipe. Unfortunately, I have brought more disheartening news today. I'm afraid the City Council has decided to divide the proceeds among the robbery victims when the bank goes up for sale. And, at the house sale, you will be able to receive only half of the profits. The other half will also go to the victims."

Carrie gasped at their audacity. She and Ruth needed that money to start over, without it, they would be left with nothing. She would be left with nothing. Was it not enough that she had lost her husband, her honor, her reputation, the last thing she had left was the roof over her head and they must take that from her too?

"They can't do that, can they, Sheriff?" she asked breathlessly.

The sheriff cleared his throat and tugged at his collar. "Wagner stole what was theirs and refuses to say where the money is now. We asked him to comply multiple times, but he refused. The money he stole did not belong to him. It was the bank customer's money. They needed it; even if they didn't, it's theirs. Now that Wagner's property is for sale, proceeds from his estate will legally go to the victims. They agreed to give you fifty percent of the proceeds of the house if you leave Columbus." The sheriff sighed as if freed from a heavy load. "However, if the robbery money turns up, they will reimburse you for the house and the bank. Just leave me an address to send it to."

By then, it could be too late for them. Bile rose up in the back of her throat as she registered what the sheriff had said.

"You can inform the townsfolk that I've already decided to leave."

They would not get the pleasure of throwing her out of town. She would not allow it. All her life, she had seen how the people in town had treated the orphans. As if they were all nothing more than delinquents, a burden. That had changed to an extent when she had married Phillip but now that Phillip had turned out the way he had their masks had come off and they were back to their old selves. They no longer had to pretend.

She did not rob the bank, yet she was the one who was getting punished.

"Good, the City Council wants you to settle comfortably at any other location. Their deal is legitimate. You have the City Council's promise on that." He retrieved a contract from his coat pocket and handed it to her.

Uncertain about what to do and with Ruth visiting a friend, she asked, "Did they already try to get Philipp to sign the deeds over to the City Council?"

The sheriff took a deep breath. "Yes, they tried, but he said the assets belonged to you. He signed the deeds over to you last week." He sipped the tea.

Why would Philipp do that? Why wouldn't he let her talk these things over with him? Does this mean he loved her? No, it couldn't mean that. The way he's treated her is not the way of love. Those who love you do not humiliate you and leave you to fend for yourself. She felt a pang in her heart as she remembered her parents leaving her at the orphanage all those years ago. Yet, here she was, going through more or less the same.

She nodded her head in agreement and signed the documents as requested.

"Heaven knows where I'm going, but I'll send you my address once I get settled. And I won't leave this house before the hanging."

"Make a note of it on the contract." Advised the Sheriff.

Carrie fetched pen and ink to make the notation on the contract and signed it. Then, she escorted the sheriff to the door. Her cordial mask slipped away with the closing of the door. She slammed her back against the door, closing her fists tightly.

The City Council bamboozled them. She and Ruth needed to sit down, rethink their budget, and decide what to do. Thank God she had five years of savings from working at the mercantile. She may have to give up brandy, though. Drat!

<u>1 Samuel 12:3</u> *Here I stand. Testify against me in the presence of the LORD and his anointed. Whose ox have I taken? Whose donkey have I taken? Whom have I cheated? Whom have I oppressed? From whose hand have I accepted a bribe to make me shut my eyes? If I have done any of these things, I will make it right."*

Chapter Three

December 21, 1859, Go West

After Philipp's confession, Ruth moved into the cottage with Carrie for support. Carrie and Ruth had spent the last two days decorating their little cottage to boost their morale, but Carrie strenuously vetoed mistletoe for obvious reasons. However, pine boughs, pinecones, and candles decorated the hearth and other deserving horizontal spaces, crying out to take part. Ruth added peppermint drops to the candles when she made them and tied a red ribbon bow at the bottom of each one. The peppermint scent from the liquid candle wax reached into every crevice of the house and lingered. Holiday spirit flowed from room to room, keeping the problems of everyday life at bay while they worshiped the birth of Christ.

That evening, huddled around the parlor fireplace, sipping hot chocolate with Ruth, Carrie came to a decision. Philipp will be hanged and she can't stay here after he's gone. The whole town suspects her as an accomplice. Rumors of a female accomplice have been making the rounds. She's not the accomplice, but no one believes her. Of course, no one knows he was bedding another woman but Carrie was not willing to divulge that bit of information. Besides, it would do no good. They would still find a way to blame her and accuse her of not keeping her husband happy which is why he resorted to such means.

She knew she had to redirect all her focus towards planning for the future.

Carrie broke the silence. "I told the sheriff I'd leave town on Philipp's hanging day. Everyone here hates me. They'll never let me forget my husband was a bank robber and a murderer. What do you think about moving away?" Recently, Ruth, the laundress, took over the sewing tasks. She told Carrie her stitches looked like she experienced a seizure while sewing. Ruth dropped her current sewing project onto her lap.

"I didn't think you'd be ready to leave Philipp so soon. Yes, I'm ready. What do you have in mind? What do you think of Canada?"

"Heavens, no. It's cold enough in Ohio. Why do you want to go to Canada?" Carrie said.

"Because I'm a freed darky, and I ain't going anywhere near most of this country where they will drag me by my head back to the fields, Even for you." Replied Ruth staunchly.

"I completely understand. I'm not going to force you to go. Hopefully, we can decide on a place together. I don't want to go anywhere without you. You're the only family I have." Carrie placed her hand on Ruth's.

Ruth thought for a moment. "War is gonna break out soon. I don't want to be near this country's eastern half and not the south. I could get kidnapped and sold back into slavery."

"Well, let's see, how about something out west that we can reach on the Oregon trail?" Carrie said.

"That's a tough journey, and we got no men to help us."

"You think we need men? Can we send a telegram and find out the requirements to join? Maybe we can hire a man to help get us there." Suggested Carrie.

"First things first. If we throw in together, how much money do we have between us?" inquired Ruth.

Carrie drew in a deep breath, worried they'd fall short. "I've saved $412. Please tell me you didn't put your money in Philipp's bank." Not wanting to hear the confirmation, she covered her ears.

Ruth's turn to inhale deeply. "The only thing I'd leave in your husband's vicinity would be turds." She nodded for emphasis, then pinched her nose, feigning a reaction to a revolting smell.

Carrie's eyes almost bulged out of her head. "Ruth!"

"You heard that." Then, changing the subject, she said, "I saved $679." She shared a self-satisfied grin.

"Washing and sewing pay that well?" But then she remembered Ruth had worked for two years longer than she had. "Dang, Ruth, we have $1,091 if I carried my leftovers correctly. Wonderful!"

"A thousand dollars is a good start, but is that enough? Ruth paused, then said, "Can we at least wait for the response to our telegram? I will not commit until we have gathered all the information and agreed we have enough money to do so."

Her friend was the practical one who kept her from making foolish decisions at least once a week. Yes, the telegram was step one. At least they were making progress. "Yes, bright and early in the morning, send a telegram to the experts to find out where we stand."

Ruth stated, "I can't wait to hear your plan for avoiding Indian attacks, poisonous snakes, floods, or getting over the Rockies and into San Francisco before winter without a man's help. You want to pray for something. Pray for that." Ruth returned to her sewing project in her lap.

Carrie stopped to think about what Ruth had said.

Ruth squirmed in her seat and sipped at her hot chocolate. "I hear there's good land in California. Are you considering buying a house in a town or starting a farm?"

Carrie's turn to squirm. "Well, that depends on how you feel about my next suggestion."

Ruth stared at her, "You're not planning on busting Philipp out of jail and taking him with us, are you?"

"Don't be silly."

"You've got something up your sleeve. Let's hear it."

"Don't laugh. I want to build a family of our own. Before we leave town, we should adopt the neediest orphans, giving them what they've prayed for—a home and family. Maybe we can buy some land and build a farm to support ourselves if we do. I was going to suggest adoption to Philipp, but that dream will hang with him."

Ruth leaned forward, "You've got a big heart, my friend, maybe too big. Where's the money coming from?"

"The sheriff says I get fifty percent of the proceeds when the house sells."

"I know you, Carrie. You'll go in there and adopt nearly all of them. We can't afford that. We can afford perhaps two at best." sighed Ruth.

Carrie counter offered. "Four. Please, Ruth. Don't you remember what it was like praying every night your parents would return and get you or that some kind family would want to adopt you? We're that kind of family now. So, let's answer some prayers."

"Kids are expensive, Carrie. Maybe we should adopt after we reach California."

Ruth was not getting her point. "We don't know those California kids. We know what it's like to be abandoned at our orphanage. We know their prayers. More importantly, we aren't strangers to them."

"We don't know if we can support ourselves long enough to get to California. And you want more than two kids. So, adopt more in California after we've settled in."

Ruth has always been her voice of reason. Carrie smiled and wiggled her shoulders to and fro. "Can we go to the orphanage tomorrow and discuss the details with the Headmistress?"

Ruth paused, trying to put her words in the proper order. "Can we at least send a telegram to the Oregon Trail experts first? We need to know the worst of it before committing ourselves." I would feel much better if there was a man with us.

"I remember you brought that up before. How can we find a trustworthy man to go with us?"

"I've been thinking on it, and I think we should ask the sheriff if he knows of anyone wanting to go west without the means." Replied Ruth.

Carrie's eyes lit up. Of course, Ruth was right.

"Great idea. The sheriff would know if they were reputable." She exclaimed.

"Oh, another thought, before we go to the sheriff, let's go to the library and the newspaper office to see if they have the information, we need on traveling by wagon train. I bet they have it, and we don't have to spend money to send a telegram."

"You're right. One of the two will have it."

Ruth poured herself a cup of coffee and sat at the kitchen table. Carrie did the same. "Carrie, neither of us has birthed a baby before, but I have observed the patience, energy, and lack of sleep expended on one baby at a time. Besides, neither one of us has milk for a baby. They are helpless and will depend on us to survive. We have a journey ahead of us. How can we stretch our budget and have the patience to manage everything that needs doing? The trip alone could kill us."

Ruth was right about her; if she could, she'd adopt every child in the orphanage. The pain of being tossed away by her mother drove her desire to save children from such a fate. But Ruth's trip through reality lane revealed her impulsive decision-making. Neither of them has a husband and likely will never have one. There are only two of them to go around. "I didn't think of it from that point of view."

"I'm not saying no children because I know you love those children. But please don't adopt babies. We need children who can dress and feed themselves and no more than two. I don't think we can afford more than that. After the journey, if you want more, adopt more. I think that's a fair compromise."

Psalm 16:11 *You will show me the path of life; In Your presence is fullness of joy; At Your right hand are pleasures forevermore.*

December 23, 1859, Manna from Heaven

At breakfast, the following day, the sound of elegant cutlery on the ceramic plates and bowls on the table resounded as the two friends sat quietly and devoured the delicious breakfast that Carrie had prepared for them. Yet, while they ate in silence, their gaze was drawn to the sight outside their window, where the town was embracing the Christmas Spirit with decorated houses, children running around in the snow, and people singing carols. Their warm spirits were enough to make the streets feel less frigid, but this warmth had not been extended to Carrie or her friend. They sat there calmly watching. The same streets that did not welcome them seemed like an open and welcome place for all. Excited children and parents wandered the streets, greeting one another and enjoying family fun—an activity they had missed out on as children as they had no family but each other.

Carrie was the first to break her gaze as she instead redirected her focus on chasing a pat of butter around her bowl with a spoon fresh from stirring her coffee, hoping to melt it.

"Do you think I should stay here while you search for Oregon Trail information?" asked Carrie.

"Yes, I think that would be best for now." Ruth caressed Carrie's right hand and continued, "I'll go alone to keep you safe, the last thing we need is to draw attention towards our plans."

Carrie expected her to say as much but she could not hide her disappointment as she barely managed to contain her reaction to having to stay back as grumbled under her breath, "Thank you, my friend."

Ruth looked at her reproachfully and Carrie felt a small twinge of guilt, she instead decided to set her mind on planning their trip. That would occupy her time and take away some of the annoyance she felt of not being able to do anything substantial to help with their escape plan.

Ruth said, trying to cheer Carrie up, "Stop twisting yourself into a knot. Enjoy your breakfast. Maybe there's only good news about the Oregon Trail."

"From your lips to God's ear. Amen." Muttered Carrie begrudgingly.

Hours later, Carrie adjusted herself on a rickety chair, pulling boxes and papers from the upper shelf of Philipp's closet. The suit in which he would hang lay across the bed. She did not care about Phillips. All she cared about was getting rid of all this stuff that she can't take with her. She unloaded the boxes and opened the boxes one by one. In one of the boxes, she found letters sent to Philipp from his family in Germany.

Carrie paused for a moment. She had no knowledge of communications between Phillip and his family nor had he ever mentioned them. Perhaps they were aware of his plans to partake in criminal behavior. Either way, she decided she would let them know of what had happened and his sentence of death by hanging.

She set one letter aside to remind her to respond. Soon, as she was buried up to her neck in the second-floor bedroom closet, she heard Ruth return home.

"Carrie, where are you?" Ruth's voice echoed.

Her tone of voice gave away a touch of frustration. "I'm upstairs cleaning out a closet. I'll be right down."

"Thank you. I found Oregon Trail information, but it's not encouraging." said Ruth gravely.

"Coming." Sighed Carried. She didn't know why she expected there to be good news, it wasn't like God had made life easy for her. She carefully stepped down from the chair and descended the stairs in time to witness Ruth pouring brandy. Vacant eyes looked past her as she and the brandy slumped into a dining chair and remained reticent.

"Tell me," asked Carrie gently, "What has discouraged you?"

Ruth's chin quivered.

Carrie took both her hands, which were cold enough to keep ice cycles from melting; however, Ruth kept her chin down. Her monotone voice slowly formed words. "The wagon train information was at the newspaper office. My hopes blossomed about adopting after listening to you, and now, dreamers, that's what we are, dreamers. But unfortunately, the cost is prohibitive to travel to California."

Carrie's face went slack, paled at the thought of losing their dream of adopting and going west. Rubbing Ruth's cold hands, she tried to get them functioning as a team again. "Listen, we're still leaving town on January 27. We must not let bad news discourage us. I will not stay back. Please tell me what you discovered. We must move somewhere, and we've run out of direction. Then, if we can discuss it, maybe we can think of a way to proceed."

Nodding, Ruth raised her head and fixed her eyes on Carrie. " Brace yourself. The wagon costs $200, and food per person costs $600." Sighing deeply, she deferred to the sheet of requirements. "The other requirements are six oxen, tools, camping supplies, a first aid kit, food for the oxen, firearms, ammunition, medicinal spirits, clothing, and bring no personal belongings. The cost of which is unknown. Each pilgrim, you're called a pilgrim while on the trail, buys them when you arrive in Independence, Missouri. Plan to be early in case they run out of supplies. To top that off, a man for every wagon is required. If we find someone, we must be there three months before the wagon train departs Missouri to learn how to survive the trip. That means we leave next week."

"This new side of you is scaring me. Please try to snap out of it and help me figure this out?" urged Carrie.

"This is the new me after some thief stole our adopted babies and my ticket to California." Ruth covered her face with her hands as she tried to hold back her tears.

Carrie, unwilling to give up yet, remembered what Ruth had said. Finally, she blurted out, "It's just two children and us, right?" Hoping Ruth could pull herself together.

"Don't forget the mandatory man that counts as one member of the four-person wagon." With elbows on the table, Ruth used her fingers to rub her forehead.

Carrie snapped her fingers. "Simple. You, the children, and the driver take the Oregon Trail, and I'll work my way there alone."

"We'll need all our money for the Oregon Trail, and we're still short three times over. How will you finance your solo trip to California and pay the wagon driver? The money only stretches so far."

Usually, Ruth cheered Carrie up. But occasionally, the table turned. "My dear, are you suffering from a headache? How about a headache powder and a nice hot cup of cannabis tea?" smiled Carrie.

Ruth's hands dropped to the table. "Bless you, Carrie. A headache plagues me, and I'm worried about what to do."

Ruth's bunched shoulder muscles begged for a massage. "Please relax. We will figure this out. We're orphans and exist on pure gumption; who taught me that, I wonder?" Carrie rubbed Ruth's taught shoulder muscles.

"Oh, that feels so good," Ruth moaned.

The massaging stopped while Carrie searched for a headache powder and combined the cannabis tea ingredients.

"Where did you go? That felt so delightful." Reproached Ruth.

"Headache powder and tea, remember? Concentrate on calming down. Close your eyes." Replied Carrie gently.

She pulled two cups and saucers out of the cabinet, then tossed a pinch of cannabis, cream, ground lavender, and black tea in Ruth's cup. "Take deep breaths and blow out slowly to calm down while the water heats." She picked up where she left off on Ruth's shoulders. "Have faith in the Lord. We'll think of something."

"Your fingers are magic and could turn the meanest tempered, half-bald, garbage can pilfer alley cat howling to keep you up all night into a purring kitten who follows you around as if you bathed in catnip. So how do you do it?" Ruth asked in rhythm with the massage rotations.

"Because I love you. Doesn't work on anybody else."

The teapot whistled. Carrie placed teacups on the table. Then, she stirred the headache powder into half a glass of water. "Here, drink this down."

Ruth obeyed, finishing the headache powder, and focusing on the tea.

Carrie sat opposite, stirring in sugar and cream. It's time to come up with a good idea. Think Carrie. She absentmindedly tapped the end of the teaspoon on the table.

"Please stop. That tapping isn't helping my headache. Besides, you'll make dents in that beautiful wood." Grumbled Ruth.

Carrie snapped out of her thoughts and looked down at the spoon. "Oh, I'm sorry, dear." Droplets of tea had fallen onto the table. The dining table was made of walnut and boasted a mirror finish that demanded quick action. Using her napkin, she brushed the droplets away, admiring the table's beauty instead of usefulness. Her upbringing never included the admiration for fine-quality furnishings. In the orphanage, the functional furniture received a coat of white paint every other year. No one lost sleep over quality. This table matched all the other furniture in the house. Philipp, proud of his German heritage, no doubt ordered his furniture from Germany after he settled in America. Pushing her teacup aside, she swept her palm down the length as far as possible, marveling at the grain in the wood.

A realization came into sharp focus. "I own all the furniture." Hope flickered in her heart. The timbre of her voice rose. "It's been in front of us all this time, and we didn't even notice it before. All of Philipp's furniture was fancy German-made for show. Maybe other folks in German Village would like to buy some of it. This could be our ticket."

"Oh my God, Carrie, what a relief." Ruth stood and braced herself on the table. "How much do you think we can make on it?"

"The deed. Let's study it in case it says different." She dashed up the stairs to Philipp's office and plopped into his leather chair.

Ruth arrived a close second and planted her hip on the chair's right arm. "You've got a bird on your shoulder if you don't mind."

"Of course, I don't mind." Unfolding the deed, Carrie held out one side for Ruth to take, and she held the other. She moved her finger along as she silently ingested each word. But there was no mention of furniture in the deed. Ruth slumped into her.

"Drat!"

Pacing the room with slow, heavy steps, Carrie also felt a headache coming on. After a few minutes, she suggested, "Let's look at this differently. If they did not list the furniture in the deed, which the City Council drew up, that means it is mine, right? If it belonged to the city council, they would have said so, after all, they did mention they would be taking the house, they never said they would take what came with the house."

"Thank the Lord." Ruth nodded, and a trembling smile developed. "They didn't say anything in there claiming the furniture. That would make it yours, wouldn't it?"

They joined hands while jumping for joy and squealing their delight. Carrie smiled, hugged her friend closely, and then they singsonged, "No contract on the furniture."

Ruth proposed, "Let's set up a sale, but they can't take possession until Philipp hangs. Then, if we're breaking the law, I'm sure someone will show up and tell us."

1 Peter 5:7 *Cast your cares upon the Lord, for he cares about you.*

Christmas Day, 1859, Let's Talk Adoption

Carrie, Ruth, and the Headmistress were the only ones still up and doing the dishes. Christmas day, they had been glorious. First, she and Ruth sang Christmas songs with the children. Then they broke into groups after lunch to play Christmas games she and Ruth had played when they lived there. Finally, after dinner, the children opened one gift. The scent of roasted ham and sweet potatoes still lurked in the air, mingled with the tang of pine nuts, apple, cinnamon pie, and candied fruit cake.

To verify its cleanliness, Carrie held a platter next to the lantern. "Mrs. Overton, there's a matter I would love to ask your advice about." When they graduated from the orphanage, she and Ruth quit calling the headmistress by her title instead of her name.

"What could that be? Please call me Katherine. Both of you are ladies now." And now, they were on a first-name basis. At least Carrie had one friend in the world.

Ruth, drying the dishes, spoke up. "She's got it in her head to adopt children."

Katherine clapped her hands together in joy and said, "What wonderful news. tell me what you're thinking." She carried a stack of clean, dry plates to a cabinet with an empty shelf.

"I'll never marry again, but I love children. The answer to my dilemma would be adoption. Ruth has talked me down to only adopting two. But we plan to go to California and recently found out how much that costs. And the money to carry out such a dream is nonexistent. So how much does it cost to adopt a child?"

"Well, girls, it doesn't cost a thing except for proof the adopting parents can afford to take care of an additional child. That's all. What age are you looking for?" asked Katherine.

Shaking her head, Ruth pleaded, "Please, Katherine, don't encourage her. We can hardly afford to take care of ourselves, we can't afford children on top of that."

"Ruth says the little ones must be able to feed and dress themselves."

Katherine added, "Don't worry so much, Ruth. God doesn't share his plans with us. When is Philipp scheduled to hang? Oh, forgive my forthrightness. Do you know yet?"

Carrie lowered her head and replied, "Yes, he hangs on January 27."

"There's your answer. There are thirty-some days to pray for it. But, Ruth, having more faith in the Lord wouldn't hurt you." Smiled Katherine.

A little after midnight, Carrie knelt beside her bed and instantly regretted it. A wave of exhaustion overwhelmed her. She feared the power to rise again had abandoned her. Yet, what a blessed day this had been. She scanned her Bible pages, searching for the quote for today before beginning her prayers. From now on, maybe she should say her prayers after snuggling into bed. After all, she's all grown up, as Katherine said.

Psalms 27:14 *Wait for the LORD; be strong and take heart and wait for the LORD.*

December 26, 1859, Pony Express is Hiring

An advertisement in the Columbus newspaper caught Carrie's attention. The Pony Express needed cooks. The job sounded perfect for her. As cooking positions opened closer to the west coast, she could transfer to that station and work her way west, but she had to interview for the job first in St. Joseph, Missouri. She had money, but the extra cash would be a blessing in an emergency. Besides, you could never have too much could you?

Jeremiah 24:6 *My eyes will watch over them for their good, and I will bring them back to this land. I will build them up and not tear them down; I will plant them and not uproot them.*

December 28, 1859, The Adoptees Arrive

Carrie answered the soft knocking at the door, wondering why whoever it was didn't knock with added enthusiasm. When she pulled the door open, she could tell a little girl had knocked on the door. Tears tumbled down her face.

Headmistress Katherine and Judge Adams stood there, each with a four- or five-year-old girl in their arms. They were their girls. She knew it but stared in disbelief. Carrie didn't know what to do first; grab the children or fetch Ruth. Bouncing on the balls of her feet, she hollered, "Ruth, come see who's here."

These little girls deserved parents. These were not some random girls Katherine had picked out, Michelle and Carla had both been under Carrie's care since birth. The memories rushed forward to real-time: play, story, bath, and mealtime through the bumps and bruises, plus chickenpox and measles. Carla had an adorable habit of hanging off Carrie's leg, and Michelle adored her cooking. These two children were the ones she would have picked out for herself. This adoption day will always be cherished and celebrated because she knew in her heart that she would never be this happy again. She loved both these girls with all her heart and being a mother to them would be the highest honor.

Carrie ushered their guests inside out of the cold and wind, then closed the door. "Please make yourselves comfortable." She looked at Katherine. "They're our girls, right?"

"They're for you, Carrie. Ohio law won't let darkys adopt white children." Replied Katherine gravely.

Carrie heard Ruth's footsteps come to a halt behind her. One girl held out both arms for Carrie to take her from Katherine's arms, but Carrie's mind slipped back to the day she held both arms out in the same way, imploring her mother not to leave. Frozen in pain, she balked and kept her hands to herself.

"Carrie, what's the matter? All you talk about is adopting children, and now you turn to stone. They're precious." Ruth came from behind Carrie and held out her arms to take Michelle, five years old, with dark curly hair and missing her two front teeth, from Judge Adams.

Seeing Ruth with the child snapped Carrie out of her trance. Carrie threw her arms around Michelle and Ruth. "Thank you, Ruth." She kissed her cheek. "And welcome home, Michelle. We've waited for you a long time." She kissed Michelle all over her face from her cheeks to her forehead until she giggled.

Then she held her arms out for Carla, a four-year-old with straight blond hair and spindly legs, to come to her. She hugged Carla tightly and kissed her cheeks and forehead. "But we can't afford them. How is this true?"

Katherine said, "I think these two little girls would love having you for a mother, Carrie."

The two little ones spoke with a chorus of "Yeses." Finally, Carrie broke down and sobbed at the epitome of happiness. The room spun, and her knees wilted a little. The next thing she knew, as if from a distance, Ruth patted her cheek, called out her name, and she woke up.

Judge Adams said, "We better get the legalities done before we lose Carrie again." He pulled documents out of his coat pocket.

"But according to Katherine, we can't afford these girls." Carrie traded girls with Ruth. "There's coffee and cookies in the kitchen. Please, let's go sit while I clear my head." She covered Michelle's face in more kisses, hugged her close, and then traded girls with Ruth again to kiss Carla's face. The little one threw her arms around Carrie's neck and said, "Mama." That's all it took to steal Carrie's heart. "Ruth is Mama, too. Don't forget." Tears soaked her face.

After signing all the papers, including those Ruth would need to take the children to California without Carrie, Judge Adams had one more surprise. Pulling another envelope from his suit pocket, he said, "Ladies, I created an adoption fund for Michelle and Carla.

Every member of the City Council contributed to helping your children arrive safely in California."

He held the envelope out for Carrie to take.

Ruth and Carrie stared at each other. They couldn't believe their ears. The townspeople wanted to help them? This could not be, not after the treatment they had subjected them to. Ruth was the first to recover from the shock and she hurriedly pulled out a handkerchief for Carrie who was reduced to a blubbering mess as the third waterfall of the evening began.

Ruth tried to calm her down and after a moment, Carrie was able to catch her breath. "B-B-But I don't understand. The City Council took all the money away from us, they hate us."

Katherine smiled, adding, "Let's just say the sinners have repented."

Carrie jumped to her feet and dived into Katherine's arms as she thanked both her and Judge Adams for taking care of them and giving them the resources they needed to flee and save themselves. Thank you, Lord, for this precious answered prayer.

<u>Psalms 68:3</u> *But may the righteous be glad and rejoice before God; may they be happy and joyful.*

Chapter Four

January 2, 1860, The Jeweler

The final day in Columbus for Ruth and the children arrived, kicking, and screaming. Chaos reigned with one pouting child, the other clinging onto Carrie's leg with the strength of a thousand men refusing to let go, as Mr. Lafferty took trunks to the train station one at a time.

It surprised Carrie just how little she knew about children, despite having been one and volunteering to care for them for years. Things were different when it was a full-time job and not a few hours of volunteering.

For example, they wake up before you every day and do not leave you alone. If you're not out of bed and dressed in a hot minute, they search for food alone, leaving the kitchen like a battlefield and then wail like a banshee should they not get their way. She reminded herself that kitchens in homes were a new concept for them. They're curious about a lot of things, unfortunately, and this is how they subdue their curiosity by exploring and stretching their little legs.

Somehow, the little people managed to lay siege to their house, and she thought she'd be in charge. Ruth fared better with the children because she held them accountable and kept a short leash. Carrie, on the other hand, was too soft on them and she couldn't bring herself to do that just yet. She'd be fine with practice because she loved them awfully. Wrapped around Carrie's legs, Carla squabbled with Michelle, who had just entered the room.

Just then, there came an ominous knock at the door. Boom, Boom, Boom.

She couldn't move, Carla was locked around her legs. She stooped down and gently gathered the girls into her arms, and went to answer the door. A stranger stood at the threshold.

"Mrs. Wagner, my name is Benjamin Stein, and I own a jewelry shop downtown. Your husband commissioned a special order for the woman he loves. He designed it himself and paid for it upfront. I don't give two gelt for either your husband or yourself. I must admit I almost kept it since he's going to hang, and my money got stolen from his bank, but he may have mentioned the gift to you since then."

Contemptible low-down thief. "Could you wait a moment, please?" Carrie left the man standing at the door and put the girls in the parlor on the settee. She told them not to move. Returning to Mr. Stein, she said, "Mr. Stein, I'm shocked at how close you came to becoming a thief yourself. If only my husband had asked about your skill in resisting criminal tendencies. He never mentioned anything of the special gift to me."

What trick has Philipp pulled this time? A gift for her after what he's done. Or was it even for her? We'll see what Ruth thinks of this. Dear Lord, help me keep a civil tongue in my head.

His fist shot out, and he flattened his palm. A ring. No, not any old ring. It epitomized 'special order.' The gold band was hardly visible to the naked eye because of all the jewels. She supposed there were diamonds of every size. It practically blinded her in the sunlight. The biggest one sat in the middle like a roosting hen. Slivers of diamonds proudly presented the roosting hen to the world. And a circle of round diamonds encased the fiery presentation, causing fractured rainbow colors to dance wildly. Philipp special ordered this for her. Why? It screams, "I love you," from the highest peak. Carrie held her hand out to take it from Mr. Stein.

"Are these genuine diamonds?"

Mr. Stein placed the ring on her wedding finger. "Yes, every single one of them. It took me months to make it. I'm quite proud of it."

"What did it cost?" asked Carrie breathlessly.

"Since he commissioned it as a surprise, I think I better not share that information." Muttered the jeweler.

She's done with this conversation, and there are many other things to do. "I need to know its value for when I sell it. And I require a receipt as well." Replied Carrie stonily.

Mr. Stein's face blanched, "But I made it for you, special order."

"Mr. Stein, I'm sorry, but it means nothing when gifted from a convicted bank robber and murderer." Then, a thought came to her. She yanked Mr. Stein's creation off, then pulled her wedding ring off, sliding the diamond ring back onto her finger. "How much can you give me for this ring?"

"I made that one, too, but it's your wedding ring, madam." He protested.

"Yes, I had a wedding, but no marriage, and I need money. How much?"

Mr. Stein, clearly unhappy about this turn of events, threw out a low price, "$100."

Carrie countered with, "$200."

"Now wait a minute, Mrs. Wagner, that's more than I charged in the first place." He protested again.

"Very well, $150. You know you can resell it and make a profit." Bartered Carrie.

His eyes cut to hers, and he grumbled, "Fine, $150. Mind you. I'm never dealing with your family again." He pulled out his wallet, counted the bills, and handed them to her.

"Thank you, Mr. Stein, nice doing business with you." Smiled Carrie as she managed to stifle a giggle.

Stein pivoted on his heel and fled from her door as if she had chased him away.

After her guest left and she shut the door, she decided she should enlighten the sheriff about the jeweler's tendency to cheat people. Then she'll ask the lawman to accompany her to the jewelry establishment, searching for a receipt. Maybe an unexpected situation like this one tempted Philipp into crime.

This gift from God is the insurance she needs to ensure she will make it to California. Their fortune had turned. Katherine had been right, all she needed was to place a little faith in God. Philipp's pending hanging now remained the only other responsibility to check off her list before embarking on her wild west adventure and new life.

1 Timothy 6:9 *Those who want to get rich fall into temptation and a trap and into many foolish and harmful desires that plunge people into ruin and destruction.*

January 6, 1860, Prepared For the Oregon Trail

The only thing she owes her convicted husband is attending the hanging. Philipp got sentenced last week. "You know, Ruth, I still feel that Philipp isn't capable of murder. Robbing the bank, maybe, but not murder."

"Carrie, the man confessed. What more do you want?" asked Ruth.

"I feel I must defend him if for no other reason than his gift of identity to me. I'm Mrs. Carrie Wagner now, a flesh and blood person with a legal name and social standing as the wife of a bank owner. Carrie, no last name, abandoned by her parents, no longer exists. No criminal would care about rescuing an orphan girl from the invisibility she's dwelled in almost all her life. Why would he care? He must have loved me at least a little."

"Girl, how's that new social standing working out for you? Oh, I forgot, the high society ladies meet here every Wednesday for sewing circle and they eat out of your hand, too." Ruth batted her eyelashes at her and fanned her face with her hand.

Laughing, Carrie joined the joke, "Didn't I tell you? I canceled my membership. Mrs. Landover took offense to my epileptic stitches, and my tea sandwiches lacked a professional presentation. I could tolerate that, but I drew the line when starchy old Miss Miller insisted on tea instead of coffee. How un-American."

"Philipp won't talk to you or see you. You're right; he's a peach."

Carrie stuck her tongue out at a distracted Ruth, but there was some truth in what she said. "Well, I'm unlovable. I know it's true. My mother deserted me, and now my husband would rather hang than spend his last hours with me the common problem I can find is none but myself."

88

Ruth set her tea aside and leaned forward to take Carrie into her arms, "Stop saying that. It's not true. I love you."

"You don't count. We're practically sisters. All we have is each other. So, why did he ask that I not visit him in jail? What drove him to rob and kill? It's making me crazy. If only I knew why. If only he would tell me what I did wrong. Perhaps, I did not make a very good wife?

Ruth shrugged her shoulders, "Why do fish swim? Why do birds fly? Sometimes people are plum crazy. All I know is, trying to figure him out will make you crazy, too and any man would be lucky to have a wife like you so don't think that way again. We have daughters now and we cannot let them grow thinking that being orphans means you call trouble to yourself." She drew circles in the air with her index finger beside her temple.

Just then a weeping Carla entered the room.

"Mommy, Mommy, I fell and bumped my head," four-year-old Carla wrapped an arm around Carrie's legs and held her other hand to her forehead. The room descended into chaos when Michelle ran in, denying responsibility for Carla's phony injury.

"How did you bump your head playing checkers?" Carrie bent to peruse Carla's forehead. "No blood, Carla, you might have a bruise, but you'll be fine." She kissed her on the forehead and patted her shoulder. "All right, you little darlings, it's time to brush teeth."

"Aw shucks, just because Carla bumped her head." Michelle's pre-bed protestation, there's one every night the evening nurse at the orphanage informed her.

"Don't take it out on Carla. We are a family now and do things best for the family. Remember we talked about that at the noon meal." Chided Carrie gently.

Still wrapped around her legs, Carla asked, "Are you sure you can't come with us tomorrow."

She tousled her hair, "Yes darling, I'm sure. Remember, I have business to take care of in Columbus before I can leave. You all will be perfectly safe with Ruth and Mr. Lafferty." Then adding Michelle into the group hug, she instructed them, "I want both of you to be good and do what Ruth says. I'm so jealous of the great adventure awaiting you. I hear California is the perfect place to build a new home, and we will have plenty of land to farm. We're going to have our own home. Aren't you as excited as I am?" She hugged them both again. "I will miss you very much."

Ruth brushed them out of the room with a sweep of her arm. "Come now, shoo, get ready for bed. We have a busy day waiting for us tomorrow,"

Releasing a deep breath, Ruth said, "This will be their only night under Philipp's roof, thank God."

Carrie glanced up at Ruth. "Please don't tell me you warned me about Philipp. I know you did."

Ruth sat beside her, "I wasn't going to say that, but since you brought it up...

Carrie pinched her upper arm.

"Ouch." Ruth rubbed her arm. "It's not a blessing, girl. I wish I could keep my big fat mouth shut."

"No, don't ever do that." Carrie snapped her fingers while jumping to her feet. "Oh, my goodness, your freedom papers. They're in my purse. You'll need them, the adoption papers, and the judge's letter authorizing you to convey the children to California and care for them until my return."

"Lord, a mighty girl, we almost put the whole shebang out of business, I don't understand where my mind is these days," sighed Ruth as she ran to get her purse while Carrie returned with hers.

They hastily transferred the documents. Train tickets, too.

Carrie took a deep breath, "Oh, here's Judge Adams's letter to that Judge in Independence, Missouri, in case you have any problem joining the wagon train. He did mail a copy to the Missouri judge if you couldn't get anyone to take the letter to him for you. I still need to write a permission letter to give you legal guardianship over my children. Maybe I better do that next."

Ruth required special permission to join the wagon train outside the state lines of Missouri because of Missouri's slave state status. Fortunately, the wagon train wouldn't leave until April, but the travelers had to report early for training on surviving the 1,700-mile trek. Mr. Lafferty and Ruth would have to make the grade or be left behind. Carrie wasn't worried about that. Ruth would become a pro twice as fast as the others, leading the wagon train by their appointed arrival date.

Following behind, Ruth held her purse wide open toward Carrie and asked, "What about that pistol that's supposed to keep us safe on the trail?"

"In the top drawer behind you," Ruth pulled the drawer open, then looked over her shoulder at Carrie.

"Oh, I meant the top drawer under the top drawer. Can't you read my mind?"

Ruth laughed and retrieved the pistol, "No, I can't, and thank you, Jesus."

"Take all the ammunition, too." Then Carrie's brain came up with something new to worry about, "What if some street thief or pickpocket snatches your purse? What's plan B?"

"Plan B? I'll tell you what plan B is—plan B is Plan A. These papers are going between my shift and the corset. I'd like to see some low-down thieves get a hold of these papers without me noticing. Anybody tries, I'll introduce him to Mr. Colt here." Ruth checked to see if the gun was loaded, then shoved the pistol into her skirt pocket with a nod. She then placed boxes of shells in the trunk.

Carrie stood and wrapped her arms around Ruth's neck, "What am I going to do without you? How will I manage?

"Ain't like I got a passel of friends," Ruth replied weakly while she wrapped her arms around Carrie's waist. "If I did, I wouldn't tolerate your contrariness."

"Take that back."

"No."

"I'm not contrary."

"You are, and I love you anyway."

"Me, too." Rubbing the spot on Ruth's arm where she had pinched her, Carrie knew her friend was nearly always right and apologized, "Sorry, I pinched you."

Ruth pinched her upper arm.

"Ow, dang it, why did you do that?"

"To remind you to show up in California on time, or you'll get more from where that came from."

Carrie laid her head on Ruth's shoulder, "Don't worry about that. I can hardly wait to get there."

"I'll apologize when I see you again. This isn't goodbye, we will see each other again."

They stood there with each other's heads on their shoulders and shared prayers and hope for the future.

Then Ruth said, "I will put the children to bed. You write that permission letter. Nobody is going to arrest me for carting around two white children."

<u>Jeremiah 29:11</u> *For I know the thoughts that I think toward you says the* LORD, *thoughts of peace and not of evil, to give you a future and a hope.*

January 15, 1860, Columbus, Ohio, Digging Up Dirt

"Sheriff Huffman?" JT braced himself against the door momentarily while he sized up the lawman. The Sheriff looked up from the paperwork on his desk. "Guilty as charged. Come on in. The Sheriff waved to invite him in. "George Huffman. How can I help you?"

The man was pushing forty and had a thin build, but those were lawman eyes giving him the once-over. JT sat in a battered wooden chair opposite the sheriff's desk. He gave the office the once over and decided it had to be the most cluttered, dustiest office he'd ever seen. The only dust-free item in the room was a rifle on the wall behind the sheriff. It gleamed as if ready for action. How does this man get anything done?

"Afternoon. My name is JT Grant. I'm a Pinkerton Agent following up on the Hank Lipton murder."

The sheriff moved the toothpick in his mouth to the other side. "Oh, son, there's a fly in the buttermilk. Back up a minute. The city council didn't request another Pinkerton agent. We don't have a budget for that. Besides, the case is closed, the man confessed he will be hanged what more do you want?"

"Yes, I understand. The agency won't be charging you for my services." Replied JT firmly.

"Well, why are you here?" The sheriff pushed back from the desk, pulling an ankle up to the opposite knee.

"Hank Lipton was my best friend, and rumors of a female accomplice to his murder exist. Captain Pinkerton waited to see if more information would come up at the trial, but that didn't happen." JT paused, searching for a place on the sheriff's desk for his hat.

The sheriff grabbed a stack of wanted posters and dropped them on the floor beside him, revealing an empty dust-free spot on the desk where JT's hat could reside.

"Thanks. I'm here to find out whether there was a female accomplice. Can you tell me what you grasp about it?" JT rested his elbow on the arm of the chair.

"Well, the whole town thinks it was Carrie Wagner, the bank robber's wife." He replied hesitantly.

"You mean the murderer's wife?" JT felt the distinction was critical.

"Well, yes, have it your way, the murderer's wife. She seems to be the logical choice, but it doesn't fit with her background. She's a sweet girl wouldn't hurt a fly."

JT thought he'd make up his mind about the circumstances being what they were. "What do you mean?"

"Carrie's parents abandoned her when she was five years old. The Women's Benevolent Society took her in and raised her. She stayed with them for eleven years. Then she worked at the Mercantile for five years before marrying Philipp Wagner. In that whole time, she never so much as spit in the street or look at anyone the wrong way."

"Interesting. How long were the Wagner's married? No criminal record? What made her snap?" JT asked.

"Let's see." The sheriff tapped his chin while calculating in his head. "I think they were hitched about two weeks when the bank robbery happened."

"Were they happily married?"

"Oh yes, until he robbed the bank and deserted her."

"Then why would a happy new bridegroom rob the bank, travel 120 miles to Cincinnati, wait for a Pinkerton Agent to murder, get arrested, and get dragged back to Columbus?" The idea had to sound as ludicrous to the sheriff as it did to him.

"I agree. It's a cock-and-bull story from beginning to end, but Philipp never saw fit to clear it up for us. He never uttered a single word in his defense, not even to his wife. After a few weeks, he told her to stop visiting him in jail. I felt sorry for the pretty little thing. She looked heartbroken."

"What about her made you feel sorry for her? She probably assisted in Hank Lipton's murder." JT felt a sneeze coming on. The dust in this office would choke a horse.

"You're chasing the wrong dog, Mr. Grant. Carrie's a beautiful petite scrapper whose husband deserted her while she waited for him—"

Ahchoo! "Sorry, it's all the dust," JT said.

Nodding, the sheriff continued, "He freely confessed and calmly waited for the hanging. Carrie stood by him the whole time."

"Sometimes women fool you into thinking they're as innocent as a farm girl." But, as Jenny had done to him, if the wife doesn't fit the bill, maybe it's the other woman. "Can you think of any other woman who could have been the accomplice? Did Wagner have a Saturday night woman?"

The sheriff chuckled. "Hardly. I can't comprehend how he landed Carrie. He's not what I would have called a catch."

"You've got my attention."

The sheriff pulled open a drawer in his desk, shuffled papers about, and came out with a photograph. He handed it to JT. The figure in the picture looked like a boy masquerading as a man. JT would describe the man as arrogant and foppish. "That picture is from when Wagner inherited the bank. Philipp's dad had owned the bank. That's how he ended up as bank manager. Old man Wagner died years ago, and his wife soon after. I guess a gal, especially a gal like Carrie, could consider him attractive. But man to man, Philipp never measured up. He couldn't look a man straight in the eye. Too passive and unobtrusive.

And he wasn't much for small talk either. Kept to himself mostly."

"He couldn't have been that bad. Everyone put their money in his bank." Said JT.

The sheriff lowered his leg to the floor and pulled himself to the desk. "Yeah, well, most of us had been putting our money in that bank back when old man Wagner was running it. There were no problems then; we didn't expect any when Philipp took over. Essentially, Phillip was merely running things as they were, we did not expect any changes. We trusted Philipp until the day he robbed us blind." He shook his head. "While looking for that accomplice, if you come across any of that bank money, let us know. I think the city council would make it worth your while."

"I'm not sniffing out your bank money for you, sheriff. A noose awaits Carrie Wagner, and she's overdue." Snarled JT.

"Don't be such an anxious boy. Wait until you meet her, then you'll savvy what I mean."

JT shook his head, "I don't let a wink and a smile deter me from my job, sheriff." JT retrieved his hat, signaling the end of the conversation.

"I don't know about you, Pinkerton men, but I like my prisoners to be guilty before I string them up." The sheriff rose from his chair and walked toward the office door. With one hand on the doorknob, he turned toward JT, removed the toothpick, and spoke. "Philipp Wagner hangs tomorrow. You barely got here in time. Mrs. Wagner agreed to leave town directly after the hanging."

JT extended his hand to shake the sheriff's.

"You'll need proof, Mr. Grant, and you'll need to bring her back to Ohio if she's guilty. I don't relish your job. And I'll remind you she's not wanted dead or alive."

"I chase murderers for a living, Sheriff. I don't become what they are."

"Is that so?" The sheriff asked, "Then you better wipe that murderous look out of your eyes.

Chapter Five

January 27, 1860, Philipp Hangs

Carrie's fairy tale turned murder mystery marriage of only two months concludes today at the end of a hangman's noose at noon, which left an hour for her to catch the southbound train to Cincinnati. Instead, Carrie curled up in a leather chair in the parlor to gather her thoughts before her brain shut down and checked her purse and valise to ensure she didn't forget something.

The law and townsfolk believed her husband deserved the sentence he received. But they knew nothing of the man she married. She would not have dreamt in her wildest dreams that Philipp would be capable of committing a crime as heinous as murder, but he did. He saved her from an 'invisible' state of being to establish her in society as the banker's wife, only to throw her back into invisibility. Actually, he took her from invisibility and made her the center of everyone's attention in a terrible way. Every time she left her house, the people stared at her as if she was naked. Since he banned her from visiting or writing, her opinion of her husband disintegrated. Carrie didn't know what to believe anymore; all the time she spent having faith in the love she shared with Phillip had become a taudry nightmare.

Maybe it depends on how you describe love. For some people, true love comes softly and miraculously. But unbeknownst to her, there's what some call true love that's full of secrets, lies, and betrayal. Deadly narcissistic hearts with poisonous agendas—like Philipp's. When he disappeared, she worried herself sick, having gone nearly four weeks without a word from him.

Philipp's betrayal left a new gaping hole in her heart to rival her mother's. Both apertures remain raw with jagged bloody edges, like the devil's kiss sucking at her soul. The heinous grievances lie inside each pit like committed, constant reminders that she was undeserving of love.

And what of her innocence? Burned to eradication like Sodom and Gomorrah by her wedded husband. Each passing day wore a little of her devotion away and increased her contempt. The taunts she received on the city streets, the vacant seats around her in church, and when she discovered he left her no money to survive drove her to incertitude.

For the first time in her life, she'd learn how to take care of herself, not uncommon at twenty-one years of age, but she had thought marriage settled her future. After he's hanged, unlike a newborn babe, she starts out knowing nothing except cooking and childcare and how to shoot an 1851 Colt Navy Revolver.

When she told Ruth she had to stay behind to attend the hanging, she did it out of respect for her husband, but today, respect is as rare as an albino horse. He refused to set the facts straight. Somehow, he's mixed up in these heinous crimes, and his wife has difficulty believing it. She had considered him innocent, but no more. He must have been guilty. He must not have the courage to meet her in the eye and give her an explanation.

Today she must perform her last duty as his wife, witness his hanging. Thoughts of escape kept her restless all night long. Her soaked linens clung to her despite the near-blizzard conditions reigning outdoors. Fear of relapsing into her 'invisible' state had her leg muscles bunched in preparation to run. Loss of security was the flaming playing card dealt her way today. She cannot leave it on the table for the next player. Betrayal was a repeat offense for her; her mother left her first. Philipp's brimstone-ish-horrific betrayal left her as soul-crushed as the first time.

Uncurled from the leather chair, she headed toward the kitchen.

The truth she must face today—he's guilty. Of what? She's unsure, but he deserved punishment for taking a sledgehammer to her life.

She crossed over to the north window of their neighborhood cottage. The sky matched her mood, gray and foreboding. Last night's snowstorm raged as a thick layer of pure snow would somehow blot out the evil at work today. A large bloodthirsty mob gathered two blocks up in front of the courthouse. She could smell their bloodlust from here.

The teacup she held in her cold, trembling fingers rattled against the saucer as the two came in contact. Those vultures, her supposed neighbors since she was five years old, stood out in blizzard conditions, demanding a pound of her husband's flesh. They will have to get in line behind her. He's killed all her dreams. Now her wrath would see him off to hell.

A faint shadow appeared, walking away from the crowd in her direction. It must be the sheriff. He promised to escort her to the hanging to help keep her safe and help her board the train afterward. Someone in a buggy stopped next to him. The sheriff climbed into the buggy, and the driver stepped into the street.

Thank goodness she won't need to trudge through the snow, wind, and ice. It looked like Dr. McGee's buggy. Bless him for his kindness.

Bundled up against the weather, she scanned the cottage, taking the disappointment and anger shared with those unsympathetic walls with her. She hoped the next tenent would fare better. Then, a knock came on the door; she grabbed her valise and answered it.

The howling wind ripped the door out of her mittened hand, and it slammed against the wall with Herculean force. The sheriff reached in and grabbed the doorknob. Carrie walked with the Sheriff, and he helped her up into the buggy.

The sheriff leaned toward her to say something. "You sure you want to witness this? I don't recommend it. You look as white as a ghost. I can take you straight to the train station."

What? Shirk her duty? She shook her head and said, "I owe him that much, at least." Then leaned back into the buggy, blocking some of the fierceness of the storm. She loved the scent of freshly fallen snow, so crisp and clean that just inhaling it should calm her troubled soul. But her husband shared no sense of duty regarding her heart. She needed to see him again to see if her battered heart reacted. The man had betrayed her. She may have to dig her heart out of her chest with a well-sharpened knife if a fraction of empathy for him is left. She wouldn't miss this hanging for the world.

I don't know how you figure that, but here we go." The Sheriff encouraged the horse forward.

After turning around, they gradually closed the distance between the bloodthirsty crowd and the murderer's wife. The carriage gave a bumpy ride over the ice lumps the iron-rimmed wheels conquered. Sheriff Huffman carved a path through the crowd to get her up close and private to the gallows. The worst of the crowd of vampires complained the buggy blocked their view. For heaven's sake! Hanging was not the county fair. Go home!

A few minutes passed, and before long, a deputy escorted Philipp out of jail and up the gallows stairs, dressed only in his suit. The din of the crowd tripled as they demanded Philipp hang immediately. The barbs the unholy mob threw out crushed her soul, if not Philipp's.

"Where's our money, thief?"

"You're going to hell, murderer."

"Did your wife help you rob us?"

If she said anything to him now, he wouldn't hear her. He looked frozen solid, with clamped jaws, a jailhouse beard, and purple lips. His blond hair whipped back and forth, and the frigid wind chaffed his skin pink.

His appearance shocked her; he'd lost weight. Would it have killed them to loan him a coat? They'd get it back in a few minutes. The perimeter of his suit, the part not flattened against his body, flapped violently in the gale-force winds. She half expected pieces of it to tear off and fly away. The solemn hangman stood and stared at his pocket watch as if the devil only accepts cursed souls when the big hand struck due north. Wringing her hands, she wondered if any of the crowd behind her had ever seen a loved one hang in the middle of an angry crowd? The man she loved faced a terrible death, and suddenly, she wanted to leave, to be far away, but it was too late; she had to stay and face the morbidity of Philipp's end.

His desperate eyes scanned the crowd frantically, but he searched farther back, not in front of where the buggy sat. For whom does he search? Not her. Can't you spare a glance at your wife? He knows this buggy, under his nose, conveys his wife. His wild eyes proved she was the last thing on his mind. The hangman encased Philipp's head in a black bag and tied it shut.

The dam broke, and she sobbed. Nothing that happened in the last two months made any sense. He never loved her. That's the only conclusion that made sense. Why the elaborate charade? Where could she find the truth?

She observed Philipp's now-bag-covered head through eyes overflowing with tears and clutched her hands to her chest. Her shoulders curled to hide the pounding of her battered heart. This can't be happening! He didn't kill anybody. A remembrance of his sweet proposal to her flashed through her mind. My darling Carrie, I ask for your hand in marriage. Take pity on a man deeply in love with you.

The hangman moved to pull the lever.

Every cell in her body screamed, No! She slammed her eyes shut. Hanging is too brutal even for Philipp's crimes. And the mob brought their children with them.

Please, God. No! The loco crowd howled their approval.

Thwack! The trap door snapped open.

Carrie's body jerked involuntarily, but the mob roared in approval. Gravity fractured his neck. She heard it despite nature's fury and the hatred from the pack of wolves behind her. Or she thought she did. A feral, haunted scream burst from her throat. An ethereal arrow pierced her heart as her palms reacted to cover the imaginary wound. His body swayed as the glacial winds battered it. Carrie glimpsed at the crowd, suspecting the pitiful howl originated from one of their tortured souls. Maybe a coveted dream sounds like that when it dies. Suddenly, the bride had become a widow in the blink of an eye. Carrie's short-lived love and confidence disappeared like a card trick in a magician's hand. The man she loved, the betrayer, was dead. Her heart lay shattered in her chest.

Now she's back where she started; betrayed, unloved, homeless, and invisible. Thank God the hanging was over, and she could put this nightmare behind her. The cold and violence of the winter storm seeped into her body, which helped her remain immune to the horror. Closing her eyes, she sank back into the carriage seat, numb.

The Sheriff came to her aid, folded her into his arms, "Look away. You don't need to see this." Then he yelled into her ear and pleaded, "Let me take you to the train station. This flock of Christians looks like a pack of ravenous coyotes waiting for nightfall."

She nodded as she wiped her eyes, but just then, despite the heavy snow coming down, she clearly saw one of Philipp's shoes fall off, undoubtedly because of the knee-jerk reaction to the fall. Her arm shot out to keep the sheriff from leaving yet. A hole in the heel of his sock telegraphed to the crowd what an inadequate wife she had been. Ruth's the one who worked in the orphanage laundry and could mend anything, giving it a second life. Eleven years as a cook in the orphanage proved her expertise.

What does it matter if his sock is holey? Who cares what this town thinks? But he saved me from obscurity by marrying me. So, I have a name now. She stuck one leg out of the buggy, intent on saving her husband's dignity.

A heavy hand jerked her back into the buggy. "What do you think you're doing? They'll tear you apart."

She blew her nose into her handkerchief. "I can't let them bury Philipp with only one shoe."

The Sheriff nodded at her and climbed out of the buggy. He walked the short distance to Philipp's corpse, retrieved the fallen shoe, and replaced it on his foot.

Someone reached into the buggy and tried to drag her bag away. They probably thought she kept her money there. She didn't, but she still needed to save her meager belongings. She latched onto the handle and leaned over to bite the thief on the hand. The sheriff returned, pulled the thief away from the buggy, and punched him. He rushed back into the buggy and urged the horse to turn toward the train station. The brunt of the storm hit them square in the face as if to say, 'you thought this would be easy.' The frozen droplets stung like broken slivers of glass driven into her face with an unholy force. She covered her nose and mouth with part of her woolen neck scarf and sighed in relief to put the nasty business behind her. Once again, she was betrayed and unloved.

The multitudes of hatred concentrated on her from the crowd sent chills down her spine. Carrie empathized with them. If anyone knew anything about the ever-growing pus-filled ball of anger in your belly festering like an army of red ants on the prowl, she's your person. Betrayal consumes your mind and heart. She's not giving anyone a chance to betray her ever again. Take your lies somewhere else. Your fickle nature can betray someone other than her for a change. The cure for what ails her rests just beyond her fingertips. Ruth's the only person she can trust, and she won't see her again until November.

The orphanage, where she volunteered daily to help with the children, put lit candles in all the windows in her honor. Yesterday, they shared goodbye, kisses, and hugs. She gave the cook her recipe for Thanksgiving dressing to please the children. Then, with her mittened hand, she waved to whoever might be at those windows. That building and its inhabitants held a warm place in her heart. They were her family and the only people she would miss.

The other half of the town, who missed the hanging, waited for her at the train station. She plastered her emotionless mask on as she passed through them, depriving them of the joy of seeing her wounded. But the ones who breathed down her neck bruised her heart with their barbs.

"You shoulda been hanged right next to him."

"You make me sick, stealing from honest folk."

One of the hordes reached out to grab her. She shrank away, but the stranger smashed a rotting gourd in the middle of her chest. Could this day please end?

"Where's our money?" One mob member shouted, but now the entire crowd chanted it.

Please stop asking me that question. I don't know.

The train whistle split the crisp morning air with an arrival warning. Finally, the sheriff helped her at the station and walked her to the train.

As she turned to board the train, a young man stepped forward. "Excuse me, Mrs. Wagner, do you have any parting words for the city of Columbus?" The reporter blinked snowflakes away and stood eagerly awaiting her words of wisdom to jot down on his pad.

The boy deserved a cold shoulder from her, but the crowd, visible over his shoulder, earned a headline above the fold that would keep Carrie Wagner in their memories for decades. "Columbus should be proud of itself today. The heart of Ohio is as dead as my husband."

The reporter swallowed hard. "Good luck, Mrs. Wagner," he tipped his hat and turned away.

The sheriff escorted her onto the train just far enough to cut the wind and cold and stopped her there. "This is as far as I go." He reached into his coat pocket and pulled out a folded paper. "This is your copy of the agreement with the City Council. Next, he produced a Bible from under his arm. "Your Bible, which Philipp asked me to return to you after the hanging."

Carrie snuggled it under her arm, wondering where the sheriff had hidden it up to that point. "Thank you for your kindness, Sheriff Huffman."

"Good luck, Mrs. Wagner." He stepped back into the storm and cursed as the wind sent his hat sailing.

The conductor gave instructions, but she couldn't catch his meaning with the combined noise from the train, crowd, and weather. Carrie went in search of the perfect seat.

She found a straight wooden seat facing forward, close to the heat source. Settling in like a roosting hen with a deep cleansing breath, she placed her valise next to her on the seat. The sweet but masculine aroma of cigar smoke permeated the train car. It didn't bother her other than reminding her of men. Finally, she had achieved a semblance of peace and relief from the bloodsuckers and the elements. It's over. Her sigh began at her toes.

The pot-bellied stove glowed with hostility, and she welcomed the heat. The window glass and pressurized steam muted the hateful taunts. She pulled off her mittens and used her handkerchief to wipe her face free of tears. Her new dream is California. Cincinnati's the goal for today.

When she opened her bag to store the Bible and the contract for the house sale and her half of the profits away, she found Little Ed, a handmade rag doll from her best friend Ruth, staring back up at her. The rag doll served as a reminder of her little brother Eduard. She slept with it every night. "Oh no, his smile unraveled." His grin was number one on her priority list when she checked into the hotel tonight.

Carrie unwrapped her woolen scarf, and her damp chestnut hair, with its bold streak of gray at her left temple, tumbled loose around her. Though wet, thick, wavy hair keeps your neck much warmer than a scarf.

The conductor bellowed, "All aboard."

The iron savior lurched and chugged away from the station platform, speeding up. She resisted the urge to glance back over her shoulder. There's nothing back there for her anymore.

Her feet felt positively glacial. She pulled a lap blanket from her bag to wrap around her feet. She can't loll about crying over past misfortunes; it's time to grow up and care for yourself. Then, of its own volition, the word "How?" escaped from her mind to her lips.

She coiled her damp wool scarf and placed it against the vibrating window. Carrie leaned against it and hoped for a nap. Summoning a vision of kicking insomnia in the seat of the pants, she slowly exhaled and closed her feverish eyes. Sleep had become an infrequent visitor during the last two months. She ordered her knotted muscles to relax, starting with her head and working her way down. Thoughts of hangmen, vampires, her dead husband, and the devil gathering more miserable souls fretted her mind for a while, but the rhythm of the railroad car swaying on the track helped. Somewhere in between, she fell asleep.

***

A loud commotion startled her awake sometime later. Two men wrestled in the dirty wooden aisle, not three feet from her. The object of the scuffle was her bag. Both men gripped it while they punched their foes with their free fists. His blood and the angle told that the taller sandy-haired man suffered from a broken nose. The black-haired man had the upper hand and looked unharmed. She threw herself into the melee to retrieve her valise and stumbled over her cobbled feet. She fell toward the vortex, squealing. Before she could hit the floor, a right to the side of her face sent her back to oblivion.

Coming to, Carrie felt a strong arm encircle her shoulders, preventing her from harm. Looking for her bag, she twisted in his hold, and pain on the side of her head throbbed.

"I have your bag here, ma'am." He sounded a little breathless.

She pressed her fingers to her temple and tried to focus. Then the softest, bluest eyes a man ever possessed came into view. A girl could be struck dumb by those eyes, other girls, not herself.

He smiled at her with trouble emblazoned across his forehead. "May I help you up?" the stranger asked while scanning her head to toe.

"Yes, please, things are a little bleary, and my head is pounding." He scooped her up fluidly like a cowboy who has handled hay bales for years.

"Now I can see why you fell," He said while nodding at her feet. "Trying to keep your feet warm?" The lap blanket indeed circled her feet. He wasn't tall, but he was taller than she. Everybody towered over her five-foot frame. She guessed he stood five foot nine. He placed her upright on the train seat, and she scooted to the wall of the train car.

"Sir, kindly tell me what happened?" She didn't want to miss the opportunity to scan him head to foot. His hair was black as sin, and he had veiled cobalt blue eyes and a travel-weary aura about him. Maybe the aura was just her headache pounding away at her brain. What game is the good Lord up to now? He's the most handsome man she's ever met. She's practically drooling.

The dubious one offered his hand, "Allow me to introduce myself, JT Grant, adventurer."

Adventurer? Like in Africa? She placed her hand in his, "My name is Carrie Wagner." His touch set off a tingle up her arm. That's never happened before. His grip assured rather than subdued, but he didn't release her immediately. Looking into his eyes, she felt his thumb rub over her clasped hand. It must have been her imagination. Oddly, when she was 'invisible,' no one greeted her, but protocol changed to kissing her fingers after she married. Now it's handshakes. There's a lot about functioning within society she truly doesn't understand.

Miss, take some traveling advice from a recent stranger. You need to be more careful in the future."

Tucking her skirt aside, she sat. That strong jaw of his begged for a caress. She twisted her fingers in her lap to teach them a lesson. "It's Mrs. Wagner," she corrected him. It dawned on her that the best gift she received from Philipp had more than one use--warding off unwanted attention. Mr. Grant slid into the seat next to her. Now what? Carrie glanced over her shoulder to see if the car was vacant. They had company.

"Place your valuables strategically. Lift your knees a few inches." Then, demonstrating, he pushed the bag under her knees where she could feel its presence, and he did it without personal contact. "That way, a thief will wake you before he's off with the goods."

He pulled a handkerchief out from somewhere and wiped dirt from her face. "That punch to your face will make a pretty shiner by morning."

Using his handkerchief and her mirror retrieved from her purse, she searched for dirt to eradicate. "Did you give it to me?"

"Yes, but I hope you know it was accidental, and I apologize."

"Thank you." Looking around for the other man, she asked, "Where's the other man?"

"I threw him off the train."

"He deserved it." There's nothing on her face except the beginnings of a black eye. She dispatched the mirror and held the handkerchief for her rescuer to reclaim.

He used the handkerchief to indicate the remains of something on the front of her coat. Taking the hint, she spied the mess.

"Thank you, it was a goodbye gift," she growled. She accepted the handkerchief again and busily scooped the mess onto the cloth.

"Bravo," he slapped his knee, "Use humor when you're down. It drives them crazy."

"So, you're aware of my sad story."

"No, but I saw the fond farewell they gave you. I'm dying of curiosity, but ladies with a mystery about them are far more charming."

She closed the handkerchief around the scooped mess and tied the corners together. Now what to do with it? "Mr. Grant, would you be kind enough to toss this into the potbelly stove for me? Of course, I assume you don't want your handkerchief back."

"Well, ma'am, I can't think of a better plan for your going away gift right now."

She watched him dispose of disgusting rotted vegetation with the help of a portion of a branch propped in the corner used to open the door on the stove without burning himself. She once again took the measure of the man. Dark hair peeked out at the throat of his shirt, and his muscled chest and arms filled out the rest of his shirt. When he returned to his seat, he made himself at home by pulling his left ankle to his right knee. She slammed her knees against the train car wall to avoid touching him. "Please, sir, I did not invite you to travel with me. We are strangers."

"I beg to differ. We shared a greeting and introduction only moments ago. I don't usually call myself a hero, but I did save your bag from a thief."

"I didn't mean to seem ungrateful. Thank you for being so kind, but I prefer my company alone."

"And that's how your bag ended up almost being stolen from you. I can protect you as far as Cincinnati."

He's arrogant. But only an idiot would turn down an offer of protection from a champion. So deep inside her gut, Carrie's courage, a lamb masquerading as a wolf, stood down, happy to allow the fight's winner to take guard duty. Maybe there would be a second day of her new life.

"Thank you, Mr. Grant, very kind of you."

Carrie paused for a moment. Wasn't that what she said when Philipp first asked her to dinner? Idiot! Why did you say that? You certainly don't need an offer of help from yet another man. You have no idea what he'll do next. Why doesn't he go away?

Drat!

She gave her pistol to Ruth and didn't think of buying another, nor did she carry a knife. She doesn't even have a hatpin because she wore her hair loose today. It seems her brain hibernated when she needed it most. She's had enough of this. She's already disposed of one man today.

"Mr. Grant, a mangy ole tic-filled dog bit me a week ago. I almost bit someone this morning, but his reflexes were too fast for me. I'd sit across the aisle for your safety if I were you?" He glared at her, waiting for the "just joshing you," she supposed. Then, after enduring her death mask stare for a few seconds more, he bolted to the opposite side of the train car and admired the Ohio countryside. There's nothing to see in winter in Ohio: just trees, fallow fields, and snow.

Job 7:16 I despise my life; I would not live forever.

January 27, 1860, Cincinnati, Ohio, The Truth Hurts

Mr. Grant and Carrie bundled up against the slashing icy wind and the menacing black clouds that kept the cold confined to the ground because the weather system over Columbus also covered Cincinnati. Mr. Grant held her close and guided her with an extended elbow or a touch on her lower back as they walked to the hotel. He even waited until she checked in. Without his help, her arrival might have been dicey at best. She thanked him for his kindness and apologized for siccing an imaginary rabid bite on him. But thank goodness he's gone. She needed some time alone.

Carrie raised her heavy head long enough to see the hotel had above-average hospitality staff, bathing facilities, and a bellboy who took her valise to the room and opened the door. Two windows, a soft-looking bed with freshly laundered sheets, and lace curtains lured her into the room. This place seemed secure enough for her heart to implode. She closed the door after tipping the bellhop. She leaned against the locked door and let out a hopeless sigh.

At last, in her Cincinnati hotel room with the dark of night creeping into her bones, she fetched Little Ed from the valise to hug him, but one look at his face reminded her of his unraveling smile. Carrie proceeded to a vacant corner of the room and slid down the wall to hug her knees. She gave into the pent-up need to sob and let it all out. Today was the worst day of her life, more so than her abandonment day. Brokenhearted sobs rang out as loud as demanded until a dripping nose drove her to yank a handkerchief from a pocket in her skirt to mop up her face. She knew the good Lord had a plan for each of his children, and she must have faith. He also allowed his children to suffer, as for her. *Carrie begged for the end of this trial. Lord, have I not suffered enough? Please forgive me my sins so that I may serve you.* But the stake driven through her heart tortured with every heartbeat.

"Hotel Services, Mrs. Wagner." Someone called out from the other side of the door.

Wiping her face again, she stored the handkerchief away and went to answer the door.

"Your fresh hot bath awaits you in the bathing room at the end of the hall to your right. For your information, that bathing room serves six guest rooms.

I wouldn't dally if I were you. Someone else might commandeer your bath."

"Thank you for your kindness." Then, tipping him handsomely, she closed the door and prepared for bathing. The warm bath will assuage her shivering, goosebumps, and soul.

Carrie spent half of this dreadful day wishing for a tub of hot water. All her scattered thoughts required organization, and a plan forward from here would lower her stress level.

A hot bath clears your mind and relaxes your body, like waking up innocent and peaceful. Could she ever use one right now? Another bather could appear, so once inside, she fortified the bathing room door against intruders, stripped, dipped her toe into the water, then slid in her whole body. Nice and steamy. A long "Ahhh" escaped her lips as she settled in. And her abused skin rejoiced to soak in the remedy.

Bracing her neck against the natural roll of the back of the tub, Carrie lathered up a washcloth full of flowery-scented soap suds and erased the dirt, lies, and betrayal off her tender skin. It felt glorious, like her bones were melting, and her brain wandered through a rose garden. Every home should boast a bathing tub.

Then, violence in the world would tumble. She leaned back and closed her eyes.

California moved one hundred and twenty miles closer to her tonight.

As for Philipp, she figured he claimed a bit of her heart, although knowing Philipp's true feelings toward her would also soothe her soul, be it good or bad news. Some things are between God and the sinner. Was there a credible reason for Philipp's elusive and troubling presence in her life? Someday it would please her no end to discover that information. Perhaps he possessed good causes in his mind for his crimes. But, no matter the reason, she needed to move on.

Carrie's hand closed on the diamond ring hanging from a pink ribbon around her neck. A better hiding place eluded her. It worried her that somewhere, somehow, the ring would slip out in public, perhaps while trying to pick something up and instigate her death. Expensive baubles similar to this one attracted trouble. Opening her fist, she studied the ring. The colors of the rainbow reflected off of it. She slid it onto her finger and found it fit perfectly. Why wouldn't it? Philipp ordered it for the 'love of his life.' That's part of the story that drove her crazy.

Carrie informed the ring. "Philipp didn't love me. So why did he special order you for me? What's that, you say? You fit me, so wear it. Hmm, perhaps you're the apology Philipp never delivered." Carrie grunted, and a few of the bubbles surrounding the ring popped. How would she know if a note didn't accompany the ring?

One thing was for sure; it was the most beautiful object her eyes had ever beheld. And it's another mystery to be solved since the crucial witness, the ring itself, refused to talk. Maybe Philipp wanted her dead. Wearing this ring would accomplish that task. Carrie pictured Philipp at his desk designing the ring, cackling as he drew diamond after diamond. "Yes," he muttered, "you'll be the asp for my Mrs. Cleopatra." God in heaven, she paints Philipp as more despicable as the days pass.

Removing the ring, Carrie lathered more soap and washed her face and neck. Then, she submerged in the water to soak her hair and came up to lather it. After rinsing the soap out, she squeezed as much liquid as possible and laid back against the neck of the tub again, but the room-temperature bath water encouraged her departure.

Carrie raised herself so that the water would sluice off her body. She then reached for a large, fluffy white towel on the stool beside the bathtub. If Ruth had to learn to care for herself, she should too. Don't rely on random people offering to help; keep your goal in mind. Some dreams passed away gradually, giving the dreamer time to adjust, but Philipp poisoned hers.

Donned in a nightgown and wrapper, she unlocked the bathing room door and dashed back to her room, locking herself inside for the night. *I've kicked your dirt off my shoes, Philipp. Tomorrow is the first day of the rest of my life without you.*

Forcing herself, Carrie sat huddled close to the lone lantern, sewing Little Ed's smile right with a blanket from the bed wrapped around her shoulders. The window rattled in the strong night wind, allowing cold air to seep into the room. When first abandoned at the orphanage, she cried herself to sleep every night over Eduard. As siblings, they were close, even sleeping in the same bed. She loved and missed him so much. Taking pity on her new friend, Ruth spent months gathering loose patches of material and yarn to create this doll version of Eduard. And now his smile was as good as new. She yawned.

Exhausted, Carrie climbed into bed, hugging Little Ed close. Then she searched for a Bible verse after saying her nightly prayers. Each night she chose a verse that was her Bible lesson for the day.

Lord, I have a lot of questions without answers. Please show me the way to my path and give me the strength to persevere. And, Dear Lord, I am trying to work on my deeply held rage. Thank you, and good night.

Freezing, she thumbed through the Bible, hoping for a quick find for tonight. Ah, yes, this one.

Psalm 109:21 & 22 *But do thou for me, O God the Lord, for thy name's sake: For I am poor and needy, and my heart is wounded within me.*

Chapter Six

January 28, 1860, Rescued

Carrie purchased the morning newspaper the following day before checking out but found her departure delayed by the most annoying hotel manager. The odious man tried to convince her to sit for a photograph for the third time to benefit his pocket. Now he summoned the lobby stragglers to gather around.

"Mrs. Wagner, your husband, acquired his notoriety in Cincinnati and Columbus. Why the law clapped him in handcuffs in this very hotel."

Thanks for reminding me. Not used to being the center of attention, Carrie pressed on, "Let me pay my bill, sir. A riverboat awaits me." A crowd must be forming behind her by the sound of scraping shoes and rustling clothes. "Please, I need to be on my way."

"Let the photographer take one photograph. That's all I ask." The manager indicated the wall behind him by spreading his arms. "I will hang it here. Now that the widow of a Pinkerton detective murderer has slept here, I can charge double for that room."

Barely able to speak through clenched teeth, she asked, "How much do I owe?" Next time she'll ask about the rate before checking in. It's good that she got up early to leave herself some extra time because if this keeps up, the riverboat will depart without her.

"Now that I think about it, I think a sign on the room door labeled, "Mrs. Philipp Wagner slept here accomplishes my goal. But unfortunately, the night clerk didn't put you in the same room where Hank Lipton died. I wonder why?"

How morbid, Carrie blessed the clerk for his sensibility.

The misogynistic manager beamed at her like his senses had taken a long walk. A less-than-kind thought popped into her head. If only she could be a man for thirty seconds to punch him squarely in the nose. Why do men never listen when a woman says 'no'? Enough of this. She tossed two dollars on the counter, saying, "Whatever else you figure I owe; I charge you for the inconvenience. Good day." But her five-foot-tall and one-hundred-and-ten-pound frame failed to part the crowd.

Mr. Grant chose that moment to come to her rescue once again. Stepping up from behind, he whispered into her ear, "Need some help?"

She nodded, fully aware she should decline and learn how to handle the situation herself. Then she cursed that scared little girl, representing her flagging courage, cowering in her psyche.

With an arm around her waist, he tucked her in close. But that's not the kind of help she needs.

His attire had changed entirely from yesterday. Today he sported western apparel with a gun strapped to his hip, cowboy hat, and rawhide coat. He looked in his element and appeared in control.

"Step aside, ladies and gentlemen."

No one moved. Mr. Grant pulled his revolver and fired a round into a vacant corner of the room. The crowd parted as the sea had for Moses. Women squealed as men pulled them to the side. In haste, the photographer bumped past her with a tripod and camera on his shoulder. Too late to capture the likeness of the murderer's widow. She had to smile at that.

During all the commotion, her rescuer eased her out of the hotel. "Where to, ma'am?"

In the daylight, Mr. Grant's magnetism grew twice-fold. First, that coal-black wavy hair of his dared her to run her fingers through it. Although he must have shaved, his jaws appeared darkened with stubble. For that reason, and his square jawline, she struggled to keep from caressing his face. And, Lord, save her from those deep blue eyes of his. They're positively sinful. Because of appearances, she unwrapped his arm from around her waist. "To the docks. I have a riverboat to catch." Threading her arm through his bent elbow, they turned toward the docks.

"Why didn't you mention staying at the same hotel last night?"

"Like you, I needed a place to roost for the night. I was already there; why not just check in?"

Somehow, she felt guilty and remained undecided as to his intentions. Time to change the subject. "Do you often shoot guns off indoors? How shocking."

"Honestly, Carrie, if you insist on traveling alone, you must learn to care for yourself. Particularly if you plan to travel west. As the saying goes, 'There's no law west of St Louis and no God west of Ft. Smith.'"

"Call me Mrs. Wagner," she said. If only she had his self-confidence and comportment. Mr. Russell would hire her in a minute. Where can she learn that?

Mr. Grant's next question sounded like he was scolding a child. "Do you own a gun or know how to use one?"

"Yes, I had one and knew how to use it."

"Do you have it with you?" he asked, bordering on disbelief.

"No. I gave it to a friend who needed protection." Unfortunately, Ruth needed it more than she did.

The information stopped him dead in his tracks and caused her to misstep. Then he questioned passers-by repeatedly until success. "Excuse me, could you direct me to the location of the closest gunsmith?"

Gun oil and gunpowder scented the air and greeted them when they entered the shop. Weapons of all sorts hung on the walls behind the counter. A horseshoe-shaped counter kept customers honest. Product description labels dangled by a thread, handguns, rifles, shotguns, and specialty items. The proprietor walked over to their part of the horseshoe. Not understanding why, they had to visit a gun shop, Carrie let Mr. Grant control the conversation. "This young lady needs a weapon to defend herself. I think a derringer will do fine."

Carrie's jaw dropped at the lie. Did he not hear her when she said she knew how to use a pistol? Is this a trait you must master to become a member of the men's club? After all, she's invisible to the hotel manager as well. Hoping to gain equal standing, she stepped forward to line up beside him instead of behind. The proprietor quickly placed three derringer models on the counter before Mr. Grant, not her.

"These are my bestsellers," he pronounced.

"Does the price include a cleaning kit and ammo?" Her companion lifted each derringer to peer down its barrel.

The proprietor said, "Includes the kit. No ammo."

Well, she never would have thought of asking that.

"Could you please hold these one at a time, so I can see which fits your hand the best?" Mr. Grant held one gun out toward her.

An action she would never have thought of taking. Maybe the man is helpful after all. She turned toward him and palmed the first derringer. "Is it loaded?"

"No, ma'am, not when a woman is holding it." The store proprietor laughed at his joke, but she found no humor in it.

Choosing the middle derringer, JT said, "We'll take this one and a box of shells, please."

"That'll be five dollars."

Five dollars? Now her dubious companion is spending her money. How does he know if she has five dollars? Mr. Grant reached into some pocket on his person and produced payment for the proprietor.

"Oh no, you can't pay for it. The gun is for me, isn't it?"

"Yes, but my idea." Taking her valise, he stored the weapon inside for safekeeping. "Find someone to teach you how to use it. Don't forget," he admonished. "And remember, it's for close range only."

"Thank you. How can I pay you back for such kindness?"

"By staying safe."

Maybe Mr. Grant, genuinely concerned about her safety, performed a gentlemanly service. And maybe Philipp Wagner was as innocent as a new born babe. "Thank you for your concern, and now I think you had better take me to that riverboat before it leaves without me."

"Don't worry. I'll take you there. My train leaves in forty-five minutes."

Inwardly she sighed; he saved her from coming up with an excuse for their separation later. However, when the time came, she watched him walk away proud and confident. Two traits she envied. What a treat for some woman somewhere.

Galatians 4:1-3 *Now I say that the heir, as long as he is a child, does not differ at all from a slave, though he is master of all, ²but is under guardians and stewards until the time appointed by the father.*

January 28, 1860, An Answered Prayer

Carrie boarded the Ohio Pride in the early afternoon. Columbus, founded at the confluence of the Scioto and Olentangy Rivers, paled compared to sprawling Cincinnati and the width of the Ohio River. Yet, the sights and sounds of the crowded boat docks delighted her, no matter which direction she gazed.

Cargo boats of various designs were loading and unloading everywhere. The docks overflowed with cargo bound for up or downriver. Fishing boats unloaded their morning haul, contributing to the riverport's scented charm. Dock supervisors shouted orders to their workers, assorted steam whistles blew, and bells clanged.

She quickly boarded the boat, weaving through the crowds of passengers and their families trying to make it to the loading dock and get her ticket checked. Once she had boarded the boat, she gathered with the rest of the passengers at the rail. Departees waved and threw kisses to relatives and friends bidding goodbye, and those onshore shouted their endearments. She watched the throngs of people with tears in their eyes, mothers with children shouting goodbye to the father of her children and Carrie couldn't help but wonder, why were passengers leaving their loved ones behind? What could have possibly possessed them to leave their families and travel all the way to another part of the country? No reason could be big enough to separate her from her family if she had one.

As she stayed there, leaning against the rail, the ship began letting out six short blasts from its whistle, indicating that the ship was about to leave. She picked up her things and headed on inside before more people could get trampled by the crowds. As she made her way inside, the boat let out one final long blast through the boat's steam whistle shrilly, announcing their departure. No one wished her a pleasant voyage or threw vegetables, just peace. She was leaving no one behind who would miss her, and she was okay with that. She could get used to the peace that came with it.

Curiosity drove her to the south side railing to take in the view of a slave-holding state. After everything she's read in the newspapers about the southern states and all that Ruth had told her, undoubtedly, they differed vastly from the rest.

On the opposite bank of the river stood Covington, Kentucky. Also, a busy river port like Cincinnati, but the difference was immediately noticeable. Only darkys worked loading and unloading boats, closely supervised by white men with whips. She pulled her eyes away, silently praying for all their souls. She couldn't bear to see such things. She was much too fragile to bear it. Ruth read newspaper articles to her about slavery explaining what new poor darky had been killed, hunted, or punished before she could read English very well. Carrie had shuddered then, and she shuddered now. Slavery was worse than anything she had experienced. Compared to that, being abandoned, betrayed, or cast into hell did not seem so bad.

Luckily, Carrie found a lone deck chair that stood near a window, bathed in sunlight and quickly climbed into it to read her newspaper. Later that evening, she changed into her nightclothes and climbed into her cot for the night, welcoming the rest after the long day. She knew she needed it, she had a long journey ahead of her but no matter how hard she tried to catch a wink of sleep, rest eluded her. Every rotation of the paddle wheel produced a loud squeal. As fickle as luck was, her economical aft cabin put her right next to the contraption, so each squeal was irritatingly audible and loud enough to ruin her peace. It seemed that sleep would evade her for another night if this night resembled those since Philipp's conviction.

An unusually high-pitched squeal grated her nerves, causing her to wake. Trying to muffle out the sound by practically smothering herself with a pillow did not help. Tomorrow, she must ask the captain if he could remedy the noise or perhaps move her to another cot. This would never do. Since sleep shunned her, she decided to read for a while, perhaps that might make her sleepy. After shrugging into her wrapper and lighting the oil lamp, she turned but then she froze.

"Don't holler, lady. I mean no harm. I wouldna steal nuttin,' I swear!" whispered the raggedy boy anxiously. The poor boy appeared to be about twelve years of age.

He seemed out of place in the relative warmth and comfort of the riverboat cabin. The ragamuffin wore a light shabby shirt and pants without a hat or coat to protect him from the cold. One toe poked through the worn-out leather of his shoe, and his hair spiked up from the embedded filth and grime.

"How did you weasel your way in here unnoticed, young man?" asked Carrie not unkindly.

Avoiding her question, he answered, "I woulda skedaddled before mornin', so's you wouldna seen hide nor hair of my mug, miss."

"Odd. I did not feel a cold draft when you came in." Arms akimbo, Carrie glared at the boy. "What are you doing here then, boy?"

"Stowaway, ma'am." Clarified the boy, "If I do sneak on board, I find a hidey hole, but tonight it's colder than a miner's pecker ain't it." Two bony hands rubbed his arms for some warmth, "Ma'am, you ain't no bigger 'n me. You been ailing?" he asked curiously.

"I'm not sick. I'm petite." Huffed Carried as she pulled the blanket back on her cot, "Come now, get in bed before you freeze to death."

"Don't fret 'bout me miss. I ain't pushin' up daisies yet." Replied the boy.

"I can see just how fine you are young man. Into the cot, please, no arguments."

The boy didn't need to be told twice. It had been apparent he had been extremely cold; his teeth were chattering as he spoke. He jumped at her command, kicked off his shoes, and slid into her cot, pulling the blanket to his chin, sighing in relief.

Returning to her original question, she asked, "Well then, how did you weasel in here?" The boy's dirty blond hair covered half his face; she couldn't resist pushing it back.

"I picked the lock and sidled through quick as a rabbit." The boy yanked the ends of the blanket tight around himself. "What's poteet mean?"

"Petite means this is as tall and wide as I'll ever be." Explained Carrie. The boy nodded. Something about him seemed familiar. "Does the lock still work?" she inquired.

"Yes' um, I didna break it." He rubbed his feet.

After locking the door, she found terrified brown eyes following her around as she came back, pleading with her for mercy.

"So, young man, what do people call you, and when did you eat last?" This time, she recognized the frightened, deserted look on the boy's face better than most would have. That's why he seemed familiar. The abandoned always identify with their ilk.

"Billy, ma'am, I ain't ate nuttin' fer a spell." He swiped his dirty finger under his runny nose and wiped the wet digit dry on the blanket.

She filed his nasty habit away in her mind to address later choosing to ignore it for now.

"Well, I'm Carrie Wagner," she gifted him with one of her warmest smiles. "And if we can refrain from referring to miner's peckers again, here's something for you to eat."

For the passengers' convenience, cubbyholes stretched across the wall between the cot and the sole wooden chair in the cabin. A quarter-round of bread, cheese, and an apple huddled in one crevice. Showing him her cache, she offered an invitation, "Why don't you sit up long enough to have something to eat?"

Again, there was no need to ask twice, and, of course, he dragged the blanket with him. Then she spread the food by laying a handkerchief in front of him. It seemed like he couldn't decide where to begin for a few seconds, taken aback by the spread, and then one hand latched onto the cheese and the other onto the bread.

"Dank ya, ma'am," he noisily chewed until they disappeared. She reckoned she could have blown a spoonful of soup cool enough to sip simultaneously. The entire apple met the same fate. Core, seeds, stem, etc. She refused the urge to check for wounded digits. After he ate, she tucked the worn-out boy into her cot, losing the argument with herself to scrub him first even though that had been her first instinct.

"You ain't gonna snuff the lamp, are ya, ma'am?"

"Please call me Mrs. Wagner." She knew why he wanted to keep the lights on. The night terror stage stayed with abandoned children longer than others. "No, I got up to read for a while. Why?"

"Only babies otta be affeared of the dark, but ya never know whatta befall a feller in the devil's darkness." He punched the pillow into submission and yanked the blanket to his chin. "That evil bastard won't catch me unaware." He muttered.

"Don't you worry about the devil, okay? We've tangled before. He'd sooner take on a prairie twister than Carrie Wagner again. And Billy, please do not say bastard either. It's a nasty word that brands innocent babies for their whole lives." There were a dozen or so children in the orphanage classified as such. Those kids were teased mercilessly, despite the headmistress's constant warnings to stop and could never escape the title they had been branded with at birth no matter what they did or where they went. Some people went as far as to call them the devil's spawn.

Propped up on an elbow, he asked, "What do I say instead?"

"Let me see, um...how about heel or louse?" suggested Carrie.

"Didn't have da same punch to it, but I'll use one or another." Grunted Billy in response.

He yawned and stretched his hands before lying flat on his back and rolling toward the wall. Why did Carrie reassure him? Because he couldn't keep the fear and loneliness from showing all over his dirty freckled face. And, because she couldn't pretend, she didn't understand.

After all, she used to be a lost, lonely child like him with more than one fear on her mind in bed when the mistress came around to put all the candles out and the fear of the dark would stifle her. After that, there would be nothing but shadows chasing the wall as the silence deafened and the darkness blinded her. Lucifer comes for you when you're defenseless and plants moot questions in your head which have no purpose in the present.

Why did they give me away? Why did they not want me? Am I not lovable? How can I find my family? Will I ever belong? Endless questions would plague her while tears ran down the sides of her face, spilling into her ears. Ruth would hear her silent sobs and would crawl into bed with her. She would comfort her and they would pray together until they fell asleep.

She couldn't read anymore. Instead of reading, she thought about Billy and his struggle to survive. She silently prayed for him. Realizing that you've been tossed away with no more thought given than that to yesterday's newspaper was a pain she wouldn't wish on her worst enemy let alone this poor defenseless child. It was an abscess of the soul, a pain that no amount of medicine can cure.

She could not let this boy keep wandering. Her conscience did not allow her to do so but she couldn't afford to support him either as her mind so crudely reminded her. There wasn't a fiber in her body that would allow her to pat him on the back in the morning and wish him luck as she sent him on his way to the bleak future that awaited him.

How could she let him go. After all, look at him; he has no money, no roof over his head, is not attending school, and needs clean clothes, new shoes, and a winter coat, gosh darn it he had nothing. He would freeze himself to death and people weren't kind. She shuddered at the thought of how she would have managed to survive had she not been sent to an orphanage and instead had to survive on her own as a ragamuffin.

Oh Lord, is this a new trial you have set before me? Or, she paused for a moment to think, perhaps Billy was the sign which she had been praying for? The Lord knew she couldn't turn the boy away despite having limited funds and a strict deadline, yet the boy was here sleeping in her bed.

Father, I will care for the boy and trust you to provide. Thank you for this gift.

She pulled her winter coat from the hook on the wall and curled up in the rocking chair. The noise from the paddle wheel sounded louder in the semi-darkness. Carrie kept herself busy counting the shrill squeals the paddlewheel made until sleep claimed her.

Isaiah 63:8 *For He said, "Surely they are my people, Children who will not lie." So He became their savior.*

Chapter Seven

January 29, 1860, Who's the Adult Here?

What on earth was keeping Billy? It didn't take a twelve-year-old boy this long to bathe at the orphanage, but then again having a waiting line did seem to rush you. Carrie sat alone at a dining room table, waiting impatiently. As she deliberated getting up and going after him to see if he is doing okay, his clean face appeared at the dining room entrance. To catch his attention, she waved at him, and he bounded over happily sliding into the chair next to her.

"Am I eatin' clean?" He asked, flashing a broad smile that displayed every tooth in his mouth.

"Yes, I think you'll do, but we must buy you some clean clothes as soon as the boat docks. Scarecrow rags are in better condition than what you're wearing, my dear boy." Sighed Carrie.

"Where do ya think I got dese?" He fisted the front of his dirty, torn shirt for emphasis. "I ain't allowed new clothes."

Carrie frowned. What does he mean he's not allowed? Was he in an orphanage, too? No, of course not. The orphanage provided clean, suitable clothes to wear to school. That person Billy fled from must be the culprit behind this. Just then the server arrived at their table to take their orders for breakfast. He stuck his head in the pages of the menu.

"Ma'am," the server said, "the captain has dining room rules."

Carrie looked up at the man with a warm smile. "I'm sure he does. Riverboats run on a tight schedule, do they not?"

"Yes, ma'am," the server said.

"Let the captain know I plan to arrange passage for the boy once we've eaten, and he'll have clean clothes later today after our next stop." Carrie reached over to close Billy's slack jaw. "Stop dawdling and order yourself some food. It is not polite to keep someone waiting. The man has other tables to wait on."

"My belly can't decide 'tween hot cakes, sausages, eggs, and coffee or four eggs, bacon, biscuits, and sausage gravy with coffee. So, can I gets both?" he asked hopefully.

"No, you may not. Choose what I can afford." Replied Carrie.

"My belly button done worn a hole plumb through to my backbone."

Laughing, she dismissed the remark. "That's not the issue." When was the last time she laughed? Gosh, too long ago. She chose scrambled eggs, bacon, and coffee for the both of them, which sounded absolutely delicious.

The steward nodded and informed them their food should be out in fifteen minutes and hurried off.

"Why aren't you allowed new clothes? Allergic?" The playful grin on his face disappeared like a blown-out candle. His eyes fell away, and he fidgeted in his seat and ran a finger under his runny nose. She fished around in her purse until she located a handkerchief for him. "Wipe your nose with this, please."

Billy pocketed the handkerchief and asked, "What does a-ler-jik mean?"

"Oh, how to explain that? Well, it's when something doesn't agree with you. Other people can handle whatever is just fine, but it gives you a rash, makes you sneeze, gives you a headache, or some such reaction."

"Yeah, that's it! I'm allergic!" He slanted his eyes up at her. "New duds gib me airs."

Laughing again, her hand flew to cover her mouth. Smart Alec or boy in need? Which is it? Both deserve care and guidance. The truth is that she needed Billy more than he needed her. Nothing else has brought this much happiness since she adopted the children, and she wouldn't dare spoil that.

The server returned and unloaded plates of food from the tray. Billy's mouth dropped open as his eyes darted from one breakfast item to the next as if he couldn't decide where to start. He approved by sniffing his breakfast like a 'coon hound with a swoosh of his head from left to the right.

Mr. Grant slipped into a chair on Carrie's left and wished everyone a good morning.

Carrie thought he had a train ticket to 'leave me alone.' "Good morning, Mr. Grant. What a surprise."

"Now I knowd they's a heaven. Step aside, lady and gent. Right afore yore peepers, I'm gonna disappear all this grub!" Billy speared a forkful of egg, topped them with bacon, and washed it down with coffee.

Ah, another opportunity to teach him some manners. "Billy, in polite society, all those going to eat must wait until everyone is plated." Explained Carrie patiently.

Carrie's reward was a cocked eyebrow. "I ain't polite when I'm dog hungry. So, dig in afore I gulp this down and start in on yores."

"Don't you dare touch my plate. I'm starving." Chided Carrie.

Turning to Mr. Grant, Carrie asked, "What are you doing here? What happened to the train?"

He shot his hand up and snapped his fingers hard to summon the server.

Carrie flinched at the sound.

The server responded. What a rude way of summoning service. After he dismissed the server, his cobalt blue eyes fell on her.

"Well, Mrs. Wagner, I'm an adventurer headed west. And you're headed west as well, destination unknown at this point. My mother taught me to be respectful and helpful to defenseless women. Therefore, I couldn't let you go alone, do you see what I mean?" he grinned.

The server returned and filled Mr. Grant's coffee cup. While he sipped, he glanced past Carrie and asked, "Who's the urchin?"

Taking offense, Carrie defended Billy. "He's not an urchin." Before Mr. Grant had the opportunity to say anything else, she added. "Well, I guess he does look like an urchin right now, but I haven't asked about his circumstances yet."

"Where did he come from?" Mr. Grant stared unapologetically at the rapid pace of food consumption being packed away by the so-called urchin.

Billy said, "I might ax ya the same, Mr. But-in-ski. So, happens. I don't know wheres I came from. Mz. Wagner, why don't ya tell that hayseed to tell his story, walkin'? Yore too old for a what do fokes call it, oh, cha-per-one ."

"True, I don't need a chaperone, but please don't talk to people in such an aggressive manner. And do not refer to a woman's age." Explained Carrie. Billy rolled his eyes at the new lesson Carrie had given him on manners but Carrie chose to ignore it for now.

The server approached their table and placed breakfast in front of Mr. Grant. The assortment of delicacies rivaled Billy's original order.

Budget-conscious Carrie said, "server, separate checks, please." The server nodded, but Mr. Grant winced.

A wealthy woman of middle age and her lapdog husband interrupted their revelry. A fox fur draped the woman's shoulders, a massive, feathered concoction perched on her head, and Mr. Moneybags puffed on a gigantic cigar. Mr. and Mrs. Wall Street, no doubt. Carrie raised her eyes to the couple standing not two feet away and steeled herself. There were dozens of these "I'm so rich that you don't matter" types that crawled out of their fifty-room mansions to demand an orphan or some other dubiously labeled person vacate the vicinity like they're contagious or devoid of any value.

"Madam, excuse our interruption. I'm Mrs. Penworthy, and this is my husband, Mr. Penworthy, and we paid for first class. But this boy is not first, second, or third-class. It is rather offensive. Please remove him from the premises at once." With her nose tilted up, the matron motioned toward the main doors of the dining hall.

Billy ate to his content and never looked up.

People can insult her and get away with it, but not one of her children. That's all it took to decide about

Billy. Forcing steel into her backbone, she rose to face the matron. "I'm Mrs. Wagner, and this boy is in my charge. May I suggest that if you are offended, you could take a walk on the deck or play bridge in the card room? For you, it's impossible to see my boy from those vantage points." Then Carrie motioned toward the dining hall door.

"That doused her fire good and proper!" Billy slammed the table with his fist. "Squawk, no more of yore la-te-das around here, lady," then stood and pointed at the woman with his knife.

Carrie took the knife away from him.

"People in some parts disappear from time to time. I'd sure hate to see somethin' happen to Mr. Moneybags there." Billy pointed at the man in case she suffered from any confusion as he smiled.

Carrie rounded on him. "I don't hold with threatening people."

Billy stuffed a forkful ofegg into his mouth. "Yes 'em, I'm on your side," he protested around his mouthful.

"Well, upon my soul!" Mrs. Penworthy said.

Interrupting, Carrie said, "Excuse me, ma'am, if you could allow me a moment."

The woman nodded.

Eyeing Billy, she said, "Apologize this instant, young man."

Billy dropped his fork, his mouth agape and asked, "Fer what?"

"For threatening someone's life. That's unacceptable behavior that I won't tolerate." Said Carrie firmly.

Mr. Grant opened his mouth to say something, but she raised a palm to silence him.

"Is that so, Mz. Wagner?" Billy turned to the high society couple. "Sorry, Mr. and Mz. My manners ain't so good."

Her negative approach toward the couple had most probably encouraged Billy's outburst; she added," I, too, owe you an apology. I'm buying a ticket for him right after breakfast and new clothes at the next stop. I am aware he doesn't fit well in this atmosphere. So please forgive my behavior as well."

Sometimes pent-up anger from the past clouds her judgment on current events. Ruth says Carrie has the worst temper and likens it to a tornado. That must improve, she couldn't possibly have her children adopt this behavior.

"Thank you, Mrs. Wagner. Come, Montgomery." The matron swung her ample hips as she shuffled out. Watching those ample hips sway in that blue dress could cause a nasty bout of seasickness. Montgomery followed with hands clasped behind his rail-thin frame and puffed on his cigar as if smoke signals might save him.

Carrie slumped into a chair, noticing Mr. Grant. He would be guilty by association, so she offered an apology. "I beg your pardon, Mr. Grant. I forgot you were here."

"Oh, I'm not here, Mrs. Wagner. So, you needn't scold me." He fled his chair before she said another word, taking his plate and coffee.

Drat! Carrie handled that all wrong. She picked up her fork, and in the time to consume two eggs and bacon, Billy ate every morsel of food on his plate and rubbed his satisfied stomach serenely.

After breakfast, Carrie sought Mr. Grant's cabin and knocked on the door. Mr. Grant opened the portal. "Mrs. Wagner, how nice of you to visit."

He looked surprised to see her.

"May I come in, or do you want to walk on the deck?" asked Carrie.

"Please come in. I think all is proper if we leave the cabin door open." JT led Carrie to a chair near the potbelly stove. Then he shrugged into his coat before sitting on his cot. "I assume we are here to discuss Billy."

"No, we are not. Mr. Grant, I am a full-grown woman and will not be requiring a chaperone." Then, thinking herself harsh, she followed up with, "Rather, shouldn't I be learning to take care of myself?"

"Stop right there," he said, "who will point out to you never to tell a stranger your business? You're as green as a four-leaf clover and ripe for a disaster."

"What do you mean by that?" she demanded as she felt her forehead scrunch into a tight scowl.

"Yesterday, for example, without provocation, you told me," He spread the fingers of one hand out on his thigh, "a stranger, that you were unarmed and had money."

"I did no such thing." Her intertwined fingers were in danger of popping off.

"Let's review, shall we? Do you remember when I asked if you owned a gun?" He raised his first digit.

"Yes, of course."

"You answered yes, but you gave it to a friend. Somebody needed to step in and stop you if you planned to conquer the west without a weapon. What option did I have other than to remedy that, or my conscience wouldn't give me a second of sleep the rest of my life?" He added a second digit.

Carrie chewed her bottom lip and blinked at him a few times. He was right of course.

"I went to pay for the derringer, and you popped up and announced to the world that you possess enough money to pay for the purchase." Another digit. That makes three.

Shamed, Carrie glanced at the floor. "Oh my, how badly I behaved."

"There was nothing for it but that is why I decided to tag along with you since we are westward bound either way and I would hate to see such a beauty get robbed or murdered."

Carrie snapped at him, "Don't say that. No one has ever referred to me as beautiful nor do I wish them to. I am not. Stop lying to me."

"Well, they're blind. I first noticed your creamy skin that's as clear as the sky above, not a blemish anywhere. And that turned-up nose puts all others to shame."

"Thank you," Carrie flipped her palm in the air, "but never mind, sir. Solid old maid material here. Whatever you're thinking, you can erase it from your mind right now." Anymore, and she would be beet red until morning.

JT shook his head, "and now the pigeon admits thieves and murderers need not be wary because there is no husband or guardian. Widow or divorcee? Don't worry about me. Your rather charming personality keeps me at bay." Digit four.

Carrie chewed on that for a moment, admitting that it stung. Then, she changed the conversation. "Is crime as rampant out west as you make it out to seem?"

"Mrs. Wagner, there is no law enforcement out west. None. That means every low-down crook and cold-blooded murderer flees to the west, where they are free from prosecution, free to do as they wish." JT reached out to take her hand, and his tone softened. "I'm not trying to frighten you, but you must know the reality if you insist on traveling. It is unsafe for a lone woman, especially one as beautiful and petite as you."

Carrie sighed at his reference to her supposed beauty as she resisted the urge to roll her eyes.

"There are men who would take advantage of you," the chaperone warned her again.

She pulled her hand from Mr. Grant's and covered both flaming cheeks. This conversation hasn't gone the way she planned, and she did not intend for it to stay this way. Instead of shooing him away, Mr. Grant convinced her of the needed precautions. Unpredictable precautions for which she now realized she was unprepared.

Drat!

Now she didn't know what to do. On the one hand, Carrie could not let this man follow her everywhere she goes after all, how well did she know him? The only thing she knew about him was that he craved adventure. But even that might be a lie. According to him, you can't trust anyone so why should she trust him? What sets him apart? Worse than that, he thinks she's beautiful, and he's magnetic. Her eyes caressed his dark, wavy hair, slid down his molded chest, and admired his corded thighs. A need to touch him flared inside of her. She's a pillar of determination, all right. How long ago did she swear off men? This urge was odd, an unwelcome and annoying feeling. Philipp never raised this kind of attraction to her. She stuffed both hands in her skirt pockets to reinforce her failing resistance.

Carrie tried to respond, but words failed her. "Um, Mr. Grant," she pushed a loose strand of hair behind her ear, "while, I mean, ah, since it seems I would be remiss if I declined, I accept your kind offer of help." Her eyes met his as he smiled like a cat with a full milk dish. Why do I have the feeling he's up to something? A voice inside Carrie's head told her she was making a mistake, but she pushed the feeling aside, "I must ask in the future that you don't touch me. Women come into this world with a reputation to defend."

"Then we have a deal, Mrs. Wagner?" He offered a hand to shake.

"Please call me Carrie." They shook hands.

"Thank you. My Christian name is JT. Please use it."

Crisply spoken, she assumed he took offense to the dining room meal payment from that morning. "I'm sorry if I offended you this morning. Can you explain my error in hopes I don't repeat it?"

JT raised an eyebrow but obliged, "In polite society, it's customary for a gentleman to pay the check in an unattended woman's company."

Not something you learn in an orphanage. "I did not know. Thank you for the lesson. Oh, and may I ask? Is it proper in society to summon service with a snap of your fingers? If it's proper, I would like to change my habit." She replied sweetly knowing full well it was not.

Chagrined, he had the decency to look away momentarily, "Touché, Carrie, well played. I shall apologize to the server the next time I see him. Can we talk about that urchin next? I was under the impression that was why you wanted to see me."

His features changed, and now he looked annoyed. Carrie said, "His name is Billy. You don't like children, do you, JT?" After that, she can quit admiring his physique because she has no use for anyone who doesn't love children.

JT stood. "I don't like pickpockets or thieves who think they've found a pot of gold and intend to latch onto their mark until the money runs dry."

Affronted that he would say such a thing about Billy, she said, "One could say the same about you."

***

Carrie needed to arrange Billy's passage with the captain. At least for a few days, until she talked to him and discovered his story. She knew she couldn't let him go on alone if he was an orphan.

The next riverboat port came at mid-afternoon. Carrie and Billy disembarked to buy essentials. "Look, the mercantile is across the street. The one I worked in was larger than this one, but what we need should be there." Carrie tugged him by the hand, and he pulled back, coming to a stop. Then, when their arms couldn't stretch any further, Carrie also stopped. "What's the matter?"

"Dat place is plum full of moneyed folks. No way I'm goin' in dere so's I can be made sport of." He pulled his hand free from Carrie's. "And I ain't no baby, stop holdin' my hand."

"Sorry, it's a reflex. I've been taking care of a lot of small children." Carrie scanned him head to toe, remembering her school days when she hated to go because she could be wearing a dress one of the other girls in class donated to charity. "There's a changing room in the back. Walk straight to the back, and step into the private room. I'll pick things out for you to try on. That way no one will see you. How's that?"

"I ain't gonna wear somethin' that's gonna pick a fight everywheres I'm at."

"Understood, pinky swear. Now, can we go before we miss the boat?" Carrie struggled to keep the irritation from her voice.

"Can I have socks? My road thumpers froze solid a 'coon's age ago. Ain't had socks since the last blue moon." He pulled his pant legs up to show his sockless ankles. Those blue-tinged ankles indeed proved his feet suffered from freezing temperatures. "Yes, we'll get socks." She admonished herself for not thinking of it before now.

"Red ones. Can I have red ones?" They linked elbows. "Fokes can spot 'em a mile off."

Carrie thought about that request for a moment; it was odd. Why would a boy without socks for a while ask for red socks? Wouldn't any color do the job? But he said he wants folks to see them a mile away. He's looking for attention. "Yes, if they have red ones, but everything will turn pink if you wash them with anything else. Just warning you."

The riverboat's whistle sounded for the third time before Billy, and she scrambled across the walkway back onto the boat. Loaded with packages, they had to stop twice to retrieve the 'runaways,' as Billy called them, that found their way to the ground. They rushed the packages to the cabin, where a tired Carrie flopped onto the bunk. The boy threw torn package paper about the room, trying on his new treasures. Nothing delighted him better than his two pairs of red socks.

Shocked by how much money she had to spend to clothe him for winter, Carrie's brain ached. But how could she not? Billy needed them. but she needed to get to California too. Promises were made to her California family. Tonight, she knew she had to sit down and inspect her budget. She didn't have that Pony Express job yet. And what if she doesn't get it? Groaning, she covered her ears to block out Billy's joyous revelry and talked herself out of a drab of brandy.

My Lord, when did trouser prices go up to $1.00? Please bless me with super budgeting skills. Amen.

Psalms 22:19 *But be not thou far from me, O LORD: O my strength, haste thee to help me.*

Chapter Eight

February 3, 1860, A Meeting of the Minds

After two days of questions, conversation, and sharing a little trust, Carrie enjoyed the afternoon sun despite the chill in the air with Billy seated beside her on deck. During that time, she had arranged Billy's passage with the captain in exchange for passage to Cairo, Illinois. They would transfer to another riverboat, taking them north, this time on the Missouri River to St. Louis. The captain put Billy to work supplying wood for the boilers and daily cleaning the deck. Not enviable jobs since the boiler consumed enough wood daily to heat several neighborhoods back home, and many of God's creatures, accompanying their owners on the trip south, occupied the deck. Carrie shared her plans with Billy.

Tomorrow morning, they arrive in Cairo, and decisions still need to be made, these decisions depend on their pending conversation. Billy could end up as another betrayal, Mr. Grant could turn out to be right about him was that was a risk she was willing to take? What if his family shows up to claim him after Carrie's heart becomes invested? What about the inability of others to love her? It's imperative to discover Billy's thoughts sooner rather than later. It isn't easy to know who to trust.

It was time for her to overcome her fears and ask Billy about his situation before sharing hers. "Do you have any living family?" she inquired.

He removed his lips from the mug and said, "Me, family? 'Less yore talkin' 'bout fleas, no."

The way he talked always garnered a smile. There was something about the way he perceived life. "Have you, by chance, thought about staying with me?" Carrie turned to catch his expression. He grinned.

"I'm stickin' to ya, whether you like it or not." He pulled his knees to his chest adamantly.

Carrie laughed at his flippant response. "A little spoiled, aren't we??"

Billy's eyes roamed the shoreline momentarily, and he said, "How ta say it? I've beat wallops and starvin'. I didna have a ma or pa. Yore the kindest lady I ever met. Please don't chase me off. I have nowheres else to go."

Carrie didn't expect a panicky look but received one anyway. "I will not chase you off. Don't worry. But I should tell you my plans before you commit." She handed over the ad clipped from the Columbus newspaper about the Pony Express hiring. "I'm headed west, and my first stop is St. Joseph, Missouri, to land a job as a cook on the Pony Express, but Mr. Russell, the hiring manager, declined to hire me because I'm a woman and can't step into a pony rider's shoes at the drop of a hat. So, the mail must go through no matter what. I can ride a horse, but not for eighty miles at a gallop."

"You cain't run no Pony Express all on yore lonesome, Mz. Wagner." Billy stood at the boat railing, prodding goats out of his way with a stick. Secured with rope, the goats had enough leeway to wander toward him. "I'd be a help to ya. I knowd horses better dan da back of my hand—worked like a whore on payday at a racetrack in Kentuck for a spell. Not gonna lie. I stol somthin' and had to work it off. Please let me tag along. I wanna be with ya."

Carrie wondered if he learned his colorful language at those stables. "Before you beg to come along on my journey, young man, you must know I have rules. I call them my survival rules and intend to live by them. I'd expect you to do the same."

'No question about it. Billy answered most of her prayers. It was clear that the boy thought the world of her just like she did of him. Carrie hugged him and kissed his cheek. And then admonished him, "Don't say whore."

"What do I say instead?"

"Well, I'm not sure," Carrie said. "If you must use the term, how about a tramp? Although that's only slightly better. You shouldn't be referring to this type of woman at your age. Before you beg to come along on my journey, young man, you must know there are rules. These are my survival rules, and I intend to live by them. My question is, will you?"

"Well, let's hear dem rules. Sugarcoat 'em so's I don't havta toss myself to da fishes." He grinned toothily.

As any practicing Catholic would have done, he performed the sign of the cross and waited for the dreaded information. Someone in his past taught him about God.

"Simple,

One: Trust no one, not even family

Two: Keep your word

Three: Don't abide liars, and

Four: Lead a Christian life and be an example for others."

Carrie noticed beads of sweat on Billy's upper lip and fished out a handkerchief for him to use.

He took the handkerchief and finished the job himself. Carrie knew how to stand firm because she lived a godly life and must demand the same from those close to her. But she's agitated at the thought of him saying 'no.' "If you can't do it, we're done." While waiting for Billy to respond, she sipped hot chocolate.

Billy contemplated the rules for a full minute and said, "So far, I ain't been goin' to church socials, eatin' my fill, or bein' treated like I was human, much less kindly. Dose rules suit me just fine."

Before Carrie's grin made it to a smile, she asked, "Can you ride for 80 miles at a gallop?"

Billy licked his lips. "Yep, ya reckon Mr. Russell will grab us bof, two for one?"

"There's no way to be sure. The highest priority is getting the mail through, no matter what. They're hiring boys as young as twelve. Can you do it if our pony rider can't?" she inquired hopefully.

The idea lit up his face with excitement. "Ya said dem horses are gonna be good stock, not plow nags-- they'll need special care, feed, and exercise. I be yore boy. Nobody else will treat dem horses any better. I can ride or take care of horses. Dose riders be coming in bone-ass tired and starvin'. And the pony riders will be acussing and 'chewin' tabacca. Men tend to scratch and spread out, you know." For emphasis, he demonstrated by scratching at an armpit. "I can help swat the men away from ya."

Having admonished Billy for saying whore and pecker, Carrie let 'ass slide. He says many words that should never see the light of day but that is expected from a child who has had no one to guide him. He hasn't done too poorly in raising himself. Carrie had to admit his point did hold credence. Spending nights in an isolated cabin with strangers sapped the starch out of her perfect plan, even with a derringer tucked under a pillow. Mr. Russell stated in his return letter that part of the benefits promised to the riders was a warm cot inside the cabin. So, men would sleep in the same cabin. Another reason he couldn't hire a woman. Billy tagging along would solve the horse wrangler dilemma, address Mr. Russell's concerns about getting the mail through, and discourage the occasional roaming male libido. What other option is there?

"There will be eight to ten high-maintenance horses and a barn. Are you sure you can handle them?" she asked.

He rubbed his hands together. "Yes, ma'am. First, we're gettin' to St. Jo early, right?"

"Yes, about a week early."

"Great, fer seven-whole days, I'll learn ya about dem ponies so's ya don't make a fool of yerself." That toothy grin of his reminded her of a kid on Christmas morning. "You want a little brother? Mr. Russell will take bof of us ifn we's related. Been house-broke and don't eat much to speak of."

Billy's confession answered her prayers. Mr. Russell could hire a two-for-one deal if he hired them. What a rascal. "A wolf couldn't out-eat you."

A well-fed, cleaned-up young man stood in the place of that raggedy little boy. Nothing made him happier than his new socks and a double order of anything to consume. Ultimate happiness turned out to be two pairs of red socks. Wear a pair, wash a pair.

"No lying, remember, and you want me to lie to Mr. Russell about who you are?"

Billy nodded and said, "But ifn we ain't family, what ifn he wants one and not t-other?"

That's feasible. If Billy had accrued experience working in stables as he claimed, Mr. Russell would likely hire him as a horse wrangler and send her packing. Besides weighing the outcome of their separation, Carrie's heart had already accepted Billy as a brother despite common sense warning otherwise. "Promise me you're not a runaway. I would be devastated if I kept a boy from his parents. It's illegal, and I would end up in prison for kidnapping." His lack of family had to be verified because she can't be the wedge that divides a family.

"My folks is pushin' up daisies. Nobody ain't never gave a hoot 'bout me before." He replied quietly.

Billy's happiness and determination reinforced her own. Carrie cared about him and reached out to squeeze his hand. In mere days, this boy had offered more compassion than the entire city of Columbus had in the last sixteen years. Neither of them had kith nor kin, which had created an affinity between them. Together, their relay station would give Mr. Russell bragging rights.

"All right, young man, we agree to tell a little white lie to Mr. Russell, but this is a special circumstance, and no future exceptions are allowed. Understand? No more lying."

"Gotcha, I knew when I met ya, you were the prize-winning hog at the county fair." Grinned Billy.

Gee, thanks. Someday soon, Carrie needs to teach Billy how to give a compliment without hiding it as an insult. "Let's talk about my long-range plans if I land the job on the Pony Express. I'm hoping to work my way west as cooking positions open up. My goal is California. If that doesn't suit you, I understand."

"I'm goin' where ya go whether it's California or Antarctica." He replied adamantly.

As advised by JT Grant, giving up too much personal information could be detrimental. So, she decided not to tell Billy about Ruth and the children yet. In case their paths diverge at some point.

"I'm putting all my trust in you. Please don't disappoint me." She said quietly.

"Da sun would trip and fall out of da sky afore I disappoint ya."

The hope in his eyes rejuvenated her tired soul. But what would they do if the Pony Express jobs didn't work out? Carrie aimed to earn money on the way to California and arrive there before November. Instead, she's adopted a brother, which will deplete their funds faster. If she doesn't land a job and gets stranded in St. Joseph, what's the alternative? Maybe sell the diamond ring as a last resort, but who would pay a reasonable price for it in the west? If I show it to anybody, they'll steal it from me. There had better be an alternative plan soon because God help the soul who will try to divide them.

Jesus, I pray for your support. He eats like all eight or ten horses that may be in that barn if we get hired. Amen.

"Call me Carrie from now on, brother." They shook on it.

Psalm 46:1 *God is our refuse and strength, an ever-present help in trouble.*

February 15, 1860, The villain Frets

Leticia Brown, a truly beautiful woman, paced what the proprietor called a hotel room. It's been almost two months. Where is that dang kid? He better show up soon. That bank loot should be here by now. He can expect another harsh thrashing for being absent for so long. Wait until my hands are around his throat. He'll wish he never was born. She'd tracked his sorry ass this far, but he's an expert at disappearing. Over the years, she had trained him so well that the Artful Dodger of Charles Dickens acclaim would be impressed. Curse his eyes! I'm out of money again.

Shapely hips sashayed of their own volition as the vixen crossed to the hotel room's dirty window, if you could call this dump a hotel. It reeked of disappointment, failure, and ruin. Yanking the dank curtains aside, she viewed the collective malaise below. Cairo, Illinois, must be the armpit of America and the pickings were slim.

The seductress tried hanging out near the stage line looking for a "mark," disembarking with a money belt tightly strapped to his waist, but either the suckers were going elsewhere, or she's lost her touch. The manager of the gambling hall chased the wanton out of there two weeks ago. She needed a report from that boy on where the bank money was.

Something's happened. Must have. He'll come through. He's never failed an assignment before. It surprised her how much she missed the little shit. He'd be history if her delicate hands could stretch around his scrawny neck.

One of the local prostitutes roughed her up last night for working the incumbent's beat. Being at this trade since age sixteen, she gained control of the fight and sent the floozy running away with a beautiful black eye. The streets of Philadelphia will teach you many things, but brotherly love is not one of them. The filthy streets of Philadelphia taught her everything about men. The striking blonde woman reflected in the cracked mirror smiled as she tried to refill the whiskey glass. "You don't look a day over twenty-five, even if I say so myself." Not bad at all. You've still got what it takes, honey! Stroking her long golden hair, she tucked invisible strands back into place, then reached into the revealing neckline of the red satin dress and plumped her bountiful breasts. Satisfied, she sought out more whiskey, but the bottle stood empty.

After exiting the shabby hotel room, she leaned over the iffy railing across the hall. Compared to their evening rake-in, the deserted hotel lobby lay almost empty on the floor below. "Hey, desk clerk, bring me a bottle of whiskey."

The desk clerk had a couple of customers checking in and never gave her a passing glance. "You haven't paid for the last two bottles."

"Put it on my bill, honey. I'll pay at check out." Or when the devil comes to claim me.

This time the clerk stopped, looked up, and growled. "That's another topic altogether. Exactly how long are you going to stay in that room? This is a hotel woman, not your home!"

Who does he think he's turning surly on? "That's not what the manager said to me last night, dear boy." Holding the empty whiskey glass out toward the clerk, she wiggled it. Let's find out how well he knows the manager. "The manager said whatever I desired inside these walls was his to give and mine to take."

"You a sporting girl?" The second man in line with a bulldog face asked.

The man failed the once-over test. He can't have much money or wouldn't be checking into this dump, but she's bored and hungry. Maybe he's good for a dinner if his mug doesn't kill her appetite by then. "Well, sir, why don't you bring a bottle with you, and we'll discuss how sporting I can be." She grinned slyly.

The customer in front of the john piped up, "Never mind, I'm frugal, but I have standards." He threw the room key back at the clerk and turned to leave.

"Oh, honey, don't go away mad. We all have standards. My standard is handsome men with oodles of money, but I'm experiencing a temporary lull." The harlot pursed rouge-smeared lips and blew the tight-assed Bible-thumper a kiss. How long will it take to find another sucker to replace that dead Columbus sugar daddy? The bastard had proven himself to be her best mark in thirteen years. How often do you find a chump who owns a bank? The fool ate out of her hand until one of his wealthy clients threatened to move their money because he disapproved of the tramp with who he slept with. He opted to salvage his reputation by getting married to that orphan.

The banker deceived her; she should have cut his heart out, saving the law the trouble.

The mirror beckoned, and she responded by smiling at the breathtaking woman's reflection. How could the bank manager want that, that orphan, that washed-out imitation of a woman, that ghost who stole her man? How could he have humiliated her like that? She wanted to strangle the ghost, too. *I'd show the bitch what happens when you cross the wrong woman.* Ask Hank Lipton's ghost how it worked out for him. The john burst through the hotel room door, holding a whiskey bottle in both hands. The john slammed the door behind him with a kick, placed the whiskey bottles on the rickety bedside table, and began shucking down to his birthday suit. "Take those clothes off, woman. My johnson's harder than a democrat's logic."

"That's your johnson's problem if I don't see the money first." She cocked a red satin-covered hip toward him and placed her hand on it. He dug into his coat pocket, pulled out his wallet, and flipped it open.

To reassure herself, she pulled open the drawer on the decaying piece of furniture loosely referred to as a dressing table and verified that the loaded revolver still rested there. Better safe than sorry. And the stiletto knife her first love, the first man to run out, had given her many years ago, remained laced to her curved thigh. Back then, the girlish version of herself made two promises regarding that first lover. One of them had already come to pass while she waited to give that boy a beating when he showed up.

She purred while slithering toward the bulldog, "Don't worry. You'll get your money's worth." Down to only his red long johns, his jutting problem became obvious. He promised an enjoyable ride if she kept her face averted. Her words must have excited him. He selected a few bills from the rest and tossed them toward her.

"Take it, bitch, just get in the sack with your legs spread wide." He threw his wallet to the foot of the bed. He tore open the front of his long johns and shuffled them off his feet.

While the john preoccupied himself, she pried the leather wallet compartment open. Oh yes, he's quite the Republican. He's flush. What's he doing in this hotel? The money in the wallet could satisfy any crook for a while longer, maybe until that boy showed up. Let's see—what sounds delicious for dinner tonight? Steak or pork chops? First, removing more bills from his wallet and then yanking her skirts up, she placed one small slender foot on the mattress. "Now, baby, tell me what I can do for you?"

March 5, 1860, Job Interview

Carrie and Billy stepped off the steamboat in St. Joseph into a crowded port with light rain. A boy took their luggage to the hotel because they needed to go straight to the express office and arrange a meeting with Mr. Russell. "When we get there, please let me do the talking. We don't know if Mr. Russell is averse to children." Absent from wrinkles, she smoothed Billy's coat and picked off lint from nervous habit.

"Sis, yer wound up tighter than a whore on her first night."

Carrie grabbed his earlobe and asked, "Why do you know so much about the activities of...of women led astray? And please don't call them whores. I've never said that word in my entire life before, and now it rolls off my tongue with ease. I will not have it, do you understand me?"

"Sorry, I meant evening dove...em, tramp."

Please, Lord, don't let the boy say anything when we arrive. "What have we discussed about vile language, young man?" She freed his ear.

A repentant face glanced up at her, "Ifn you want, I can lay low at the hotel."

"No, silly. Mr. Russell hires both or neither of us. That's our agreement, isn't it?" she held his gaze, waiting for compliance.

"Yep."

Carrie turned and resumed her path to Mr. Russell's office. Afraid to say more to the boy, she clamped her jaws shut unless her tongue lost control. This interview with Mr. Russell meant everything. Billy had better not botch this opportunity. Maybe it's best to walk away. But even though her insides quivered and her breathing elevated to panting, she must land this job.

Another block and Carrie pulled open the door to the headquarters of the Pony Express office. A dozen men milled about, waiting their turn to talk to Mr. Russell. Some looked like bronc busters and reeked of body odor, horse, and tobacco. A couple seemed to be mountain men, as wild-looking as the pelts on their backs. The rest resembled store clerks.

Moving away from the stench of the mountain men, Carrie stood next to the harmless-looking store clerks. This job sounded like the perfect solution for her, but many others are also starting over in the west. The office door opened with a jerk, startling Carrie to attention. A tall, broad-shouldered man she assumed was Mr. Russell shook hands with a gentleman who seemed to be leaving and thanked him for his interest in the Pony Express. Once the man departed, he scanned the pool of candidates, and his eyes fell upon her as he approached.

"Ma'am, I'm Mr. Russell. How can I be of service to you?"

Embarrassed that Mr. Russell walked up to her, ignoring the men waiting before she arrived, Carrie guiltily stepped forward. "Well, Mr. Russell, I'm Carrie Wagner. I hope to discuss a business matter, but I don't want to keep you from these patiently waiting gentlemen."

"A business matter, you say," he scratched his head and tapped his chin while studying his shoes for a moment before realization dawned in his eyes and he replied, "Ah yes, aren't you the woman who wrote me from Ohio?"

"Yes, Sir, I'm Mrs. Philipp Wagner from Columbus, Ohio, requesting an opportunity to discuss the matter of my employment face to face in more detail, please." With all the mail he must receive and interviewing hundreds of people, she's surprised he remembered her letter.

"Etiquette demands I don't keep a lady waiting while conducting business. Where are you staying while you're in St. Joseph, Mrs. Wagner?" he asked.

"At the Beacon Hotel."

"Ah yes, may I suggest meeting there tonight for dinner **to** discuss what's on your mind?"

"Why yes, of course. What time?"

"Would six p.m. work for you?"

"Yes, I'll wait for you in the lobby."

"Fine." They shook hands on it. "Do you need an escort back to the hotel, Mrs. Wagner?"

"Thank you for the offer, but my brother is all the protection I need." Mr. Russell glanced over her shoulder. Then she realized she had neglected to introduce them. "Oh, my manners are lacking. Sorry, Mr. Russell, this is my brother, Billy."

"Pleased to meet you, young man." Mr. Russell sized him up as he extended a hand to shake.

"And you, sir," her brother said as he stood to shake Mr. Russell's hand.

"Well, another year or two, and we could use you somewhere between here and San Francisco." Russell tucked his thumbs into his pants pockets and rocked on his heels.

"Whatever yer thinking I can do tomorrow, I can dang sure do today!" Billy's chest puffed out as if daring Mr. Russell to argue the point.

Mr. Russell's eyebrows nearly shot off his forehead. Carrie groaned, but luckily, the man smiled. "Yes, dinner will be enlightening. Pleasant day, Mrs. Wagner." He turned, snagged one of the waiting men, escorted him into his office, and closed the door.

"What happened to I'll be quiet?" Sometimes she wondered if he was an aide or a nuisance.

The hands on the clock in the lobby crawled through quicksand, coming to a stop at times, she'd swear. All she worried about was how to convince Mr. Russell of their value. Her verbose sidekick promised again he would remain quiet at dinner, but the good Lord knows he'll blurt out something scandalous. She can't fault him, he's a child trying his best to learn, but everything rides on this dinner. There's nothing for it, Chatterbox stayed in the room, and she promised to return with food.

Mr. Russell chose the steak house across the street from the hotel. After ordering, she finally had his undivided attention. "Mr. Russell, I wish you would reconsider not only my application for a position on the Pony Express but also one for my brother. I have a solution to the objection you mentioned in your letter. If a rider becomes incapacitated, who will get the mail through? Billy rides like the wind and knows horses because he worked at a Kentucky racetrack for a time." She paused to catch her breath and realized she hadn't given him a chance to speak.

"I don't doubt your brother's abilities and wouldn't challenge him." He chuckled to himself.

"I'm so sorry for Billy's language this afternoon, Mr. Russell. We're orphans and were raised apart." *Oh no, I'm embellishing the lie. Stop.* "It's a burdensome task smoothing out his rough edges, shall we say." *Oh, dear Lord, I keep lying. My prayers tonight will be exceptionally long.*

He laughed a deep belly laugh and slumped back in his chair. "Well, Mrs. Wagner, I wish you luck with that. However inappropriate his language is here in St. Joseph; I assure you he has the sand to survive in the west." Russell laughed again, shaking his head. "I pity any trickster who crosses his path."

"I'm so relieved you're not offended." Carrie smiled at Russell and leaned toward him across the table in excitement. "Are you willing to discuss a position for me?

"Perhaps I should seek out this orphanage for further candidates." He laughed to himself. "You're no wilting flower yourself, Mrs. Wagner." Russell pulled his chair closer to the table. "I'm going to ask you straight out; did you have anything to do with your husband's plans to rob the bank or murder a Pinkerton man?"

"Of course not, and, for the record, I don't believe my husband guilty of murder."

His gaze roamed her face. "I've always been a sucker for a pretty face, and this one needs a place to start over, right?"

"Yes, sir. It does."

"Can you cook?"

"Yes. I cooked three meals daily for an orphanage full of children for eleven years.

"Fine then. I have an offer of employment. Take it or leave it. A couple of stations in Nebraska will serve a double purpose as a stagecoach stop for Central Overland California and Pike's Peak Express. The stage will run three times a week, eastbound and westbound. The Latham's have a ranch if any man annoys you, but I need someone who can feed the stage passengers, express riders and take care of the station." Russell folded his hands and rested them on the table.

Carrie carefully considered the offer and wrestled with asking about a job for Billy but broached the subject with an inquiry on wages. "And the wage?"

"Ten dollars a month and found. And send the boy to me tomorrow morning. I'll see if he can ride and what other skills he may have." He sat back in his seat as the server arrived with their meals.

A desire to shout out in glee gripped her, but she successfully held it in.

Carrie's mouth watered at the delicious sight and intoxicating aroma of the thick-cut t-bone. Butter sat melting in the middle. The smell of grilled beef overwhelmed her senses. An overwhelming scent of mesquite made her mouth water. The layer of fat around the edges sizzled, and the steak lay in a warm puddle on the plate. She had never ordered a steak in a restaurant before. It looked heavenly. As a guest of the Pony Express, she intended to enjoy this complimentary meal to the last bite, even if Mr. Russell thought her a glutton.

"We've agreed, Mr. Russell. Thank you for giving us a chance." Armed with a fork and sharp knife, she devoured the gastronomic delight.

"At the risk of sounding bold, if Nebraska fails your expectations, please return to St. Joseph. I'd love the opportunity to acquaint you with the city." Mr. Russell's eyes, as well as his smile, lit up.

"Sorry, sir, our eventual destination is California. I'm getting as far away from Ohio as I can without drowning. My name rang a bell for you. That means I'm not far enough west yet. We'll leave on the next freight wagon, stage, or mule you're sending to our station."

2 Chronicles 5:13 *The trumpeters and musicians joined in unison to give praise and thanks to the LORD. Accompanied by trumpets, cymbals, and other instruments, the singers raised their voices in praise to the LORD and sang: "He is good; his love endures forever."*

Chapter Nine

March 9, 1860, The Big Sandy, Nebraska

Three weeks before the Pony Express's launch on April 3rd, the first supply wagons destined for the Nebraskan Big Sandy Pony Express station departed. Billy and Carrie accompanied the drivers on their ride.

They were startled by the plains' bleak desolation.

After crossing the Missouri River, civilization disappears into an endless expanse of grasslands. Roads weren't there. They had to keep the sun to their southwest to locate the station. Central Overland California and Pike's Peak Express Stage Line had established a track for the supply wagons. The ruts on the ground caused a bumpy ride. But they also seemed comforting. She's not alone. So many had come here in search for their fortune before her, and many will come after. The lack of trees allowed the frigid wind to assail them relentlessly. Out of necessity, they bundled up in many layers of blankets, coats, scarves, and socks; gosh, Carrie couldn't help but wonder what people would think if they saw them, after all, they must resemble two loads of laundry ready for wash day.

But she's headed west while admiring the setting sun, coming closer every day to her California family, her children, and Ruth.

March 12, 1860, The First Stagecoach

When the pounding of horses' hooves and a stagecoach rattling signaled the first stage, Carrie looked up from churning the butter. Setting the churn aside, she draped a woolen shawl around chilly shoulders and checked out the window. A dusty coach and six exhausted horses gave the impression of racing directly toward her. The horses were different colors but heaved together like a machine with foamy chests and breathing like a railroad engine in a short distance. The coach tried to steal attention from the horses by displaying red, yellow, and black painted surfaces. Not to be outdone, above the coach door in gold lettering emblazoned from back to front: Central Overland California and Pike's Peak Express. The collective parts come together under one man's control, the master of all, the experienced driver. Look at all that raw power. What a beautiful sight.

She rushed out the door to welcome the visitors as they disembarked and sat down for their noon meal in excitement. The aroma of hot cornbread and beef stew that had just come out of the oven filled the emptiness.

On the stove, a fresh pot of coffee awaited visitors, and a batch of molasses cookies would travel with them as they headed west. Her eyes didn't deceive; three weeks of planning went into today. The coach arrived at last. She mentally checked each item off the list of preparations as she bounced on the balls of her feet, caught up in the excitement. Finally, the coach wheeled into the yard in a cloud of dust and tall grass. Suddenly, her mouth went dry. The driver stood on the brake and pulled on the reins while yelling, "Whoa," at the weary, winded beasts, who snorted to a noisy stop. The chickens announced their disfavor by flapping their wings and cackling their opinions.

"Howdy, Mrs. Wagner, I'm Busby." Said the driver.

"Welcome. Nice to meet you." "The coach is plum full, and this crowd ain't had vittles since dawn. Better stand back."

Busby, encased in frontier leather clothing and a beaver hat, leaped from the driver's seat, and jerked the stage door open.

"All right, folks, noon meal. Keep to the schedule. We have the same time it takes these folks to provide fresh horses. Step lively."

First, a middle-aged man stepped down and reached to help the ladies. Then, after greeting everyone, Carrie ducked back inside and ladled out the stew.

"Please, ladies and gentlemen, settle in around the table, and I'll ladle the stew." Calling it a dining table was like comparing donkeys and thoroughbreds. The humble table was comprised of several untreated wooden planks and some two-by-fours. The first time the Big Sandy Station appeared, the urge to return to St. Joseph almost consumed her. She'd describe the place as serviceable. Nebraska's tall grass grew as far as the eye could see. Mr. Russell described the place as a cabin that sounds comfortable. It appeared more like a hut because it lacked all creature comforts. When someone mentions a cabin, don't people think of logs like those seen in Ohio? That is not the case in this instance. This modest building consisted of a frame, plank siding, and a roof. She succeeded in finding a worse place to live than the orphanage.

The passengers helped themselves to the extra chairs that hung on the wall. Everyone passed the dishes down to the end when the stew bowls arrived. They had established mores as a group traveling together to save time and foster unity. The door opened as people poured coffee cups halfway around the table, allowing another man to enter. He must be well-known to the noontime snackers because they paid him no attention. The stranger sat in a chair close to the fireplace to observe the activity in the space.

Wrangling a clean cup from the sideboard, she filled it and headed toward the stranger. The stranger's blue eyes scanned from the top to the bottom of her five-foot frame, lingering here and there, to the well-worn shoes as if sizing up a side of beef for purchase, then dismissed the object of his assessment as inedible. Right back at you, JT.

"A man can change clothes, but those blue eyes give you away in a room full of blue-eyed men. So, to what do I owe this visit?" inquired Carrie.

JT stood, "I wondered how long it would take before recognition lit up your beautiful face."

Did my *face light up? Poppycock. Why would he dog my trail?* Could he be one of Philipp's cronies sniffing around? Oh, good Lord, won't she ever be far enough away? Avoiding eye contact, she held the coffee cup out.

Strong fingers overlapped trembling digits, searching for a grip on the cup, but his fingertips lingered too long, attracting her attention.

"We'll discuss that later." He said as her dainty fingers tried to release from under his on the cup.

Carrie grabbed the cup by the handle with one hand and ripped the caressed fingers of the other hand away. *What is he doing?*

Later? Isn't he traveling with this group going west? "I'm assuming you like your coffee black. Doesn't everyone west of the Mississippi? Cows must be in shorter supply the further west you go. Want something to eat? Busby said there isn't much time before leaving again."

Deep breath. I sound like a raving lunatic.

The pony rider perused the crowded table, and her eyes followed his. Every seat had a warm body in it.

"Don't worry. I can wait until later; I'm the assigned pony rider for this station."

What? Why did he get himself assigned as my pony rider? Why won't he stay gone? That explains his uniform, with his gun strapped to his hip. A telltale muscle twitched in his jaw, indicating a person under stress or an attempt to subdue anger. It seemed like she would never rid herself of this insufferable man.

Emotionless blue eyes locked onto hers, with a day or two's worth of beard growth and an "I-mean-business" expression. Didn't he know a hider can't hide from another hider? Orphans make the best hiders. When the headmistress walks in where the assembled children await, everything depends on who can keep the angelic look on their face longer than the next orphan, guilty or not. Ruth taught her how to do it. So, what is Mr. Innocent trying to hide?

Billy popped his head through a slightly open shack door. "Mr. Busby, da best nags in da whole Nebrasky territory, are ready and waitin' fer ya.

"Well, folks, you heard him. Let's load up and move on." Busby downed the dredges of his coffee. "California ain't coming to us."

A few minutes later, she handed cookies to the passengers and wished them a safe trip, then closed the door to the coach. Everything went well. Now you can work on lowering your pulse rate and catching your breath and perhaps controlling yourself.

Billy ran up and slid his arm around Carrie's waist. "How'd da first time go, Sis? Betcha dem coach riders swalered dat stew and beat der bowls on the table fer more."

"Yes, they did. Come on in and meet the new pony rider." The shack door banged against the wall in Billy's haste to meet the pony rider.

"A new pony rider! Oh, Boy! Cain't wait to show em da horses." The chaperone stood at the stove, pouring coffee. "No, not the chaperone again. You're the new pony rider?" The starch slid out of him.

"None other." The "all business " mask chiseled a grin for the boy as if pleased to find a kid with whom to swap yarns.

"What do you want here? Sis, this is bullsh...leavings." Then, as confused as Carrie about this sudden reappearance, he meandered over to JT's area of the shack.

"Good to see you again. I owe you an apology for my past behavior." JT gulped down coffee and said, "The way you see to Carrie impressed me. I'm sorry about my urchin remark." JT offered his hand for Billy to shake on it. The two other pairs of ears in the room assumed neither could believe anything he said and shared that belief at a glance.

Ignoring the offered hand, Billy said, "Ya slithered yore way to Nebraska territory to sorry me to death?"

Carrie had never heard such high octaves from Billy before. "Liar."

Man, and the boy looked at Carrie in surprise when a reprimand failed to follow the accusation. "Come, eat while it's hot." But he didn't budge. "How did you talk Mr. Russell into sending you to this station?" Carrie asked.

"Simple, little lady, I told him you make me weak in the knees, and I intend to make you mine."

The coffee pot shook as she held onto it with both apron-covered, trembling hands. It clattered down on the stove with a clunk. Shocked, she couldn't move for a second. *Is JT insane? What does he hope to gain by saying such a ridiculous thing?* "Could you not speak of such rubbish to me? I am not interested."

Billy said something while she pulled herself together. "Why do ya upset her with lies? She's had a bellyful. I hates it when she cries. Take yourself back to where you slithered from and leave Carrie be."

JT's expression warmed as he turned his attention to Carrie and strode toward her.

"How do you like working with horses, Billy?" JT asked.

"Horses can't talk. It suits me tolerably. Why ya here, chaperon? And don't shovel dat cock 'n bull lie Carrie snatched ya dead heart. Not buyin' it." He crossed the room to Carrie's side, putting himself between the two.

Carrie's battered heart isn't in danger of falling for that crap. "Chores wait for you in the barn," she nudged Billy gently on the shoulder. While figuring out what trouble JT planned, he didn't need to be underfoot. She kissed Billy's sweaty forehead, and he absentmindedly wiped it away with the back of his hand. Even a slight gesture brought a smile, such as wiping off her kiss. Someday, he'll miss those kisses.

JT strolled to the other side of Carrie at the stove. "Did I hear you call Carrie Sis just before you came in?"

The man can't help but hear everything. She said, "Billy and I told Mr. Russell we were siblings, so he wouldn't hire one of us and not the other." This is a lie she told. She was irritated by his presence in the Pony Express station. He is there not because she won the state fair's beauty contest, and he wants to court her, but rather for another reason. He'll be sleeping in the same cabin as her. She has made two attempts to get rid of him because she must learn to manage things independently.

Additionally, she is unable to think clearly when he is nearby. She will not repeat that error. But now he's back. What does he believe I possess? Is he attempting to rob her of money? He is not a Columbus native.

"Now, see here, both of you. I came to apologize for my previous behavior, hoping we could start over again. And I needed a job, too."

The unwelcome visitor struggled with what to say next, but she didn't come to his rescue.

Focusing on Carrie, JT said, "I'm serious, Carrie, you might be destined to be mine, and I used my feelings for you to get assigned to the Big Sandy. Aren't you interested in finding out if we have a chance?"

Carrie shook her head. "Not interested." A pregnant pause—as if he thought someone else would comment.

"I'm here to apologize to both of you. I misjudged Billy and now believe he seeks love and belonging, not your money. And Carrie, I found I missed you and worried for your safety, as any prospective beau would."

Did he say, beau? Carrie stared him down.

"Let me clear up this misunderstanding. I do not intend to marry again, and YOU ARE NOT MY BEAU." She placed both palms on his chest and pushed him away to create breathing room between them.

"Damn straight." Billy's profanity drew her attention.

The blue language machine bolted for the door to outdistance his new sister and save his ear, then turned to leave this piece of wisdom. "Wait till you chomp down on that stew, chaperone. You ain't had nothing that good since you left your momma's teat." Then he flew through the portal and slammed the door behind him, leaving a deafening silence.

Oh, my God. Billy, I'm going to kill you deader than dead.

Closing her embarrassed eyes didn't help because now the term 'momma's teat' ricocheted around the inside of her skull. Please open the earth and swallow me before I face the 'prospective beau.' Heat climbed up her neck and spread across her pinkened cheeks. She placed a bowl of stew and a spoon on the plank table and covered her face with both hands as she turned away.

He coughed, "I, um, ahem, I can't wait to try it."

Embarrassment filled the shack and overflowed the windows. The only occupied chair scraped along the floor as JT pulled it toward the table. Peering over her shoulder, she watched as he tested his first bite.

He gingerly scooped a spoonful of steaming stew and brought it to his lips to blow on for a few seconds. "Smells delicious, Carrie." He shoved the whole spoonful in and chewed hungrily, despite being fresh off the stove. Then he hummed and shook his head a little. Next, he buttered up his cornbread.

After all that, what if he hates it? She looked away, not to be caught watching, and sliced some cornbread for herself, arranging the slices on a tinplate. The children at the orphanage loved her cornbread. Her secret ingredients were sugar and bacon grease, plus allowing the batter to sit overnight before baking.

"Carrie, Billy's right. You could serve this in any Chicago restaurant. And the cornbread is heavenly."

What should she say in reply? Ask him to rate it against his mother's teat. "Thank you, JT." *I'm going to kill you, Billy.* A fresh wave of heat engulfed her as she joined him at the table.

"You don't believe I'm soft on you?" he asked in a hushed tone.

"What do you think you're up to with all the flowery statements worshiping my nonexistent beauty and declarations of tender feelings? You can stop it anytime now. I've caught on to those lies. I am not as naive as you wish to believe I am." She sent him a withering glance that hopefully said don't start with me.

Then, feigning injury to his wounded heart, he said, "Your physical beauty is a given, but the woman inside is more attractive. Your pure innocence, hungering for impossible dreams, a delicate soul screaming for protection, and a woman with impossible rules."

"How did you become aware of my life rules?" Two lowered eyebrows shot him a warning. One he ignored.

"Yes, I heard you when you shared those rules with Billy. But for an orphan stowaway on a riverboat, you'd break any law to protect him. And enough determination to sacrifice herself barreling through the west with only a derringer. You need me, Carrie, and you know it." murmured JT.

"This time, you've overstepped yourself." Her foot tapped against the floorboards.

"If you insist, I don't want to share this, but if it will make you happy—Russell worried about his decision to hire a woman. The Pony Express is no place for a woman alone. So, I shared my adventure stories with him and added my growing affection for you. That's the truth. The man's a savior. He helped relieve my misery and assigned me to the Big Sandy station as a pony rider. But also, to take care of you."

Shocked, Carrie rose and deposited her empty stew bowl in soapy water. He can't go back. So, it's another betrayal set up by Mr. Russell, and Mr. Grant delivers the kill. Her heart broke that Mr. Russell felt he had to second-guess his hiring decision, but she was pleased he didn't issue a recall. Carrie focused on the positive. Instead of firing her, he sent someone to help. Mr. Russell didn't know she had chased Mr. Grant off two previous times.

Testing her boundaries, after a moment, as she gazed out the window over the wash pan, she asked, "Are you going to change your attitude about Billy?

"The two of you come as a package deal?"

"You bet."

"That makes him my best friend. You're not the only one with a bad relationship history. Had me a wife once that I need to tell you about."

"Please, no..." Carrie thought about escaping, but chores awaited her. He paid her objection of no consequence and continued.

"The little wife cleaned out my bank account and disappeared. Never found the little thief. She learned how to steal the money and disappeared from listening when I shared my cases with her over dinner. At least she got something out of the marriage. That marriage was the most embarrassing event of my life. Like you, I swore to dedicate myself to better pursuits. Then you walked into my life. But don't worry. Our courtship will be one step at a time. No snap decisions."

One step at a time? Why can't the man seem to keep his hands to himself as it is? Then, turning to face him, she asked, "When I talk, do you listen to what I'm saying, or do you think only a man's opinion is the gospel?"

"Can't say I've thought that over before." Ignoring Carrie, he asked, "Where did you learn to cook so well?"

"If we can't talk about why you ignore me, then we can't talk about cooking.

"You leave me no choice; let's talk about you. I won't deny I find you attractive. That you're a head-turner can't have escaped you until now."

"Will you please stop complimenting me? Whether I am attractive is neither here nor there. There's a man in my life, and his name is Billy."

"Well, I bought a half Arabian mare once. I sure admired that horse, but she had the prickliest temperament.'

"No, not a horse story." She held her palm out in his direction.

Nevertheless, JT pressed on. "Every chance she got, she would bite or kick me for no reason I could see. So, I sold her. Would you like to hear what happened next?"

Carrie blissfully ignored him, shoving her hands into the soapy dishwater.

"As soon as I turned to leave, that dang-blasted horse followed me down the street. How do you like that?"

No comment from Carrie.

"In my experience, females think they know what they want when they have no notion."

You're comparing women to horses now?" How romantic. "I'm no horse expert, but the mare had a bone to pick with you." She waved a soapy fork at him while delivering her message.

"That never occurred to me before. Which bone, I wonder? Now, don't ruffle your feathers. With you, I will always be a perfect gentleman." He offered his hand as a truce.

"My hands are busy, and the time for that has passed."

"I'm curious; hasn't any man remarked on your beauty before?"

"Not even my husband mentioned it, perhaps because it isn't true," Carrie said.

Looking around, JT located a mirror on a wall and brought it to her.

"What do you think you're going to do with that?"

Show you how beautiful you are." He took a tea towel, dried her hands, and then led her to the table. Sitting at an angle from her, he propped the mirror up. "Look."

Not the least interested in this game, she vacated her chair, but not fast enough.

He snagged her elbow. "Not brave enough are you? Come on, Carrie, stop running away from the truth."

"How dare you manhandle me! Turn me loose." Both hands tried to push him away. "I'm not running away from the truth; I'm protecting myself from..." As anger rose in her chest, she yanked her elbow out of his fingers. She went back to washing the dishes.

"I'm sorry. I meant no disrespect." JT said.

Carrie's barely restrained temper snapped, and she smashed her fist on the counter. "Yes, you did." Those three words coated in brimstone surprised her. JT stepped on a sore spot. She had been the only child at the orphanage whose parents came to the orphanage door and begged them to take her. The children teased her over the years about being so ugly. Even her parents didn't want her. A mirror was not her friend, and JT was sticking his tongue out at a tornado. "Your compliments somehow serve your plan, but they're lies. Stop lying to me. I've told you I am not interested in another affair of the heart. You're up to something. I haven't figured it out yet, but I will. In the meantime, stay away from me."

JT responded with a long, low whistle, showing his surprise at her speech. "Thank you, Carrie, for sharing those insights straight from your heart, but if I go back to St. Joseph, no doubt Mr. Russell will recall you and Billy both. I wouldn't want that to happen, would you?"

She had forgotten about Mr. Russell but nailed JT. He so much as confessed to being up to something involving her. "No, of course not, but I see the real JT now—a blackmailer." He's successfully kept her from traveling west on the Pony Express—another reason not to swoon at his feet.

JT sipped at his coffee and shook his head. "I'll use blackmail if forced. You're right. You can deny your beauty all you want, but the fact remains that I'm attracted to you. It may not be in my best interest, but it's true. And you, my stubborn little woman, continue to offer yourself as a target of violence, trotting around the wild west without care. Believe it or not, I cringe to think of you maimed or murdered. I must watch out for you if only for my sake."

"Fiddlesticks."

"And one more thing I want to bring to your attention. You always remember my blue eyes, but you possess the most interesting shade of brown eyes— maybe amber. Quite unusual and remarkable."

"Honestly, JT, they're hazel and unremarkable."

"That's all the flattery I'm giving today. Anymore, and it'll turn your head." He returned the mirror to the wall. "My curiosity has been running wild. Do you mind if I ask a question?"

"Asking a question doesn't guarantee an answer. Take your chances."

"You can satisfy my curiosity about how you came to work way out here in the middle of nowhere and exactly how far west you're aiming for?"

"So, you can follow my every step. No, thank you."

"You're learning—right answer."

"Well, Mr. Gr....sorry, I meant JT..." JT cut her off.

"I'm glad we're past the Mr. Grant stage. When someone calls me Mr. Grant, it reminds me of my father, and the Lord knows I don't want to remember that low-down skunk."

Referring to your father in such a disrespectful manner shocked her, but comparing him to a skunk caused an involuntary giggle stifled behind her palm. "Why would you say such a thing about your father?"

"Maybe because it's true. Town drunks lack redeemable traits. So, my sainted mother, scared one of her boys would turn out like him, gave us names we must grow into, hoping we'd turn out better than him."

"JT?" Confused, her spoon stopped in midair. "What's so righteous about JT?"

"Promise not to laugh?"

She nodded.

"Mom slapped a newborn baby, me, who had never done her any wrong with the Christian name of Justice. Justice! Can you believe it?"

He never forgave her based on his crossed arms and incredulous expression.

"My next brother, Royal, is two years younger than me. We call him Roy."

Ignoring the promise she made, she laughed out loud.

"Mom didn't stop there. My little brother, Judge, is four years younger than me. We call him Jud if you don't want a fat lip."

Carrie said, holding her sides, "No sisters?"

"No, just the three of us, and it would take all three of us to run this place. What possessed you to take all this on?" A sweep of his open arms indicated the station.

"In the days leading up to today, maybe I bit off too much to chew, but I'm headed west and need the money. I don't have a choice." She gifted him with a weak smile that didn't reach her eyes.

"Since I don't want to converse with a lady about money, I'll renege on my promise and compliment your hair. It reminds me of a chestnut mare I used to have. A real beauty."

"Part Arabian?"

"No, not this one."

He shared a warm smile and laughed. This demeanor matched his magnetic eyes; he was friendly, inviting, and handsome. Now, this is the honest JT. Her defenses loosened, but her blood pressure shot up.

"You have such beautiful chestnut hair—unusual and striking. Back home on the ranch, my Aunt Tildy also has a gray streak in her hair. But hers originates from her crown."

"Billy says the streak is the mark of the devil. I'm glad my hair reminds you of your aunt rather than reminding Billy of the devil." Carrie rose to wash the dishes that remained from the stage passengers.

"Now that I think about it, that didn't come out quite right. Sorry, no woman enjoys being compared to a horse."

"So, tell me about that ranch. Where is it?"

"The Triple-A is a cattle ranch in Texas near New Braunfels. Owned by my Aunt Tildy, she gave half ownership to the Grant boys ten, twelve years back."

"Are you headed there?"

"Eventually." His chair scraped across the floor as he stood. "Which one of these rooms is mine? It's time to settle in before joining Billy at the barn."

"The one on the left. By the way, JT, I sleep with a derringer under my pillow and know how to use it."

"I recollect that derringer. I'll keep it under advisement, ma'am." He retraced his steps. "By the way, Carrie, you're stirring the fires of desire deep inside me. Your amber eyes mercilessly devour me whenever you think I'm not looking. Between you and me, there's no denying that." He tipped his hat and said, "Good night."

"Drat!" This will never do. How is she getting to California now? Best think about it.

<u>Luke 12:5</u> *But I will forewarn you whom ye shall fear, Fear him, which after he hath killed hath power to cast into hell; yea, I say unto you Fear him.*

March 15, 1860, Hire a Detective

After a week of arduous effort devoted to preparing the relay station for the opening day of the Pony Express on April 3rd, the three of them, JT, Billy, and herself, had fallen into a routine. Carrie wiped her hands on her apron, feeling the satisfaction of a hard day's work. Her palms were rough and calloused from the endless scrubbing and cleaning she had done, but she didn't mind she was grateful she could earn.

As the sun dipped below the horizon, the sky turned a deep shade of orange, casting long shadows across the rugged terrain, Carrie finished the dinner dishes. She washed the pots and pans, scrubbed the wooden table, and swept the floor. When everything was in its place, she lit a lamp, casting a warm, golden glow around the room.

Then, holding the lamp out for Billy to take, she said. "Here, sleepyhead, take this and go to bed."

"Why do you need a lamp if you're going to your bunk, boy?" JT chuckled. "It's not like your pallet danced around the room and came to rest somewhere else while you mucked the barn."

Billy rounded on him angrily. "Mind yer own darn—"

Carrie interjected before he could say anything else, "Off to bed with you." Carrie hugged him and kissed his cheek.

"I'm too old for ya to be a kissin' on me." He muttered as he wiped his cheek with one sleeve. "I'm bunkin' in the barn tonight."

"Too old? Well, I'm glad you pointed that out to me." She smiled at his sleepy, grouchy countenance. He rewarded her with a small smile and wandered off. Now it was time to deal with the jokester.

"JT, Billy does a man's job every day without complaining. If he wants a lamp next to his pallet at night, I don't consider it to be an unreasonable request." Fists akimbo, she said. "For some reason, he is afraid of the dark. I let it pass. I'd appreciate it if you do the same."

"Whoa, I meant no harm by the comment." JT pushed his chair away from the table and onto its two rear legs. "Just joshing him a bit, is all. The kid does it all the same."

Carrie grabbed the bread bowl and worked on setting the bread batter for tomorrow.

"Does he still believe in the bogeyman?" JT asked solemnly.

"I have no idea. Aren't you afraid of anything? Scared something you fear will happen?" She said after adding cup after cup of flour into the bowl and stirring.

"You want to know what scares me?" he asked while pushing his chair back.

"Yes, I do. Let's hear it." Carrie set the batter aside.

"Snakes." He spit the word out.

"Snakes don't count," Carrie said, unable to contain a laugh. "Everyone in their right mind is afraid of snakes."

He fidgeted in his seat, which he returned to all four legs, and buried himself in thought for a moment. Finally, his eyes rose to hers. "I'm scared my best friend's murderer will escape justice."

Carrie gasped, and a hand jumped to her heart. Three months and several hundred miles separated her from that sickening word--murder! Carrie stood frozen. Her heart raced, threatening to pop from her rib cage. She could feel the blood pounding in her ears, drowning out the sounds of the station around her. The memories came flooding back, unbidden, and unwelcome. He said the one word she hoped never to hear again. And that word sent her right back into those bitter, hopeless months leading up to Philipp's hanging. Instead, she averted her eyes and struggled to maintain her composure.

"Are you all right, Carrie?" He abandoned his chair to approach her.

Carrie waved him off. After a moment, she said, "Yes, of course, I'm fine. I'm sorry about your friend, JT." Pausing to gather herself, she said. " Two strangers in the middle of Nebraska, both of their lives impacted by murder, what a mighty coincidence. "I ah...I agree with your need for justice. A burning desire to set the record straight still haunts me about my husband's death, but I failed."

"I suspected you were widowed. Did he die under suspicious circumstances?" JT clasped his hands together and leaned toward her as if her answer was one that he had been waiting for.

"Suspicious enough for me. Did the authorities come to a dead-end in your friend's case?" If she heard "dead end" once, she heard it a thousand times. No evidence existed to indicate an accomplice. All of the leads dried up. Sheriff Huffman advised her to accept the truth; Philipp was a thief and a murderer and to close this ugly chapter of her life.

"Yes, but a Pinkerton Detective is on the case now. They always get their man." JT assured her.

Carrie's mind raced as she sat in the main room of the cabin. The realization hit her like a bolt of lightning. A detective! Why hadn't she thought of that before now? The murdered man was a Pinkerton detective sent to find the bank money. That's what they do; they investigate. Carrie must be daft not to have thought of this before. What a great idea!

Her thoughts scattered in a hundred different directions at once. Cost? Possibility? Should she go back? Should she stay here? How to contact them? How was she going to afford to pay for them? But the one thing she knew for certain was that she couldn't let this opportunity pass her by. The man she married might be innocent. But, of course, she couldn't prove the fact. If any chance existed, she needed to clear his name and, in the process, clear hers. It was time to clear that debt.

Carrie knew that she had to act fast. She stood up, her mind buzzing with ideas. She had to find a way to contact the Pinkertons. But how? She had no idea how to get in touch with them. Should she go back to where her husband was held? No, that would be too risky. She couldn't afford to be caught.

Then, an idea struck her. She remembered hearing that there was a Pinkerton office in the nearby town. She could go there and ask for help. But what about the cost? She had no money to pay for their services.

Carrie knew she had to take a chance.

"JT, do you know anything about hiring one of those Pinkerton detectives?" Carrie turned toward JT and noticed the monolith had returned. "Is something wrong?"

Leviticus 5:5 '*And it shall be, when he is guilty in any of these matters, that he shall confess that he has sinned in that thing.*

Chapter Ten

March 15, 1860, Innocent?

JT couldn't believe his ears. The woman thinks there's something wrong with him. She's good. Who's playing whom here? The more questions he asked her, the more she led him around in circles. He's beginning to realize the full extent of Russell's ordeal when Carrie plied him for a job. And now, she's asking him for advice on how to hire a Pinkerton detective. He decided to play her game for the time being.

"Ah, nothing. Oh, I think I'm getting a headache." JT rubbed his forehead for effect.

"What a shame. I'll brew you a cup of cannabis tea." As she rose, his arm shot out to restrain her.

"Never mind." Carrie relaxed in her chair again but appeared concerned. Would she be so excited about hiring a detective if she had murdered Hank? No. Her reaction didn't make sense. "Carrie, are those suspicious circumstances surrounding your husband's death what scare you at night?" Keep fishing; there's more to this puzzle.

"That's a rather personal question, don't you think?" Carrie picked at a loose thread on her rolled-up sleeve. Then, abandoning the task, she intertwined her fingers and placed them on the table.

"Turnabout is fair play." He threw the comment out there like a gauntlet.

"I loved my husband." She paused and sighed.

"Yes, I'm sure you did."

"When Philipp and I met, my whole world turned upside down." A reminiscent smile appeared briefly. "I guess you could say it was a whirlwind courtship. He was a man of action." She bit her lip to steady the trembling. "My greatest fear is finding conclusive proof I married a thief and a murderer. I'm sorry. I shouldn't be burdening you with this. Please forgive me."

Carrie's amber eyes were glistening with unshed tears as she looked up at him, her eyes raw with barely constrained emotion. He almost lost himself in those eyes before his instinct kicked in and reminded him it could be an act. *It's not her beauty that draws you in as much as the aura of innocence. It makes a man feel like he must protect her. But darn it all, he's sipped from the same cup as Philipp, the Sheriff, and Mr. Russell. The odds are stacking up against him. Could they all be* right about Carrie? Is she as innocent as she appears? The longing expression he had witnessed nearly convinced him to bend to her will.

April 4, 1860, Carrie Darns a Sock

Yesterday afternoon the Pony Express opened to grand fanfare in St. Joseph, Missouri. The stage driver's bulletin they received last week said the rider would leave after the 3 p.m. ceremony.

Today, Big Sandy's first rider will be thundering in right about supper time. As the first rays of dawn crept through the windows, Carrie leapt out of bed, eager to begin the day. She quickly washed her face and dressed in her best clothes, a simple cotton dress that she had made herself. As she dressed, she hummed a favorite hymn, feeling the joy and energy of the day coursing through her veins. Peering into her small mirror hung on the wall, she wound her hair around the crown of her head and pinned it. She smiled, and with the grey streak, she looked like she had a pastry pinned to her head. Just what she needed—a food craving with no ingredients to satisfy it. She entered the kitchen, lit a lamp, and poured water into the coffee pot.

Next, the grinding of coffee beans was sure to run everyone out of bed. Carrie put her back into twisting the handle, and the silent blackness of night choked and died. "Rise and shine, boys; this isn't a vacation resort." A devilish grin pulled the corners of her mouth up as the two hibernators stumbled out of their respective dens. "The cook can use some wood for a fire. And if you want eggs for breakfast, somebody should check if the hens have obliged us."

JT shoved his fingers through his hair, pushing it out of his face. "This is how you want to greet the day. So, be it?" He ducked back into his room. She assumed to wash up and dress.

"Come on, Billy; no one could sleep through that." She dumped the grounds into the coffee pot and refilled the grinder with more whole beans. Once again, the shack rattled with a bone-jarring noise.

"Cut it out, Carrie. A feller needs time to jump into his pants." Billy howled.

Carrie laughed as she visualized Billy hopping around, trying to bound into his pants.

"Sorry, boys, I'm so excited our first rider is coming in today. I can't wait to meet him. I want to make sure everything is ready. Aren't you two even a little bit excited?" Carrie jumped when she heard JT's voice coming from just behind her.

"You are aware he's not getting here until later?"

After dusting the coffee grounds off her palm, she turned. JT now sat at one of the dining chairs, struggling to put one of his socks on. She noticed a hole in the heel and was struck dumb by the glacial force pushing her back in time. She shivered as she focused on a different sock with a similar hole in it. He's gone! She should have fixed his sock. But, instead, she let them bury him with a hole in it. Why didn't she mend his sock? He was her husband, and he'll wear a holey sock forever. She gasped for air as her fist covered her heart. "No, no, no." she crouched before JT and pulled at his holey sock, pulling it off his foot.

"Carrie, what's the matter with you?" JT asked.

Carrie stared at the sock, with its hole, reminding her that maybe she could have been a better wife. She took the sock to the supply shelf and retrieved her sewing kit. Billy appeared as she concentrated on threading a needle in the dawn light and one lit lamp. He stopped short.

"What's the matter with her, JT?" Billy stepped forward and laid his hand gently on Carrie's shoulder. "Carrie looks mule-kicked, but we ain't got no mules."

"I'm not sure." JT dropped the boot in his hand and remained barefooted for now. "She saw my sock had a hole and went into a trance."

Carrie's hand covered Billy's on her shoulder. She patted it. "Billy, I need an egg to darn this sock."

Billy couldn't help an attempt to gain her attention. "Sure, Carrie, you mad because his socks ain't red like mine.?"

Carrie's head snapped toward him, and her eyes nailed him to the spot. "I said I need an egg!" Billy stepped back, stunned at her reaction. "Won't take me no time," he said as he ran to light another lamp and dashed out the door to the hen house. Carrie sat with the sock crushed in her palm and her eyes closed. Tears ran down her cheeks unhindered.

"I'll fetch some wood for the stove, Carrie." She heard the chair creak as JT rose, and the door gently sighed as he exited the cabin. She felt a storm brewing inside her, getting stronger and stronger. Helplessness grew, and all her thoughts became fuzzy, making it harder to think. She cursed her parents for abandoning her. Ordinary people grew up in families with mothers, fathers, sisters, and brothers to talk to, seek advice, and learn life lessons from. Who could she have asked if her marriage was typical? Ruth had opinions, but she was unmarried. Since Philipp didn't testify on his behalf, did that prove his guilt, as the Sheriff suggested? Just married, why would he go out and rob his bank and kill a Pinkerton agent two weeks later? It has never made any sense to her. Was she an inadequate wife for burying him with a holey sock? What else could she have done to help him? She didn't know. That's the problem.

Carrie had always felt like an outsider, never quite fitting in no matter how hard she tried. She had grown up in an orphanage, where she learned to keep her head down and stay out of the way. But everything changed when Philipp asked her to marry him. Suddenly, she had a full name, a place in the world, and someone who wanted her by their side.

It was a strange feeling for Carrie, to have someone who cared for her in that way. She didn't know how to act or what to say, but she knew that she owed Philipp a debt of gratitude. He had given her something of immeasurable value, something she had never had before: a sense of belonging.

Of course, that gift had been tarnished by the accusations against Philipp. Carrie didn't know if he was guilty or not, but she knew that he deserved her respect. After all, he had given her a name, a home, and a place in the world. That was worth something, even if he had made mistakes along the way.

At the very least, he deserves her respect.

She spread JT's sock out in her palm. Wherever you are, Philipp, I'm doing this for you.

Billy returned with an egg, and Carrie focused on her task. Quietly, JT and Billy sat as if shocked by the sock. If she had ever conquered sewing skills, this would be much easier.

Carrie knew what a darned sock looked like after Ruth had repaired one. Whatever she must do, this sock will be whole again. Once finished, Carrie slid the sock onto JT's foot and caressed the sock focusing on the darned area. Sighing, she looked up at JT and said, "That's the best I can do. Thank you for allowing me to address one of my demons."

And just like that, she snapped back into the present, putting coffee on the stove and asking Billy where the harvested eggs for breakfast were. The activity in the cabin had resumed. Warmth emanated from her heart as if Philipp appreciated and forgave her gesture.

Isaiah 41:10 *Fear not for I am with you; Be not dismayed, for I am your God. I will strengthen you, Yes, I will help you, I will uphold you with My righteous right hand.'*

April 4, 1860, Zeke in & JT and Billy Out

The boys, JT, and Billy, had made nuisances of themselves by checking in on her every fifteen minutes or so the entire day. At least she completed washing the dinner dishes without one of them popping in. They meant well. And they laughed at her expense when she produced the darned sock for JT to slide onto his foot. JT held it up with his thumb and index finger. The color of the thread differed from the sock, but that's common in the middle of Nebraska. And the craftsmanship itself begged for comments. "It's a good thing my boot will cover this," JT said.

Billy broke out laughing. Ya, best check and see if she done sewed bof sides together."

"Very funny, both of you." She said, but their teasing had snapped her out of her remaining melancholy. "Both of you realize that I'm the cook and you do not wish to be on my bad side, right?"

"Yeah, JT, best not to prod her until she turns on us."

Both had been at it all day with their sewing skill barbs, slipping one in every time they saw her. JT even limped in at noon to eat, saying the patch on his sock had cut off the blood flow to his foot. Then, she heard the sound of a horse plodding along. Billy must be bringing the fresh horse up for JT. He'll be riding out when the exhausted rider comes in and passes off the *mochila* to him. Carrie had the incoming rider's dinner waiting for him on the back of the stove and put clean bedding on JT's cot since the two riders must share accommodations.

JT stepped out of his room dressed in his Pony Express uniform and called, "Billy, is that you?"

"No other."

"Come fetch this war bag." Billy bounded in to fetch it. "Wait. I must shove the danged Bible in, or the whole enterprise will collapse. I can't have that weight on my shoulders."

"JT, please watch what you say in front of Billy. That's blasphemy. He's got plenty of time to pick that up for himself."

JT glanced in her direction. "Sorry, you're right. It's just how Russell said it to me rubbed me the wrong way."

"You're all grown up, JT. Let it be." She dried the last plate and added it to the stack. "I'm a little busy raising two boys."

"Oh!" He flinched as if from pain. "I wondered how long it would take you to retaliate for the sock. Nice."

"Come on, both of you. Let's sit on the porch and wait for our new rider. I'm so excited." Carrie dashed out first, grabbed one of the rough-hewn chairs on the porch, and positioned it to face southeast so she could have the perfect view. The boys followed suit.

Noticing Carrie sitting upright in her chair and scouring the horizon, JT said, "You'll hear him before you see him." He raised the horn for her to see and then gave it to Billy to add to the arraignment on the horse.

"I forgot all about the horn. Do you think we can hear it from that far away?"

"Try it, Billy," JT encouraged.

"You bet," Billy filled his cheeks with air and blew through the horn as hard as he could.

The resulting sound thundered against Carrie's eardrums. "Thunderation!"

An answering horn blast came from the prairie. All three stood to look but couldn't find anyone on the prairie. Carrie bounced on her toes. "He's coming!"

JT left the porch and stood beside his mount, waiting for the *mochila* to arrive. The incoming rider would dismount, remove the mochila, and hand it to JT to place over his mount's saddle. Then JT would mount up and be off. They heard the horn blast again, louder this time. Soon after, faint hoofbeats lofted on the breeze.

Carrie hugged the porch post and could finally glimpse the rider. "There he is! I can see him!" She had never been this excited, except maybe on her wedding day. "This is going to work. We're going to California." A vision of clear streams, lush forests, and meadows for farming all waited for them to arrive. The pony rider came at full gallop and thundered into the yard. Chickens scattered in every direction. He and the horse sweated profusely and fought for air. Finally, he pulled on the reins and yelled, "Whoa." The animal stiffened its front legs and staggered to a stop blowing hard. The rider bounced off, dragging the *mochila* with him.

JT grabbed it, threw it on his horse, mounted, and rode out in the blink of an eye.

The rider yelled at JT's retreating back, "We're a half-hour ahead of schedule."

JT was out of sight in seconds. Carrie turned to the new pony rider. "Hello, my name is Carrie; you must be exhausted. Come on in, I've kept dinner warm for you, and there's plenty of coffee."

"The name is Zeke. Some food will fix what's ailing me."

"And this is my brother, Billy. Billy, please take Zeke's horse." She glanced at Billy as he said, "Here, I'll take care of her."

Carrie turned and opened the cabin door to welcome Zeke inside. After he passed through, she indicated where he should sit. "I hope you like beans and ham." She moved toward the stove to serve up a portion. "And there's freshly baked bread."

"Ma'am...."

"Call me, Carrie, please."

"Uh, Carrie, that sounds better than Sunday dinner at grandma's right about now." Where can I wash up?"

"Oh, I'm sorry. I should have shown you that while we were on the porch." She led him back outside to the washing station.

Returning to the cabin, Carrie placed his serving on the table. She busily put butter, bread, coffee, and the usual dinner accompaniments on the table for him, poured herself a cup of coffee, and sat across the table. If she had to guess, her opinion would be that Zeke was a prospector before riding for the Pony Express. She wondered about the life he led before becoming a rider for the Pony Express. Perhaps he was once a prospector, panning for gold in the nearby rivers and mountains. Or maybe he worked on a farm, tending to the crops and livestock. Whatever his past, it was clear that life had not been easy for him.

Older than JT by ten or fifteen years, with leathery skin, shaggy hair, an overgrown beard, skinny, short, and dirt under the fingernails. Obviously, hungry. She knew what it was like to struggle and fight for survival. At the orphanage, she had learned to fend for herself at a young age. She had never been given anything in life and had to work hard for everything she had. It was the same for Zeke, she surmised.

As he came in and sat at the table, Carrie said, "The room behind me on the left is yours. You share it with JT. JT is the rider that just left."

"Oh, by the way..." He paused while trying to swallow and guzzled some coffee down. "Mr. Russell asked the riders to relay a message to you. Some fancy woman in St. Jo is asking around about your brother, Billy."

The information hit Carrie like a train barreling down the track at full speed. The icy fingers of betrayal squeezed her heart as they did when Philipp turned on her. *Why did I let myself love this boy? I deserve this pain for being a fool! I forgot--never trust anyone.* That's what her parents and then Philipp taught her, and now Billy served up the same dish. She kept getting in line for another heartbreak. Billy swore to her he had no family. Why would he lie to her about such a thing? *Maybe the woman isn't related to him.*

"Thank you, Zeke. I'll inform Billy."

After finishing off two bowls of ham and beans and several cups of coffee, Zeke lingered at the table to share his Pony Express ride story with her. Carrie assumed she nodded at the appropriate times, smiled back at the humorous intervals, and managed to conceal how much she didn't give a horse's patootie about his story. Zeke must retire before Billy returns to the cabin. She can't discuss the fancy woman with Billy without waking Zeke. The little chat with Billy needed to happen elsewhere in case she lost her temper.

When she inquired on the riverboat, Billy lied about having any other family. The longer Zeke's story went on, the more she stewed. Try to calm down. Ask Billy to explain before your tea kettle of a temper blows. There's no explaining it. He lied.

"I'm sorry, Zeke, I'm getting a little worried about what's taking Billy so long. I'll check the barn and make sure he's all right." She rose and indicated the door to Zeke's room.

"This is where you bunk. Please ask if you need anything else."

"Best beans and ham I've had, Miss Carrie." He tore off a piece of bread and pushed it around his plate to sop up the drippings.

"Thank you, is there anything I can do for you before you retire? You must be exhausted." Asked Carrie politely.

"Well, that's nice of you, Mrs. Wagner. You go on and check on the boy. I'm old enough to tuck myself in." He didn't rise from the table.

Carrie left. At first, pacing in front of the barn door, waiting for her temper to abate, seemed like a good idea, but she soon abandoned the fruitless thought and pulled the doors open. The fresh hay, leather, horse, and manure aroma assaulted her senses. Only one lamp hung in the back of the barn. So, she advanced toward it. "Billy!" A couple of the horses objected to her tone and nickered.

"Yeah, just finishin' up. Had to walk the mare fer a spell to cool her down."

Carrie heard someone scooping grain and stepped into the glow of the lamp. "You claimed to be an orphan when we met, did you not?" She couldn't keep the angry tone out of her voice.

Billy straightened and turned toward her with shock written all over his face. "What happened?"

"What do you mean, what's happened? I want to know if you lied to me." She couldn't help following up her demand with a foot stomp.

Billy walked past her to the aisle, then turned to face her. "Carrie, what happened? What makes you think I lied?"

"Zeke says a fancy woman in St. Jo is looking for you. Is she a family member?"

Billy's face blanched, and he raised a palm to his forehead. "Nobody snitched, did dey?"

He did know her and had been hiding it from her.

"No, Russell didn't tell her anything. He wanted to warn me first."

"Did Zeke say what name she's going by?"

"No, but you can ask him. Billy, what's going on?"

"This story will take a while, Carrie." He dragged himself over to a hay bale and sat down. She joined him. He sighed deeply and looked up at her, "She's my real sister." His words were like a physical blow to her chest. She had lowered her guard and let herself love him. There's no one to blame but herself. Her eyes began to water, and she fought hard not to cry.

"Despite promising me you wouldn't, you lied to me?" She hoped desperately that somehow Billy could clear this up with the next sentence he spoke.

"Well...if you think back, I said no one but you ever gave adang about me before, and I wasn't lying." Billy made a prayer gesture with his hands under his chin and bit his lip as he locked eyes with her. "I wanted to stay with you."

"That's the same as a lie. I told you I wouldn't be deceived again--"

"Carrie, don't say it. Don't make me go." His eyes pleaded with her. She fought the urge to demand he leaves instantly.

He reached out and covered her lips with his palm. "Don't say it, Carrie. Let me try to explain, please."

Her stomach lurched, and she pushed Billy's hand from her face. "Tell me." She held eye contact with him as she waited for an answer.

He wilted, his arms dropping to his sides. "She's my sister but the devil's disciple." He twisted his fingers together. "I ran away from her. Been wantin' to for a spell, but I warn't grown enough to make it on my own."

"She's your sister?" Carrie's fists flew to her waist. "I have to send you back to St. Jo. I have no right to keep you here."

"Ifn you do, I'll bolt again. I won't go back to her." shrieked Billy.

Spoken as a promise. Despite a Herculean effort, tears rolled down Carrie's face. He has a family. She has to send him to his sister because she can't be responsible for separating family members. "I'm sure she only wants the best for you, Billy."

"No, she dudn't. Ya figure I come into this world knowin' how to pick locks? She's a thief and a fancy woman. I ain't a gonna back even ifn you say so." Now tears fell on Billy's face as well. "Ask me why I'm afraid of the dark, go on, ask me. Ever since I remember, she'd lock me in a closet and sometimes leave me for days. Without checking on me or knowing if'n I croaked in there." Billy rose from the hay bale and paced in front of Carrie. "She did it regular 'til I's big enough to fight back."

"How could she get away with that?" Vignettes of a cowered Billy in the dark flitted through her head. "Weren't you missed at school or church?"

He gave her an incredulous look. "Sometimes I wonder which one of us had book learning." He picked at the hay bale choosing a strand to worry between his lips. "I ain't never seen the insides of a church, and she sure didn't send me to school."

Carrie's hand rose to cover her mouth. Growing up in an orphanage had been Carrie's idea of the worst childhood possible. But even an orphanage sends you to school and church. The worst punishment consisted of a paddling--a fate Billy probably would have chosen over being locked in a closet. She searched his face but saw only despair and fear. "Are you telling me the truth this time?"

He returned to the hay bale next to her. "I'll swear on da Bible in the cabin if'n you want me to."

Carrie looked into the tear-filled eyes of the boy in front of her, feeling a sense of empathy and sorrow that she had not experienced in a long time. As she wiped his tears with the hem of her apron, she couldn't help but think of herself as a child in the orphanage, longing for someone to come and rescue her.

The boy looked up at her with a pleading expression, and Carrie felt her heart ache with sympathy. She knew that he might be lying to her, but she couldn't bring herself to turn him away. After all, he was just a boy in need of help, a boy who reminded her of herself.

As she gazed at him, she saw his vulnerability and his desperation. She could tell that he was afraid, afraid of what would happen to him if he was sent back. And yet, she knew that she had to do what was right. Whether she liked it or not she was not his legal guardian.

"Even if what you say is true, you know I have to send you back," she said firmly, trying to keep her emotions in check.

The boy's face fell, and Carrie felt a pang of guilt.

How many nights had she gone to bed at the orphanage, praying her family would return for her? She considered herself a pretty good judge of desperation. This desperate boy might be lying through his teeth. If so, his sister would have taught him well.

He threw his arms around her neck and tucked his head under her chin. "Please don't, Carrie."

Carrie returned his hug, patting his back. "But, Billy, she is your legal guardian. I'm not. She could charge me with kidnapping or something. I can't go around the country gathering young men willy-nilly."

Billy pulled slightly away and looked up at her. "Let's push on to California. She cain't never find me der" A hopeful smile split his damp face.

Now it was Carrie's turn to pace. "I want to do right by you, Billy, but I don't want to end up in prison." Carrie wrung her hands. "I need to point out that you brought this on yourself." She unwound him from her neck. "You knew one of my rules was don't abide by liars. I don't appreciate being betrayed, especially by a twelve-year-old boy. Get some rest. I'm expecting you to start back to St. Joseph tomorrow. I wish you a safe trip." If she said another word, her resolution would fold, and she'd hug him to her. Betrayal seared her heart, leaving pain and emptiness in its wake. Please deny you have a sister, brother, grandfather, or a'dog.

Carrie ran from the barn into the cabin, straight to her bunk, and sobbed her heart out. Don't you dare let Billy's tears sway you. After a long while, the sobs gave way to hiccoughs, and she got up to get water. She found the door open wide when she entered the cabin's main room. Zeke stood on the porch in the early dawn light watching the barn. She wondered what was going on, but thirst claimed her attention first.

As Zeke returned, she went to the water bucket on the counter next to the wash pan. "Ma'am..."

"Call me Carrie, Zeke."

"Miss Carrie, what happened last night? Are you all right?" The corners of her mouth curved up, somehow finding humor in his question. "Well, it depends. I'm still here, so I suppose I'm fine."

"No, ma'am, you ain't fine. You cried half the night, and your brother...."

She rounded on him. "He's not my brother!" *Please, momma, daddy, don't leave me here. I'll be good. Please. Please.* Billy deserted his sister in much the same way as her parents abandoned her. Carrie knew the anguish Billy's sister must have been experiencing since his disappearance. She could probably recite her nightly prayers word for word. Under what situation did he leave his sister? How could he be that callous?

"Sorry, Zeke, I didn't mean to snap at you."

Carrie, go on home. Don't come back to this jail anymore. I'm as good as dead. Philipp, her only remaining family, forced her away from him. Neither her parents nor Philipp gave any explanation for their inhuman treatment. I'll build battlements around my heart to avoid future heartbreak.

Zeke pushed his hat back on his head and scratched. "Well, whatever he is. He's saddling up fixing to leave."

Carrie dashed to the doorway in time to witness Billy's rump settle into the saddle. He turned his horse toward the cabin. She relaxed a little. He meant to say goodbye before leaving. "Tell him I'm writing a note and to wait."

Carrie penned a note to Mr. Russell and started for the door, but she couldn't let Billy go without something to eat or a jacket. So, she grabbed an empty flour sack, tossed in some food, snatched his jacket, and flew to the porch. Carrie glanced up at the boy slumped in the saddle with downturned facial features. His chin trembled, and he wiped his nose on his shirt sleeve. She must look the same. He looked like he never slept a wink last night. *Don't let him go.*

"This is for Mr. Russell."

Billy stuffed the letter inside his shirt.

"You didn't eat yet. There's enough food to last until the next station." She lashed the bag of food onto his saddlebag. "And it's April. In case you get cold, take your jacket." Don't abide liars. He lied once; he'll lie again. Trust no one, not even family. Tears fell from her eyes. "Wait, you need a hat to protect you from the sun." She ran inside and returned with Billy's hat and her derringer. She would never forgive herself if something happened to him. She held them out for him to take. What did he hope to gain? Why did he lie to me? He knew this would happen eventually.

He placed the hat on his head. "Carrie, this is your pea shooter." He held it out for her to reclaim. She made no move to take it. Then he shoved the gun into his waistband. He lifted his head, and they locked bloodshot, teary eyes.

"Take good care of yourself." Carrie wiped her face with her hands. Billy's broken-hearted eyes held her captive. Neither of them looked away. She didn't want to blink for fear he'd vanish. You don't leave your family behind.

"You take good care of Little Ed and tell JT goodbye for me, will you?"

She nodded.

"Goodbye, Carrie." Billy turned his horse southeast and kicked him into a gallop. He slapped the reins against the horse's rump as he rode into the dawn horizon.

Clods of Nebraska prairie flew up behind him as he went. Long golden strands of grass floated back to earth forming a hazy cloud giving the scene a dreamlike quality. She reached out toward him and almost called out but did not. Carrie stood there, watching as Billy rode away into the distance. She couldn't help the sense of longing that washed over her trying to sway her into going after Billy. But she knew better than that. She had already made the mistake of falling in love once before and she wasn't going to make the same mistake again. She admonished herself. Just like Billy, you brought this on yourself. You allowed love for him into your heart. Try following your own rules for a change. Lowering her head, she returned to the cabin to prepare for the day ahead and planned how to explain Billy's absence to JT.

<u>Song of Solomon 3</u> *By night on my bed I sought the one I love I sought him, but I did not find him. "I will rise now, I said, "And go about the city; In the streets and in the squares I will seek the one I love." I sought him, but I did not find him. The watchmen who go about the city found me; I said, "Have you seen the one I love?"*

Chapter Eleven

April 7, 1860, Where Did Billy Go?

JT turned at the sound of Carrie's voice calling out from the cabin, "Breakfast is ready.". He had risen early that morning, with a sense of urgency gnawing at his gut. The absence of Billy had troubled him deeply, and he had spent the better part of the night trying to make sense of what had happened. All he had managed to glean from Carrie was that Billy had been sent to his "real sister," whatever that meant. That's all he managed before passing out in bed last night.

The question of why Billy had been sent away nagged at JT's mind as he made his way to the barn. There had to be something important that had prompted the decision. Something that would bring him closer to solving Hank's murder. But what was it? And where was his lead? Eighty miles away, that's where.

He slid into his seat at the table, "Smells terrific, Carrie." He picked up his utensils and dug in.

Carrie carried her plate and coffee to the table and sat across from him. "Thanks, JT."

"You feel like telling me more about what happened to Billy? His leaving seems a little abrupt, doesn't it?" He glanced across the table at her while slicing ham. He'd give anyone who asked ten to one that Carrie chewed on more than a biscuit.

"Zeke brought me a message from Mr. Russell when he rode in last time. A fancy woman is asking around St. Jo looking for Billy." Carrie paused to wash the biscuit residue down with coffee. "I confronted Billy about it. He admitted to having a sister."

"Billy's sister is a prostitute?"

She snapped her angry eyes up to meet his. "A prostitute? Why would you think she's a prostitute?"

"That's what fancy woman means; didn't you know?" he asked, confused at her reaction.

"How would I know that? I thought she dressed to suit her station." Grunted Carrie.

"Sorry, no. At least, in semi-polite conversation, that's another name for a prostitute." He shoveled a forkful of egg and bacon, "Russell probably used it so he wouldn't offend you."

"You mean I sent Billy back to a prostitute?" Using both hands, she pushed her hair away from her face and parked both elbows on the table.

He saw dark circles under amber eyes. They were red and puffy from crying.

"You honestly didn't know that's what fancy women were?" asked JT.

"No, JT. I didn't." whispered Carrie defeatedly.

"How naïve are you? Born yesterday?" He couldn't help but chuckle. What woman of similar age hasn't heard the term before?

One fist hit the table. "Orphanages don't teach you about prostitutes or fancy women." She shook her head at him.

What about those years working at the mercantile, he thought? One or two of those customers must have been a fancy woman. Putting that aside, he tried to look at it from Carrie's viewpoint. He could sense the conflict within Carrie's heart, the love she had for her brother battling with the fear of the unknown. The decision to send him to a prostitute was not an easy one, but perhaps it was the only option she could see at the time.

He imagined the weight of the responsibility she must have felt, knowing that the fate of her brother was in her hands. The guilt of doing what was right and what her heart wanted and the pressure of making the right decision must have been overwhelming.

She sent a boy she cares deeply about to an uncertain fate with a prostitute. Well, yeah, that does sharpen the picture a little. "You didn't have a choice, that is, if she's, his sister?"

"I hoped against hope that she wouldn't be his sister, but what other reason would she be looking for him so desperately?

JT cleared his throat, "You mentioned that Billy said she mistreated him."

"Yes, he did say that. Probably another lie." She snarled.

As JT contemplated the situation further, a nagging thought crept into his mind. What if the woman in St. Joseph wasn't really the boy's sister? What if she was mistreating him in some way, and that's why he had run away on a riverboat?

He imagined the boy, alone and scared, navigating the treacherous waters of the river, hoping to find a better life somewhere else. He must have been desperate to leave his current situation behind, and the fact that he had chosen to run away on a riverboat spoke volumes about his circumstances.

"The woman in St. Joseph may not be his sister; if she is, she may be mistreating him. Maybe that's why he ran away on a riverboat."

Carrie's jaw dropped; a sense of realization dawned.

Miffed at how she handled the misunderstanding that may have cost him an ally and her lack of investigation into the woman who claimed to be Billy's sister, JT spoke.

"If it had been me, I would have asked more questions to ascertain why he felt lying to you was the better option, assuming he lied. Although he thinks he can survive by himself, we both know a boy of that age is no match for the realities of life." His mouth ran dry, and he paused to guzzle more coffee. "I had to take on a man's job at fifteen. It's not easy."

It was hell trying to keep a roof over his family's heads and feed them three times a day. JT's words revealed a vulnerability that he had kept hidden until now. The memory of having to become the breadwinner of his family at such a young age still haunted him. It had been a difficult time for him, and he knew that it was no different for anyone else who had to face similar circumstances.

He took a deep breath before continuing, "I know how hard it can be for someone to make it on their own at that age. It takes more than just grit and determination; it takes help, support, and understanding. And if we don't provide that, we are failing as human beings."

JT's eyes were filled with an emotion that she couldn't quite place. It was a mixture of anger, sadness, and frustration. She realized that he was not just talking about the boy who had lied to her but about all the children who had to face such situations.

"Lies and more lies, that's what he would have given you," said Carrie. "He would've said whatever to get me to do what he wanted. I can't trust him after that." She twisted her fingers until the skin turned white or purple in various areas. Finally, he captured a hand for himself.

Those beautiful amber eyes of hers, a mirror capable of accurately reflecting emotions.

JT repeatedly prayed to God, 'Please, Lord, let Carrie be innocent,' because the man inside the ruse had fallen in love. JT was in love with Carrie, and he would do anything for her. God knows if she's guilty, it'll be the first time he would have to choose a person over the law.

JT's feelings for Carrie were strong and undeniable. He had fallen for her from the moment he met her. Her beautiful amber eyes and her compassionate heart had captured his attention, and he couldn't help but feel drawn to her.

He knew that he would do anything for her, even if it meant going against the law. But the thought of Carrie being guilty of anything was unbearable to him. He couldn't imagine having to choose between his love for her and his duty to uphold the law.

JT knew that he had to tread carefully, especially since his feelings for Carrie were becoming more and more intense. He didn't want to jeopardize this case or his relationship with her.

He took a deep breath and tried to push his emotions aside. But no matter what happened, JT knew that his love for Carrie would never waver. He was willing to do anything to protect her, even if it meant risking everything he had.

Still holding her hand, he yearned to kiss each fingertip. But, instead, her desperate fingers clamped around his. "You're not his legal guardian. You could have been arrested for kidnapping if the woman was his sister." JT explained to Carrie.

JT's heart swelled with warmth as Carrie's hand nestled in his. He couldn't help but feel a sense of comfort and safety when she was near him. Her palm was delicate and soft, and it fit perfectly in his hand.

JT was lost in the moment as he rubbed his thumb across the top of her hand. He felt a deep connection to Carrie that he couldn't explain. Every day, he discovered something new about her that he liked. It was as if they were made for each other.

Recently, he had found himself drawn to her exquisitely curved hips. Whenever she walked by him, he couldn't help but stare. He was mesmerized by the way her body moved, and he longed to hold her close.

JT knew that he was falling deeper in love with Carrie every day. He wanted to take care of her, to protect her, and to love her with all of his heart. As they stood there, hand in hand, he felt as though he was finally where he was meant to be.

"Don't torture yourself. You're not Billy's legal guardian. I will do my best to find out whether the boy is okay or not." promised JT.

JT couldn't help but feel a sense of responsibility towards Carrie and the boy. He knew that she was genuinely concerned for the young boy's safety, and he wanted to do everything in his power to help. So, he sent word to his contact, Russell, to learn more about Billy and his sister. After all, the boy may be desperate.

As he waited for a response, JT found himself lost and confused. He would have liked to solve Hank's murder and go home before he fell totally or this impossibly helpless, genuinely naive woman. He could spend hours caressing her fine, creamy skin, even with dark circles and puffy lids. From what he saw, there was not an imperfection to be found.

He was drawn to Carrie's beauty. He couldn't help but imagine running his fingers along her smooth skin, caressing her face and body, and exploring every inch of her.

But as much as he was attracted to her, JT knew that he needed to focus on the task at hand. He couldn't let himself be distracted by his feelings for Carrie, especially when there was a murder to solve and a young boy's safety to consider.

Still, he couldn't deny the pull that Carrie had on him. Her innocence and helplessness made him want to protect her, to keep her safe from harm. He found himself daydreaming about a life with her, where they could be together and start a family.

JT knew that he needed to tread carefully. He couldn't let himself fall too deeply in love with Carrie, not when there were so many unknowns in their situation. But as he looked at her, he couldn't help but think that she was the most beautiful woman he had ever seen.

April 15, 1860, Philipp's Guilty

Balancing the laundry basket on a curvy hip, Carrie headed back to the shack's overhang, where she could comfortably fold the laundry rescued from the drying line. Today the sun rose uncommonly warm for this time of year, and they are taking advantage of it. As she came around the corner, JT approached from the other side. Carrie's heart skipped a beat as she watched JT approach her. She couldn't help but notice the droplets of water running down his chiseled chest and abs, glistening in the bright sunlight. She swallowed hard, trying to keep her composure. JT's towel-clad head and wet hair made him look even more ruggedly handsome than usual, and Carrie found herself drawn to him like a magnet.

As he got closer, she noticed the look of amusement in his eyes. "You caught me," he said, grinning. "I was just taking a dip in the creek to cool off."

Carrie lowered herself into a chair and teased him, "Isn't the water still too cold for bathing in the creek?" Then, she positioned the empty laundry basket next to the full one in front of her and selected the first item to fold.

He toweled his hair, but she still admired wild black waves dancing around his head. The towel began life as a bag for Baker's Beans. But, of course, everything west of the Mississippi River has a second and maybe a third life.

"I'll say I nearly froze, but it woke me up. And I found out why it's called Big Sandy Creek." Leaning against the cabin for support, he dusted the sand off his bare feet with the towel.

Carrie couldn't help but smile at JT's description of his creek adventure. She could imagine the shock of the cold water and the thrill of discovering something new. "I'm glad you survived your morning dip," she said with a chuckle, folding a pair of socks.

JT tossed the towel aside and stepped closer to her, his gaze locking onto her delicate features. "Surviving was the easy part," he murmured, his voice low and husky.

The grains of sand scattered as they hit the raw wood-planked porch.

"Oh no, I just swept the porch." She jumped up to retrieve the broom from the cabin.

"Wait, I'll do it. I made the mess." He lunged to intercept her, and they collided in the doorway.

Immediately, Carrie's whole body went stiff. The doorframe pressed snugly on the back as JT's bare chest pressed against her from the front. To save embarrassment, she forced hungry eyes downward, but, my God, never had she seen anything in her whole life that invited her to pounce upon it like JT's bare chest. With all the muscles, hair, and smell of soap, she couldn't help but take a deep breath.

Her hands begged permission to touch him, so she tucked them behind her at the waist, the only place with space to do so. The pelt of curly black hair on his chest captivated her. The combination of his body heat and the inviting soap scent called out something feral inside. A month or more seemed to pass before she could drag her eyes from his muscular chest to his face. She swallowed hard and forced her gaze to move slowly until their eyes met, drawn together like magnets. Endless cobalt pools drew her closer. She longed to wrap her arms around him and never let go. His deep, soulful gaze held her captive, and she found herself lost in those endless blue pools.

As they stood there in silence, time seemed to stand still, and the world around them faded away. All that existed was JT and Carrie, locked in an intense, wordless exchange. The air between them crackled like lightning, and she felt a sudden rush of desire that threatened to consume her.

An old proverb popped into Carrie's head. Fool me once, shame on you, fool me twice, shame on me. This attraction was doomed. You don't deserve to be loved. She pushed herself away from JT and backed into the cabin, surprised by the resulting sense of loss. As she retreated, Carrie felt a coldness settling in her chest, an emptiness that threatened to swallow her whole. The heat and passion that had been building between them just moments ago were replaced with a sense of disappointment and shame. She couldn't believe she had let herself get swept up in the moment, again.

She couldn't help but feel like a fool for allowing herself to fall for JT's charm once more. She had been down this road before, and it had only ended in heartbreak.

The sense of loss was palpable, like a heavy weight pressing down on her chest. It was as if she had lost something precious and irreplaceable. She had known from the beginning that this was a bad idea, that falling for someone like JT would only end in tears. But somehow, she had let herself believe that this time it would be different.

As her thoughts weighed her down, she began to leave but he caught her hand and pulled her into his arms, sharing a passionate kiss. Yes. Yes, kiss me. Without permission, greedy arms wrapped around his neck, burying one hand into his damp hair. Corded arms crushed the air out of her lungs, and her breasts rejoiced as she smashed her nipples into JT's rock-hard chest. Previously unknown fires smoldered then flamed to life. She's never felt like this before. This lack of control. The power your body can wage against reason. The bombardment of desires that consume you all at once. She didn't want him to find her lacking, but when her knee lifted to curl around his leg, her brain screamed, stop. Another moment and she'd become a fancy woman herself. Carrie's heart was pounding in her chest, her body still humming with desire.

Lightheaded, she pushed herself away from making another mistake. Wiping strands of hair away, she fumbled for the broom. Using it to steady herself, she kept her face averted. "Per...perhaps you should do the sweeping." With the broom in hand, she extended her arm in his general direction. He took it gently from her fingers. As he took the broom from her hand, his fingers brushed against hers, sending shivers down her spine. She dared a glance up at him, but quickly averted her eyes again, not wanting to meet his gaze. She could feel her face flushing with embarrassment and the lightheaded feeling only intensified.

He watched her for a moment, his eyes studying her intently, and she could feel his presence looming over her. She wondered what he must be thinking of her, with her clumsiness and her nervousness. But she was too afraid to ask, too afraid to even look at him again.

Instead, she turned away and busied herself with other tasks, trying to hide her discomfort. But she couldn't shake off the feeling that he was watching her, that he could see right through her.

Perched again in the chair she had vacated on the porch. She reached for a shirt to fold. Behind her, JT blew out a cleansing breath and closed the distance between them, extending the Baker's Beans towel. "You may want to...um... there's water on you..." He stopped and indicated the front of her blouse with his fist-clenched towel. She spent a couple of seconds admiring his strong fingers.

Then she glanced down. The damp material of Carrie's blouse hugged every curve and revealed puckered nipples. Working for the Pony Express proved too strenuous to wear a corset. Hence, JT's soaking-wet bare chest drenched her when she desperately clung to him.

Embarrassed, she snatched the towel from his hand to cover herself and ran for the sanctity of her room. Once inside, she slammed the door and buried her head under a pillow. Then she pulled the edge of the blanket up around her, intending to curl up and die. She heard him shuffle around in his room next door, which forced her to roll away toward the outer wall.

"I'm headed to the barn, Carrie. I needed a shirt and my boots."

Carrie finally released the breath she had been holding as the shack door shut. How am I going to leave this room once more? She fought back the tears that he saw her breasts in that condition and cried in frustration. After roughly five minutes of feeling sorry for herself, rationality finally overcame her, and she recovered. Traveling west alone, incidents like this were destined to occur. You have work to do; stop being a snob. Mr. Russell forewarned her that incidents like these might happen. She wiped her nose, got out of bed, and hung the wet shirt and camisole from pegs to dry. Carrie took a deep breath, trying to calm her racing heart. She couldn't let this incident hold her back. She was on a mission, and she couldn't let anything or anyone stop her.

Shelves on the north wall held neatly folded replacements. Carrie tugged on one, and the Bible hit the floor and came to rest open with its pages fanned out. A loose piece of paper darted under the cot. Finishing dressing, she picked up the Bible and retrieved the note. She wondered how long the letter had been in the Bible and who wedged it in there as she placed it back on the shelf, she had never noticed it before. Could it be from her mother?

Turning the note right side up, she recognized the handwriting.

Shock froze her solid.

It was from Philipp.

Carrie trembled as the words on the page refused to come into focus. After all those weeks of denying her to visit him in jail, what could he say now? Taking the note out to the table, she spread it out to read it in daylight. Please don't be a confession.

January 6, 1860

Dearest Carrie,

I humbly ask for your forgiveness, if you are able to find within the depths of your kind heart. I am ashamed to confess that there is a secret aspect to the man whom you wed. None of this burden falls upon your delicate shoulders. I must reveal that I have fallen deeply in love with another woman. Alas, how I wish it were not true. My decision to marry you was motivated by a desire to regain a measure of respectability, and to rescue my bank from certain ruin. But all is lost, for she has sealed my fate. I must face the gallows for a crime that she committed. My hope is that this letter will serve as a gesture of goodwill towards you, my dear wife.

You must be wary, for she will surely come for you. I cannot fathom why she believes that you possess the funds that were stolen from the bank. I have assured her that this is not the case. However, her anger towards me for taking a wife has caused her to be blinded by her rage. If she crosses your path, I implore you not to have her arrested. Please remember that upon my demise, all of my property has been entrusted to you. In doing so, I request that you do me a favor now.

Please be cautious. The woman in question is far more treacherous than I could ever describe. The very least that I owe you is a warning. I have requested of Sheriff Huffman that he not return this Bible to you until after the execution.

It is with a heavy heart that I admit that you deserved far better than what fate has bestowed upon you.

Yours in sorrow, Philipp

Matthew 6:14-15, *For if you forgive other people when they sin against you, your heavenly Father will also forgive you. But if you do not forgive others their sins, your Father will not forgive your sins.*

Oh my God, he's guilty! And he's quoting the Bible to me? Is this a joke? Another woman? Did she murder the Pinkerton man? Anger boiled up her throat until she thought she'd choke. And he begs me for forgiveness. The snake is as guilty as Judas. It's no use after what she's done. How romantic, he went to the gallows protecting the real murderer, his true love.

Carrie's hands trembled as she re-read the letter, her heart heavy with a sense of betrayal. How could Philipp have done this to her? She had trusted him with her heart and her future, only to discover that he was a liar and a thief.

The words on the page twisted like a knife in her chest. "None of this burden falls upon your shoulders," he had written. But that was a lie too. She had been foolish to believe in him, to think that their love was real.

A bitter rage rose within her, as she imagined Philipp and his lover conspiring to steal from the bank. She couldn't believe that he had gone to the gallows protecting the real culprit, without so much as an apology to her.

She threw the letter down, the paper crumpling under her furious grip. The Bible on the shelf seemed to mock her, its pages filled with words of forgiveness and redemption. But how could she forgive Philipp for what he had done to her?

His one true love? Oh my God, Philipp ordered the diamond ring for his paramour, not his wife. Now it makes sense.

Why did he do this? Her mind's eye propelled her into the depths of hell, where she searched amongst the worst of the cursed for her once-beloved husband's cursed spirit.

Come out and face me, you cowardly son of Satan!

Our marriage vows meant nothing to you. Yet you ask me for mercy on behalf of your murdering fancy woman. No. Can you hear me now? NO. And, since when do you quote from the Bible? How about this Bible quote, my twisted husband?

Genesis 2:24 *Therefore, a man shall leave his Father and his mother and hold fast to his wife, and they shall become one flesh.*

Carrie's rage simmered beneath the surface, threatening to boil over at any moment. How could Philipp have done this to her? How could he have betrayed her so thoroughly?

Her hands shook as she held the letter in front of her, the words blurring together in a haze of fury and hurt. "You broke the sanctity of our marriage vows," she muttered under her breath, her voice filled with bitterness. "You defiled me."

But as she read on, a sickening realization began to take hold. Then, like a lightning strike, a sickening revelation came to light and fell into place, deepening the betrayal Philipp dealt. Philipp had not just betrayed her with another woman. He had forsaken their marriage bed altogether, leaving her alone and unfulfilled. And all the while, his paramour had seen to his every physical need.

Carrie's mind reeled with the depth of her naivety. She had believed Philipp to be kind for giving her time to adapt to marriage before consummation. But in truth, he had never intended to make love to her at all.

The image of Philipp and his paramour trolling with laughter at her expense filled her with a burning rage. How dare they mock her innocence and trust? How dare they twist the sanctity of marriage into something so sordid and base?

Carrie's hands curled into fists at her sides, her fingernails digging into her palms until they drew blood.

Blood ran cold in her veins, but her late husband's hypocrisy reddened her with anger. The depth of her naivety rocked her to the core. She conjured an image of Philipp and his paramour trolling with laughter at her expense.

The shack wall held the very tool she needed to express her anger. The iron frying pan, hanging on a peg, served as a cudgel, and the stove served as a suitable stand-in for Philipp.

Slam! "You mangy dog!"

Slam! "Snakes look down upon you."

Slam! "Satan quakes in your presence."

The heavy iron frying pan defied Carrie's quivering arms to lift it again. "If I could dig you up right at this moment..." Running across to the shack door, she tossed the frying pan as hard and as far as possible, frightening the chickens. Flapping wings and raucous cackling erupted in the yard. Returning to the wall, she grabbed another pan and pounded the shack's interior wall while sullying Philipp's entire lineage. Each blow resulted in clouds of wood dust and caulking, making her sneeze. Speaking of something to sneeze at, her late husband's heartfelt proposal came to mind.

"I know we haven't known each other long, but please put me out of my misery and become my wife. Tomorrow if possible. "

Oh God, how she loved him or thought she loved him. Finally, my existence mattered to someone, but no, you betrayed me instead. The rotting corpse of her dearly departed lay six feet down, pried forever from his lover's arms. Relief proved elusive, and the pan joined the iron frying pan in the yard.

Realizing the anger wouldn't abate anytime soon, Carrie fought outside to keep from destroying everything in the cabin. What a two-timing miserable excuse for a man. A boil on the backside of society!

The ax caught Carrie's attention with its glinting blade half-buried in a woodblock. Standing on the block, a foot on either side of the ax, she levered the ax back and forth until the dangerous edge came loose. The momentum landed on her bottom in the yard as the dirt clod settled. Unceremoniously, she fought to gain her footing and grabbed the ax. The more massive logs would defy satisfaction, but the smaller ones better run because they can't hide. Selecting the first victim, she put a branch on the block and swung the ax rather clumsily.

None of her pleas submitted to the Sheriff intended for her husband reached him, and he banned her from visitation. The reason why is clear as a bell to her now. Because his paramour didn't want to run into the useless wife, the two halves of the branch jumped in opposite directions. The smaller end of the branch flipped aside. Repositioning the larger end, she swung again. Half of the branch hit one of the hens this time, and she broadcasted her displeasure in a flurry of feathers and screeching. The boiling caldron within demanded a worthier opponent. A thicker branch stepped forward. He went to the gallows for another woman! How noble! Thwack! The hacking sound the ax made egged her on for another.

That freezing day in January, when she attended the hanging in a snowstorm, with the angry citizens of Columbus looking on, and witnessed Philipp hang, popped into her mind. Feverish eyes scanned the crowd, searching for his wife, she thought at the time. No. Those God-forsaken eyes searched for the murderess. If memory serves her right, a foolish girl tried to say goodbye to her bag of lies. And you dare ask me not to turn the tramp in? That is if she doesn't kill me first. How dare he treat her worse than a dog! Even Carrie's parents left her in reliable hands before turning their backs. Curse you, Philipp! He's one hundred percent right about one thing. She deserved better! She mattered! She had value!

I am not trash you arbitrarily decide to throw away one day!

A tightly coiled snake squeezed her heart. Lack of breath caused little black spots to dance before her eyes. When she boarded that southbound train that day, she was gravely mistaken about going west and being able to start over and forget all about the past. Thanks to Philipp, the past will be coming to find her.

Muscled arms jerked her back against a chiseled chest, forcing the wind out of her lungs and lifting her from the ground.

***

JT wrestled the ax from Carrie, then turned her loose. "What in the blazes is going on? You can lose a foot by abusing that ax." He hefted the ax over his shoulder and buried the blade deep in the woodblock.

A dirt clod raced across the ground toward him, kicked by the little whirlwind, "I hate men. Remove yourself from my sight."

A dirt-covered Carrie stood before JT, huffing like a locomotive, amber eyes bright as a hawk, and hair loose and tangled. What a firecracker! Fire blazed in her eyes; sunrise pink glowed on her cheeks, and the tip of her tongue flashed across her bottom lip. Those tantalizing rosy lips captured his attention as he remembered how sweet they tasted only minutes ago. Never had he seen anyone as angry or beautiful as Carrie Wagner in her current state of utter devastation. The aberration pushed past him to retrieve discarded pans from the yard.

"Are you all right?" he asked gently.

"No, JT, I'm not all right. Does it look like I'm all right?" A hen took up residence in the iron frying pan. "Out," she demanded. The hen received a glancing blow for her rudeness and retreated in protest. "What are you wailing about? Sunday is chicken dinner day!"

Entering the cabin, she noticed the unfolded laundry she had abandoned earlier. After placing the pans on the wall, she dragged the laundry basket inside.

Following close behind the beautiful cyclone, JT noticed that one sleeve of Carrie's blouse had ripped at the seam and came loose at the shoulder, presumed from exertion. The exposed flawless creamy skin called out to be touched, but that's for another time.

"What's got you all churned up?" For safety's sake, he stood one step outside the cabin door in case objects grew wings again.

Carrie retrieved the wadded-up ball of paper from the corner of the cabin. Then she held it up to his nose. "This! I'm churned up about this letter!" One by one, her fingers closed around the wad. "This cursed note from my departed husband. I found it in my Bible."

"I don't understand. What about it disturbs you this much?"

"Don't squinch your eyebrows at me! I'm pretty fed up with being run over roughshod by men." The wadded note received more abuse when she slammed it on the table.

JT watched in awe as the tangled mass of Carrie's chestnut waves claimed her attention, and she attempted to corral them into submission. Frustrated, she huffed off into her room and fetched some hairpins. Seated again, she pinned the tangled mess up regardless of the manner or means. He felt a powerful urge to help her, to reach out and offer his assistance. But as he imagined his fingers threading through her chestnut waves, he became acutely aware of other desires that were bubbling to the surface.

His heart raced as he imagined what it would feel like to run his fingers through her hair, to cup her head in his hands and breathe in the scent of her. His gaze lingered on her delicate neck, imagining the sensation of his lips brushing against her skin. He knew he should resist these urges, but the temptation was too great.

As she finished pinning up her hair, he felt a sense of loss. The moment had passed, and he had let it slip away. But he knew that the desire he felt for Carrie would not go away so easily. It would linger, growing stronger with each passing day, until he could resist it no longer.

What made her this angry? He tore his hungry eyes from the tempting glory of chestnut hair. "Please tell me what that wadded-up paper ball set you off." Either Carrie's aim stunk, or his head was the target.

With a huff, she rose again, but this time to start a pot of coffee. "Read it for yourself. I don't think I can get through it a second time."

He couldn't imagine why a parting note from Carrie's dear departed husband angered her. Smoothing out the wad, he scanned the letter. He couldn't have been more mistaken about the situation. Mr. Inferior had another woman! How? The guy screamed middle-aged milquetoast. How the bank robber and murderer landed Carrie boggled his mind. How could the idiot think any other woman would compare?

The fool mentioned the bank robbery but said his paramour had plans for his bank, not him. And the money turned up missing! How do you misplace thousands of dollars? But he said he went to the gallows for the woman who murdered a Pinkerton agent. That agent, his best friend, Hank Lipton, saved his life twice and taught him everything he knew about the detective business. That's why he's investigating this case, even though he had retired.

And what do you know? My new suspect is coming after Carrie. All he has to do is wait, but this note might be hogwash. If Carrie is innocent, she won't lie about the letter. She wouldn't hand it to him to read. Glancing at Carrie, he stood by as she used residual anger to abuse dinner ingredients with a sharp-looking knife and beat Satan out of every pot on the stove with a heavy wooden spoon.

Justification for her anger flooded him. Oh, hell yeah, let's not forget the part where he said he's in love with someone else. Just what every wife wants to hear. And her reaction to the letter sure seemed valid enough for him. Carrie's innocent. The itch he can't scratch is how much she must have loved Philipp to be this angry.

The coffee pot sat brewing on the stove, and she started on the batter for the cornbread. If the way she stirred that cornbread batter showed her anger, it's good that Wagner was dead. Done with the note, he tossed it back into the corner of the cabin. He briefly traded mental places with Carrie and remembered how she hated betrayers. No wonder she's hopping mad— I can't blame her. I've been there myself. This tragedy might top his wife Jenny's theft and disappearance, leaving him penniless and heartbroken three years ago. Especially mortifying because of his profession.

"I'm sorry. But a man like that, you're better off without him." As soon as the words left his lips, he knew he had chosen the wrong approach. Women are a breed unto themselves, and she's angry enough that she didn't hear him.

The batter bowl plunked down on the table. Then Carrie braced both hands on the table's edge and looked him square in the eyes. "Thank you, JT. You're in good company. My Father, my dead husband, and you all know what's best for me without asking for my opinion! Well, I don't need to hire a Pinkerton agent anymore. I'm sure of Philipp's guilt."

Any way you look at it, Carrie benefited from becoming a widow. But she shouldn't blame herself for not knowing about the other woman; even Sheriff Huffman missed that. "How did this note get into your Bible?"

The stirring of the cornbread batter stopped, and she clamped her round eyes and scrunched eyebrows at him before settling her fists on her hourglass hips. "Really? What interests you most about that note is how it got into my Bible?"

If ears could belch steam, Carrie's ears would fuel several trains. Sometimes he should think before speaking. If he knew anything about women, which he doesn't, he'd know it's not a favorable sign when she places her fists akimbo. Ignoring her question, he shuffled, "Do you believe this note is true?"

Carrie set the cornbread batter aside to rest. Next, she grabbed a soup pot and scooped water into it, saying, "Oh, it's real. It answered a lot of my questions."

What questions?

"Like, did he have an accomplice? Did he love me? Why did he disappear without a word? Was he guilty of all the counts they charged him with?"

"He covered those answers in the note. Are you satisfied?"

"I don't know if I'd call it satisfying, but yes."

"Does the Bible quote mean anything specific to you?"

Adding the water-filled pot to the stove, she responded, "My betrayer husband should have asked for forgiveness in person. Then I would have told him I'd forgive him when evil is purged from this earth. That goes for his fancy woman, too. What's with all the questions?"

"There's a confession I need to make to you, but please try to remain calm before I do. I can help you with the mystery surrounding your husband's death." JT rose from his chair, facing her, and reached into his pocket to retrieve his Pinkerton identification papers.

"After you read this, please give me a chance to explain. I'd be honored to help you in any way I can."

In the last couple of weeks, Carrie, his prey, had shown behaviors that didn't quite fit a bank robber or murderer. In his experience, women who conduct bank robbery and murder do not turn from crime on a whim and work their fingers to the bone to make an honest dollar. He'd suspected her innocence for a few weeks, and Philipp's note proved it. She was an example of why he became a Pinkerton man, to bring in criminals and help people in crises. And the city of Columbus has victimized beautiful Carrie Wagner in spades. A wronged woman he had hoped he would never have to arrest.

He hoped she would melt into him out of gratitude. He held the identity packet out to her. However, she flipped the envelope open and grasped it with quivering fingers as she read and reread the contents. His forehead glistened with sweat. She took a deep breath and gave him a hard smack across the face, causing him to crick his neck. Then threw his identification at his chest. She experienced pain from that slap as well. She waved the troublesome hand around to make the stinging go away.

"A Pinkerton agent! Lying to me all these weeks?" She paced back and forth like the proud cock of the yard. "Tailing me because you thought me guilty. Just like the town folk of Columbus." With her delicate fists planted at her waist, she pinned him to the spot with her best accusatory stare.

Instinct kicked in, and he tried to defuse the situation. "Now, Carrie, honey. I did offer to help."

"Don't call me honey, you betrayer." She hissed through clenched teeth and stomped her foot in disgust. "Lurking around, spying on my every move...oooh. But, good Lord, is there a betrayer under every rock?" She looked over her shoulder at the shack's wall with burning eyes and straight lips.

Quick as a jackrabbit, he placed himself between Carrie and the pan-covered wall. Pushing her fists straight down at her sides, she stared a hole through him while her head bobbled like a hen on the prowl. He expected objects to retake flight. But she showed him her back while taking a brandy bottle and a tin cup from a cupboard. The gurgling sounded like a liberal pour. Now he wished he hadn't blocked her access to the pans because he'd rather she threw pans at him rather than resort to liquor. For her nerves, he supposed. That's what women always say about their drinking. So much for explanations.

Confronting him while hugging her bottle, she threw down the gauntlet. "I swear to God, you're a dead man if you say one more word. Liar! Betrayer!"

She wiped her lips with her forearm and proclaimed, "And never kiss me again!"

The anguish on her face made him want to get the ax for her. Heaven knows he deserved more than a slap in the face. She knocked back the cup's contents in the blink of an eye, goading him into saying something. No problem, he'd rather jump in front of a five-mile-long stampede, murdered drunken Father or not. The little soldier conceded the battle and sought the comfort of her room. But the war isn't over yet. He retrieved the evidence supporting his case from the corner of the cabin. Captain Pinkerton would need this letter as evidence.

JT, Pony Express rider turned Pinkerton agent, the man she may have had budding feelings for, died today without valor.

Chapter Twelve

April 20, 1860, Carrie Resigns

Behind the closed door of her room, Carrie's handkerchief, once crisp and pristine, was now sodden with the tears that streamed down her face. She climbed into her cot, braced her back against the wall, tucked the blanket across her lap and around her feet, and sipped brandy while sobbing. Whatever qualities a person must possess to qualify as a functioning adult, she stood in the wrong line on Creation Day to receive them. But she visited several other lines multiple times, like betrayal, heartbreak, and being unlovable. Abandoning sipping, she finished the finger of brandy in two swallows and suffered through the fire trail, working its way to her stomach. But the pain that cut the deepest was the knowledge that she was unlovable. She had been hurt too many times, betrayed too often, to believe that anyone could truly care for her. It was a thought that filled her with despair, and as she downed her brandy in quick succession, she felt the fire trail of alcohol sear through her body, a temporary balm for her aching heart.

She dragged in a deep breath and poured another. The fiery liquid burned its way down her throat, leaving a trail of heat in its wake as it settled in her stomach. But she couldn't stop now, not when she needed the numbing effect of the alcohol more than ever. She took a deep breath and poured another, the amber liquid splashing against the sides of the glass.

Carrie leaned on Ruth's imaginary shoulder and remembered the warnings.

"I told you to come with us on the wagon train." or maybe,

"I thought you swore off men." And then her favorite,

"How often did I warn you that Wagner feller loves only himself, eh?"

But after venting her spleen, they would hug, share each other's love, prop her up, and send her back into the world.

But Ruth wasn't there, and she needed to learn how to self-soothe.

Carrie sipped some brandy and suddenly realized how exhausted she felt. Hugging Little Ed close, she spoke to him. She said, "We loved each other, then I lost you. I'm sorry, Eduard." I am never to be loved.

She brushed her tears away with a corner of the blanket.

Placing the cup on the floor, she wrapped the blanket around her and soon fell asleep. When she awoke, the darkness confused her. Once again, she pulled herself into a sitting position and knuckled her eyes. She awoke feeling hollow and needed to think through the recent events and devise a plan. Needing another sip of brandy, she searched carefully for her abandoned cup on the floor.

As she reached out her hand, groping in the darkness, her fingers brushed against a rough surface. It was the cup, cold to the touch, as if it had been left there for hours. She wondered how much time had passed since she had last taken a sip, but the answer seemed irrelevant now. All that mattered was the icy liquid that awaited her.

Let's deal with that backstabbing liar, JT.

As she sat alone, deep in thought, the memories of her encounter with JT flooded back to her mind. She couldn't believe that she had allowed herself to be swept away by his charms, only to be left feeling foolish and used.

First, why did she let him kiss her? That kiss conveyed her desire for him. All her effort went into it, only to find out minutes later that everything he'd said and done was a lie since she met him. The memory of the kiss burned in her mind like a flame, a reminder of the vulnerability that she had allowed herself to feel. She had put all her effort into that kiss, only to have it thrown back in her face like a discarded rag.

And then there was the incident with the water-drenched blouse, a moment of humiliation that still made her cheeks burn with embarrassment. How could she have been so careless, so reckless in her actions?

Her face burned now, thinking about it. This two-faced Pinkerton stalked her to determine if she was Philipp's accomplice.

Carrie sat in her room, replaying the memory of that kiss over and over in her mind. She couldn't deny that she had enjoyed it, that her body had responded to JT's touch in ways that she had never experienced before. But even as she indulged in these thoughts, she couldn't help but feel a sense of shame and regret.

For she had given herself over to a man who had proven himself to be a liar and a betrayer, someone who had manipulated her for his own purposes. And in doing so, she had revealed her own desires and vulnerabilities, laying herself bare to someone who had no intention of reciprocating her feelings.

As she thought back to the moment when he had pulled her against him, she couldn't deny the intensity of the passion that had passed between them. Muscled arms holding her tightly, hungry lips consuming her, it had all felt so real, so genuine. But now she knew that it had all been a lie, a ploy to gain her trust and use her for his own purposes.

She kissed an adventurer-turned-pony rider-turned-Pinkerton, and he kissed a suspected murderer. Where's the trust to build a relationship in that? The answer is nowhere.

Carrie continued to sip at her brandy as her brain shifted topics, Philipp's letter. Her husband loved another woman. He couldn't have chosen a worse way of annihilating his wife. So, why didn't he marry his paramour instead? If he had, her life would be so much simpler now. He thought marrying her would save his reputation, but how? She had no credentials to add to anyone's respectability. She was an orphan and invisible. So, how in the world would she save his bank? Instead of rescuing his bank, he allowed his true love to talk him into stealing all the money in his bank's safe.

And Philipp admits to going to the gallows in his paramour's place. You don't go to the gallows for bank robbery, but you do for murder. He desperately needed to save her. There was her answer. He's guilty by association but still guilty. If he had told the truth, he wouldn't have been hanged. He would have gone to prison as an accomplice. She had been right about him. The Philipp she knew wouldn't have robbed a bank or murdered anyone. At least she knew she didn't judge him wrongly. His true love murdered the Pinkerton man sent to bring Philipp back to justice. What kind of woman was the tramp? She doesn't have to answer that herself because Philipp painted the woman as dangerous and angry over his marriage. Philipp's woman will come for her, but don't expose her name to me, and please don't have her arrested. Because she, as his wife, owes him a favor. Bull!

Carrie received all of his material possessions, which puzzled the other woman. She somehow thought Carrie had the stolen bank money. How did they lose track of the money? And why does the paramour believe Carrie possessed it? She would have returned that money to the Sheriff if she had it.

Wait, a cotton-picking minute. JT, the Pinkerton betrayer, read Philipp's letter. It's proof she didn't rob or murder anyone. She got up in search of the letter.

Her fingers searched around in the pitch-black corner of the cabin and felt the cold seeping in from the gaps in the wall, some dust, and debris, but she couldn't find the letter. Her hand snapped back in fear of discovering a spider. *Drat!* She then searched the tabletop, but nothing. Did he destroy it? Why would he do that?

Wait—didn't he say he would like to help me if he could? Help me with what? He's looking for the person who killed that poor Pinkerton man. She wouldn't mind knowing who killed the poor man herself. She knows it's Philipp's sweetheart, but what's her name? They should have hanged her instead of Philipp. She'll have her chance; the murderess is headed straight for yours truly. Her identity, well known to this murderess, makes Carrie easy to find. What can she do to prepare? How could she prepare for something like this? How could she protect herself from someone who had already proven themselves to be a cold-blooded killer?

More important than any of this was finding Billy. She had run him off, only thinking of the consequences to herself, refusing to hear his story. No decent person does that. Indeed, no Christian would. She neglected to give him money to survive on and would not go back to his sister. He took nothing with him except the clothes on his back. How could she have done such a horrible thing to a helpless boy? She must find him. She sent him to a fancy woman, possibly an abusive fancy woman. Now she must save him.

If JT still wants to assist, he can find Billy and locate that murderess before she becomes the fancy woman's next victim. All of this means the end of her short Pony Express career. She must inform Mr. Russell he'll need to hire a replacement.

But she's not speaking to her latest betrayer. Sitting up, she wrapped some blankets around her shoulders, took her brandy bottle and cup, and moved to a chair outside the cabin for serious problem-solving.

<u>Numbers 6:3</u> *says they must abstain from wine and other fermented drinks and not drink vinegar made from wine or other fermented drinks. They must not drink grape juice or eat grapes or raisins.*

April 20-21, 1860, Baptismal of Sorts

After Carrie sought her room, night fell, and JT found his bed, too. Carrie never made her presence known for the rest of the day. He removed the coffee and soup pots from the stove.

On second thought, he didn't want to see her that distressed again, despite the passion it brought.

He lay in bed, listening to Carrie grieve. Later, he heard her slight movements in the main room; she broke down into sobs again. Finally, he heard the cabin door open and close, which filtered her cries. Her pain pulled at him, keeping him awake, but he stayed put. A method of solace eluded him. That question is as old as humanity—how do you mend a broken heart?

Carrie's innocence also kept him up at night. He pretended to be an explorer while expressing care for her well-being and love. And he now needs her as bait to entice the killer. How will he get Carrie's participation now that the hoax is no longer necessary? Whether she is aware or not, he would remain by her side till the completion of his task. Until Hank's killer is apprehended, he can't let her ride off into the sunset with Billy.

Even then, he may not part from her. His traitorous body craves not just her kisses but her desirous body. It's a relentless fact he needs to accept. Maybe pretending he's soft on her has gone straight to his libido. She's gentle on the eyes, and her kisses are the stuff of angels, but we talk about baggage. She comes with a complete set and several carrying cases. But when she's not screaming at him, he catches glimpses of the woman behind the façade. The woman who loves Billy fiercely as if they were mother and son, her habit of giving away guns to others in need because she would worry about them if she didn't, and the heart she puts into running the relay station. You'd think she owned the place. And those amber eyes and velvety skin.

JT couldn't help but feel drawn to this complex and intriguing woman. He knew that she came with her own set of baggage, but he couldn't deny the strong connection that he felt towards her. The more he notices, the more he wants her in his bed. Just how heavy is that baggage? No, I don't need a woman who drinks. That's the end. He rolled over and went to sleep.

JT woke with the first streak of pink on the morning horizon. He hoped to talk some reason into Carrie this morning. He took a few minutes to make himself presentable, then looked into the main cabin. Empty. Her bedroom door stood open, and the room was vacant. He thought so. He didn't hear her come in last night. Opening the cabin door, he found her wrapped in blankets and leaning against the chair. When he stepped in front of her to check if she slept, the shock froze him in his tracks. He didn't have to be a Pinkerton detective to determine why she slept so soundly. An empty bottle of brandy lay in the crook of her right arm. Her left hand clutched the earlier discarded Bible to her heart. Fury rose in him of volcanic proportions.

Carrie's road in life lay strewn with muddy holes, boulders, and wrong turns, but drugging herself senseless didn't help. Is this the first time the vile liquid passed her tender lips, or did she have crates of it stashed inside somewhere? Dang, if he'd stand by and watch it happen all over again. Alcohol had dictated his father's life. JT had not one memory of his father sober. He carefully lifted the Bible from her grasp and set it aside. He pulled a bucket of water from the well and baptized her. The cold water hit her dead in the face, drenching her hair, clothes, and the porch area where she sat. She snapped awake screaming, bolted to her feet, rubbing water out of her eyes. Gathering her wits, she looked him up and down, her eyes settling on the bucket in his hand.

"Good morning, sunshine! Welcome to your new life." JT said.

He bent to retrieve the empty brandy bottle from the ground. She probably pulled the wet blanket to her chin to avoid another embarrassing display of feminine charms.

"I believe this is a Pony Express relay station and stagecoach stop. Best get to doing your job!" grinned JT.

He bounced the bottle in his hand to inform the lush there was more to this conversation by a long shot.

Even in dawn's weakened light, soaking wet, pale with red-rimmed eyes, something about Carrie Wagner beckoned to him. No, he's not falling for a chump move. *She thinks she doesn't want to marry. I call and bet the deed to my ranch.* His eyes settled on her wet, opaque nightgown plastered against petite but muscled legs where the blanket didn't reach. *Why is everything about her so darn feminine? Add some starch to your spine, boy. It was only one kiss.* Yeah, one kiss that brought him to his knees. He doesn't want a woman who swills alcohol. It'll be difficult training his body not to react to Carrie Wagner. Why? Why did she have to pick up that bottle?

Carrie pushed her chin out and forced a smile on her lips. "I'm a full-grown woman who doesn't need to be told when to work, especially by a betrayer. I want to stand here and pass the time with you, but I feel chilly. So, excuse me, Mr. 'You're-not-my-father,' while slipping into some dry clothes. Then I'll see to breakfast."

With a gentle pull, she grasped the edge of the blanket that rested atop her delicate form, and slowly unfurled its folds. It yielded to her touch, much like a serpent uncoiling from slumber. As the blanket slipped away, it revealed a figure shrouded in a flimsy, wet nightgown, now tightly adhered to every feminine contour. The dampness of her gown had given it a molding effect, which left nothing to the imagination. As she shed the blanket, beads of water cascaded down her drenched gown, falling in droplets onto the wooden planks of the porch beneath her feet.

"JT, please hang this blanket over the clothesline for me," Carrie said with seemingly no embarrassment about her nearly naked state. His mind's eye likened the request to a wood nymph casting a spell on her suitor. So why isn't she angry? She held the blanket out for him to take. Dumbstruck, he complied.

"Thank you, sir." Then she straightened her shoulders, turned, and entered the cabin as if he had been misbehaving instead of her.

He would have better luck forgetting his name than the image of her breasts heaving under a wet nightgown rendered opaque and form-fitting for the second time in as many days.

Jeremiah 4:18 *"Your own conduct and actions have brought this on you. This is your punishment. How bitter it is! How it pierces to the heart!"*

April 21, 1860, Hangover

She dragged herself through the preparations for the impending arrival of the stagecoach passengers, her movements slow and lethargic. Her head felt as if it were being ruthlessly attacked by a team of miners using blasting powder, each explosion causing an excruciating pain that reverberated through her skull. To make matters worse, her stomach had officially declared its separation from the rest of her body, citing egregious acts of abuse. Despite feeling thoroughly wretched, she pressed on with her duties, determined to see them through.

Once everything was in order, she collapsed onto her cot in hopes that her throbbing headache would subside. She drifted off into a deep sleep, and when she eventually awoke, she was disoriented and unsure of what had stirred her from her slumber. As she attempted to rise from the bed, a heavy weight in her head shifted and slammed into her skull with a vengeance. She let out a low, pained moan and lay back down, closing her eyes in an effort to quell the overwhelming discomfort. She became acutely aware that the pounding in her head had intensified, the incessant throbbing now akin to the sound of railroad spikes being driven mercilessly into railroad ties.

"Oh, sweet lord, what have I done to myself? How much did I drink?"

Both of her palms held her forehead in place. The taste in her mouth would drive flies away. She grabbed her boar-bristled toothbrush and baking soda and scrubbed her teeth, tongue, cheeks, and the roof of her mouth. Then rinsed twice and repeated.

Something deep within her, perhaps her spleen, was stirred to life and began to wave its fist in protest, demanding a pound of JT's flesh for his impudent behavior. The voice within her head was much too loud and refused to be ignored. The man had acted as though a mere dram or two of Brandy consumed by a woman amounted to high treason. It was an affront that she would not abide.

She couldn't recall there being much left in the bottle when she had taken a sip. But when JT held up the empty bottle for inspection, she was shocked at the sight of it. Nevertheless, judging by her current condition, which was a first for her, she surmised that she must be suffering from a hangover. Perhaps she had imbibed a little too much of the potent brew. Even so, that did not give JT the right to treat her so brazenly. Who did he think he was to douse her like that?

As soon as the full effects of the hangover subsided, she vowed to have a few choice words with Mr. Grant. Her eyes were still sore, and the pounding in her head persisted, but she remained resolute. She would not be cowed by his impertinence. And as she contemplated what to say to him, a word emerged from her lips - handsome. It was a word that she had not intended to say, yet it spoke to a part of her that remained untamed and rebellious.

When she finished rubbing the water out of her eyes after being baptized this morning, she received a shock to her system. JT stood between the rising sun and herself, surrounded by the fiery fingers of dawn. His wavy hair was all tousled from sleep and shining bluish black. He meant to give her no quarter by the look in his eyes, but his threat remained unspoken. What had set him off like that? That look he gave her, all tight-jawed and steely-eyed, with his chin, tucked in. Yes, it was his eyes; they were different, like her behavior had disappointed him somehow. Why should he care what she does?

She remembered how masterfully he swept her off her feet the other day, simultaneously divesting her of the ax. JT's corded arms and muscled chest put Philipp's to shame in comparison. He held a wild woman up off the ground, kicking and screaming with his left arm while swinging an ax and planting it firmly into the wooden block.

Physically, he was neither taller nor broader at the shoulder than Philipp. However, Philipp had never created the sense of security she experienced snugly crushed against JT. Philipp smelled of shaving soap and starch. The bank manager preferred his starched shirts. Pleasant aromas. Nothing to complain about there. While spending a few seconds as JT's hostage, horse, manure, leather, and sweat had assailed her. A real working man's essence. She found it more appealing by half than shaving soap and starch.

What's wrong with her? There's work to be done, and she wastes time mooning over a man. Anyone would think she had never seen a man's chest before. Well, maybe she hasn't. She could kick herself for drinking so much. She only kept brandy around for when the painful monthlies attacked. Never more than a few sips. If she had known about the after-effects of over-imbibing, she'd be sober as a judge instead of enduring a skull-splitting headache and vomiting. Blast the hide off those soldiers marching around in her stomach with spikes on their boots. She prayed to all the saints in heaven to save her.

After dutifully feeding the passengers on the dinner stage, the hungover and exhausted Carrie Wagner collapsed onto her cot, determined to fend off any and all disruptions for the next century. She could barely keep her eyes open and her mind was awash with aches and throbs, but she refused to let anything or anyone disturb her much-needed rest. And so, she drifted off to sleep, her head sinking into the softness of the pillow.

When she woke up, she was surprised to find that the sun had risen again. Despite the trials and tribulations of the previous day, she had been granted another chance at life. As she lay in her cot, she heard the distant hoot of an owl and the shifting of the wind, carrying with it the pungent scent of manure. But even these mundane sounds and smells couldn't dampen her spirits.

Carrie had come to a realization--Philipp Wagner didn't deserve any more of her time or thoughts. She was done shedding tears for a man who didn't value her, done feeling inadequate and naive. Her decision to adopt children, move to California, and build a loving home with Ruth rang true to her. It was the right path for her, one that would allow her to find joy and purpose in her life once again.

Please stay away from men; she doesn't understand them at all. But, thanks to her late husband, she had bigger things to worry about today. His woman is trying to find her, so she must get to California immediately. The Philipp Wagner experience has been a profound life lesson; she will learn from it and move on the best she can. Besides, the JT Grant betrayal has now taken first place ahead of the Billy betrayal.

Maybe she should thank JT for breaking her heart. He reminded her that she was not worth loving. A notion that keeps proving itself right as rain. Why was she surprised by his evil revelation? Because of that kiss? It must have been obvious I had never kissed a man before. The heat of embarrassment consumed her. Devoid of emotion, he talked to her like she was less important than last night's dinner. And he's a Pinkerton. She covered her eyes with a palm. I asked him how to hire a Pinkerton to help solve Philipp's case. He's probably still laughing about that one. How did he keep from laughing in my face every time he complimented me? She sat straight up in bed as a revelation hit her.

"Holy smoke."

Mr. Russell didn't send JT here because he had a crush on her. Now that she thought about it, that would be an excellent reason not to send him to this station. Instead, JT told him he was a Pinkerton and that she was under investigation.

"Oh, Lord!"

JT told Mr. Russell to hire the hapless siblings! She didn't land this job on her own merits. JT Grant's manipulation began when she stepped on the train steps in Columbus. The loathsome spy does hate children. Since Mr. Russell didn't want to hire her, she needed to relieve him of her presence. But before fleeing to California, she had to find Billy. She had to apologize and listen to his entire story.

The westbound stage rolled in about an hour late, but everything was ready. Westbound passengers differ between night and day from eastbound passengers. The California-bound folks are excited about their new adventure and dressed in finery, but the eastbound lot showed up weary of travel, dirty, and broke. This batch was eastbound, but the friendly, easy-going Carrie had taken a sabbatical, and her ghost had no personality. She got the cookies and cornbread bagged for them to take along, and they left for their not-so-warm homecoming. While doing dishes, her brain returned to planning. Now that she's in danger, she no longer has her derringer, having given it to Billy for protection. She'll have to arm herself because when that woman catches up to her, she plans to be the dangerous one. Well, Carrie girl, the road starts with the first step. Let's get moving.

Carrie's peaceful evening evaporated when JT entered the cabin. He helped himself to food and coffee and sat down to eat.

"I hope you feel as bad as you look. You deserve it." JT said.

Rising from the dead, Carrie said, "I wanted to talk to you about yesterday, but I was going to wait. But, since you rudely approached it first, let's kick it around until it's dead, shall we?"

A sharp pain stabbed through her brain, and she struggled to keep it from showing on her face.

He looked up at her, appearing genuinely shocked at her challenge. Then, he shot out of his chair and claimed her by the upper arm.

"You were passed out drunk! How long have you been swilling liquor down like that?"

As Ruth calls it, that caldron that simmers inside her, known as her temper, came to her rescue.

"It's none of your business, and take your hand off me." She pushed against him.

He loosened his grip but did not remove his hand.

"You never stop surprising me, girl. Carrie, listen to reason. Where did you get that? You're drunk. You can't drink and…."

She jumped up out of his grasp.

"What did you say?"

"I said you're a drunk."

"I'm not a drunk. I felt sorry for myself and overindulged in the brandy a little. That doesn't make me a drunk."

He shook his head, grinned, and slapped his palm against his thigh. "I know a drunk when I see one."

The urge to strike him overwhelmed her. She pivoted on the ball of her foot and sought refuge in her room. "Stay away from me."

He called after her, "It's addictive, Carrie, don't let it ruin your life."

Before he could gather steam, she said, "I am not a drunk." Then, she turned to face him. "Do you understand me? I am not a drunk. Do you get this upset whenever a gentleman of your acquaintance has a nip or two?"

"Yes, Carrie, I do. I don't hold with drinking. I don't drink, and I disapprove of drinking. When we first met, I told you my father was a drunk. It muddles your mind and ruins your life. And besides, are you kidding me? A drop of two?" retorted JT.

Exactly who does he think he is? Certainly not my husband, not a blood relative, nor have we ever claimed to be friends. He's just another man making decisions for her.

"Then, I agree with you. You shouldn't drink. It upsets you too much. I'll worry about my non-existent drinking problem, and you worry about yours. That way, we'll both be happy."

JT's hand flew up, signally for her to stop. "Good, we're calling a truce?" JT asked, "You know men like your husband give men a poor reputation, don't you?"

Carrie cocked her head at him. "Really, JT, men like my dead husband give men a bad name? Not the sack of skunk meat eating at my table daily?"

He paused. His eyes roamed over Carrie's hair and came to rest on her face.

"We need to discuss a lot, like tracking down Philipp's fancy woman."

She opened her mouth. "

"No, not yet. It's not your turn to talk. I don't care what order we discuss our tasks, but we will discuss them."

"When a man gets bad news, he walks into a saloon and orders a whiskey, and no one gives it a second thought. A woman gets bad news; men expect her to sniffle into a handkerchief, accept a few there, there's, and wonder how long it'll be before she stops crying and makes dinner or does the laundry. You handle your grief your way, and I'll handle my grief my way."

Finally, she stunned JT into silence. The silence gave way to awkwardness. So, Carrie thought she'd bring up her plan.

"JT, I'm resigning from my position at the Pony Express. I'm sending Mr. Russell a letter with the next pony rider. After that, I intend to return to St. Joseph to find Billy. After that, I'm headed straight for California." She pushed back from the table to return to her room. She didn't know if she had the guts to pull off the coup de grâce.

She heard JT say, "But Carrie, I need you...." She slammed her door shut in the middle of his sentence and threw herself upon her cot.

JT's footsteps stopped at her door. "Carrie, I'm sorry I upset you so much. I don't enjoy seeing you hurt this way."

"Please go away, JT." His name left her lips with a sob. "I don't much like being made a fool."

"I had no intention of making you a fool. I had a murderer to catch. That was my goal." He spoke in quieter tones now.

"You lying dog, you buried me in compliments you never believed. At least Philipp never lied to my face." Sitting up, she pressed a corner of the blanket to her wet cheeks.

JT pushed the poor excuse of a door open.

Carrie said, "You're not allowed in here."

He sat down next to her as if he slept there every night. "They weren't lies. I love your hair. You're the most beautiful woman I've ever met. And that kiss we shared nearly had me begging. But…" He had Carrie hanging on every word.

"But?"

"The truth between us--no more lies."

She nodded.

"Just like you, Carrie, I have no plans to get married again. Once was enough for me. You told me you didn't have plans to marry."

He pushed errant tendrils of her hair behind her ear.

"So, now, don't get your feathers ruffled again. I thought you'd be a willing partner in a dalliance. You certainly don't plan to spend the rest of your life celibate? "

"I didn't know my celibacy was up for discussion." Carrie stood, yanked the blanket off the cot, and folded it.

"I'm making this worse, not better. I don't know what to say."

Carrie stopped and chanced a glimpse at his face. He looked perplexed, worrying his thumbnail with his index finger and keeping his eyes averted.

"JT, I am not interested in a dalliance. If true love exists, it's avoiding me. I refuse to marry again without true love. And I'm only going to dally after a marriage ceremony."

JT tugged at his shirt collar and cleared his throat. "Don't you think it's getting warm here?" He rose to his feet. They stood inches apart. That twinkle in those darn blue eyes of his drew her in hook, line, and sinker.

Carrie's heart raced as she threw herself into JT's arms, consumed by an unbridled passion that she had never felt before. Without a second thought, she pressed her lips against his, eager to explore the depths of their desire. JT responded with equal fervor, wrapping his arm around her waist and pulling her close. His lips were rough and urgent against hers, his fingers tangling in her hair as he deepened the kiss. Carrie was lost in the moment, her mind consumed by the sensations that JT's touch was igniting within her. As they pressed against the cabin wall, Carrie could feel the heat of JT's body against hers, his hips grinding against her belly. Every nerve in her body was alive with pleasure, and she could feel her self-control slipping away with each passing moment.

Oh, dear God! Flames from a new and soul-sucking desire threatened to consume her as surely as Sunday came after Saturday. Wedging a hand between them, Carrie had to push him away before she collapsed. She placed her palms on his chest, but her hands had other plans and caressed the muscled expanse. Her conscience woke up and reminded her that she's kissing a betrayer. Gathering her remaining willpower, she pushed against his chest. Weakly at first, then with a little more pressure.

When his lips left hers, she almost begged for their return like the apparent wanton that she was. Instead, she jerked her arms from around his neck. JT dragged breath into his neglected lungs. After her hasty display of affection, lust, desire, or whatever else, she struggled to find something appropriate to say and came up with, "Blame your darn blue eyes."

What surprised her? She didn't feel embarrassed. She wanted to kiss him and did so. Maybe she did it to relieve herself from the heartache and betrayal. If so, it didn't work. Her headache once again grabbed her attention. She could tell him she was out of her mind in pain. Shoot! Not another lie.

"Is there more where that came from?" The handsome lout smiled at her. One of those smiles with a message. This one said I'm holding all the cards now, baby.

Not if I can help it.

JT caressed her bottom lip with his thumb. "Yes, we should take it one step at a time."

Carrie bit his thumb. He waved the offended thumb as if it was on fire.

Sans guilt, Carrie informed him, "You know you're no better than my parents or Phillip? You knew I was vulnerable and lied to my face for the last four months. I think it's time you vanished from my life."

"I was doing my job, Carrie. Being a detective, you use any ruse you need to catch the bad guy. I'd do it even if I had to dress like a woman."

Carrie snorted and sought a handkerchief. "Oh, stop, you're incapable of the truth."

"Come on, don't you want to see Philipp's fancy woman go to prison? I do. I told you Hank Lipton was my best friend. I'm not sure if they will hang her. Few will hang a woman. But, don't forget, she's coming closer every day. Wouldn't it be great if we teamed up to bring her down? Do you think a derringer alone will save your life?"

"I gave the derringer to Billy. Yes, I would like to get my hands on that woman, but I have a deadline to keep. So first on my list is finding Billy."

"That works perfectly because that's where we need to go first. I need a telegraph station."

"Hopefully, to clear my name."

"Of course, I'll notify Mr. Russell that we're resigning immediately." JT turned on his heel and vacated the room. Sighing, Carrie had two words for JT. Get lost.

<u>Romans 6:12</u> *Therefore do not let sin reign in your mortal body, that you should obey it in its lust.*

Chapter Thirteen

May 1, 1860, The Muddle

JT figured the barn would suit him just fine while he tried to sort things out in his mind. While a man mucks stalls, his mind can solve the world's most complex challenges. He realized he had to return to the beginning to see if he had missed any clues. The pieces of the puzzle aren't coming together. It's more like a detail here and there getting ruled out. Assuming Philipp's letter is true, which he'll believe until proven otherwise, the female accomplice is still at large. But the bad news, whoever the genuine accomplice was, she would eventually find Carrie. It chaffed him to use Carrie as bait, but he didn't see any other way to lure the murderess out at this point in the game of justice. That chestnut ball of fire was under his skin, making herself comfortable despite struggling to keep his hands off her. But that kiss did him in. The second one, not the first, she brought him down like David felling Goliath. Never in his wildest dreams did he think the minx would up and take what she wanted? And that kiss wasn't any old kiss. Dang, if he didn't feel branded.

Carrie still referred to him as Mr. Grant or Sir, indicating her anger toward him. Fully aware of his hatred for beans and hardtack, that's all she's been serving him for the last two days. But he's figured out a way to get her talking to him. Her weak spot was Billy. He waited until Carrie called out, 'dinner's ready,' and headed for the cabin. As per the last two days, she ate before summoning him and stood with her back to him washing dishes. He spied the plate of beans, minus a chunk of salt pork tonight, and hardtack waiting for him on the table with a steaming cup of coffee.

"Looks great. I'm so hungry I'd chow down on a loin of polecat." JT settled at the table, scraping his chair forward and licking his lips while humming. Then, forcing himself to imagine a steak, he dug in. Halfway through his plate of beans, he asked, "Why do you suppose Billy didn't like your husband?"

"What are you talking about? Billy never met my husband." Each word was spoken succinctly.

"But he did. He let it slip that Philipp was the coldest-hearted banker of them all. Why would he say that if he's never met him?" asked JT.

"I don't care why maybe to make me feel better." The circling washrag slowed.

"He also mentioned that Wagner was crazier than a horse on locoweed." JT reminded.

How would he know that?" Waiting on the verbal Gatling gun, JT cringed. At least she'd be talking to him again.

Carrie turned, revealing her raised eyebrows, and asked, "You were listening to us that night? You're lower than a snake in a mile-deep crevasse." His plan worked. Curiosity nipped at her heels. She folded the wet washrag and draped it over the edge of the dishpan. Then, pulling the chair on his right for her, she sat down. "How could Billy have known Philipp? Billy and I met on the riverboat trip south after Philipp's hanging. That doesn't make sense."

"I agree. That's what I mean. If Billy met Philipp, did he meet him in Columbus or elsewhere before boarding the riverboat? I have a nagging feeling about him showing up in your cabin that night. Odds are, it wasn't an accident. I have to figure out what part he plays in this investigation." JT shoveled in another spoonful of beans. "That's why I appeared miffed when you told me you sent him away."

"Billy in Columbus....what would Billy be doing in Columbus?"

"Well, I've got a theory, but we must find him to learn the whole story." JT grimaced as he bit off a chunk of hard tack.

"What's your theory?"

"It's the way detectives think. You get a clue and ask yourself, what if this happened? What if that happened? Until you come up with a rough idea of the situation. Billy is involved in this bank robbery or murder somehow, I don't know how yet, but he is. Sometimes criminals use kids to case their jobs for them. It could be something like that."

"Case?"

"Watched the bank to note when the employees and the money came and went."

"Billy, a criminal?" She grabbed him by the forearm, forestalling the next spoonful of beans.

"I'm talking theory, not fact, Carrie. Don't upset yourself." After lowering the spoon to his plate, he took her fingers from his arm and held them gently.

"Oh dear, that means Philipp used Billy to---how could he treat a child--I married a stranger, didn't I?" She brought her gaze to his.

Avoiding that question, JT moved on, "How did the note avoid your notice for so long?" The time-lapse didn't make sense to him.

"I can't read German. It's the Bible my mother left with me at the orphanage. I've been thinking things over for the last two days, too." She fought against the tears, struggling to keep her composure. "After two days of deliberating, I'm no closer to a plan of action. I don't know where to start, how to find Billy, the fancy woman, or the money to pay the Pinkerton agent, which turns out to be you."

"It's your lucky day. I'm already working on this case until it's solved. And since I retired, my services are free." He studied Carrie as she worried her bottom lip.

"I have to start at the beginning and reinvestigate this whole case. Billy knows Philipp and Philipp having a Saturday night woman, are new leads. And the note in the Bible might be gospel or a bald-faced lie. The point is we need to find out. You want your name cleared, and I want to find my best friend's killer. So, what do you say about throwing in together to solve this?" It's the only way he could think of to keep track of her while reinvestigating the case.

"Your best friend's killer?" She snatched her hand away from his. "Is that true?"

"Yes. I tried to explain it to you the other day. Hank Lipton was my best friend. That's why I'm investigating this case."

Standing and turning away, "From the first day I got on the train in Columbus, you've been ahead of me the whole time, haven't you?"

"Yes, Carrie, no more lies."

Carrie nodded her head as she paced. "What about Mr. Russell? I finish what I start and promised to run this station to the best of my ability." She clamped her upper arms with both hands and rubbed while pacing.

Seeking to relieve her concern, JT shared, "Don't worry about Russell. I told him to hire you and Billy and to assign me to your station. I couldn't think of any other way to stick to you then. He won't care if we move on. He's expecting it."

Carrie turned her flinty eyes on him, pushed her fists straight down to her sides, and her ragged breathing alarmed him. A flush rushed across her face as she stepped into his personal space. Then, looking him in the eyes, she said, "You're the most contemptible person who ever drew breath."

Her reaction surprised him. Expecting to be slapped again, JT was surprised when Carrie backed out of his personal space, began pacing, unbuttoning a few buttons at the top of her blouse, and rolled up her sleeves.

"Your bait has news for you, Pinkerton man. You work for me now, and my priority is finding Billy. Nothing and I mean nothing, else happens until we find that boy. And if you treat him as a sub-human as you have treated me, you will regret it." Her tone in the last four words rang true.

"Carrie, I never meant--" started JT.

Her arm shot out toward him with the palm of her hand in his face. "After we locate Billy, he and I will depart for California.

"What do you mean? First, we must catch the murderer," JT pointed out.

"Write a note to Russell telling him he needs to send replacements for us as quickly as possible." The offensive limb fell to her side.

"I've done that."

"Good, hmm, you have the makings of a fine errand boy if this Pinkerton thing doesn't work out for you. Oh, and thanks for doing this job for free." Carrie grabbed a towel off the shelf, "Excuse me, I don't feel quite as clean as I should."

May 10, 1860, St. Joseph Rebound

Billy crouched in his secluded hiding spot, peering out from behind the dusty crates stacked high. His eyes were fixed on his sister, Lettie, as she paraded her latest victim, a foolish doctor, around town, making a mockery of his naivety. Billy had done his research on the man and knew that Dr. Champlain was a vulnerable target, a middle-aged widower with children studying in a faraway boarding school. But if Lettie continued to drain his finances, there wouldn't be any money left to pay for his kids' education.

As Billy watched from the shadows, his mind raced with the urgency of the situation. If Lettie continued to lead Dr. Champlain around by the nose, his children would suffer the consequences. He knew that Lettie had no idea where Carrie, was, or she would have already been on her trail to Big Sandy. Billy needed to act fast to throw Lettie off Carrie's scent and protect his sister from harm.

The mere thought of Lettie getting too close to Carrie made Billy's blood run cold. The memory of their last encounter was still fresh in his mind, and he knew that he couldn't take any chances. He had to find a way to mislead Lettie, to make her think that Carrie was in a different direction altogether. But how?

Billy knew that he couldn't let his sister, Lettie, find him. The mere thought of her discovering his whereabouts sent shivers down his spine, for he knew that she would unleash hell's banshees upon him if he didn't have the bank riches that she so desperately craved. And those riches, he knew, were still with Carrie.

Despite his resolve to protect the doctor from Lettie's grasping claws, Billy knew that he had more pressing matters to attend to. For the last time, Lettie had deprived him of food and clothing, tanned his hide, and confined him in a cupboard, leaving him to rot like a common prisoner. He couldn't afford to let her get her hands on the stolen bank money, for the consequences would be dire.

He knew that Lettie was a force to be reckoned with, a cunning and ruthless adversary who would stop at nothing to get what she wanted. And what she wanted, more than anything else, was the stolen bank money that she thought Carrie had taken and hidden away.

Billy had to find a way to protect Carrie, to keep her from Lettie's grasp, and to ensure that the money remained hidden.

When Lettie sent him to case the bank and watch the banker's wife back in Columbus, he had no idea he would fall in love with Mrs. Wagner. The extraordinary woman had a heart of gold, always volunteering her time at the local orphanage, attending church every Sunday, and planning her upcoming wedding with great enthusiasm. Her kindness knew no bounds, and Billy found himself completely intoxicated by her selfless spirit.

He often caught glimpses of her in her room at the boarding house, where she and her friend Ruth would sew her wedding dress and giggle over silly girl talk. Even in the mercantile, where Mrs. Wagner worked, she treated every customer with the utmost kindness and respect, even those who looked down upon her.

For Billy, Mrs. Wagner was the polar opposite of his sister Lettie. Lettie was cunning, selfish, and manipulative, using any means necessary to get what she wanted. In contrast, Mrs. Wagner was kind and giving, always putting others before herself.

Billy couldn't help but be drawn to Mrs. Wagner's radiant spirit, her warm smile, and her gentle demeanour. He longed to be near her, to bask in the glow of her goodness, and to forget the dark and tumultuous world in which he lived.

If Billy had chosen a sister, it would have been Carrie for in a world full of darkness and deceit, she was the shining light that gave him hope, and the one person who could make his life worth living.

As Lettie and Philipp went to dinner in Cincinnati on the night of the bank robbery, Billy took the stolen money and headed back to Columbus. He couldn't bear the thought of Lettie's mark or Carrie's worthless husband getting their hands on the loot. He knew that they didn't deserve a single cent of it. His plan was simple: hide the money in Carrie's house, and when she found it, she could return it.

But things didn't go according to plan. Lettie decided to take matters into her own hands and murder a Pinkerton agent. Philipp was arrested for the murder of Hank, the Pinkerton, but he refused to speak a word. Billy knew that his sister was the real killer, but he couldn't prove it.

Billy was sent to spy on her on the riverboat and the more he got to know her the more he grew desperate to protect Carrie from Lettie's wrath. He knew that Lettie was getting dangerously close to Carrie's trail, and he couldn't let her get any closer. He had to protect Carrie at all costs.

That spineless banker couldn't stomp a spider. Spending time with the banker's wife gave him his first experience of what 'normal' life might have been if he'd had one. Instead, Carrie gives smiles, hugs, kisses, or discussions instead of orders and persuasion instead of slaps or work. He would do whatever it took to keep Carrie safe from Lettie, even if it killed him.

Dang, their hides; what are JT and Carrie doing in St. Joseph? Billy's heart raced as he watched JT and Carrie disembark from the stagecoach in St. Joseph. He quickly ducked into an alleyway, hoping that they hadn't spotted him. His mind raced with thoughts of how he was going to keep Lettie from finding out that Carrie was in town. With Lettie and her mark out of town, he knew that he had a limited amount of time to come up with a plan.

When he arrived in St. Joseph, he went into hiding. No way he's letting his sister find him again. Lettie and her mark were out of town, but how will he keep the two women from bumping into each other? Lettie returns by tomorrow. Before thenAW©S, he had to keep Lettie thinking about anything except going west to find Carrie. All four will simultaneously be in the same town—an authentic recipe for disaster.

As Billy stood there, contemplating his next move, the gravity of the situation weighed heavily on his mind. He knew that it may very well come down to the ultimate sacrifice - giving up his life to protect the woman he loved. But he was prepared to do whatever it takes to keep Lettie from finding Carrie.

If he had that ragdoll, he'd give it to Lettie, and she'd disappear. Perhaps the news of his death would send Carrie and JT packing. First things first, find out why they are here. And he'll have to devise something else to preoccupy Lettie when she returns. Let's see, maybe a doctor or another banker. This berg is large enough for more than one doctor. One must possess low morals, have money, and an eye for the ladies. Yep, go out there and find Lettie her next mark. She won't come up for air, much less notice two newcomers to St. Joseph.

Billy set himself tailing JT and Carrie. Thank God they checked into a different hotel from Lettie. Peering into the hotel window, he waited until they left for their rooms upstairs. Then he walked up to the check-in counter.

"Hey, mister, did Mrs. Wagner and Mr. Grant say why they were visiting St. Jo?" asked Billy casually.

"Mr. Grant asked where the newspaper, telegraph, and sheriff's offices were. Mrs. Wagner asked if I had seen a blond-headed twelve-year-old boy with red socks and a tendency to swear." The desk clerk leaned over the counter to look at his socks.

Shaking his middle finger in the desk clerk's face, Billy warned him, "Listen here, you nosey turd, you ain't seed me, don't knowd me from Bob's uncle. Unless you want a blade in your gizzard, forget I was here."

The clerk swallowed hard, "We haven't met."

Billy retreated across the street and waited for one of them to leave the hotel. Not ten minutes later, JT emerged and headed to the sheriff's office. He cut around to the back of the building and ran to the right, counting the premises. Number seven, the sheriff's office, he ducked into the shaded side alley. He crawled to the open window and crouched to listen to what JT had to say. He only had to wait a few seconds before JT entered and introduced himself.

Billy's heart raced as he pressed his ear against the window, straining to hear the conversation inside. JT's voice was deep and steady, but he spoke in hushed tones, making it difficult for Billy to catch every word. Nonetheless, he remained patient, focused on every syllable that escaped through the open window.

"Sheriff, I'm JT Grant, a Pinkerton agent. I'm working on the Hank Lipton murder, which occurred in Cincinnati, Ohio."

"I remember reading something about that case. Wasn't it solved?" The sheriff asked.

"Halfway. The bank manager who robbed his bank and murdered Hank was hanged in January, but he had a female accomplice that I believe is in this area, and I may need your assistance to bring her in." explained JT.

"Who is she?" asked the sheriff.

"Unknown at this point."

Billy heard rustling.

"I have this letter the murderer wrote to his wife just before the hanging, located only a few weeks ago."

Billy about swallowed his tongue. Ask him what the letter says, sheriff.

"In it, he warns his wife that the woman will come after her because of the mistaken belief that Mrs. Wagner has the bank money. He tells his wife he never loved her. Instead, he loves the female accomplice. To save his accomplice, he went to his grave. And he also asked Mrs. Wagner not to hurt his one true love." JT drew a cleansing breath. "Sheriff, Mrs. Wagner is the bait. I'm sticking to her like glue over at the Beacon hotel. This letter is now evidence. Please ensure it gets to Sheriff Huffman in Columbus, Ohio."

Back to the wall, legs sprawled in the dirt, Billy sat dumbfounded. That bastard sent that piece of shit letter to Carrie. Tears rolled down his face at the thought of Carrie's heart-shattering. Philipp and Lettie, destined for each other, didn't have enough redeeming qualities to fill an inside straight.

"Sure, I can take care of that."

JT said, "I've written a copy. I'm going to the telegram office and sending it to Sheriff Huffman. I'll inform him the original letter is on its way."

Billy heard the office door open. The cadence of JT's voice had changed since their separation. He spoke with a slight variance in tone and a businesslike manner. Something's happened. What's eating at him?

"Oh, Sheriff, have you seen a blond-headed twelve-year-old boy wearing red socks and cussing a blue streak?"

"That sounds like every boy in town except for the red socks. I'll keep my eyes peeled. Why? Is he associated with the accomplice?"

"No. Mrs. Wagner is looking for him." JT left the office and headed to the telegraph office.

Billy walked across the street, ran around a corral and livery stable, then straight down to the backside of the telegraph office. The window is where the customers go. So, he slid under the plank sidewalk on the side and waited.

JT sent the information in the letter to his Captain at the Pinkertons' office in Chicago and Sheriff Huffman. "How close to New Braunfels, Texas, can you send a telegram?"

"Well, let me see." The clerk thumbed through a handbook.

"Nothing west of the Mississippi River, I'm afraid."

"That's what I thought. How about you send a telegram as close as possible and ask the postmaster to mail it to my folks? I'll give you enough money for postage."

"All right, what's the message?"

To Mrs. Matilda Ackerman, Circle A ranch, New Braunfels, Texas. STOP ON MY WAY HOME, STOP MIGHT BE THREE- OR FOUR-WEEKS STOP DON'T WORRY, STOP JT"

"That will cost you $1." JT paid and walked away.

Flipping over, Billy lay on his back. I'm on my way home, JT said. What does he have in mind for Carrie? He had better not intend to abandon her like everyone else in her life. He suddenly recovered his composure and went to the newspaper office, where the din of the press had all but silenced any dialogue. Fortunately, all the windows were open. JT entered.

"What can we do for you, mister?" As JT stepped into the newspaper office, the sound of the printing press roared like a lion in the background. Billy watched as JT surveyed the room, his eyes scanning the space for the editor. His demeanour was calm and collected, his posture confident and unwavering.

Without hesitation, JT approached the editor's desk, and Billy leaned forward to listen in. The editor's eyes flicked up from his work, and he regarded JT with a quizzical expression.

JT said, "I want to run an ad in your newspaper."

"We're always open to ads. What do you want to say?"

Billy imagined the news clerk with pen and paper in hand.

"Missing, in capital letters, searching for Billy. Blond-headed twelve-year-old boy with red socks and a penchant for swearing. Please contact JT Grant at the Beacon hotel. Let's run it for three days and see what happens."

Got it, $1 on the nose."

Another surprise—why are these two so eager to capture him? Especially after Carrie's moving farewell speech at the Big Sandy. Hearing this, he must find Carrie. Something is wrong. But he needs to set up Lettie's mark before she comes to town. You can't check into Carrie's situation while protecting her from Lettie. As soon as he wriggled out from under the planked walkway, the red socks found a new place to live. He put those treasures in his pocket, of course. He needed a hat! He required one to cover his mound of dirty blond hair. And the swearing? Until he locates Carrie, the use of swearing is forbidden. That desk clerk better not give him away.

Chapter Fourteen

May 15, 1860, Mrs. Lipton's Letter

Carrie and JT managed to avoid each other the next day. She wrestled with the thought that she should apologize for how she delivered the bad news message to him. But that would only lead to another argument.

The next morning, she didn't leave her room until noon and ate at the restaurant. The waiter showed her to a table at the window where she could be alone. She placed her order and enjoyed the view outside while she waited. Then, JT walked up to the window outside and knocked, gaining her attention. He signaled he would come inside to join her. Carrie's heart skipped a beat at the sight of JT outside the window. She felt a mix of emotions, unsure of what his intentions were. When he gestured to come inside and join her, she hesitated for a moment before nodding.

He slid into the chair across from her, "Greetings, Sunshine, you're beautiful today. Can we call a truce? There's still a murder to solve."

She expected a stormy greeting instead of praise and said, "Of course."

A server approached to take JT's order, then left.

"I got a telegram and wanted to share it with you. We are still partners trying to catch Hank's murderer, are we not?

Carrie nodded.

"It's from Captain Pinkerton.

JT slipped his thumb into the envelope's flap, freed the telegram, and read aloud.

"SENDING VIA US MAIL LETTER FROM MRS LIPTON STOP FOUND AMONG HANK'S THINGS STOP FRONT OF ENVELOPE READS JT IF ANYTHING HAPPENS TO ME, I WANT YOU TO FIND LETICIA BROWN IN PHILADELPHIA STOP GIVE HER THE ENCLOSED LETTER STOP I WOULD CONSIDER IT A KINDNESS STOP MAY HAVE A BEARING ON CURRENT CASE STOP CAPTAIN PINKERTON."

JT took a sip of coffee while digesting the information.

"Who's Leticia Brown?" Carrie asked.

"I haven't any idea. Hank never mentioned her to me before. He grew up in Philadelphia. Maybe she's an acquaintance from his hometown."

He handed the telegram to Carrie. They had pledged to solve this case together before their fledgling relationship hit a brick wall. Carrie took the telegram.

"We may not be here long enough to receive the letter."

"I'm aware. If we must go before it arrives, I'll leave a forwarding address with the postmaster."

Carrie pushed her chair back.

"Where are you headed?" Asked JT.

"I've finished my lunch, and no one has responded to the newspaper ad, so I thought I would look around for Billy."

JT scraped his chair from the table, "I'll go with you."

Once again, Carrie held her palm up, "No, I can search all by myself, and you haven't eaten yet."

"I agree, but you may not be safe. The accomplice may be waiting until you're alone."

Standing, Carrie ended the conversation with, "I can take care of myself. Thank you. Besides, we can cover more area if I go one way and you go the other." She patted her skirt pocket to assure him Mr. Colt was on duty. "For your information, I bought a Colt pistol this morning. And it's right here in my pocket. '

"I'm quite safe."

<u>Job 36:18</u> *Because there is wrath, beware lest He take you away with one blow; For a large ransom would not help you avoid it.*

May 15, 1860, Assaulted

Carrie walked down the west side of the street, stopping at each establishment, and skipping saloons The sun was gradually setting, casting long shadows over the worn facades of the buildings. She had yet to find a sign of Billy, but she hadn't been able to. She avoided the saloons because asking if they'd seen a twelve-year-old boy with blond hair, red socks, and a pension to cuss like a dock worker would draw a blank every time. Besides, she's not allowed in saloons.

As she reached the end of the street, she came upon a livery stable. Its dilapidated state was immediately apparent, as some sections of the wooden structure had already given way to the elements. Even the remaining aged planks creaked and groaned in protest, warning her not to venture any closer.

Carrie hesitated briefly, her heart beating faster with each passing moment. But her resolve did not waver, and with a deep breath, she stepped into the unstable structure. The stench of manure and hay permeated the air, making her wrinkle her nose in disgust. The shadows within the livery seemed to writhe and twist, as if alive, casting eerie shapes upon the walls. But she pushed aside her fear, and called out into the dimly lit space.

She opened the weathered door and stepped into the darkness, waiting until her eyes adjusted, scents like hay, manure, and horse wafted on a grit-filled hot breeze coming through the planks. A horse close on her right nickered. Stallion or mare, it asked the wrong person for a treat or attention. Horses scare her. Then she could see a lamp lit in the back of the livery. She carefully felt her way toward the light, grabbing onto stall doors or divider posts, and jumped when one of the horses snorted.

"Hello? Is anyone there?" Her voice echoed in the emptiness, bouncing off the walls and returning to her like a ghostly whisper. But there was no answer, save for the rustling of straw as a breeze whispered through the open slats in the walls.

A cowboy was bedding down his horse. "Excuse me, have you seen the proprietor?"

The cowboy turned toward her. His pinched face and sparse dirty beard jolted her into a flinch. "Sorry, ma'am, I haven't seen one yet. Is there something I can help you with?" A disingenuous grin lurked at the corners of his mouth.

Carrie felt uneasy as the man's eyes roamed over her, lingering on her chest. She sensed a malicious intent behind his vacant gaze, as if he was sizing her up for some wicked plan. Her instincts urged her to flee, to escape from the grip of his sinister aura.

As she looked into his lifeless eyes, she knew with certainty that she was confronting the devil himself. A shudder ran through her body, but she refused to let it show on her face. She steadied herself and prepared to face him head-on.

"You just arrived in town, didn't you?" he asked, his voice heavy with a gruffness that sent a chill down

Carrie's spine. She swallowed hard, sensing that his inquiry was not one of genuine interest, but rather a trap laid out for her.

Carrie remained silent, her eyes darting around the dimly lit livery aisle, searching for an escape route. She knew that if she let her guard down for even a moment, this man could overpower her and subject her to unspeakable horrors.

She summoned all her courage and replied, "I don't see how that's any of your business." Her voice quavered slightly, betraying her fear, but she refused to back down.

"I think it is, ma'am" grinned the man.

"Thank you. I don't think you can help me" Carrie turned to work her way back to the hotel on the east side of the street.

The cowboy grabbed her upper arm, jerking her backward. *Oh, no.* Her momentum met with a fist to her jaw. Darkness claimed her as she hit the ground in a heap of ribbon, lace, and petticoat, moaning as she lay there. Carrie's eyes fluttered open as she struggled to catch her breath. Her jaw ached, and her head throbbed in pain. Her vision blurred as she tried to make sense of her surroundings. The sound of shuffling and scraping filled her ears as she fought to sit up.

He shoved rags down her throat only seconds later, then dragged her into an empty stall, dropping her onto a layer of hay. Struggling to breathe, she woke stunned and clawed at the dirty rags while her other hand groped for her pistol.

Oh my God! Flashes of the night the drunken cowboy broke into her room gripped her. Was the same situation about to happen again? The same fear that crippled her then came in triple strength. Her gun snagged on something and wouldn't slide out of her pocket. The assailant's body odor surrounded her, and she vomited. *Maybe the hammer is stuck on a part of her skirt.* She jerked on the gun's grip, which was a mistake because her sudden movement drew the barbarian's attention. *Why didn't she let JT come with her? She needed him now. Please come help me.*

Both of his hands clamped down on her right wrist and twisted. Her heart pounded so hard it threatened to divert her from the pain in her wrist. She released the pistol. He delivered another punch to her face for her trouble. Then he tore the gun from her skirt and threw it over his shoulder. After the second punch, Carrie's vision blurred, and her limbs went limp. He flipped her over, binding her hands. Her hands were so tightly bound; she knew her wrist had broken. He rolled her onto her back again and spread his repulsive body across hers.

Carrie shuddered in disgust as the cowboy's foul breath assaulted her nostrils. She tried to push him away, but her limbs felt weak and heavy, still reeling from the blow to her jaw.

He spoke again, his voice dripping with venom, "You're not so high and mighty now. God, I hate you blue-blooded bitches."

She felt his rough hands tearing at the front of her dress, and panic shot through her. Thank God she had chosen to wear one of her more substantial trousseau dresses, which meant she wore a tightly tied corset. She gritted her teeth as he groped at her, trying to reach beneath the layers of fabric. Suddenly, his mouth was on hers, and she could taste the foul stench of his breath. She tried to keep her lips closed, but he forced them apart and began licking at her teeth and gums. The sensation was nauseating, and she could feel bile rising in her throat. She was about to vomit when he pulled away, a look of disgust on his face. He kissed her, not seeming to care that she'd vomited, and licked her closed lips. He pulled away before she could spew on him.

Trying to kick the cowboy off, she planted her feet and pushed her hips up, hoping he'd fall to the side, and she'd be able to rise. Instead, he took advantage of the move to yank her skirt over her head.

"Stop you heathen. Take your hands off me."

The cowboy sneered as he towered over her, watching her writhe in agony. He savored the power he held over her, the power he had over all women. "That's right, scream all you want, no one can hear you out here," he taunted, a cruel grin spreading across his face. Carrie felt helpless and violated as the man continued to assault her, tearing away at her clothes and groping at her body.

She could feel the tears streaming down her face as she realized the gravity of the situation. Her mind raced as she tried to come up with a way to escape this monster. But as he pushed her down and stomped on her knee, the excruciating pain made her gasp for air. She was completely at his mercy, and she knew it. As he silenced her screams with the rags, she felt a sense of defeat wash over her. How had her search for Billy led her to this dark place? In her desperation, she thought of JT and how he had tried to protect her. "JT was correct when he said she shouldn't go alone. Danger waited for her at every dark corner, and she found one. In spite of her stoked up anger, she needed JT now more than ever." But as the tears flowed down her face, Carrie knew that there was no one who could save her from this nightmare. She was alone, at the mercy of a cruel and heartless man.

Carrie didn't know that people this evil existed. She pushed against the rags in her mouth with her tongue. The cowboy held her down with a hip while unfastening his pants. The rags wouldn't budge. He roughly forced her thighs apart with dirty, calloused hands. She wedged her right foot against his hip and pushed with all her strength, but he was solid as a boulder. Leaving reality behind, she forced her mind far away from the livery--back to the orphanage playing with the children and listening to their laughter, closing her mind to the truth. *Lord, please don't let him kill me.*

The cowboy grunted; his total weight collapsed on her, forcing all the air out of her lungs. He wasn't moving. What's happening? She realized he had gone limp before sullying her body. She squeezed her eyes shut. Thank the Lord. She struggled to get the weight off her wrist. Then, somebody yanked her dress down and pulled the greasy rags out of her mouth.

"Carrie, ya a'right?" A familiar and most welcoming voice inquired.

"Billy, is that you?" She spat a fiber from the greasy rag out. "You found me. Oh, Thank you. My God am I glad to see you. From where did you come? I've been looking for you all day. Would you please untie my arms? I need to hug you."

"Been tailin' ya since ya bounced to St. Jo." Billy ran across the aisle, retrieved the sole lamp in the stable, and hung it in Carrie's stall, "Did da ruttin' buffalo hurt ya? Ya were here so long. I thought ya growed roots."

"Yes, my clever boy, I needed your help. He punched me in the jaw and stomped my knee. It hurts like the devil. Can you get this piece of human trash off me, please?" Carrie pushed at the corpse with her good leg.

Billy knelt next to her and shoved the assailant off her.

Amazed by Billy's feat, Carrie inquired, "What did you do to him?"

"Stuck a pitchfork clear through the bastard's backbone."

She heard that curse word plain as day but didn't give a hoot. Shocked, she realized sometimes only the curse word fits the situation—Billy's right. The assailant was a bastard. "Thank you, Billy. Thank God for you. Can you untie my hands?"

Billy tried to roll Carrie over, but she screamed. "Wait, Billy. I'll try to move a little to my left side. "Billy untied her, and she moved to her back.

"Carrie," Billy's eyes rested on her torn dress, "Whatta he done to ya?" Billy lifted one section of the torn blouse, then dropped it. Tears filled his eyes.

"Don't worry, honey. The buffalo didn't get past my corset. You saved me before he could do irreparable harm. My wrist is throbbing with pain, and my face feels like a horse stomped me, but I will be fine. Carrie jerked Billy into her arms, wincing whenever her right hand wobbled about, pulling him back down to the hay. "I love you. I love you. I'm sorry I didn't listen to your whole story. I'm so sorry. Please forgive me." The dam broke, and Carrie sobbed so hard she couldn't talk anymore. The shock had finally set in.

"Don't worry 'bout dat now. Can ya get on up?" Billy begged.

She tried to rise. The damaged left knee would not bend, and she couldn't use her right arm for support. Sobbing and praying seemed like the best medicine for her in the meantime. That piece of trash had stolen her ability to do simple physical actions. She patted Billy on the shoulder and whispered, "Get the Sheriff and JT."

Billy got up to do her bidding.

"Billy?"

He turned.

"Doctor, too."

He raced from the stable as if his real sister dogged his heels.

Alone in the sudden silence, Carrie squeezed her eyes closed to avoid looking at the corpse, then turned her face to the corner of the stall as trembling set in. Every square inch of her felt dirty and violated. She pulled the length of her forearm across her lips, removing the vile kiss planted there.

Then, she remembered telling JT she would be fine searching for Billy alone. Stupid! How could she have been so stupid? JT's tried to keep her safe since the day she met him. He deserved a profound apology.

Carrie reached under her skirts to investigate the damage. Her left side lay exposed, which meant her underthings were in danger of falling off if she stood up. She pushed her fingers up to see if he had ripped her corset where she kept all her money. In between the whalebone, the crinkle of paper money could be heard. She couldn't find any openings in the corset. Gingerly, she felt between her legs to check for damage.

Then JT burst through the livery doors. "Carrie, where are you?"

"Back here, JT." Just his physical presence alone brought down her heart rate. He grabbed the offender by the boots and dragged him away.

"Thank God you're here. I was so scared." She reached out toward him with her good arm.

He slid in beside her and took her hand. "Billy said you're hurt. Where?"

"He hit me in the jaw twice, stomped my knee, and broke my right wrist. Does it look awful?"

"Too dark to see well. I've got to get you to the hotel. Tell me where to put my arms, so I don't hurt you."

"First, please take what remains of my underthings off my right leg and roll them up for me. I'm afraid they'll fall off in the middle of the street."

JT swallowed hard. He moved to her other side and carefully tugged the exposed portions of her underthings until the whole lot came loose. He leaned across her retrieving the lamp. He carefully folded them until Carrie realized he was searching for evidence of her injuries.

"JT, don't do that. Give them to me this instant." The last word broke on a sob.

He placed fabric remnants in her lap.

"I think the best thing is an arm across my shoulders or neck and the other under my knees. Except be very careful with this knee. It already feels like my old landlady hacked it with her meat cleaver. "

JT gathered her into his embrace in one try just as Billy and the Sheriff came running in.

"Grant, where is the body?"

JT indicated with his chin, "Right over there. I'm taking Mrs. Wagner to the hotel, Sheriff. You'll have to come there if you want to question her." JT headed out of the livery briskly with Billy beside him.

"Wait a minute, boy, I have questions for you," the Sheriff called out.

"You can ask me at the hotel, Sheriff."

The Sheriff latched onto Billy, "No, I think we'll talk now since you're the one who killed this fellow."

JT carried her easily.

Carrie snuggled against his chest.

"Put your arm around my neck. It'll help me not drop you in the street."

She slowly placed her right arm around his neck doing her best to hang on with her elbow.

He pressed his lips to her forehead. "It's a good thing he's dead."

Half sobbing, she wrapped her other arm around JT's neck, "I was so scared. I had no idea something as vile as that could happen. You were right. I'm sorry, JT. I'm sorry I didn't listen."

Without a word, he continued striding toward the hotel. Carrie laid her ear against his chest. She could hear every heartbeat and had never felt so safe before. She never wanted to let go of him.

"You are never leaving my side again, got it?"

It was more of a command than a question. "Believe me, and I've learned my lesson. I don't ever want to leave your protection again. I was foolish not to heed your advice."

He backed his way into the hotel lobby, throwing the door open. "Get the doctor over here quick." He barked to the clerk.

The clerk ran toward him, "Yes, sir, here's her room key."

JT paused while Carrie took the key in her good hand. She unlocked the door to the room, where JT gingerly placed her on the bed. After lighting the lamp, he plumped the pillow under her head. "Let's talk about those underthings before the doctor gets here."

Carrie's cheeks flamed as she slid the rags between her back and the bed. "I can't talk to you about this."

"Carrie, I have to know."

"JT, this is personal, and I'm in pain. Please allow me to deal with this crisis before dealing with yours."

"I'm worried sick about what he did to you." He leaned close to view her swelling face.

She caressed his cheek with her good hand. "I told you already."

"You didn't tell me about anything involving your underthings. Did he--?"

The doctor appeared at the threshold, "Young man, you can take yourself out of here. I can tell you're only upsetting my patient."

"You don't understand."

"I already know you're not her husband. Do you want her patched up and on the road to recovery?"

"Well, yes

"Then, get out."

JT reluctantly left the room.

"The clerk told me your name is Mrs. Wagner. My name is Dr. Champlain. Let's see what we can do to make you more comfortable."

"Thank you, doctor."

It turned out that Carrie received a gash across the knee and shin caused by a rowel which took ten stitches. Her jaw would be swollen and bruised for a week or more, but thank God it's not broken. The white of her left eye had filled with blood. The beginnings of an impressive black eye and a swelling goose egg forewarned her of the worst yet to come. Dr. Champlain agreed that her wrist was broken. It sounded like she would be in bed for a while.

Carrie lay in bed, her body battered and bruised. Every movement sent waves of pain throughout her body, making her wince and groan. The room was dimly lit, with only a single candle casting flickering shadows on the walls. She could hear the sounds of the bustling town outside, but it felt far away, like it was happening in another world.

The doctor had done his best to patch her up, but there was only so much he could do. Her knee and shin had been cut deep, and it would be a while before she could put any weight on that leg. Her jaw was swollen and painful, making it difficult to talk or eat. And her broken wrist was hurting terribly.

Then nervously, Carrie pulled the abused underthings from under her back to show the doctor.

"Doctor, that man ripped my underthings half off me. He was lying on me, unbuttoning his pants. I was so scared I set my mind somewhere else, but I don't think he raped me. That's when Billy killed him." She paused, searching for words that wouldn't embarrass them both. "I sent Billy for help."

"You don't know if you've been injured there?"

"No, not certain, but I wanted you to check these for proof." She held out her rolled-up, ruined underthings.

"I'll check to be sure. You can throw those away, or I can dispose of it for you. Let's check to be sure, my dear. Now, do a favor for me and send yourself right back to your place of solace until I ask you to return. Ready?" Carrie closed her eyes. She covered her left ear with one remaining hand and turned her other ear against the pillow. "I'm ready."

These men were animals. The man who had attacked her in the livery fell directly into that category. She remembered how JT warned her how foolish it was for a woman to venture west of the Mississippi River without family or a chaperone. The very same man she assured of her safety when she struck out on her search for Billy. Maybe he does have my best interests at heart. *I should've listened.*

She felt the doctor gently nudge her shoulder. She opened her eyes and uncovered her ears. 'What did you find?"

He pulled up a chair beside the bed, her torn drawers in hand. The doctor assured her there was nothing to worry about and that he would destroy the remnants for her.

"Are you sure, doctor?"

"Of course; who's the doctor here, you or me?"

Relieved, Carrie laid back in bed. The doctor bandaged her knee and helped her out of her dress and into a nightgown. Then he gave her laudanum.

"There now. That's going to put you to sleep. Don't you worry about a thing? I'll check on you tomorrow." He pushed back his chair to leave. The screech jarred her.

"Doctor, that impatient young man you threw out of here earlier, could you please relieve his mind for me? He will not stop until he knows I'm fine."

"Oh, was I mistaken? Is he your husband?"

"No, but we might be in love if he wasn't as stubborn as a mule." Her heavy eyelids slid closed.

"He certainly displays a husband's concern for you." He patted her shoulder.

She felt a blanket cover her as she drifted off to sleep.

Judges 10:12 *Also the Sidonians and Amalekites and Maonites oppressed you; and you cried out to Me, and I delivered you from their hands.*

Chapter Fifteen

May 16, 1860, The Morning After

Consciousness came to Carrie in throbbing waves of pain. Her leg felt like it had been through a meat grinder, and her jaw telegraphed an out-of-order message. She raised a hand to her jaw, awakening Billy, whose head was on the bed beside her.

"Carrie, you awake?" asked Billy anxiously.

"Yes," she croaked.

Billy heaved a sigh of relief before saying, "I have to get JT, I'll be right back." He bolted for the door.

"Wait," Carrie implored him. "I need water."

Billy gripped the handle of the jug which was resting atop the dresser with a firm hand and poured water into the glass, the melody of the soothing flow of liquid moving from jug to glass filling the silent room. He then brought the glass over to her and placed it on the left side, where she lay propped up, weak, and tired from the events of the previous day.

The room was softly lit, and the only sound that echoed was the gentle swaying of the curtains as the breeze gently caressed them. Then, holding the glass to her lips, he shared, "Ifn I don't get JT, he's gonna wail tar outta me. The doc wouldn't let him watch over you last night."

Her fingers trembled slightly as he placed the glass of water within her grasp, the exertion of even this simple movement draining her of all her strength.

She pulled away from the lip of the glass and gently lowered herself back into the bed. The cool water brought a soothing balm to her parched throat.

"An the doc wants to know when yore awake. JT threatened me within an inch of my life if I didn't fetch him immediately." Continued Billy.

"For heaven's sake, go already, please go. Oh, and Billy, I need coffee bad. Thanks." Rasped Carrie through her raspy throat.

"Will do, Carrie."

True to his word, Billy called out as he ran down the stairs, "JT, get the doctor."

JT must have been in the lobby, "I'll send for him."

Billy returned in a few minutes with a mug of steaming hot coffee gripped carefully in his hand.

JT crashed through the threshold, then stopped when he locked eyes with Carrie. He pulled up the only chair in the room and sat on her left side. His eyes scanned her face. "Good morning, sunshine, you look mule kicked."

Thanks for the compliment." She grinned, and immediately her jaw let her know grinning was prohibited. "Ow." Her hand went to her face again.

"Sorry, I didn't mean to hurt you." He reached out to soothe her, but she flinched.

Avoiding JT's questions, she asked, "What did the doctor say about my injuries?"

"To me? As little as possible. First, he asked if we were married or engaged. I replied no to both. Then he seemed to button up on me. He did say your jaw wasn't broken, but your wrist is, and it has to stay immobile for six weeks. I don't know how you'd move that wrist if you wanted to. He's almost got you bandaged from elbow to fingertips. He'll be back again this morning to check your face and knee. That's about it."

"Would you mind helping me with that cup of coffee?" JT obliged. "Did he say when he would be here?" Carrie squirmed; she hadn't relieved herself since the assault. Things were becoming critical. She would need the doctor's help.

"I sent someone to fetch him." He studied her face. "Carrie, what's the matter?"

She'd fill this room with liquid before allowing JT to assist her. "Where's Billy?" He can help me.

JT had left the door slightly open for propriety's sake. The doctor rapped with his knuckles twice and entered the room. He took one look at Carrie and threw JT out of the room again. Then, placing his bag at the end of her bed, he asked, "What's wrong?"

"Please, I haven't relieved myself since the assault." She could feel the heat crawling up her cheeks."

A man of action, the doctor, reached under the bed to retrieve the chamber pot. He carefully moved her and tried to position her over the receptacle, but her knee couldn't bend. She braced herself against the bed using her good leg and embarrassingly relieved herself.

Her cheeks burned again. To distract them, she asked, "Doctor, JT said my wrist has to be immobile for six weeks, and now I know that knee won't bend. How am I going to perform personal functions?"

"Well, my dear, you're going to need a nurse. I'll find one for you." Assured the doctor.

Still relieving herself, she asked, "Did JT explain that I'm the bait to lure a murderer out of hiding?"

"No, so that's what's between the two of you. I couldn't figure it out. So, the man that assaulted you yesterday wasn't the murderer? He inquired.

"No." replied Carrie.

You can't defend yourself if the murderer shows up, Is your male friend a lawman?"

"A Pinkerton agent." Carrie sighed in relief. "The murderer is a woman. I'm finished with the chamber pot." He gingerly helped her back to bed. "I wondered if you had advice for what I could do to defend myself, considering my injuries." She pushed her nightgown down to cover her legs using her left hand.

"Do you have a pistol?"

"Yes, it's in the side table."

The doctor retrieved it and placed it under the bed covers where her left hand rests. "Are you, by chance, left-handed?"

"Unfortunately, no, but I get the message. What good is it if I can't reach it?"

"Maybe Mr. Grant can get a knife for you. Strap it to your left thigh so you can reach it with your left hand. Make sure you handle the grip of that pistol until it feels like an extension of your arm." He reached to untie the ribbons at the neck of her nightgown. "We have to take a look at that bite."

"Are you sure the door is locked?"

"Yes, of course." He pulled the gown down off her shoulders, exposing her breasts.

"A human bite is a nasty thing. I went to the undertakers to look at that 'man's' teeth. I don't think he's cleaned his teeth since the day he was born. Disgusting." He went to get the lamp and held it up while he rechecked the breast. "I'm going to tell you the truth, girl. He broke skin in several places. We have to keep it clean and bandaged. And hope for the best."

The doctor finished with her other wounds, then said he was off to find a nurse. He said he would speak to Mr. Grant about her safety in such a weakened condition. After all, he is the reason why she is here.

JT had her where he wanted her again, directly under his control. She must work on her attitude; without JT, she wouldn't feel a modicum of safety. She must apologize for how she spoke to him at the hotel restaurant yesterday. He was right to worry. If she had listened to him, she wouldn't be an invalid for the next six weeks.

A knock at the door startled her, and she pulled the blanket up to her neck, "Who is it?"

Billy sang out, "It's me and the chaperone."

"Come in," Carrie's lips curved into a smile. How long is Billy going to torture JT with that nickname?

"Not the right side, Billy. Go around," JT warned as Billy headed toward the bed in a headlong collision. "And stop running in here. We are going to be slow and safe. Got it?"

Dashing around to the other side, Billy exclaimed, "I can't kiss this side of her face."

Turning her head toward him, she pointed at her forehead. He promptly kissed it. "Sis, we axed for some grub for ya. Be up in fifteen minutes, dey said."

"Thank you, boys, for everything. I owe both of you an apology. Billy, I'm sorry I didn't listen when you wanted to explain everything. Please forgive me. It will never happen again. I promise. Did you find your sister?" she asked.

Billy lowered his eyes and shifted his weight from one foot to the other, "I wish I could lie, but I won't. I knowd where the she-devil is, but she cain't say the same about me. I'm keepin' a tail on her."

JT said, "Maybe it's time for the truth about your real sister."

"Yes, Billy, tell us so we can help you." Billy twisted his fingers together. "JT, we're going to need another chair. Do you think you can scrounge one up?"

JT nodded and went in search.

Billy pulled up the one chair in the room and seated himself on Carrie's left side. He sighed and ran his fingers through his hair. "I owe ya an apology, too. I never shoulda mixed you in dis. Ya too good to be tangled up in her vileness."

Carrie took his hand into hers, "You're forgiven. I'm glad you involved me because I love you and I will do anything to protect you, understand that Billy?

Billy's eyes misted over as JT entered with the extra chair. He placed the chair next to Carrie's head on her right side. Then, noticing Billy's emotions, he asked, "Did I miss something?"

"Go on, Billy, tell us," Carrie said.

"My story is pretty shocking. I'll try not to knock your socks off. My sister and I have been on the move from town to town ever since I can 'member. She completed ten years of school, but I never even completed one. She taught me to read and count money so I could help her pull off scams."

"I knew it!" JT exclaimed.

Carrie turned a warning look in his direction, but her words were for the boy. "Go on, Billy."

Billy thought he'd plow through it, "My sister, I calls her the she-devil, is a looker and can be all pleasant like when it pleases her, but that ain't her true self. Men love her. Dey never see through her. She finds a mark she can sucker until she broke him. If she couldn't find a mark, she'd fancy woman herself. She'd make me follow the mark around when he wad't with her and make sure no one was makin' him any the wiser, and she also wants to knows how much money da mark spent when by hisself. Sometimes she'd talk her marks into committing crimes fer her. I had to case the banks or other buildings before da robberies so she would have the layout down. A lot of the marks are serving time now. Dey would spend a lot of time in her hotel room kanoodling. She'd lock me in the closet and threaten me if I made any noise. Sometimes fer days. Dat's why I cain't sleep without a lantern. And if I screwed up any of her plans or cost her money, she would beat me. I'd had enough and runned away." He paused, looking at Carrie and JT's reaction so far. Addressing Carrie, he added, "I cain't let ya talk to her and get permission to adopt me. She'd go off like a volcano and probably hurt you."

Carrie squeezed his hand in understanding.

JT said, "Billy, you understand that Carrie can't adopt you if you have living family members? And she can't take you with her because she'll be charged with kidnapping if she does."

"I git that legal horse pucky, but I ain't goin' back to the she-devil, and I will foller Carrie wherever she goes. Carrie loves me, and I love her. She's my family. That's how I feel, deal with it."

Carrie brought Billy's hand to her lips.

JT brushed his palm against his prickly jaw, "We have to stay here for the next six weeks. How are we supposed to keep your sister from locating you or Carrie?" Shaking his head, JT continued, "What's her name? I'll go speak to her?"

"No!" Billy bolted out of his chair. Now he had their uninterrupted attention. "I ain't tellin' 'cause of dat."

"Carrie?" JT waited until she turned toward him. "Either you or I could be charged with kidnapping by his sister. She has to be looking for him if she's come all this way to find him."

Carrie took a deep breath, "I'll take the chance. I don't want him anywhere near that woman. He deserves to be free. He can stay here with me during the day and stay with you at night."

"Well, we'll all be in here at night. The doctor scolded me for using you as bait and laid your safety at my feet." JT's eyes again fell upon Billy, "Boy, did you help rob Mr. Wagner's bank? You stowed away on the riverboat in Cincinnati. Close enough." Billy's gaze burned a hole through him. "I overheard you tell Carrie no banker's heart was as cold as her banker's. And you told her he wasn't good enough for her. How would you know?

Reclaiming his seat, Billy calmly explained, "Are you kiddin'? Dat story was in Ohio papers fer weeks. It's not every day a banker robs his bank. The paper said he deserted his wife of two weeks. Then I met Mrs. Wagner on board the riverboat. He didn't deserve her. Carrie has a heart as big as the moon. The banker's heart was specially ordered from the North Pole. Anyone could see dat. She gibbed me vittles and a cot the night we met."

Carrie looked up at JT, "Satisfied?"

"Yes, for now."

Another knock at the door. JT went to answer it. Breakfast had arrived. JT moved his chair beside Billy's and placed the bed tray on it. "Come lock the door behind me. I have to check and see if I've received any telegrams. Do you think you can feed her properly?"

"No, chaperone, I'm gonna ram da fork in her ear. Start frettin' now." Retorted Billy.

Smiling, JT added, "When I get back, I have things to talk to Carrie about, and you can disappear."

"Kissin' agin? Ya cain't be kissin' on her. Look at her mug."

Carrie laughed, then groaned from the pain, raising her left hand to her face.

JT slammed the door. Billy locked it behind him.

"Sis, dere's one of JT's questions I paid no mind to. I dinna want to fib to you, but I cain't put the truth on it and keep you safe both." He scooped a forkful of scrambled eggs.

"I prefer the truth. Am I going to be angry when I find out?" She savored the eggs and hummed her approval. *Why does Billy need to keep me away from his sister? Unless, of course, because of my physical condition at this point. Maybe I shouldn't meet her while handicapped. The way Billy talks, I'll need all my physical and mental faculties to deal with her.*

"Oh, hell yes, yore gonna be fightin' mad, but yore in no shape to go even one round with da she-devil." He shoved home fries into her mouth before she could reply. "I'm gonna be a ghost. She cain't find ghosts."

"I thought you were going to say that."

Billy scooped another forkful of food, and she put up her hand, "Wait, can I sip coffee first?"

Divesting himself of the fork, he raised the coffee cup to Carrie's lips.

"Thank you, that's so good. Better than what I made out on that Nebraska grassland."

"Carrie, I ain't funnin' ya. She'll kill ya."

As she gazed into Billy's eyes, the gravity of the situation weighed heavily upon her. His countenance, usually so carefree and full of mischief, was now etched with lines of worry and concern. She could tell that he was holding something back, something that threatened to tear their world apart.

An eerie feeling crept over her, like a cold hand clutching at her heart. She knew that there was much that he had yet to confess, secrets that lay hidden beneath the surface. And yet, despite the danger that lurked around every corner, he seemed more concerned with her well-being than his own, in fact he seemed to not care for himself entirely.

Her mind raced with thoughts and questions, each one more troubling than the last. How could she help him out of this situation, when she was handicapped, and he was just a twelve-year-old boy? The very thought of it seemed hopeless, like trying to fight a hurricane with a feather and because of her handicap, they were unable to flee St. Joseph at will, trapped like a fly in the spider's web.

Besides, JT still must catch the murderess. The murderess will probably kill her before Billy's sister has a chance. "I know you're serious, Billy. Try not to worry about me. JT will watch over me. "

Billy snapped, "Ya think I trust da chaperone? He's thinkin' with his pecker. He's gonna get you kilt. All he cares 'bout is kissin'."

"Billy, I'm ashamed of you. You've judged JT's character all wrong. He is a tad bossy, but I've realized I'm not full grown yet. There's much I could learn from JT."

He took a sip of coffee out of her cup.

"I still haven't had the chance to tell you the news we discovered since you've been gone. JT will do his best to protect me because I found a letter from Philipp in my Bible telling me he had a female accomplice who thinks I have the bank robbery money. And, you won't believe this, he went to the gallows to save her. She's the one who killed JT's Pinkerton friend in Cincinnati, not Philipp. He was never in love with me. He loved her. Philipp said she would be coming to kill me, but my plugged nickel of a husband wouldn't give her name. I shared the letter with JT. That's when he confessed to me that he's a Pinkerton agent."

Billy uttered, "The chaperone, a Pinkerton?" Then he completely shut down.

"Whatever is worrying you about your sister, you should speak to JT about it and he will help you with it."

Biilly said nothing.

"What's the matter? Tell me," Carrie implored. "What is it?"

<u>1 Samuel 12:24</u> *Only fear the* LORD, *and serve Him in truth with all your heart; for consider what great things He has done for you.*

May 17, 1860, JT Proposes

As soon as JT returned with a telegram, Billy bolted for the door leaving his rationale floating on the wind.

Unfortunately, neither of them caught his entire declaration.

"Who set his pants on fire?" JT asked while locking the door.

Still bewildered, Carrie said, "I told him about Philipp's letter and mentioned you were a Pinkerton. And that we were here to find him and to lure the murderer of your friend out in the open. He didn't like the idea of you putting me in danger. Not enthused about it myself."

"He should have stayed; we could have answered his questions."

"He froze and wouldn't speak to me." Carrie noticed the telegram. "What news do you bring?"

"Oh, Sheriff Huffman inquired about the bank robbery money. I replied that we haven't discovered it yet."

JT settled in the chair Billy vacated on Carrie's left side, "How are you feeling? Can I get you anything?"

"Everything hurts, but my knee is the main complaint today." Carrie remembered the doctor's suggestion, "I asked the doctor for recommendations on the best way to defend myself if the murderer showed up. He got my .45 out of the drawer and slipped it under my left hand. He also suggested you acquire a knife that I can strap to my left thigh."

"Good advice. If you use that .45, don't pull it out from the blanket. Shoot through the blanket. However, don't shoot through your leg."

"Very funny," her left hand covered her face because smiling hurts. "Please stop doing that."

"Sorry. I'll get the knife for you. Let's take advantage of the fact that you can't laugh and talk about something serious, at least serious to me." He removed his hat and placed it on Billy's vacant chair. Rubbing the back of his neck, he closed his eyes and took a cleansing breath.

"JT, I'm not a firing squad. What's going on? First, Billy is struck dumb, and now you. Did you receive bad news?" He finally looked up.

He took her one good hand into his, "No, no bad news yet. I'm having difficulty putting my thoughts together to ask you something without offending you." His thumb massaged her fingers.

In a lowered tone, Carrie encouraged him, "Tell me."

Clearing his throat, he tried several openings, "You remember when…? Um, I saw you off at the riverboat. Do you remember when I revealed my feelings about you to Mr. Russell to get assigned to the Big Sandy?

"Yes, I remember when you lied to me. The nerve, following me around because you suspected I murdered someone and lied to my face with those declarations of 'fondness.'" Carrie harumphed. "Betrayal is your middle name."

He flinched, shoved his hand through his hair, and studied the door as if it had insulted him, not her. "Maybe we should talk later." He stood and grabbed his hat. Thinking better of it, he turned," You realize I was doing my job, right? I didn't set out to betray anyone." He continued toward the door.

Thinking better of it, Carrie said, "Please wait, JT. I'm a fool." He stopped but didn't turn around. "That angry little girl inside me who wants her pound of flesh, I'm working on getting rid of her. The first step is realizing she's in there waving a fist." She sighed, "I'm sorry. Please tell me what's on your mind."

He marched back to her bedside. "I wanted to tell you the truth, but you may not believe the truth, and I feared your reaction." He worried his hat brim.

"The truth about what?"

Rushing his speech, he said, "When I first looked into your eyes on that train in Columbus, I knew you were different. Hank said someday I'd meet the one, the woman who would bring me to my knees. I never thought the prediction would come to pass. Besides, you might have been a murderer.

In Cincinnati, I realized that if you were guilty, I couldn't be the one to lock you up. That boat wasn't leaving without me because I had to protect you. I prayed you weren't guilty daily and wanted to take you somewhere safe. I'd defend every square inch of your perfect body. I dream of touching that beautiful creamy skin of yours. Then you discovered Philipp's letter, and by the grace of God, you're innocent. And the clincher, when Billy told me you were attacked and injured last evening, I lost my mind and blamed myself. Because I knew you shouldn't have gone alone. Look what he did to you. It's good that Billy killed him because I would have."

Carrie said, "You're getting all worked up. Just tell me, please."

"Not yet. I have to tell my story the way I practiced it all night."

"All right, I'm not going anywhere." Carrie noticed the softening of his eyes and his gentle touch on her hand.

JT picked up where he left off. "The doctor wouldn't tell me anything because I'm not your fiancée or husband. That needs to change. When I heard about your injuries, I knew you were essential to my life. Nothing else makes sense without you. Your kisses drive me mad, and I hope you love me enough to forget what your parents did, what Philipp did, or anyone else who wronged you. Find happiness with me. Unless you tell me there isn't a chance in hell, I'm informing you that you are my woman." He ended with a heavy sigh.

Carrie's hand trembled in his, her eyes searched his face for any sign of deception or ulterior motive. She knew JT well enough to understand that he was a man of his word, but the implications of what he had just said were staggering.

Just like him to tell me instead of asking for my feelings, her mind raced with a dizzying array of emotions. How could she go down this path again, after the bitter experience of her failed marriage to

Philipp, which she had believed had been ordained by God?

JT was a handsome, capable man, with a quick wit and a magnetic charm that had drawn her in from the moment they had first met. And what about those kisses, which had set her heart ablaze and left her breathless with desire?

But even as she wrestled with her conflicting feelings, she knew that she had no choice but to go to California. It was a journey that she had longed to make for years, a chance to start anew and leave the past behind.

As much as she was drawn to JT, she knew that a marriage to a Texan would never work and she had a family who was waiting for her in California. There was no way around that. Marriage to a Texan would never work.

"Carrie, for God's sake, say something," he said.

Now he's asking. Be as truthful as he. But she hasn't a clue where to begin. She felt heat rising her neck. No one sharing such a heartfelt declaration of love could be lying. "Is this a proposal of marriage?" First, she needed to ensure she didn't make a fool out of herself.

JT sat on the edge of the bed and kissed her. "Yes, Carrie, it's a proposal of marriage."

Great! Carrie wanted to say yes and end both of their miseries. But she must go to California, and he doesn't like children. "Thank you, JT, there's a chance, but I have something to share with you as well. When that man took my pistol, stomped on my knee, and climbed on top of me, my soul called you for help. Why didn't I listen when you warned me? That brute tried to kill me. I've never been so scared in my life. I prayed I'd see you again, be in your arms, and be protected from harm. And then there you were. Are you sure you still feel that way about me after that ape put his hands on me?" He nodded. She smiled, never mind the pain. "It's true. I have feelings for you, too."

JT carefully cupped the unharmed side of her face and kissed her gently. "Thank God."

"It's those darn blue eyes. I can't resist. I felt safe in your arms, and I haven't felt safe for a long time, but I think we should slow down a little," Carrie said.

"What do you mean?" JT said.

"I'm not ready to commit yet." She locked eyes with him. "There's much we still don't know about each other. You might discover something appalling about me or vice versa. And remember, I must be in California by November. My family is waiting for me." For the first time, she reached out and caressed his jaw. Scratching an itch she acquired the day they met.

"Yes, I'm aware." JT caressed her chestnut hair. "Let's both think about that and see if we can find a solution."

"Not think on it, JT. We need to discuss it. It's a pretty big clog in the works." His fingers caressed her delicate neck, then stopped when he found something. The tie at the top of her nightclothes had become untied, and now JT's fingers pried it open a little more.

Carrie's hand flew to stop him. "JT, what do you think you're doing?"

The doctor appeared at the doorway, "Young man, I'm the doctor."

JT turned on the doctor, "You didn't tell me everything about Carrie's condition last night."

"Calm down. I don't need Mrs. Wagner upset. She needs to concentrate on healing, not what you're blowing off steam about morning, noon, and night."

"Why didn't you tell him about this yet?" The doctor asked Carrie. Then he turned on JT. "And why, may I ask, are you upsetting my patient to ease your mind?"

Carrie worried her bottom lip and turned her face away.

JT said, "I forbid you from shaming her ever again. She is the most proper young lady I've ever met."

Carrie smiled at JT's quick defense.

The doctor readjusted his glasses, "All right, out of here while I examine my patient." He closed the door behind JT.

Carrie noticed JT's reluctance to leave and remembered that he wanted to be her fiancé or husband to learn more about her condition. And probably because he loved and cared for her as well. But the gaping divide between them warned her to keep her propriety in tack. She remained quiet.

"Now, let's look at that chest and see how you are." First, he helped her up into a sitting position. Then, pulling the nightgown open at the neck, he looked inside. "Are you in pain?"

"It's tender."

"Your breasts are bruised. The bruises look like finger marks. They're very dark today." He explained.

"That's what JT saw? The claw marks left by that animal."

"Now, now, that's the least of your worries. Bruises disappear in a week." The rest of the examination passed with JT's angry, shocked face floating in front of her.

"Mrs. Wagner, are you listening to me?"

Focusing on the doctor, she said, "Yes."

"I'm prescribing laudanum for the pain. Take only a teaspoon every six hours. It's addictive." He dosed her with a full teaspoon.

After her dose, she soon fell asleep.

***

When Carrie woke, darkness prevailed, but she didn't feel alone. JT lit a match. "Where's Billy?" She asked.

"He popped in while you were having your forty winks, stayed a while, and said he had to go tail his sister."

Carrie asked, "Did he happen to talk to you about the problem with his sister yet?"

"No, why?

"He's worrying himself sick that his criminal sister will find and harm me. He has something about his sister that he doesn't want to tell me so I told him you were a Pinkerton agent, and to speak to you about it. I thought his eyes would pop out of his head. He's got me worried.

"Do I have to break her out of prison or something like that?"

Carrie attempted a smile but failed, saying, "Billy wouldn't say. I guess the doctor gave him the same warning you received."

"Don't worry. Billy and I will set everything right."

"Oh, JT, I hope it's a situation where I can adopt Billy. He talks about his sister like she's unfit. Maybe a court will grant me custody."

"Stop worrying. I'll sort it all out."

Chapter Sixteen

May 20, 1860, The Unnoticed Clue

Several days later, the Sheriff sent over a deputy to relieve JT for a while. Before they left town, JT needed to turn in his pony rider equipment. Hoping for an uneventful break, he set out for the Pony Express office. When he arrived, Mr. Russell, himself checked each item off on a checklist. The final item: The Bible. "Hold on, wait a minute. That's not one of my Bibles." Russell held the offending Bible toward JT.

"How can you tell? What's wrong with it?"

"It's in German. Look at the cover."

JT turned it right side up and read, 'Heilige Bibel.' "Oh, that's Carrie's Bible. I must have mixed them up. I'll go exchange it and be right back." On his walk back to the hotel, JT fanned through the Bible to see if any more letters with clues would fall out. You never know. After scanning back to front, he stared at the handwritten inscription inside the front cover. It read, "Verein zum Schutze Deutscher Einwanderer, Texas, #42 which he knew meant Association for the

Protection of German Immigrants, Texas #42." That's his ranch. Well, his, his brothers, and Aunt Tildy's. What's that plot number doing in Carrie's Bible? The puzzle pieces snapped together, and he ran the rest of the way. Minutes later, he knocked on Carrie's hotel door.

Carrie called out, "Come in."

JT entered, a little breathless. "I have something to show you, Carrie," he announced. He pulled a chair up to the side of the bed and planted himself, "This is your Bible. I just tried turning it into Russell. He objects to German Bibles."

Carrie laughed, "How did we get them mixed up?"

"I don't know, but I saw something interesting in here as I walked back to the hotel.

"What is it?"

He opened the cover to show her, "Do you know what this says?"

She stretched to get a good look. "No. I've never seen it before, but even if I had, it wouldn't have meant anything to me. I don't read German."

"I don't either, but I know what this says. It refers to a land grant some lord or prince gave a batch of German citizens if they would move to Texas, settle on a lot, and send a percentage of profits back to him annually. This Bible indicates lot number #42. That's Aunt Tildy's land grant that she now shares with the Grant boys. It's our cattle ranch."

Stunned, Carrie needed to let that soak in for a minute, "Why is that information in my Bible?"

"Hold on to your hat, sweetheart, because I've got a theory. Remember when I told you my Aunt Tildy had a grey streak in her hair like yours, only hers originates from her crown?"

"Yes."

"And you said your mother put this Bible in your arms on the day she abandoned you."

"Yes, of course."

"Well, my hunch is that Aunt Tildy might be your mother."

Stunned at first, it didn't take long for the questions to come. Carrie's rising temper flavored her speech, "That's not enough to make her my mother." Carrie threw her arms out. "Did she ever mention a daughter to you? Why didn't she come back for me?" You've never mentioned my brother living there. What kind of cowardly approach is 'oh, by the way, here's where I'll be in Texas? Come and visit anytime." Her flaring nostrils and high chin punctuated her tirade.

"Well, I thought I was bringing good news and you couldn't wait to give your mother a piece of your mind." JT took her hand and caressed it with his thumb. "I didn't know Aunt Tildy had any children at all. But then she never talked about her life before we came to live with her." He wiped a tear from Carrie's cheek with the remaining thumb. "She guards a sadness deep inside her; sometimes, she looks on the verge of tears. As do you on occasion."

Could this troubled woman be her mother? Carrie ran her fingers over the German words written in the Bible. She's never opened it except when Philipp's letter came flying out. It has never been an item she cherished. She never understood why her mother would push Christianity on her with one hand while forcing her away with the other. God forgive her for asking the orphanage headmistress to keep it in her safe all those years. Is this her handwriting, and did she put it here as a clue for her? Wait, why would she do that? If she had abandoned her like she's believed most of her life, there would be no clue left behind. Could she find her mother at JT's ranch? She could have found her years ago, but why didn't her mother return for her if she wanted her after all? "How could this be true?"

"I've been handling legal paperwork for Aunt Tildy for years. I know her plot paperwork better than my birth record--this is it plain as day in your Bible." They looked at each other, letting the information sink in. "I think that's enough information to warrant checking her out."

Carrie whispered, "Do you think I've been wrong about her, and she's loved me all this time?"

"I think we need to find out, don't you?"

The road home had been with her all this time. So many years wasted because she misunderstood why her mother pushed it at her during their last seconds together. The Bible seemed essential to her mother, while her daughter certainly did not think the same. Carrie remembered her mother had been crying, more like sobbing. She kissed her several times and told her she loved her and always will. Why didn't those memories come to her sooner?

"You might be heir to Aunt Tildy's half of that ranch."

Removing her hand, Carrie said, "Stop talking about your ranch. I will never live there.

"I don't get it," JT stated bluntly.

"JT, my parents traded me away for some God-forsaken piece of Texas. I'm sorry, it might be your piece of Texas. I don't want one blade of grass on it."

A whole lot of silence.

"Carrie, aren't you curious that Aunt Tildy might be your mother? Given a chance, I would want to know why she did it."

This quest isn't about you, "You haven't mentioned Eduard, my little brother. Wasn't he there with Aunt Tildy? If he isn't, maybe she isn't my mother."

"No, Aunt Tildy never mentioned a son to us."

"She probably gave him away, too. He was sick when I last saw him. Oh God, maybe he's dead. My father probably worked him to death." Could it be her mother? Or could it be more heartbreak? Her mouth opened wide but in silence. She curled away from JT.

"Carrie, baby, please."

He tried to take her hand, but she pushed him away, then he left the room. JT returned with Billy in tow. She turned to see who it was and saw Little Ed, in Billy's hand, which he had been mending for her. Carrie stretched her arms out toward Billy and motioned for him to come closer.

Trying his nurse hat on, JT interrupted, "Carrie, your right hand is supposed to be in the sling and not moved."

Without removing her eyes from Little Ed, she tucked her right arm back into the sling.

Billy approached her with Little Ed in an extended hand.

She pulled both into bed with her left hand, rocking and crying. "Eduard, Oh my God." Over and over in between the sobs. "I'll never see you again."

Billy wrapped his free arm over Carrie's embrace of Little Ed and JT used a cold, wet cloth to wipe her tears away.

***

The next day during Billy's shift, JT brought breakfast for Carrie. Carrie asked Billy, "How did the conversation with JT go? Did he help you?"

"No, I didn't speak to him. I'm afraid to tell this story because you won't love me anymore and I might end up in prison."

"Don't be silly. I'll always love you and JT will help with the prison questions."

"I'll do my best to keep you out of prison," said JT. "My girl would be right upset if you go to prison."

Billy raised his eyes to hers, "All right, here goes— I met Philipp in Columbus afore he started courtin' ya.

Carrie's shoulders fell.

"My sister is a con woman and she steals and sells herself. She taught me how to help her. I tail people for her, check out building layouts and create distractions. Whatever she needed to be successful at her current con."

Her jaw fell open.

"When we gots to Columbus, she latched onto Philipp at a gambling hall. He won a bunch of money that night. You couldn't separate her from him with a sledgehammer. She'd found her mark."

"What's a mark? Carrie asked.

JT spoke up, "It's a term for the victim of a crime."

Carrie hand flew to cover her open mouth.

"Every night they were together at the gambling hall, his house or wherever he could spend more money on her.

"His house? He didn't have that house until we married."

"No, Carrie, he had it all along. He lied to you about the house."

Billy continued, "He fell more and more under her spell. But there came a day when his wealthy chums who did business in his bank objected to his gallivantin' around with a soiled woman. Dey informed him dey would move their money if he didna become respectable again."

"That's where ya came in, Carrie. Ya were his respectability. He knew no girl from any of the families in town would marry him, so you came to his mind. You had no family, no future, no hope. You wouldn't turn him down. That's when he entered the mercantile and asked you to have dinner with him. Three weeks later he popped the question and, of course, ya said yes."

Listening to this made Carrie's stomach turn. The story so far has revealed the depths of her stupidity. She remembered all the warnings Ruth had given her at that time. Why didn't she listen?

"Boy oh boy, when the she-devil found out Philipp was getting hitched, she went plumb loco. Philipp kept saying he loved her, but it's hard to believe when you're engaged to a looker like Carrie. Philipp told her it was only for his social standin' around town. That's when she snapped. Those loaded coyotes threatened to move their money, well she thought she oughta snatch the money before any of them got the chance to move it. She had me case the bank and tail you.

"Wait! Case the bank? Tail?"

"She needed to know the layout of the bank and Philipp's habits while at the bank and tailin' means I had to foller you around and gather facts on you, too."

"She wanted to know what ya looked like so I taked her across the street from the mercantile so she could see through the glass. It pissed her off that ya were more handsome than her and that Philipp would marry some washed out piece of calico, as she put it, instead of her. But before she could act on her plans, Philipp up and married you. She nagged him for two weeks. Philipp did not want to give up his bank. But, finally, he gave in. He left da bank at noon. My sister and I waited for him at da train station, and we left for Cincinnati. Dey were all caught up with each other. It made me want to puke. I couldn't stop thinking'about what Philipp had done to ya. He didna even leave a note for ya. While I was tailing'ya, Carrie, it dawned on me how different you were from my sister. Ya kept a clean house. Cooked dinner on time for Philipp every day. Even taked noon meal to him at the bank. And ya helped at the orphanage every day. I'd look into the windows and find you washin' kids while tellin' them nursery rhymes, cooking'a big batch of something for da kids to eat or tellin' a nighttime story and tucking everyone in for the night. Ya loved them. It showed. Ya made them happy, and dey made ya happy. Sometimes dey would tease or lie to ya, but you never got mad. Dat's when I fell for ya."

Carrie reached out to caress his cheek, "I love you, too."

"Go on, Billy, "JT nudged.

"Well let me see, oh, we gots ro Cincinnati and holed up in a hotel. Dey didn't feel safe leavin' the bank money in the room while they went out to eat. And puttin' the loot in the hotel safe was the same as givin' it back to the law. So, she made me stay in the room with the money until dey got back. I was sitting there thinkin' about the raw deal dey dealt ya and I'm pissed because dey probably will forgets to bring food for me. And I gots a bright idea. If anybody deserved that money, it was you, Carrie. You were his wife and a good woman left high and dry. I taked the money and went back to the train station to Columbus. While you were sleeping, I pulled all the stuffing out of Little Ed and stuffed him with the bank loot. I knowed Little Ed was important to you and you would take him with you wherever you went. I sewed him up and tucked him back in bed with you.

"Is the money still there?"

"Yes, JT said we couldn't turn it in yet because I'd be arrested, and it would break your heart. "

"Yes, it would, but we do need to turn it in, don't we?"

"Yes, of course, but we have to time it right. Go on Billy," JT said.

"When I gots back to the hotel in Cincinnati, dere was a hassle going on 'tween Philipp and my sister, I thought, but then I heard a shot and saw her come runnin' out of the room and toward the back stairs. I was still standin' in the hall when the law came and rescued Philipp from the good citizens of the hotel. He warn't armed, but they found the pistol on the floor of the hotel room. I asxed the guy standin' next to me what was going on and he told me that the handcuffed man had killed a Pinkerton. You coulda knocked me over with a dandelion. Philipp never struck me as a man who would murder, no backbone. It must have been her that did it before racing down the back stairs. I knew dey would send Philipp back to Columbus. Dere I was all alone, so I went back to Columbus to watch over ya.

"Your sister killed that Pinkerton man."

"Yes, but I didn't see it."

"Why didn't you tell your story to the Sheriff? Philipp needed evidence in his favor."

"'Cause my sister was still loose, and I hid the money in your Little Ed doll. Besides Philipp was a no-account snake. And I can't take care of ya if I'm jailed. Philipp didn't deserve to be saved after what he done to ya, and ya knowed it."

"I see your point." Carrie dabbed her tears away. "And I thought I was the victim in this story." She took Billy's hand. "I'm so sorry. You'll never have to live like that again."

401

Carrie glanced at JT for confirmation and found him watching her. "What's wrong JT?"

"Billy, tell her your sister's name?"

"Leticia Brown. I try not to say it out loud. It's like callin' on the devil."

"Thanks, Billy, now skedaddle so I can have some alone time with my girl. We have to work out our next steps."

That name sounded familiar to Carrie. Where had she heard it before? Leticia Brown? "Isn't that the name on the...."

JT pushed his fingers against her lips.

Billy closed the hotel room door and JT locked it behind him. "Yes, that's the name on the envelope Captain Pinkerton sent to me."

Confused Carrie asked, "Does Leticia know Captain Pinkerton?"

"No, I think Leticia knew Hank when they were both young in Philadelphia. Billy said they originally lived in Philadelphia. And Hank mentioned that his hometown was Philadelphia, but Hank was in Chicago before his twentieth birthday training to become a Pinkerton agent. I believe they were lovers."

"How do you know? Did you read the letter?"

"No, I don't read private letters without permission unless it's written to or from a suspect. I'm putting the pieces together. Something happened between them, and they separated. But if there was bad blood, why did Hank ask me to deliver this letter to her in person?

Carrie added a puzzle piece of her own, "Oh, that's obvious to me, she broke it off, not him."

JT's eyebrow shot up. "Then why would she choose crime and prostitution over a relationship with Hank?"

"Think like a woman! Men make decisions and women must live with the results. No matter what. He prioritized something above her and wounded her pride. There's a wound of some kind in there somewhere. Maybe it was becoming a Pinkerton."

"Would that make her mad enough some odd years later to shoot him dead in his tracks? Seems frivolous to me."

"You need to learn more about women. The question is 'what did Hank do or say to a young girl who harbored deep feelings for him that made her reject him?' And how many years has she chewed on the pain?"

JT scratched his head, "She spurns him, but blames him for the pain."

Carrie nodded, "She's probably even angrier now that she's killed him."

"I hope I never make you that angry. If I ever do, please tell me before you shoot me. I'd like a chance to redeem myself."

Carrie smiled and held her hand out for him to take.

JT took her hand and followed her arm to her neck. He kissed her behind the ear and worked his way across her jaw and plunged into a passionate kiss on her waiting lips. How does he do that? Her whole mind and body focused on JT as she slowly curled her good arm around the back of his neck. Her fingers played in his hair. He sat on the bed where her arm had vacated. She felt his lips slide across hers turning everything he touched into desire. She moaned as she ran her tongue along his lip. He ripped his lips away breathing heavily.

"I can't wait until you're well enough to get out of this bed because you need to be strong for what I have in mind." He kissed her forehead and moved back to the chair. "You're amazing."

"Do I dare fall in love with you? I'm so frightened."

"Don't be. I'm not your parents or Philipp. I won't betray you. I'm crazy about you. "

"Would you give up Texas for me?"

JT paused, "We can worry about that later, can't we?"

"I can't give up California for you."

"Why? You haven't seen the ranch yet."

"Speaking of the ranch, there's something I haven't admitted to you yet for fear of your reaction. Ruth is a darky. She can't move to Texas it being a slave state. And a war is coming soon enough. We are more like sisters than friends. That's why I think we don't have the makings of a solid relationship."

"Damn," the curse flew from JT's lips.

"And I've been afraid to ask, but I'm asking now. Do you have slaves working on your ranch?"

"Of course not, I don't believe in owning another human being."

"Do your brothers feel the same way?"

"Of course, they do."

"You've been gone for ten years. You have no idea what your brothers think."

"I'm telling you they would never buy slaves to work our land. They've been raised better than that."

"I was positive marrying Philipp Wagner was the best thing I ever did. Betrayal gives no warning."

"I'm convinced there are no slaves. If I'm right and you like the ranch, would you consider staying?"

"You know I can't. I wish I could, but it will never work out. I'm inviting you to come with Billy and me to California."

"You want a Texican to give up his ranch and follow his lady love to California? If I did that, I don't deserve to be a Texican. JT stormed out of the room.

Carrie didn't need another heartbreak. She promised Ruth and the children she'd stick to their schedule and arrive on time in California by

November. Taking an unintentional trip to Texas would wreck her deadline. If she arrives at JT's ranch and Aunt Tildy is not her mother, or her mother didn't want anything to do with her. Not only has she given up her job with the Pony Express, but she'll be late getting to California by several months.

***

Days later, JT showed up with the stiletto knife she had requested. He pulled a chair up to her left side. Without exchanging greetings, he asked "Could you bare your thigh for me please? I have the stiletto to strap to your leg."

She pulled her gown up to her mid-thigh.

He moved to place the knife but stopped midair. His eyes devoured the exposed skin. He took possession of her knee pulling it closer to him then licked, bit, and kissed his way toward her hip.

Sporadically, Carrie asked him to stop. Her bold, desperate lover placed his palm over her mound none too gently. A desirous fire leapt to life low in her belly and quickly consumed her. Her brain screamed her need to be satisfied, but she didn't know what to ask for. This is so wrong. It's never going to work.

"Kiss me, please kiss me."

Carefully avoiding her slinged arm, JT hungrily took possession of her mouth. His lips burned their way to her soul exposing how much she needed him. She placed her palm on his chest, caressing the curly black chest hair she knew existed under his shirt. Leaving her lips, he stripped his shirt away.

JT's husky words surprised her, "I remember that day in the cabin well. I wanted you to touch me then and I need you to touch me now." He placed her left palm on his chest and kissed her again.

Somehow caressing his chest gave her a sense of security, a shared connection, magic meant only for the two of them.

JT tugged a small portion of her nightgown away exposing her breast. He froze staring.

She pulled her nightgown aright and tied the bow. Placing her palm on his cheek, she said, "Listen, that horrible bruise doesn't matter. Needs a little more time to heal that's all." She slowly turned his chin in her direction, "I love you."

He dropped his head to her shoulder, smiling, "Could you repeat that please?"

"I'm crazy about you. That means one of us is headed toward total devastation of the heart. I hope you're happy."

"I am. Thank God, because I had to make you mine."

"Maybe we can ask Billy for his advice?"

JT slid off the edge of her bed to the floor, laughing like a happy drunk even though he never drinks.

***

The following day, news of a bank robbery at a St. Joseph bank broke. The news of spread like wildfire, and Billy couldn't help but connect the dots. It was evident to him that his sister had coerced her sugar daddy into participating in the heist, and now they were both on the run. It was a wise move on Leticia's part, especially since the money from the Columbus bank robbery was en route to its rightful owner. Perhaps she had finally disappeared for good.

However, the relief Billy felt was short-lived. The very next day, they received word of a gruesome discovery the doctor who had been treating Carrie was found dead, his throat brutally slit.

***

Carrie rose early the following day after a long night of twisting and turning. Missing her California deadline can't be helped. She'll have to think of a way to make up the time.

She knew if her mother thought she was trash, she'd have to say it to her face. That rotting pit of betrayal destroying her soul one chomp at a time over the years demands a reckoning. It's time for the truth, ugly reality, or a healed heart.

She spent a restless night, plagued with worry and anticipation, as she pondered the unknowns that awaited her arrival in the state of Texas. In the early hours of the morning, she rose from her slumber and dutifully tended to her appearance, carefully combing her locks, and putting on a modest wrapper to shield her form from the early morning chill.

Her knee had healed to the point that the doc said she should be up and exercising it. Desperate for a cup of coffee, she made her way to the kitchen, her footsteps echoing through the quiet halls of the hotel. The hotel workers would be the only ones awake at this time. There, the stimulating aroma of freshly made coffee beckoned her closer to the source.

As she opened the kitchen door, JT sat at a beaten-up table, chewing on a biscuit, and sipping his cup of coffee.

"Good morning, JT."

Looking up at her, he smiled, "Good morning. What have we here?"

Carrie's left hand held her wrapper closed at the neck, "Would you please bring me a cup of coffee when you're finished dining?" She felt heat rising up her neck to claim her cheeks.

The cook, who had avoided Carrie's notice, chose that moment to chime in, "The man's eating. Take your cup of coffee upstairs with you, brazen hussy, and take your shameful self out of my kitchen."

As the cook's sharp rebuke rang out, Carrie's cheeks flushed with shame. She held a newly poured mug of coffee out toward Carrie. Carrie took it and returned to her room as quickly as a cup of coffee would allow, with JT's laughter echoing off the walls. She didn't dare ask for cream. Black coffee will serve as her penitence.

Embarrassment pushed her through, becoming presentable for the day in record time, which meant her desperate cup of coffee had chilled.

It will therefore be one of those days. Growing up in an orphanage, she had learned to value cleanliness and neatness above all else. Unfortunately, in the outside world, these norms didn't always translate.

A quiet knock came at her door, and she rose to answer it. Peeking through the slightly ajar opening, she found JT holding a cup of coffee at her threshold.

"Please come in. I know you haven't finished laughing at me yet." He left the door open for propriety.

Smiling, he held out the cup of hot coffee with cream toward her. "Oh, JT, bless you." Taking the cup from him, she sipped the welcome tonic with a moan.

"You never fail to surprise me. Where did you think you were going? Your kitchen back home?" he asked., shaking his head in disbelief.

"Not one of my best decisions, I agree." Admitted Carrie, "However, my only defense is a case of cotton-headed thinking from lack of sleep."

"Well, you managed to look adorable. I don't understand how you do it." He sat in the only parlor chair in the room.

Carrie claimed a seat on her bed near the side table for her coffee cup. "Do you mind if we discuss Aunt Tildy again?"

"I would have said yes before the kitchen stunt, but your silliness has me in a good mood." He laughed again.

She smiled back at him, admitting glee at his changed demeanor. "I decided to go to Texas, after all, to find out if Aunt Tildy is my mother. I could never rest again if I didn't. Would you consider taking me to Texas?"

His eyes nailed her to the spot. "Let's hear it." His thumb worried his index finger.

"What?"

"There's something else you need to tell me. What is it?

"Well, I planned to ask Philipp about adopting children from the orphanage, but you know that didn't work out. Ruth and I decided to adopt two children before we left for California. Ohio law doesn't allow darkies to adopt white children; there were no darky children to adopt then. So, I adopted them."

He stood before her, looking as if he had been hit with the full force of a shotgun blast. The color drained from his face, leaving him pale and trembling with disbelief. His eyes narrowed, and his lips tightened into a thin line.

He couldn't hold his reaction in. The information hit him like a fierce gust of wind on a cold, winter's day. "Two adoptees? Are you crazy?" he exclaimed, his voice shaking with anger and frustration.

Carrie slid down to the foot of the bed toward him, "I had to stay in Columbus because of the hanging and to sell Philipp's properties, but Ruth and the children had to leave earlier because they are going to California by wagon train. You know the rest. I promised to meet them the first week of November."

JT's anger forced him out of his chair. She stood as well indicating she harbors no plans to capitulate.

Waving a stern index finger in her direction, he spoke in a tone of deep frustration. "This is not funny, Carrie. Why didn't you tell me this sooner? You deliberately waited until I invested my heart in this relationship. I need you with me at home on the ranch as I've dreamed."

I'm so sorry, JT," she murmured, her voice trembling slightly, "It won't work. I wish I could, but it will never work out. So, I invite you to come with Billy and me to California."

"You have no feelings for me at all?" He stepped into her personal space, asking with soft blue eyes.

Her anger rendered her speechless.

***

Carrie couldn't calm herself down enough in two days to be able to discuss anything. Billy came and sat with her most of the time. She hugged and kissed him but couldn't speak.

On the third day, she took Billy's hand and crossed the hall to confront JT. She knocked on the door.

JT pulled the door open, standing back to allow them to enter.

"She ain't speakin' yet, JT." Sighed Billy.

Carrie claimed a chair. She attempted to speak several times, but the words were too angry.

JT broke the ice, "Carrie, all this is about those California kids. I don't believe they exist. Women have been pulling stuff like that on men since creation. And you never talked about them before. I'm on the fence about Ruth. She's a mighty convenient friend to have to keep you from staying in Texas. On the other hand, maybe you just want what you want."

She bit her tongue and kept her fists clenched. Her eyebrows nearly shot off her face. Carrie stood to leave.

On the other hand, Billy had no such infliction, "Ya brayin' jackass, dere ain't a bone in her body dat would trick another person. Her kids are as real as me. In Columbus, I lurked outside the courtroom when she adopted 'em. You coulda axed me, Ida told ya. Two little gals, cute as puppies, they were. You shoulda seen how happy Carrie and Ruth were shoppin' for their Christmas presents."

Carrie kissed Billy's forehead and squeezed him tight, "I'm leaving now." Then, she headed toward the door."

JT quickly placed himself between Carrie and the door. JT's sudden movement caught Carrie off guard, and she stopped in her tracks, unsure of what to do next. He had effectively blocked her exit.

"Wait, Carrie," he said, his voice filled with desperation. "I'm sorry. I wanted you to stay in Texas so badly that I talked myself into believing they were leverage against me. Please forgive me."

Carrie felt a glimmer of hope spark inside her, but she wasn't sure if she could trust JT's words. She looked at him sceptically, wondering if he was just saying what he thought she wanted to hear.

Billy said, "Ya know that offer about adoptin' me. I have a few things to say 'bout dat. I stick with Carrie. Suppose she adopts me, Great. Whether or not she marries you is a long shot. You can adopt me ifn the two of you get hitched, and Carrie approves."

Carrie said, "Make plans for going to Texas. I can't delay California any further." She stepped around JT and pulled the door open. She paused and told JT, "Never say you love me again."

JT moved out of the way, and she left.

Being in love with JT was like facing a firing squad whose minds changed every other minute. When she's sane, the probability of marrying JT looms over her like dead, bare tree limbs waiting to fall and crush her. But all obstacles fade when he turns her body into a desirous ball of need. Oh, dear Lord, he makes her feel like lava consuming acreage. She would accuse him of knowing nothing about her, but if she knew JT, why would his behavior shock her so often? Why didn't JT talk to her about wanting to adopt Billy before announcing it to him? It felt like an arrow through the heart. Is this love or hell?"

<u>John 14:17</u> *The Spirit of truth, which the world cannot receive because it neither sees Him nor knows Him; but you know Him, for He dwells with you and will be in you.*

Chapter Seventeen

May 20, 1860, Will I Go To Prison?

JT floated from Carrie's room to his own across the hall. She loved him. Nothing else mattered. She loved him. Thank God almighty. He pushed the door to his room open to find Billy propped up on his bed. He instantly remembered Carrie wanted the two of them to discuss something about his sister.

Hey, Billy, Carrie said that are a few things about your sister we need to talk about. I'd be glad to help you out. What's bothering you?

"Carrie tolded me ya was a Pinkerton. Ifn I spill my miseries with ya, I'll end up in prison poundin' boulders as part of some stinkin' chain gang. That's da truth of it."

"Are you saying you've participated in some criminal enterprises?"

"I don't know 'bout no enterprises, but I knowd things the law wants to know that would put dem on the scent of a major polecat. But Iif telled ya, I end up in a cage tallyin' the days for the rest of my life.

"You haven't shared this information with Carrie, yet?"

"No, chaperone, I donna wanna break her heart."

"But the information may help protect Carrie?"

"Yes. It would protect all of us."

"You already know Carrie's my girl. We are planning to marry. I want her to be happy. She's had it pretty tough so far, and I'd like to change that. You going to jail is not part of the plan. I promise to do everything I can to help in your case with the law. Do you trust me?"

"Dat's not da same as gettin' me free?"

"No, it's not, but you were an accomplice in your sister's crimes, but you, at the same time, were a minor. I think, based on the circumstances of your childhood, the court would be lenient with you."

"Lean-yent?"

"The court would give you a break because you were forced to do the crimes when you were a child.

"Courts do dat?"

"Yes, but I can't guarantee it. It depends on what judge you get. But a decent judge would never sentence you to prison after your suffering."

"I guess I trust you, chaperone." Billy gulped. "My sister, Lettie, is the low-down skunk who murdered Hank Lipton and stole Carrie's man. She's the boogyman causing all the trouble for the bof of ya.

"But the bank robbery and the doctor turning up dead? She wouldn't set foot in town after that, would she?"

"She's bankin' on everyone thinkin' dat. She's coming back for the Columbus bank loot that she thinks Carrie has.

"When?" JT asked.

"Well, I ain't rightly axed her now, have I? We aren't exactly on speakin' terms—but I know her better than the next sucker."

"Never mind all that. We stay with Carrie no matter what—both of us. I'll get you a gun in case you need it. Lettie can't get through us to get to Carrie."0

May 20, 1860, Bushwhacked

As Carrie stirred from her drowsy stupor, the hair on the back of her neck stood up. It felt like someone was watching her. She sleepily turned, dismissing her worries when suddenly a creaky floorboard jolted her out of her laudanum-induced trance. Her eyes flew open and landed upon someone lingering in the shadows. It was a woman. She had blonde hair and attractive features which were highlighted by the blue calico wrapped around her. She smiled maliciously and strutted towards Carrie slowly.

Carrie's breath hitched as confusion and fear took over. She couldn't help but recoil, yet her mouth did not make a sound. Her mind raced with thoughts. She wasn't stupid. No one else was after her. Carrie knew this had to be the infamous accomplice that JT had been looking for --the one guilty of the horrible crime that had paralyzed her town and upended her life.

Carrie knew she must stay calm. It was only a matter of time before JT or Billy came into the room. Until then, she had to stall this woman. Her voice was tinged with curiosity, but her fear was betrayed by the stammer in her words as she asked, "Who are you?" her gaze fixated on the woman in front of her. Her heart was pounding in her chest as she realized she was on the verge of a potentially fatal encounter.

As beams of light streamed through the window and etched elongated arcs on the walls, the room glistened in the gentle warmth of the afternoon sun. Carrie realized it had to be close to 3 p.m., a fact which seemed almost insignificant in the context of the peril she was facing.

Late afternoon. Billy's shift, where is he?

Carrie's gaze was drawn to the hand of the blonde woman, and there, glinting under the light of the afternoon sun, was a small but loaded pistol.

Simmering wrath flared in the blonde woman's eyes, as she walked towards Carrie and grabbed her by the chin, her nails digging deep into Carrie's cheeks. Those eyes could wither flowers.

"Who exactly am I?" She spat. "I am your day of reckoning, you wuss." I have never hated anyone as much as I hate you."

Her words were laced with venom.

The woman pushed Carrie's face away with a forceful hand causing it to slam against the headboard. "No, there is one exception," she continued, her voice dripping with disdain. "But I've taken care of him already."

Carrie's mind raced as she tried to piece together the meaning behind the woman's words. Was she confessing to Hank's murder? If Hank was the person, she was referring to then she must have killed him.

"My man married you," she sneered. "It didn't sit well with me. So, I'm here for retribution and my money."

'Goodness,' thought Carrie. This deranged woman spoke of Philipp as if he was a prize-winning bull she had won at the fair.

Carrie couldn't help but find the irony of the situation a tad bit amusing. This was the woman Phillip had accepted a death sentence for. He had loved her so much and she seemed to care about nothing. Perhaps, Phillip truly was merely another conquest.

"He never told me about you," Carrie said, her voice laced with empathy and regret. "If I had known, I never would have married him."

The woman did not say anything nor did her mask of cold and unyielding indifference betray much. "And I don't have the bank robbery money," Carrie added, hoping to diffuse the situation.

But even as the words left her lips, Carrie knew that she could not trust this woman. Whether she had the money or not, she knew this woman would try to harm her. She could see it for herself; the madness in her eyes, the seething anger that threatened to boil over at any moment.

Tensing her muscles, Carrie's fingers closed tightly around the grip of her Colt, which she had concealed under the blankets. She knew that she would need to defend herself if the situation turned violent.

The woman then began to make her way to Carrie. Her taffeta underthings rustled as she strolled to the left side of Carrie's bed. Satin with calico? This woman truly was the devil in costume. The woman pulled her skirts up and placed a foot on the bed displaying a dainty ankle and sensible shoes to match the dress.

"Allow me to tell you about your husband," the woman sneered. "He loved me, but he had some misguided idea of saving his bank by turning respectable."

Carrie's mind raced as she tried to make sense of the woman's words.

"A few Columbus businessmen threatened to move their accounts if he didn't stop carousing and sober up," the woman continued. "I convinced him that respectability is overrated but he refused to listen."

Carrie continued to keep an expression of horror planted firmly on her face. This was what the woman wanted, to hurt Carrie, to emphasize the depths of Phillip's betrayal, unaware that Carrie already knew all this.

"I got daily reports about you from Billy," the woman added, her voice dripping with malice. "What an exciting life you led. Volunteering at the orphanage, cleaning the house, cooking, laundry, and your reward? Church on Sunday."

Carrie suddenly looked up, her mask of horror betraying her bewilderment. How on earth does she know Billy?

"Where's my money, jezebel? The woman barked.

Carrie searched for her backbone, "I don't know anything about that bank robbery money." Whatever happens, don't cry in front of this floozy.

She searched for a topic to focus on if the blonde criminal stomped her. "Maybe Philipp took it," she said in an accusatory tone.

The villainess' eyes flashed with anger as she snarled, "Philipp had nothing to do with it. We were in a Cincinnati hotel room and at dinner together when it came up missing. Try again."

"Cincinnati! I wasn't in Cincinnati until after Philipp was hanged." Roared the woman.

"If you don't tell me, I'll kill Billy," she said, her voice low and dangerous. A shiver ran down Carrie's spine at the woman's whispered threat.

Carrie felt the ground shift beneath her feet. Not Billy. Not her child. Her mind raced as she tried to think of a way out of this, reeling from the shock. She had not expected this threat. Come what may her way she could not let anything harm Billy.

"Why would you do that?" Carrie asked, her voice shaking with fear.

The woman smiled maliciously and replied, "He's my brother, not yours," her eyes cold and unfeeling.

Carrie's mouth fell open, gaping at what the woman had just said. She couldn't believe what she was hearing. The murderess was Billy's sister? How could this be? And why wouldn't Billy tell her? She locked eyes with the woman, trying to see some glimmer of humanity within her. But all she saw was a monster. Her poor Billy, suffering at the hands of this awful woman all his life.

"You are as horrible as he says you are," Carrie spat, her own anger rising to the surface.

Carrie gasped as the woman's weight landed on her injured wrist, letting out a sharp cry of pain. The woman seemed to take pleasure in her suffering, snarling her threats.

"I'll put a bullet in his heart before I let him be with you," she spat, her words laced with venom.

Carrie's mind raced as she struggled to find a way out of this dangerous situation. The pain was blinding. Her broken wrist seemed like it had become mangled. She knew that she couldn't let Billy be harmed, no matter what it took.

But the woman wasn't finished with her yet. She leaned in close, her eyes blazing with a fierce intensity. "Do you know where the money is now?" she asked.

Carrie felt a surge of panic. She had no idea where the money could be if she did, she would have told the townspeople and avoided this entire confrontation.

"I don't know," said Carrie firmly .

Carrie's fingers tightened around the grip of the gun, her knuckles turning white with the effort. She gritted her teeth and drew a deep breath, trying to prepare herself for whatever might come next. Right now the woman had sat on her broken wrist, she might shoot her next just for the thrill. She had to stay on guard and whatever happened Carrie was determined not to let the woman see her pain. She tried to focus on how the house in California would look like once it was finished in hopes it might distract her.

Just then, Billy strolled in, carrying a tray of food from the kitchen, as the door burst open. He smiled warmly as his eyes landed on Carrie, but the smile rapidly faded when he caught sight of his sister standing over Carrie's head and the revolver she was holding.

"Get over here," she snarled, waving the pistol in his direction. "Put that tray down and lock the door."

Billy looked stunned, but he obeyed her command without question. He carefully set the tray on the table and turned the lock on the door, his hands shaking slightly as he did so.

Carrie watched in horror as the scene played out before her. What was Billy doing here? What would happen to him? She tried to rise up but her pain quickly sent her back. Her heart pounded in her chest, as fear and protectiveness gripped her. She tightened her grip on the gun and prepared to make her move when the time was right.

Billy walked to Carrie's side. He pushed his fists down to his side and said, "Get off her. I have the money. She doesn't know anything about it."

Carrie stared at him. Why did he say that? Was he trying to protect her?

The wicked woman sprang to her feet, her eyes blazing with fury. She twisted Billy's arm behind his back and snarled at him, "Planning on double-crossing me like your father? That is not going to happen. Where is it?"

Carrie dragged air into her neglected lungs in relief. Then, tried to take the pressure off Billy, "What do you mean, his father? Don't you both have the same father?"

The blonde beauty laughed, then asked, "What are you? Another detective?"

"Of course not." Carrie could tell by Billy's expression that Leticia had tightened her grip on his arm.

The wicked woman let out a harsh laugh, her eyes glinting with malice. "My mistake, jezebel," she sneered. "It matters not. Yes, he is my son. His father, a scoundrel of the worst kind, deserted us when I was a mere sixteen and pregnant with his child."

Billy looked stunned. How could Leticia be his mother? And who was his father?

Billy's eyes shone with a glint of desperation as he pleaded with his mother to divulge the truth about his father. "Tell me about my father," Billy pleaded, with curious eyes, of his mother and maybe to distract the villainess.

Leticia regarded her son with a mixture of contempt and amusement. She was always in control, and this moment was no exception. She took a step closer to him, her pistol still pointed in Carrie's direction, she sneered at Billy, "You want to know about him? All right, he deserted us to become a Pinkerton agent in Chicago. He didn't care what happened to us, but I showed him. I turned his son into a first-class thief. Don't you think he'd be proud?"

"But that wasn't the last time you saw him, was it?" Carrie asked.

Carrie had begun to piece the puzzle together and she wanted Billy to be here as she deciphered it. He needed to know who killed his father from his mother.

"I don't mind sharing that glorious event with you since you'll depart from us soon. Hank Lipton was his name. The fool burst into a hotel room in Cincinnati to arrest us and me. He didn't even recognize me and tried to slap handcuffs on Philipp. I had faded so much into the background for him that he didn't notice when I picked up a pistol and shot him in the head."

Billy twisted himself out of the murderess' grasp and screamed, "You killed my father! A Pinkerton agent, and you killed him."

Without so much as a flinch, through a swift motion, Leticia swung her pistol at Billy, striking him across the head. The force of the blow was so severe that he crumpled to the floor, a lifeless heap. Carrie let out a small scream as she saw Billy lying there motionless and unmoving as if all life had been drained from him. What if she had killed him?

"What did you do?" screamed Carrie.

Billy's mother did not look at her or reply. Instead, she looked down at her wounded son, her expression was cold and unfeeling and her eyes flashed with a dangerous glint as she spoke, "If you're lucky, you're dead." Her words dripped with venom and malice, showing nothing but a deep-seated hatred for her child.

She tucked the pistol under her arm and turned to face Carrie. Slowly, she pulled out the fixings to make a cigarette, holding the paper straight between two fingers, sprinkling the shredded weed on deftly, licked one edge of the paper, with both hands rolled it into a stick shape lit it, and left it hanging between her lips. Very precise and methodical. How many men had she rolled cigarettes for in the past?

Carrie's eyes misted over, but she batted the moisture away. She needed to know if Billy survived the blow but concentrated on the assailant first.

"I did my best to turn his son into a criminal. Every time I thought of Hank, I'd beat that boy. I wanted Hank to be proud of his criminal son. As it turns out, they never met. I taught him to steal, pick locks, pick pockets, tail people, and point out a potential mark. And he did it right or paid the consequences. Who knows, if the little turd survived, he'll have to pay in blood, I have plenty of ideas to punish him. I do enjoy whipping-"

Carrie listened in horror, feeling a cold sweat break out over her skin. She couldn't bear the thought of Billy suffering any longer under this monster's influence.

Bang.

The abuser's voice trailed off as the gunshot pierced the air, shattering the eerie silence that had enveloped the room. Her body slumped to the floor, her gun clattering out of her grasp. The acrid smell of gunpowder hung in the air like a sinister fog, choking and nauseating.

The breathtaking blonde lay on the floor bleeding from a hole in her heart. Carrie did not care. She had no regrets as she limped to Billy's side and found him breathing. She released a pent-up sigh.

She stared at the dead body of her nemesis. Neither remorse, fear, nor regret settled on her shoulders: just anger and a righteous calm. Smoke coiled in the air and lit up as it passed through the sunbeams. She smelled the gunpowder and realized the pistol still rested in her hand. JT wasn't the only one who came to the proper conclusion; she knew this woman suffered. There are betrayals around every corner, but Billy doesn't deserve what he had recieved from her.

Nevertheless, he had suffered years of torture because of his mother's vengeance against his father. Carrie had also suffered betrayals but never blamed the wrong party. Instead, she pitied this unfortunate woman for not knowing the difference.

JT kicked the door in and assessed the situation in the room with a glance.

Carrie said, "Please check Billy to see if he's all right. She bashed him in the head with a pistol."

JT gave the body on the floor a once-over and scooped Billy up.

"Oh, and she's Billy's mother not his sister," Carrie said.

"My God, Carrie, you shot her through the heart with your left hand. I'm impressed." He passed by the dresser, dipped a cloth into the water, squeezed it out on his way to the left side of Carrie, and sat down. He handed the rag to Carrie. Relief flooded her as she saw color returning to Billy's face. She wiped at the wound, "He'll need some stitches, but he'll be fine."

JT slapped his cheeks, calling his name. Billy came to life, looking around the room. Then, holding the cloth to his head, he slid off JT's lap, walked over to the dead woman, and began pounding on her chest. "Whore, liar, murderer. Burn in hell."

JT knelt next to him, pulling the boy into a hug. "Don't worry, son, she's already there." Then, he asked Carrie, "What happened?"

The sheriff burst through the crowd and said, "All right, everybody, disperse. There's legal work to be done here. Move on." Looking down at the deceased, the sheriff said, "She showed up, eh? Which one of you shot her?" He kicked away the pistol lying next to her hand.

"I did," Carrie said.

The sheriff nodded and said, "Is the boy all right?"

"He'll need stitches," JT said.

The sheriff turned and picked someone out of the crowd that hadn't dispersed, "Larry, could you take this boy over to Dr. Matthews for stitches and bring him right back? And don't question him."

The sheriff grabbed the broken door to push people away from the doorway. He stepped back into the room and pushed the door back into its frame the best he could. "Let's have it. What happened?" He grabbed a chair and sat. JT did as well.

Carrie started, "I woke all alone and found this woman looming over me with a gun in her hand."

JT asked, "Where's Billy?"

The sheriff interrupted. "You ask your questions later. Go on, Mrs. Wagner."

"First, she wanted to ensure I knew Philipp was her property, not mine. Then she asked about the bank robbery. money." "I lied to her. She didn't believe me and sat on my broken wrist."

The sheriff asked, "Do you, have it?"

JT checked her wrist for damage and found it wobbled, "We're going to need that doctor, Sheriff."

The sheriff sent another runner to fetch the doctor to the hotel.

"Sit down, Mr. Grant, and let me get this story for my report."

"That's when Billy came through the door. She ordered him to put the food on the floor and lock the door. Then she called him to her side. Billy told her I didn't have the money that he did. She accused Billy of being a double-crosser, just like his father.

Then I tried to divert her attention to me. I said I thought they had the same father. She laughed and agreed with me. She claimed Billy as her son and described Billy's father as a no-account double-crosser she had the honor of killing recently. When she was sixteen and pregnant, Hank left them in Philadelphia to become a Pinkerton."

JT interrupted again, "That's a lie."

The sheriff turned toward JT, "Do you want me to toss you from this room?"

Carrie said, "That's when Billy went berserk and pounded on his mother angrily for killing his father.." She completed her story without JT interrupting and answered all the sheriff's questions.

On his way out, the sheriff said, "I need to talk to the boy, too." Then, looking at JT, he asked, "Would you happen to know where the money is?"

"It's in the hotel's safe waiting for you. Please send it to Sheriff Huffman in Columbus, Ohio. He'll be excited to see it."

"Don't worry, Mr. Grant, I'll take care of it," the sheriff said as he glanced at Carrie, "Remind me not to cross you, young lady. Nice shot"

The undertaker showed up with a couple of men to remove the corpse from Carrie's room.

***

Dr. Matthews and Billy arrived in tandem. The doctor turned Billy's face away from his mother's body while they removed her.

Once the recently departed had been removed, the doctor propped up the door again.

Billy informed the room, "I got six stitches. Wanna see?"

The doctor said, "Yes, and he screamed like a little girl through every single one."

Carrie laughed, "I want to see them."

Billy knelt next to her bed on the left side so that she could inspect him for herself. He pushed his fingers through his scalp, searching for the correct spot. "Dere it is. Take a gander."

Dr. Matthews addressed Carrie "Billy tells me a ruffian sat on your broken wrist. May I have a look at it?

"Please do, doctor."

When the doctor lifted her wrist, Carrie saw it wiggle and felt a sharp pain shoot up her arm. She knew it had been rebroken before the doctor told her.

Layer after layer of bandage fell to the ground, exposing the splints. The doctor removed them. He held her wrist between thumb and forefinger, pressed a little, and then moved to another spot. "It's broken again," The doctor stated. Then he reset the bone, resplinted it, and gently reinserted it into the sling. "Now, let's look at your knee while I'm here.

After the examination, he said, "Those are professional suture marks. The scar isn't bad at all. You have a little yellow and brown coloring left from the sprain, and it's still slightly swollen. I think it's time for you to walk on that leg."

"It's about time." The three in the room celebrated at once.

"Tell me, Mrs. Wagner, who are these two gentlemen? I'll have to throw them out if they aren't family."

They must be family; she didn't want them thrown out, "You've met Billy. He's, my brother. JT Grant, here, is my fiancé." Surprised at how easily the lie sprang from her lips, she remembered Billy saying. Sometimes you do have to tell a little white lie to protect yourself or others. Those rules she's lived by all these years desperately need revision.

The doctor extended his right hand to JT, "Nice to meet you, Mr. Grant. I assume my bill goes to you." They shook hands.

JT puffed up his chest and said, "An honor, sir, for the woman who graciously said yes."

Carrie didn't dare roll her eyes with the doctor so close by.

Billy chirped, "JT, we can take her walking tomorrow."

"Now, let's look at that nasty bite you received. First, gentlemen, I'll ask you to step away from the bed for modesty's sake."

Carrie wondered how he knew about all of her injuries. JT tensed up stiff as a board next to her. He didn't know about the bite. Then he shooed Billy to the other side of the room and stood beside him.

The doctor sat on the bed beside her and loosened her nightgown tie around her neck. Carrie saw JT's face harden. Then she looked into his eyes and felt defiled. Will this be the breaking point, and he'll walk away? Perhaps she should have told him, but she hoped he would never have to know.

The doctor pulled the dressing away from the bite wound. "Oh, it's healing nicely. Thank goodness, no contamination." He retied her gown.

Then the doctor placed his palms on each of Carrie's hips. "Just as I thought, you haven't been eating enough. You must walk and eat three meals a day somewhere other than this room. And get some fresh air, young lady. It would help to have a little rosiness in those cheeks. Billy mentioned you have a nurse. I'll cancel her services for you."

"Tell Dara, Thank you for me." Said Carrie.

The door no sooner closed behind the doctor before Billy exploded, "JT, Leticia Brown, was my stinkin' ma, not my sister." he paused to spit on the floor, "And Hank Liipton was my Pa. I had me a real lawful Pa, and she kilt him." Tears tumbled down his face. "Carrie, why did ya snuff her? I wanted ta--I needed ta--for my Pa!" He threw himself at her left side, bawling and hugging her around the neck.

JT removed Billy's arm from her neck, seeing how it lay across the bite wound.

"Shhh, Billy, I'm so sorry." Tears were not far from falling from her eyes as she ran her fingers through Billy's hair, avoiding the injured area. "From what JT has told me about Hank, he was an enviable man. But your mother turned out to be a mad dog. So, I had to save you before she hurt you again. JT would be glad to tell you about your father whenever you want. And from now on, I will take care of you. You're safe now."

She didn't want to dwell on this a moment longer. Did she want to know why she shot and killed Billy's mother? Was it to save Billy from harm, or for murdering Hank Lipton, maybe to render Billy adoptable, or just because she'd had enough of lousy Leticia destroying her life?

Still angry, JT circled her bed and took her left hand into his. His thumb gently caressed the top of her hand. She hoped that meant they would never talk about this again.

No one is ever holding her down in the hay again. Now that she has been thinking about it, she needs to buy a backup weapon, and her Colt needs a holster. Dear Lord, I leave you to judge me when the time comes.

<u>Matthew 41-42</u> *The Son of Man will send out His angels, and they will gather out of His kingdom all things that offend, and those who practice lawlessness, and will cast them into the furnace of fire. There will be wailing and gnashing of teeth.*

Chapter Eighteen

May 21, 1860, Hank's Letter to Leticia

The next morning Carrie awoke to find JT camped in a chair beside her bed. He smiled at her as he offered her the cup of coffee in his hand.

"Oh, kind sir, I thank you from the bottom of my heart." Carrie gushed. "The aroma must have awakened me."

"Either that or you sensed my urgency to talk to you." Smiled JT.

Carrie glanced up into his worried blue eyes, "what's the matter?"

"I need to ask and maybe tell you something, depending."

"How mysterious. Go ahead and ask." She hoped he wasn't giving up on her and backing away now that the murderess had died.

"Did you not tell me about the injury on your...brr...I mean, your chest because you feared my reaction?" They locked eyes.

"Yes, I feared you'd leave me. And I hoped it would heal without any scars and no one would know the difference. In case one day, when I marry, the scar wouldn't be there. And I hope you know I tried my best to keep him off of me."

He leaned in close. Carrie thought he would steal a kiss but stopped only inches away. "I know it wasn't your fault. I'm not angry at you. I just need to kill the bastard again for myself." He placed his palm on her right cheek, caressing her. Then came the gentle kiss.

Relieved, Carrie returned the kiss. When their lips separated, he ran his thumb across her bottom lip.

"I have something to tell you, Carrie, and I'll have no arguments about it."

Concerned over his tone, she said, "I'm listening."

He took her hand in both of his and said, "We will consider ourselves officially engaged from this day forward. So don't keep secrets from me again."

Carrie squeezed his hand, "All right, but we still need to discuss the obstacles. Don't get mad when you hear my objections because you already didn't know about them."

"I'm talking about events that affect you from this day forward. I know we have compromises to make before we marry. And we will marry."

His insistence warmed her heart, but a looming betrayal from him would add to her numerous injuries and maybe the betrayal that would finish her off for good. She must protect her heart. "I'd feel better agreeing to your statement after we've agreed on our many obstacles."

"I agree, but we are still officially engaged. So, say 'yes,' JT."

"Yes, JT." She smiled at his beaming countenance. He looked so happy. She offered up her lips for another kiss and received her reward.

JT started to say something but got interrupted.

Billy came in brandishing a letter, with eyes for JT alone. "When did you get this, and why didn't you tell me about it."

Pulling away from their embrace, JT walked toward Billy. "You didn't open it, did you?"

"Not yet, but I sure wanted to. At least you kept yore nose outta my buzness by not openin' it either. How long have ya had it?"

"Since the morning, I was attacked by that gorilla." Carrie supplied.

"He showed it to ya and not me?" Billy said.

"Billy, I haven't had the chance to share it with you yet with all the commotion surrounding Carrie and Leticia", said JT. "Now, you interrupted something private here. Go to our hotel room, and I'll be right over. We can open it together."

Billy thought about it and said, "Don't take all day." He turned and left the room, closing the door after him.

"I wonder why he was going through my bag." JT mused.

"Why haven't you told him about the letter yet?

"Because I wanted to discuss some loose ends and ensure I have the whole Leticia Brown story straight before I write my report to Captain Pinkerton."

"Like what?"

"The timeline of events because Billy will ask questions once we've read the contents. What happened between Leticia and Hank before he went to Chicago?"

"Maybe they met in school. They were both so young then." Carrie said.

"Yes, Leticia met Hank when they were both young in Philadelphia, but not in school. Billy said they originally lived in Philadelphia. And Hank mentioned that his hometown was Philadelphia, but Hank moved to Chicago before his twentieth birthday, training to become a Pinkerton agent. So, I believe they were lovers."

"How do you know? You didn't read the letter, did you?"

"No, I don't read private letters without permission unless it's written to or from a suspect. Leticia and Hank are dead, and my conscience is clear about reading it. But I'm still putting the pieces together. Something happened between them, and they separated. But if there's bad blood between them, why did Hank ask me to deliver this letter to Leticia in person?" wondered JT out loud.

Carrie added another puzzle piece, "Oh, that's obvious to me. She broke it off, not him."

JT's eyebrow shot up. "Then why would she choose crime and prostitution over a relationship with Hank?"

Carrie proclaimed, "Think like a woman! Men make decisions, and women must live with the results. No matter what. He prioritized something above her and wounded her pride. There's a wound of some kind in there somewhere. Maybe it was becoming a Pinkerton."

"Would that make her mad enough some odd years later to shoot him dead in his tracks?" asked JT.

"You need to learn more about women. The question is, 'what did Hank do or say to a young girl who harbored deep feelings for him that triggered the rejection.' And how many years has she chewed on the pain?"

JT scratched his head, "She spurns him but blames him for the pain."

Carrie nodded, "She was probably even angrier after she killed him."

"I hope I never make you that angry.

Carrie smiled and held her hand out for him to take.

JT's lips met Carrie's skin with a feather-light touch, sending shivers down her spine. He trailed kisses up her arm, igniting a fire within her. His lips moved behind her ear, tickling the sensitive skin, and then across her jawline, planting soft kisses along the way. As his lips reached hers, Carrie felt as though she was drowning in his touch. His kiss was passionate and hungry, sending a rush of desire through her body. She wrapped her good arm around his neck, pulling him closer, and felt his lips mold against hers with an intense heat. JT's touch was electric, causing her to moan softly as she ran her tongue along his lips. He pulled away, breathing heavily, leaving Carrie craving more of his touch.

"I can't wait until you're well enough to get out of this bed because you need to be strong for what I have in mind." He kissed her forehead.

"You're scaring me." Carrie caressed his strong jaw.

"Don't be. I'm not your parents or Philipp. I won't betray you. I'm crazy about you." His palm caressed her rosy cheek.

"Would you give up Texas for me?" asked Carrie hesitantly.

JT paused, "We can worry about that later, can't we?"

"But I've already said I can't give up California for you." Said Carrie softly.

"You haven't seen the ranch yet. I'm hoping it'll change your mind." His tone echoed with hope.

Like Leticia and Hank, will their polar opposite dreams tear them apart? Carrie wondered.

***

JT strode into his shared room. As he approached, Billy rose from his bed, a look of anticipation etched on his face. "Hey, Billy, let's open that letter addressed to your mother from your father. I admit I've been curious about what's in it."

Billy pulled the envelope from his pants pocket, "Yes, JT, hurry yaself up, Ima hopin' it's about my real parents." JT tore into the envelope and retrieved the letter inside. He read aloud.

March 2, 1854

My dearest Lettie,

I hope this letter finds you well and happy. I have something that belongs to you and never knew if I should give it to you. It's the ring I bought with which to propose to you. I didn't give it to my wife when we married; it didn't seem proper. This ring was meant for our plans and dreams for the future. I never imagined you would rebuff me before I even had a chance to propose. But unfortunately, you secured a place in my heart that will never die. I loved you desperately and wanted you to have the ring meant for you. If you're reading this letter, I have gone to meet my maker. I've asked my dear friend, JT Grant, to deliver this to you after I'm gone.

I wish you happiness, Hank Lipton.

Billy crumbled the letter into his lap. "Why didn't he gib dis letter to Lettie years ago? It woulda changed Lettie's heart for sure. And we wouldna gone through all the pain of the last twelve years."

JT sighed, "Life is hard, Billy. So often, things don't work out how you imagined they would. I imagine Hank's pride took a licking when she turned him away. Was the ring inside the letter?"

Billy pawed through the crumbled letter and resorted to examining the envelope pieces. Finally, he found it tucked into a corner of the envelope. "Finded it!" It was a simple gold band with three small rose-cut diamonds set into the band. He held it up for JT to see.

"It's a beauty, Billy. You should save it to give to your wife someday."

"I donna knowd about dat. You think it's cursed or somethin'?"

"Of course not. No one has worn it before. It's brand new. Save it for the woman you want to marry someday."

Billy held the ring out toward JT. "Will ya hang onto this for me until then?"

JT took the ring and then pulled out his wallet. "Of course, I'll put it here to keep it safe."

"I hope you realize that I kept the letter without opening it until both of them, your parents died or when she was convicted. And I hope this letter cheered you up a little. Your father was in love with your mother. You were not an unwanted child."

"I wish I had knowd him, JT." Sniffled Billy.

"I know you would have loved him. He was one hell of a friend to me." JT shifted on the bed to get a little closer to him. "And any time you want to learn more about him, just ask."

<u>Proverbs 3:5-6</u> *Trust in the* LORD *with all your heart. And lean not on your own understanding; In all your ways acknowledge Him, And He shall direct your paths*

June 18, 1860, Billy's Adoption

Safely on the road to a full recovery, Carrie decided it was time to seek out a judge to adopt Billy Brown. JT set the court date, and Carrie and Billy showed up a few minutes before the scheduled time. Carrie's heartbeat drowned out her nervousness. JT accompanied them and informed the court that Mrs. Wagner and Billy had arrived.

Carrie thought JT might insert himself into the court proceedings at any second with his claim to adopt Billy. But Billy had explained his adoption parameters to JT, and those conditions had not yet developed.

Carrie sat waiting on a bench outside the courtroom with Billy on one side and JT on the other. She couldn't hold in her thoughts. Finally, she said, "JT, what if he asks if Billy has any remaining family? He might have relatives still in Philadelphia, like grandparents or aunts and uncles."

"The court may decide to search in Philadelphia for any remaining relatives before the adoption is approved. That shouldn't take more than a week." JT said.

"A week? We'll have to delay our riverboat departure. California keeps getting further away every day." sighed Carrie.

"I got a mind-boggler for ya, "Billy said. "Ya knows my family was Catholic. Lettie started in on me as long as I could remember to learn Latin. Deir church services are in Latin, and Lettie knowed the service like it was pounded into her head."

"Billy! You never said anything about speaking Latin before." said a very surprised Carrie.

"Lettie wanted to learn it to me, so's when we conversated with one another, no one would get the right of it. Unless dey also talked Latin, but Lettie said Latin was dead."

"Quite devious on her part, but the only place you can use it is to become a doctor." JT said.

"But what I'm trying to remember about is having babies without being legally hitched. I think dey have a rule on it. And those kids aren't relatives by the church's reckoning. And Lettie's fokes were high society. So don't dat mean dey donna want me?" Billy asked.

"What a clever boy you are." Carrie hugged him closely.

"Billy, you're always full of surprises," said JT. "Explain that to the judge when he asks you about family, and let's see what he says about it."

"Oh, JT, do you think they will give up a grandson?" asked Carrie.

"We'll have to wait and see what the court finds out. We don't want to give the boy false hope, but I believe Billy is right about the Catholic doctrine. Just pray."

***

It was two weeks since the judge ordered the check into Billy's background. Instead of a week, as JT had suggested. Exhausted by the waiting period and fearing someone in Philadelphia would want Billy. Carrie decided to camp at the clerk's office for news two days ago. But it wasn't until three days later that news came in from Philadelphia. The clerk refused to tell her anything; she would have to wait until the court summoned her. She had chewed her nails down days ago and now twisted her hands and mumbled to herself. When she returned to the hotel, she joined Billy and JT at lunch in the hotel restaurant to share the news.

"Well, boys, the court clerk received the information from Philadelphia just now. He said I must wait to be summoned to court to hear the results. Drat!" Said Carrie as she began to chew her non-existent nails.

"Dang, Carrie, ya the best worrier ever." Billy said.

"Stop chewing your nails, Carrie. You're supposed to be a role model for Billy. So, what do you want to eat?" asked JT.

"JT, I couldn't eat a bite. I'm slightly nauseous, and my stomach is in knots." Carrie said.

"You have to eat something. You haven't eaten properly since this process began."

Carrie closed her eyes and sighed. "Alright, tea and toast."

JT patted her hand and said, "Let me get the attention of a server." He turned to summon someone, but the room sat empty of servers. He scratched his chin confused whether he should wait or fetch one himself but one look at Carrie and he was on his feet to place an order for her, not wanting her to remain hungry any longer.

"Ya gonna pop wide open ifn you don't quit worryin'."

"Yeah, I'm a fine example for you to grow up to be." Carrie said.

"Don't worry. Ifn the court tries to send me back to Philadelphy, I'll run away and wait for ya in Californy."

"Nonsense, you can't travel to California on your own. You wouldn't know where in the state we settled."

"That's a heap better, dan going back."

"Now, Billy, if they decide to send you back because you have family, I can't steal you from them. Besides, you might grow up to take over the family business if they have money."

"Who ya kiddin'? Dey ain't gonna put a kid with no name in charge of the family business. I'd never fit in."

"Oh Lord, how true. I know all about rejection," Carrie said. She looked up and saw the court clerk running across the street toward the hotel, and continued watching as he burst through the doors and asked the hotel clerk for her location. The hotel clerk pointed toward the restaurant.

Carrie stood to greet him. "Billy, run and find JT and tell him the court clerk is here."

Billy snapped his head toward what Carrie looked at and jumped from his seat.

Running up to the table, the clerk said to Carrie, "Mrs. Wagner, the judge wants to see you in his office quickly. He's got another case in thirty minutes. Come, I'll show you to his office."

Carrie silently blessed the judge for being in tune with her fragile nerves. "JT and Billy will be here in a few seconds. Can you wait?"

"No, ma'am, I left the office unattended." said the man as he shook his head gravely.

Carrie reached into her purse to rummage for a piece of paper. She turned her shopping list over to write on the back, used the saltshaker to hold it down, and dashed off with the court clerk.

Seated across the desk from the judge, Carrie leaned forward, "What did you find out?"

"Yes, yes, I can see you're on the verge of fainting. The Brown family in Philadelphia signed away their responsibility for the boy and permitted you to adopt Billy."

Carrie sank back in the leather chair with her hand to her heart, "Thank you, Lord, thank you. And thank you, judge."

JT and Billy burst through the office door, closing it after themselves.

"It's the best news, boys! The Brown family said I could adopt Billy," said Carrie.

JT took his hat off and ran his forearm across his forehead. Billy jumped into Carrie's arms and cried.

Carrie held him close, squeezing him with love, and rubbed his back. "It's alright now, Billy, don't cry." She chided him as tears fell from her own cheeks.

JT held a hand toward the judge to shake, "Thank you, sir, for this miracle."

"My pleasure, I'm sure. I'll have the necessary paperwork drawn up. Then you can all come back and become official." smiled the man as he shook JT's hand pompously.

Billy ran around the desk and hugged the judge.

"Bless you, Billy. I'm proud to give you the good news." Said the judge.

"Bless ya judge, and ya family, 'cause I woulda rund away if you had telled me any different.

The whole room erupted into laughter.

<u>Galatians 3:5</u> *Therefore He who supplies the Spirit to you and works miracles among you, does He do it by the works of the law, or by the hearing of faith?*

June 25, 1860, Drunk

The time came for them to board a steamboat headed down the Missouri River. Dr. Matthews removed all her bandages. She now walked well enough to get around by herself. Her wrist felt stiff, but it has healed.

They were checking out of the hotel and boarding a steamboat on the first leg to New Braunfels, Texas. It was going to be a long trek from St. Joseph. The route is the Missouri River to the Mississippi River, the Mississippi River to the Gulf of Mexico, the Gulf waterway to the Guadalupe River, and the Guadalupe River to the San Antonio River. The San Antonio River originates in San Antonio. New Braunfels is twenty miles away from there.

They should all be sufficiently sick of riverboats or steamboats by the time they arrive. Billy burst through the door, "Are you ready? The hotel has a carriage downstairs to take us to the dock."

Carrie kissed his cheek. "Yes, I'm ready."

JT's voice came from behind them, "Billy, take her things down to the carriage. I'll help Carrie down the stairs."

"Hooray! We're finally going!" Billy grabbed Carrie's baggage and flew out of the room.

Addressing JT, Carrie said, "Please take your arm from my waist."

"I will as soon as you are down the stairs," he whispered into her ear, his warm breath tempting a response. But, instead, she closed her eyes and resisted an urge to curl into him.

"You look amazing today, especially your hair," JT said.

"Billy washed and arranged my hair. What a difference. You must compliment him on his work." Carrie moved forward, and JT, true to his word, released her at the bottom of the staircase.

By evening, Carrie had secured an apple and wedge of cheese and retired to her cabin, smiling as she remembered the first apple and wedge of cheese on a previous riverboat.

The next day after dinner, they decided to sit on the deck of the riverboat and enjoy the river's scenery. Five minutes in, Billy declared the pastime boring and went to watch the paddlewheel.

JT fidgeted beside her, rubbing his thumb against his index and middle finger. He looked drained and confused. You'd think a Pinkerton man would be able to solve this dilemma.

JT pushed himself out of the deck chair, "Excuse me, Carrie, I'm going to join a poker table in the lounge.

"Enjoy."

Carrie remembered when she got lost in his beautiful blue eyes and kissed him. An urge she couldn't control. The taste of him drove her wild.

Those strong arms claimed her. She pressed her fingers to her quivering lips as tears fell.

The next three days passed in isolation, except for Billy. He brought meals for her and talked about being adopted by Carrie and their future together. Having Billy for a son was guaranteed happiness. She already thought of him as such. He was an extraordinary boy who brought nothing but joy to her life.

On the fourth evening, the captain banged on her cabin door and called out her name loudly. Billy answered the door.

"Mrs. Wagner, your fiancé is drunk, causing bedlam in the lounge."

Carrie waved dismissively, "Captain, Mr. Grant doesn't drink." She rose from her chair to join the captain at the door.

"I beg to differ, ma'am. There's property damage, and he's punched at least three men." reiterated the man.

Billy, unable to contain his excitement, exclaimed, "A fight? Hot diggity." He ran from the doorway toward the lounge.

"Could you please see what you can do to bed him down for the night?" The captain begged. "He's been there almost three days straight, playing poker and drinking. "

Frankly, she couldn't resist the pious JT on a three-day drunken binge after the scolding he gave her about her empty bottle of brandy.

The captain's plea was a desperate one, and she could see the weariness etched into his features as he spoke. He had clearly been through a lot trying to deal with JT's behavior over the past few days.

As she readied herself to approach JT's table, she couldn't help but feel a twinge of satisfaction at the matter. He had always been so pious and self-righteous, judging her for the one time she had drank while indulging in his own vices behind closed doors. The irony of his current state was not lost on her.

"Let's give it a try, shall we, captain?" Carrie followed the captain to the lounge.

You heard the commotion before arrival. Nothing the captain said could have prepared her for the sight before her eyes. Several chairs smashed to smithereens, two tables flattened, and glassware and gambling paraphernalia scattered about. The pungent odor of alcohol likely meant a few broken bottles as well. But the sight for her sore eyes, JT, lay unconscious, spread out on the floor. A couple of men leaned on the bar, sporting evidence of a well-fought fight.

Carrie walked up to them. "Are you both all right?"

"Yes, ma'am, you should worry about him, not us." One of them offered.

"I don't suppose I could talk you into carrying him to his cabin?" Carrie flashed the smile she used when customers came into Mr. Simpkins' mercantile. They agreed.

JT just then looked up at her blearily, his eyes red-rimmed and unfocused. "I don't need any help," he slurred, gesturing at the room. "I'm winning."

She suppressed a sigh and forced herself to remain patient. "JT, it's been almost three days straight. Surely you must be tired. Let's get you to bed. Let the men help you."

JT scowled at her, clearly irritated by her presence. But eventually, he seemed to relent, nodding his head in agreement. "Fine," he muttered. "Lead the way."

The minute the two men hoisted him by his waist, arms flung around their necks, his head lolled to the side, too drunk to stay awake.

As they walked, she checked his waist for his money belt, shocked to find it. When they arrived at the cabin, the captain unlocked the door, the duo flopped him face up on the bed, and JT belched from his toes, proving his choice of alcohol to be whiskey.

From behind her, Billy said, "Are we sure he ain't pickled?"

"If he's lucky, he is. You take his boots off. I'll find something to clean him up." Carrie took a towel, a basin of water, and a chair to the side of JT's bed. It looks like he hadn't shaved in three days, either.

Billy fell on his backside as he pulled the second boot off. "Look, Carrie, he's wearing that poor sock you mended."

Carrie glanced at the sock and couldn't help smiling.

"Pew, his boots smell like he's worn them for three weeks straight. Poor chaperone."

"Now, you're on his side." She dabbed at the slash in his scalp.

"You can't fool me. You still love him."

"Really, Billy? That's helpful."

"JT was right. You never brought up the children and waited for him to ask. Because of that, he believed they warn't real. Moms blabber on and on about their brats. Even when they are ugly."

"You knew they were real."

Billy slapped his thigh, "I was peepin' at the adoption. He warn't there."

Carrie stopped dabbing on JT to ask, "So the two of you have been talking it over and decided I'm wrong. What do you think I should do next?"

"Carrie, I'll ignore him if it comes to that, but he's my dad's best friend. You know, the man I never got to meet."

"We must go to California. There's no way he'll go. I'd be setting myself up for more heartbreak."

"Does he look like he's happy that you're going?"

"Don't blame this drunken behavior on me. JT's a grown man."

"JT's never been pickled afore. Don't know why, but he never has. Why now?"

Carrie remembered her unspoken response when JT challenged her on her drinking, 'Sometimes the pain or emptiness is too hard to face alone. Thinking of him feeling such raw despair confused her. Remembering his drunken father and JT's guilt over not helping him at the time gave her pause. He's a Pinkerton man who solves problems for a living. Their relationship is a problem he doesn't know how to solve. He thinks he's losing his father all over again. The whole matter lay outside his reach.

Carrie stood to leave, "Stay with him tonight, Billy. He'll probably sleep until late morning. Let me know when he wakes up."

JT grabbed her hand, "Billy, I'm awake. Tell her."

"Tell her yaself, chaperone."

"All right. Carrie, sweetheart, don't be angry." JT groaned like the living dead. "I love you with all my heart, and I want to hear about all the children," he pulled her toward him, and she sank to her knees, "especially the ones you haven't told me about yet. Billy says they're puppies. That's nice, but I also want to hear about the little girls. They have names and ages, but tell me more."

A drunk JT was pretty funny, "We can talk about it later. You're drunk."

"Who me? I don't drink. Never touch the stuff." He motioned for her to come closer and whispered into her ear, "The stuff burns like hellfire going down. Nasty. I don't recommend it."

Smiling, Carrie asked, "Then why did you do it?"

"Cause that's what a man does when his life falls apart. That's what my Pa taught me."

Billy interrupted their dialogue, "I'm going to your cabin, Carrie, and get some sleep. Good night."

"Goodnight, Billy."

"Goodnight, Hank's boy," JT said.

Carrie giggled, "We'll talk about the children tomorrow if you want. Now you need to sleep it off."

"Say it, Carrie. I won't let you leave until you say it."

Both of his hands gripped hers. "Say which, I love you or I was wrong?"

"That's it. I'll take both."

"Now, go to sleep."

"Well, Carrie girl, it might interest you that I may have been a tad wrong myself." A wide grin split his face as he rolled over, seeking oblivion.

"Decent of you to mention it." She pulled the blanket up over him and left quietly. She couldn't wait until morning when JT received the bill for the damages.

<u>2 Samuel 22:28</u> *You will save the humble people; But Your eyes are on the haughty, that You may bring them down.*

June 26, 1860, The Adopted California Children

True to his word, JT arrived at her cabin at noon the next day and asked about the children. His head pounded, and the inside of his mouth tasted like he shouldn't be lighting matches anytime soon. How could his father have done this daily? It's brutal. He harbored no plans to repeat this useless behavior.

JT found Carrie in her cabin and tapped on her door.

Carrie sang out, "Who's there?"

How dare she sound cheery? "Have no fear, ma'am. It's only the dead arisen again."

Carrie giggled and pulled the door open. "I'm surprised you're awake. Are you alright?"

"No, I wish someone would put me out of my misery."

"Come on in. I just ordered fresh coffee. I'll pour you a cup. I've had lunch; would you like me to fetch something for you?"

" I can't handle the aroma of food yet." JT said.

"Why don't you go back to bed? It's the best thing for you in this condition."

"I remember promising my sweetheart to learn everything about her children. I'm here. Now I have coffee. Please tell me all about them."

"Are you sure you're in the mood? You're not afraid of them, are you?" teased Carrie.

"Truthfully? Yes, a bit. I'm not used to kids. I keep imagining what it was like when you were in the orphanage." Admitted JT.

Carrie laughed, "Well, I'm glad you've been thinking about them. I suppose it's easier for me since I grew up in an orphanage with kids of all ages. They're just like other children. They need spiritual guidance, an education, a loving home, patience, and their own family."

"But most men get to ease into it. Including Billy, you have three of them."

"JT, I'm not asking you to jump into a fiery pit of brimstone. I think you'll love the children when you meet them. They are little darlings. If you want me, they come with the package. If you want to meet them before we marry, come to California. Then, I'll understand after you meet them and want to change your mind about marriage."

"What? Now I must go to California to meet the kids before we marry?"

In frustration, Carrie drew a deep breath. "I only meant it as an option to help ease your mind about the children."

Waving her off, JT sank into a chair. "Come on now. Tell me about the children."

Carrie lit up when she talked about her children. There was an aura about her he'd never seen before. It was remarkable. A broad smile covered half her face as her animated hands punctuated her story.

The oldest, Michelle, is missing her front teeth and can't correctly pronounce words with a 't.' It only endears her more to Carrie. She doesn't walk anywhere. She runs. She's got a mop of dark curly hair that needs washing almost daily because she plays hard. There's always mud, grass stains, dampness of some kind on her clothes, burrs, bugs in her hair, and various bumps and bruises. But in the morning and evenings, she was always there to help Carla. She loves reading and insists on a bedtime story every night. Cornbread is her favorite treat. Michelle gets angry at Carla sometimes because Carla is always hogging Carrie's time. Michelle had been praying for a new Mom every night at the orphanage. She's going to be a self-starter.

Carla is four years old and the clinger of the family. She fears Carrie will disappear if she's not in sight of her. She sucks her thumb and refuses to stop, no matter how many times Carrie insists on it. JT found himself instantly infatuated with Carla. A little girl in search of a parent every day of her life. The poor little one can't believe her good luck and fears abandonment again. Carla has stick-straight blond hair, which is constantly in her eyes, but she refuses to have it cut. She sports dimples and is going to grow into a willowy woman. But now, Carla needed a father, and JT was surprised he felt he could help Carla grow into adulthood. Carrie loves the way she always hugs her legs when she's standing. The little lamb loves applesauce cake.

Michelle and Carla sound like lovable little humans looking for love and a home. He should have asked her about these incredible children long before now. Listening to her describe the children made them come alive for him. He looks forward to meeting them. He understood why Carrie needed children. She wouldn't be Carrie without them. And she took on Billy to boot. What an incredible capacity to love. She's extraordinary, and she's mine.

JT learned more about Carrie's best friend, Ruth, as well. For Carrie to trust Ruth to get her two children to California by herself, their bond must be rock solid. Now he realized how foolish his suggestion to move Ruth to Texas was. And separating her from Carrie is equally incredible.

Carrie's right. They all deserve peace and security, a place to heal and grow in California. Carrie is his only if he solves the dilemma ahead of them. What about the ranch? Will she leave Aunt Tildy in Texas if she turns out to be her mother? JT couldn't imagine so. More likely, Aunt Tildy would want to go to California with Carrie. But that ranch is his life.

<u>Isaiah 65:23</u> *They shall not labor in vain, Nor bring forth children for trouble; For they shall be the descendants of the blessed of the Lord, And their offspring with them.'*

Chapter Nineteen

July 1, 1860, War and Slavery

They were on a riverboat close to the Gulf of Mexico a week later. Carrie knew that time with JT was drawing to a close soon. She spent as much time with him as she could. It didn't take long to notice JT's yearning glances and tendency to hold onto her hand. A sense of doom hung over them.

One hot, sticky evening after dinner, JT and Carrie sought a breeze on deck in what limited shade they could find. Billy found some boys with whom to play dice. Clothes bought for her winter marriage trousseau trapped body moisture from humidity against her skin. It was causing her to chaff in various places and steam in others. Afraid someone would steal her money, she wore a corset every day. And Texas was even further south. Fantasies about lowering her nude body into a tub of cool water taunted her sanity. She needed a distraction. Asking JT about his plans when the war comes to Texas seemed appropriate conversation material. The Texas/California dilemma continued to drive them apart, and they needed to discuss it.

"JT, what are your plans for the ranch when the war breaks out?"

"Plans?" JT scratched his head. "I hope there won't be a war. I certainly don't want one over slavery. We don't enslave people and never will. We don't believe in it. So, we will probably stay on the ranch until the whole thing blows over."

Carrie shook her head, "JT, you're an intelligent man, but you are not making sense of this threat. Your neighbors will send their husbands, brothers, and sons to war. They won't take kindly of you and your brothers sitting this out. The southern army will need food and supplies. I can foresee them taking all the rations they need, including the beef on your ranch, to keep their army ready and able to fight. Every citizen must contribute."

"You feel this strongly that war is inevitable.?" asked JT.

"Yes, I do. And so would you if you had been reading the news from the East. But, instead, your Pinkerton mind is clogged with wanted posters and saving money to rescue the ranch."

"And saving you for me, too."

"Why do I feel like you're not taking me seriously?"

"Carrie, nobody is going to get away with stealing my cattle. What makes you think the Southern army would do that if it came to be?

"The government won't be stealing. The government gives you a receipt for your cattle, which you can redeem after the war, but if the South loses goodbye cattle. It's in the papers in Columbus, Cincinnati, St. Louis, St. Jo, and everywhere else we've been. There are all kinds of articles about the likelihood of a coming war and how to prepare. How to can vegetables and fruit, stock up on ammunition, calico, and bandages, how you won't be able to keep your animals from being confiscated or perhaps stolen, how to volunteer to help the wounded, and so on. From how the Democratic convention in South Carolina is falling apart, I'd say war is inevitable." explained Carrie,

"Is that what you read in the newspapers? That's what men usually read, not ladies."

"And again, you avoid the issue. Ruth and I had to consider everything regarding finding a location for our new home. We researched where to go. I'm asking that you consider the coming war more than a possibility. It's more of a probability. Consider the impact on Aunt Tildy, your brothers, and you, especially if you pay the mortgage off. You still have to pay taxes on a ranch stripped of resources."

"You sound like the south will lose." said JT.

"It's only my opinion." Carrie returned. She folded the newspaper inher hands and slid it under her arm.

"Are you bringing this up as an excuse not to stay at the ranch?" asked JT.

"No, I'm bringing it up because we are adults who must consider all options. We need to figure out our future, or we can't marry. I made the California decision before meeting you, and paying off your ranch has been your ten-year goal." She slipped an arm through JT's.

JT laid a hand on her forearm, "Carrie, you're not even going to wait to see the ranch before you decide. What about your mother?"

"Even if it turns out she is my mother, I still have to go to California. Ruth and my children are waiting for me. And the house has already been built by now. My future is in California, no matter how much I love you. You know all this already." Oh, dear God, can I or can I not trust you, not only with my life but my children's lives? Carrie wondered if she was being selfish. Should she consider moving her family to the Texas ranch if Aunt Tildy turns out to be her mother?

None of that changes if Texas leaves the union and strands them behind enemy lines for months or years. Not her idea of the dream locale she and Ruth had in mind. She had hoped somehow; maybe magically, his love would be more binding than that plot of land. But, like she, JT has previous commitments that precede their meeting.

How foolish she'd been guarding her heart against JT choosing his ranch over her. It's his ranch. Of course, he'd want to build his life there, but Ruth has been her rock since she was five. They've relied on each other through thick and thin. She is the bedrock of Carrie's family. Living without Ruth would crush her heart. Asking Ruth to move to Texas is a betrayal of her trust. It's a decision she's never going to make. So, JT and she remain at an impasse.

Isaiah 45:21 *Tell ye, and bring them near; yea, let them take counsel together.*

July 1, 1860, Billy Kidnapped

Billy's dice game broke up early because all the other boys had parents who enforced bedtime rules. It's not like they were playing for money anyhow. They used matchsticks. His pants pocket bulged with them. He slid down the aft stairs handrail on his way to find out what JT and Carrie were up to and barreled into a burly man turning the corner to ascend the stairs.

The man regained his footing in the blink of an eye.

The stranger grabbed Billy by the front of his shirt with a single ham-fisted snatch.

The other fist slammed into Billy's eye.

"Ow, gib me a chance to sorry ya, will ya?" screamed Billy.

The man dragged him toward a lamp. Under the light, they recognized each other simultaneously. Judge Edgar Pullman, one of Lettie's marks a couple of years ago, that she fleeced out of $20,000 if memory serves correctly. Billy looked for someone to call out to, but no one lingered on this side of the deck.

"I thought I recognized that voice. Billy boy, well my, my, my. Where's that lying, cheating whore of a sister of yours? I want my money back." The judge buried the fingers of his free hand into Billy's hair and closed his fist, jerking his face up for a more personal conversation.

Uncontrollable trembling set in. "Lettie's d-dead." The aroma of bourbon, lots and lots of bourbon, and the overpowering stench of cigars engulfed Billy.

"Isn't that convenient for Lettie?" The judge shook Billy's head furiously. "Where's my money?"

Billy felt his shoulder and leg muscles tighten like strings on a guitar, "She n-never gib me any g-grift money. Lettie died wifout a single penny."

The honorable Judge Pullman freed Billy's shirt only to hit him with a rear hook perfected in his boxing days. Billy fell unconscious. The judge hauled him up by his clothes and tossed him overboard. Then dove in after him.

***

JT and Carrie vacated the riverboat deck to retire for the night. Later, Carrie pulled on a wrapper to answer the door. There stood JT with worried eyes and a clamped jaw. "Is Billy here with you?" He asked. "He's not in my cabin." JT walked past her into the cabin, quickly checked her room, and darted back to the door.

"No, he's not. What's happened?" She paused to think. "Have you searched for him?" A dark pit of fear revealed itself in her gut, and her leg muscles tightened in preparation to run.

"That's next. I'll let you know what I find out." JT shouted to her as he turned to leave.

"Let me go with you." She pleaded.

"No, you stay here in case Billy shows up," JT said over his shoulder just before the door closed.

"All right, JT, please hurry." She wondered where Billy could be. He played dice with some boys earlier, but JT knows that and will check it out. Carrie lay down before collapsing and closed her eyes to the horrific thoughts of what might have happened to the boy. The more she pushed the thoughts away, even more scenarios popped into her head. A good mother always knows where her children are. She should have been watching over him.

After ten minutes, she couldn't stand not knowing for one more second. Billy had to be on this boat somewhere. They were in the middle of the Mississippi River. She pushed panic aside and struggled into her clothes as quickly as possible. Fortunately, she hadn't brushed out her hair for the night yet. She left her cabin in search of JT.

Crossing to the port side, Carrie found a small crowd surrounding one cabin, asking questions of the occupants. JT stood among the group, and Carrie joined them. Both the boat's captain and JT were asking questions.

"If you didn't see anything, tell us what you heard, Mr. Barnstaff." TJ's voice sounded panicked, and she began to worry.

Carrie breathlessly waited for Mr. Barnstaff's reply.

"Well, I had just laid down for the night but hadn't fallen asleep yet. And I hear a man say, "It's you again. Now, I got you. Where's my money?" The other fella who sounded young said, "I ain't got your money." Then one or the other got slugged with a hell of a punch, and things got quiet. Then I heard a splash as something got thrown overboard and another splash. That's all I know."

The captain asked, "Did you come out after the second splash to find out what happened?"

"Nope. I don't mix in anybody else's trouble."

JT asked, "Captain, please check the passenger log and determine if anyone besides Billy is missing?"

"Good idea." The captain pulled away from the group and headed to the pilothouse.

Carrie followed him. "Mr. Grant did not find Billy?"

"No, Mrs. Wagner, we did not find the boy anywhere on the boat."

Billy's missing. What happened to him? Is he all right? If someone threw him overboard, does he know how to swim? Oh, my God, he can't be dead. Carrie nervously rubbed her hands together. Maybe one of those boys in the dice game hurt him. "Captain, has someone questioned the boys he played dice with earlier this evening?"

The captain entered the pilothouse and latched onto the passenger log, "Mr. Grant did that already, ma'am. If you don't mind, I'll begin surveying the passengers."

"I'm going with you," Carrie announced. "I can't sit in my cabin and wait. I'll explode."

As they stepped out of the pilothouse, JT caught up with them.

"Don't tell me to go to the cabin and wait," she tried to walk past him.

JT snagged her elbow, pulling her back, "The captain can do his job better if we stay out of his way." She pulled her elbow from his grasp, fully intending to ignore him, but he folded her into his arms.

"Stop it. I must find Billy, JT." She squirmed against the trap that held her. "Turn me loose. I can't lose him again."

"All right, we'll follow behind the captain at a short distance, but don't interfere."

Carrie nodded like a woodpecker, "Yes, now let's go find out what's going on." Her gut felt overly wound, as if a boa constrictor had squeezed the life out of her.

They quietly walked behind the captain as he checked each cabin. Then the captain came to a cabin where no one answered the door. The captain announced himself again but met with silence. Using his master key, he opened the cabin door. There were personal effects, but no one. Turning toward JT and Carrie, the captain said, "Well, it appears the second splash belongs to U.S. Marshall Ambrose Stanton. Does the name mean anything to you?" The captain held up the Marshall's badge for verification.

JT responded, "No, never met him." Beside him, Carrie slid to the deck out cold.

"Oh my, Mr. Grant, I don't think we have a doctor on board."

"Don't worry. She fainted. She'll be fine," JT bent to scoop her into his arms. "Captain, I will need a week's worth of grub. Could someone pack it up for me? I'll be going after them. Can you pull to the shore long enough for me to get off?"

"Can't do that, too shallow, but we've got a dinghy that will do the job. Just let me know when you're ready, Mr. Grant." Replied the man.

JT lifted Carrie's limp body in his arms and carried her to the bed. As he laid her down, he noticed her once rosy complexion had turned an unsettling shade of white. Fear gripped his heart as he searched for any signs of consciousness creeping back into her. He quickly grabbed a washcloth and dunked it into a bowl of cold water, wringing it out before gently placing it on her forehead. The water dripped down her face, but she didn't stir. JT's heart sank as he realized how serious the situation was. He knew Billy was missing but he needed to make sure she was okay before he could go after him.

Desperate to revive her, he continued to wash her face, hoping the cool water would wake her up. But when that didn't work, he resorted to more drastic measures. He slapped her cheek gently, hoping the sensation would jolt her back to consciousness.

Carrie's eyes popped open and focused on him, "Are you going to find him for me?"

JT heaved a sigh of relief and replied, "Of course. Nobody's taking him away from us. I won't come back until I have. You have my promise."

Carrie put her arms around his neck and pulled him closer. JT slid into bed next to her. "Don't forget to return to me—I love you."

JT kissed her trembling lips and hugged her to him. "I love you, too, sweetheart. Please continue this trip to the ranch and wait for us there. I don't know how long it will take, but don't leave for California until we come home." He unbuttoned his shirt, removed his money belt, and quickly removed some cash. "Make sure this money belt is always safe with you. If you need money, you have my permission to use it." He stuffed the cash into his pocket. "I'm going now. You stay here."

One second, he was with her. The next, gone. Dumbfounded that JT left his money belt behind after his former wife had stolen all his money, she hugged the money belt to her heart. Somewhere in Carrie's addled brain, it warmed her heart that JT loved her that much. He trusted her. Now, she must trust him.

Insidious fingers of panic crept into the dark pit in her gut, twisting and turning like a plain's tornado torturing her. Carrie crisscrossed her arms over her belly, hoping to alleviate the pain. Like the worst kind of twister that U.S. Marshall stormed in, recognized and arrested Billy, leaving her heart shredded and scattered to the four winds. The echoes of the mournful howling wind haunted her as it dragged her son further away.

Billy, I'm sorry. A mother is supposed to keep watch over her children. I failed you. Please forgive me.

As the weight of the situation dawned on her, she felt her heart sink with despair. The thought of Billy, an innocent child, being locked away in prison was unbearable. In this moment of dire need, she knew that she must act quickly, but alone she could not protect him. She needed JT, the man she loved, by her side.

With a sense of desperation, she pleaded with the heavens for a way to bring Billy back to safety. But she knew that the law would not be on their side. JT would have to go against all odds, against the very system he had sworn to uphold, to rescue Billy. She could not bear the thought of losing both the child and the man she loved.

Her mind raced with thoughts of how to convince JT to come with them to California. She knew that his sense of duty was strong, but she hoped that his love for her would be stronger. She needed his strength, his courage, and his unwavering determination to see this through. She not only loved him but she also needed him, more than he could ever know.

She rolled over in bed and filled the mattress with tears. Tomorrow she would find the courage from somewhere to press on. *But, please, God, bring them safely back to me.*

Job 5:11 *He sets on high those who are lowly, And those who mourn are lifted to safety.*

***

Before his eyes opened, Billy became aware of stifling heat and body odor and woke tied and gagged to a chair in a dirty flophouse room alone and thirsty. The side of his head throbbed like a fourth of July parade. He flipped his head to the right, and the pain lessened somewhat. Judge Pullman burst into the room and slammed the door. Billy flinched at the noise.

Pullman pulled the gag out of his mouth and said, "You're back, good. I hit you a little too hard. You should see that shiner you're sporting. One of my best."

Billy glared at him. "What's the point of this? There's no money for you."

"The point is I don't believe you. Lettie can't have gone through $20,000 in two years." The judge sat on the bed opposite Billy. "You see, I'm not Judge Pullman anymore. Never was. That money came from a train robbery. Now I'm a U.S. Marshall, except I'm not that either. Somebody bushwhacked the Marshall and left him to rot. I came along and claimed his identity. Ambrose Stanton at your service, thief. If you don't cough up the money, I'll turn you into the nearest Sheriff."

Billy gripped the wooden chair seat on both sides and closed his eyes. How will he get out of this situation? The derringer lay at the bottom of the river.

Billy felt his heart race as he clenched his fists, trying to calm himself. The sound of the water rushing by echoed in his ears as he sat in silence, deep in thought.

He could not afford to give up, not when his life depended on it. He had to be strong, to find a weakness in his captor and make a plan to escape.

With eyes closed, Billy took a deep breath, allowing his mind to focus. His thoughts raced as he tried to think of ways to help JT. He had to find a way to let him know where he was being held captive. Billy knew that he had to be clever and subtle. He couldn't afford to be caught trying to escape, or worse, trying to send a message.

Stanton punched him in the stomach, "Wake up. This ain't nap time."

The blow landed with a sickening thud, sending shockwaves through Billy's body. He doubled over, gasping for air, his ribs aching with every breath. The room spun around him, and for a moment, he thought he might pass out. But then, the pain brought him back to his senses. He gritted his teeth and tried to steel himself against the next blow, but it came faster than he could prepare for it. Stanton didn't hold back, raining down a barrage of fists and kicks on Billy's defenseless body. Billy tried to shield himself, but there was no escape. Every impact felt like a hammer blow, sending jolts of agony through his limbs. He gritted his teeth, trying to endure the pain, but it was too much.

He collapsed to the floor, a crumpled heap of broken bones and shredded flesh.

Stanton laughed as he cut Billy free of the chair, his eyes glinting with sadistic pleasure. He dragged Billy to his feet and resumed the beating, each blow landing with a sickening thud. Billy could feel himself slipping away, his consciousness fading as the pain overwhelmed him. But he refused to give up.

Billy tried not to cry out and give Stanton the satisfaction of knowing how badly he hurt, but when the kicks came fast and furious, the moans escaped his trembling lips unheeded. The blackness gratefully returned once again. He rushed toward it with open arms.

Stanton wasn't there when he woke up again.

Billy didn't try to move.

Everything ached.

His legs were tangled.

Billy tried to straighten one of them, only to bring on a streak of pain shooting up from his ankle. It's broken. Now he can't run away. Then he tried to untwist his body to lay flat. It seemed to him that his hip bones creaked in protest, so he joined in. Finally flat, he ignored his thirst and the need for an outhouse to figure out how to help JT find him. Of course, if he ever got left alone when someone was around, he could message them. But Stanton probably isn't that dumb. And he's not sure if he can talk.

Billy tried to move his jaw. It hurt like hellfire but remained solid. He flexed his fingers to see if they still worked. His left hand had bruises and swelling, with several broken fingers. His right hand appeared bruised but not broken. He placed his hands on the floor and tried to push himself up into a sitting position. The ankle protested, which brought Billy's eye to the red sock covering the maimed appendage. An idea struck him. Red socks were not ordinary. What if he unravels his sock and ties little bows along his path for JT to follow? JT will recognize instantly the thread was from his socks. He raised his left hand for inspection again. His forefinger and thumb remained unbroken, and he could still tie bows.

A while later, Stanton came in and flopped down on the bed with a plate of food. "You amaze me, boy. You're still alive. As soon as I finish my grub, we'll be moving on. Can't stay in one place too long."

Billy stared at him while he shoveled food into his gaping maw. "I need water and an outhouse. That is if you want to keep me alive."

"There's water in that pitcher," he pointed at it with his fork, "and a piss pot under the bed."

"That's helpful, but my ankle's broken."

Stanton laughed again. "If you think I'm carrying you, you're crazy. Figure it out for yourself."

Billy slowly came to his hands and knees and crawled to within reach of the chamber pot. After that uphill task, he crawled toward the table with the water pitcher. Pulling the pitcher down to his level, he drank to his pleasure, noticing his blood mixing with the water. Then quickly tied a red bow around the handle. Finally, he left the pitcher on the floor under the table, pushed into a corner.

His captor announced, "Time to go."

"I cain't walk like dis. Cain't I took care of my ankle before goin'?"

Stanton pulled the sheet off the bed and tore several strips off. He wound them around Billy's ankle, one after the other, tying it off. "That's the best you're going to get. I'm not spending money on you. Now get up!"

July 14, 1860, The Red Bows

JT had been following a series of Billy's red bows for days. What concerned him at the first bow's location was blood on the floor and a chair in the room. Even though someone had tried to clean it up. Angry and concerned, he now knew he stalked a beast. The beast hasn't turned Billy into a Sheriff's office yet. That's odd. Why not? Isn't that the reason the Marshall snatched him in the first place? What other reason could there be? Is this a personal vendetta? Marshalls aren't the only people who would recognize Billy. Leticia and Billy's past victims would also remember him in a heartbeat. How could a Marshall be one of Leticia's marks? That doesn't fit this puzzle.

So far, he checked if they had gone west or north from the last red bow. This road goes east. He's desperate to find the next red bow.

Carrie must be worried sick. He hated thinking about what she endured. He's not doing so well himself, worrying about how injured Billy must be. When he catches up with that blackheart, he will need divine intervention to refrain from killing him on sight.

When he arrived in town, he stopped at the livery stable first for his exhausted horse. While brushing his horse down, a bit of red caught his eye. A sloppy bow sat tangled in the mane of the white horse in the next stall. JT went to check the horse over. He found the mare drenched in sweat. Another clue he tracked a beast, for only a beast would put horses up without bedding them down. They were only minutes ahead of him. JT moved the bow higher up in the horse's mane so that Billy would know he had located him if they missed each other. Now, where would Stanton hold up with a gravely wounded boy?

He walked down the east side of the street while crossing unlikely places off his mental list. That hotel looked too prosperous and kept walking. Then, he came to a crossroad, looked down at the new street, and noticed it led to a seedier section of town. That's more like it. The further he walked down the street, the more raucous it became. A drunk sat on the boardwalk, his head on his bent knees while sleeping. JT nudged his foot.

"Leave me alone. I ain't bothering you none."

"Can you point me to the cheapest, dirtiest flophouse in town?" JT asked.

"Somebody always wants something."

JT slipped five dollars into his shirt pocket.

Without looking up, he said, "You see that sign on the left that says, 'Cat's Eye Saloon'? The flophouse is next to it."

With another five dollars in his fist, JT stepped into the flophouse and approached the clerk. Did a seedier description than flophouse exist? Whatever it was, it applies to this burn pile. "I'm looking for an injured twelve-year-old boy traveling with a mean-spirited man. Have you seen them?

"Maybe."

JT shoved money into the man's shirt pocket.

"Mean-spirited isn't the half of it. That guy would scare the cursed out of hell. The boy didn't look well and limped."

JT spoke through clenched teeth, "Where are they?"

"Last room on the right down that corridor." The man pointed the way with his thumb. Then he asked, "Should I find the Sheriff?

"Yes, tell him to hurry before I kill the bastard."

The clerk bolted for the street.

JT reached the last door, kicked it in, and froze at the sight before him. Stanton had Billy tied backward in a chair, branding him with a running iron. Billy, hardly recognizable, bit down on a piece of wood.

JT recognized Stanton immediately.

That particular memory blazed its way to the present. He couldn't believe his eyes.

Stanton ran to the window to throw the branding iron out. Turning, he lunged at JT. It didn't take a millisecond to figure out the massive bulk of the man would crush him in a fight. JT pulled his gun and shot him in the thigh. The behemoth wallowed about on the floor, cursing and bleeding. JT ran to help Billy.

"Billy, it's JT. I'm here." He got no response. He pulled the piece of wood out of Billy's mouth and was going to tap him on the cheek, but the left side of his face looked like a three-day-old gouge wound from a steer. He stepped into the corridor and called for someone to fetch the doctor. Back in the room, he checked out Billy's injuries. From what he could see, there was a broken ankle and fingers, devastating branding wounds on his back, and whatever happened to his face.

JT felt a muscle contract in his jaw.

Billy didn't deserve this.

Nobody deserved this.

He had found him as quickly as possible but still felt guilty. He wanted to comfort him by pushing the matted hair out of his eyes, hugging him, assuring the bond between them would never break and take him somewhere he'll never be recognized again. He lifted Billy's right hand to his lips and kissed his palm. He almost arrived too late to save Billy. Now he knew what Carrie meant when she said she couldn't lose him twice. This is my son. It's my job to keep him safe.

JT separated Billy from the chair as the Sheriff arrived.

"What's going on here?" The Sheriff bellowed. Then he saw Billy and winced.

"Sheriff, I'm JT Grant, retired Pinkerton agent, and that man," JT pointed, "Murdered my father ten years ago. I'll testify to it in court." The man's eyes locked onto JT's in confusion. "And he kidnapped my son here from a riverboat and tortured him. Lock him up before I reshoot the no-account madman.

"Can't say I'd blame you none." Said the Sheriff.

"Oh, and he had identification claiming to be a U.S. Marshall, Ambrose Stanton. I don't know how he got it, but my instincts told me he stole them or killed the Marshall. After I take my son to a doctor, I'll drop by and furnish details." Explained JT.

The Sheriff turned toward the clerk and said, "Louie, we'll need a wheelbarrow for this one." Then, he pulled handcuffs from his belt and approached the squirming mountain.

Stanton tried to defend himself, "How could I have murdered his father? I don't even know him. Yow. My leg hurts. Take me to a doctor, too."

"Sure, sure...first we gotta roll you onto a wheelbarrow and put you in jail, then Louie and I need a couple of drinks after all this commotion. It's been a hard day, right Louie?"

"The worst Sheriff."

"I noticed he's caused some damage to this room, Louie. Submit the charges to me, and I'll add them to the charges against him."

JT asked, "How far away is the doctor?"

The Sheriff stepped out into the corridor. "Which one of you owns that wagon out front?" One man raised his hand. "We're borrowing it to take this boy to the doctor.

"Thanks, Sheriff," JT replied.

It seemed like Billy had been with the doctor for hours. *Please, will someone come to tell me what's going on?* Deemed too anxious to be in the examining room, he sat waiting just outside the room. He worried his beard stubble with his palm back and forth and then paced for a while.

The examination room door opened, and the doctor didn't hesitate. "He's in serious condition, Mr. Grant. I splinted his ankle and fingers. Those burns on his back were quite another matter. Those wounds need cleaning and bandaging daily. Infection is a high probability. He's got a skull fracture and three gashes on his scalp. I sutured the left side of his face. I'm afraid he's scarred for life. He's missing a couple of teeth. Three of his ribs broke. I wrapped them tightly. He's got contusions and abrasions from head to toe, and I suspect internal bleeding. We must keep a close watch over him. He's not out of the woods yet."

JT didn't think his head could hang any lower. It's a good thing the doctor stopped listing ailments. "Can I see him?"

"Of course, I sedated him, and he'll remain sedated for a couple of days so his body can rest and heal." Nodded the doctor.

"I'm not leaving his side unless you throw me out." Said JT.

"I'd feel the same way if he was my son."

JT grabbed a wooden chair and entered the examining room. He placed the chair next to Billy's shoulder and walked around the bed, taking in the damage and subsequent doctoring. Billy lay on his stomach because of the burns on his back. Carrie will be shocked, happy he survived but shocked about what Billy had to endure. JT's going to make sure she gets him back. They're a family and belong together.

JT slumped into the chair, slid his hand under Billy's palm, laid his head against his mattress, and slept for the first time in three days.

The next morning when the doctor returned, JT slipped out to give his report to the Sheriff.

"Good morning, sheriff. I'm here to give you my account of what happened yesterday."

"Let me introduce myself. I'm Pete Flanagan, sheriff of this little corner of the world." They shook hands. "I looked through wanted posters last night and came up with this one. It looks and sounds like him. What do you think?"

JT took the poster to review, "This is probably not his real name either. But that is his mug, and he's been active since before my father's murder. So, I think this is him. And look at that bounty, $5,000." JT whistled his delight.

"It's yours. Here's the voucher. Go to the bank across the street, and they'll pay it out for you." Sheriff Flanagan held the voucher out for JT to take.

JT felt odd about accepting the money for some reason he couldn't name. He's been bringing in murderers and thieves for the last ten years without bounties, but this money could send Billy to school one day. "Thank you, sheriff." He stuffed the voucher into his pants pocket. "What about the report?

Sheriff Flanagan fished around in his desk and came up with a few sheets of paper and a chewed-up pencil.

"Write it out as it happened. Don't forget the dates and times. Sign it at the bottom."

JT sat in a chair facing the sheriff's desk and began his tale. It took five sheets of paper and an hour and a half of his time. "There, sheriff, it's done." He got up to leave.

"Hold up, will you stay and testify at the trial?"

You'd have to lock him up to keep him away, "Do roosters crow at dawn? Has it been scheduled?"

"You're lucky, the circuit judge will be here a week from Saturday, but he doesn't hold court until Monday. Does doc think the boy will be able to give testimony by then?"

JT swallowed hard, "Too early to tell. For now, the doc is keeping him sedated. If you need me, I'll be watching over my son."

The doctor took Billy off sedation on the third day because of possible addiction. JT thought his heart had taken all the blows it could handle, but watching Billy in constant pain twisted him in knots. He ordered himself to stay strong. Billy needed JT to remain strong despite wanting to curl into a fetal position. Relief remained elusive no matter which position he lay in.

Billy cried while holding JT's hand in a vice-like grip. Then delirium set in, and he called out to Carrie morning, noon, and night. On the seventh day, JT begged the doc to sedate him again. He bear-hugged the doctor when Billy calmed down and soon fell asleep. The doctor's wife made a pallet for him beside Billy's bed and insisted that he sleep while Billy slept. He didn't even remember lying down.

***

The morning of the trial arrived. JT and the doctor pronounced Billy could not attend the trial. The judge ruled the court would go to the doctor's office to receive the vital testimony.

Sheriff Flanagan came yesterday to take Billy's statement for the trial. That's when JT learned Stanton had been one of Leticia's marks. Not surprisingly, Stanton was known to Billy as Judge Edgar Pullman, who was angry over the $20,000 train robbery money that Leticia bilked from him. When Billy told him Leticia had died, he went berserk, and the torture began. Billy had to testify to all his injuries at Stanton's hands. He'd never been prouder of anyone more than he was of Billy taking the stand and telling his story while looking straight at his offender unflinchingly while never leaving his bed. Finally, the judge asked Billy if he could show his wounds to the jury. JT, knowing he couldn't do that alone, went to Billy's bedside and lifted the sheet carefully, pointing out the injuries. Some jury members shook their heads while others blanched and pulled out handkerchiefs.

The judge thanked Billy for his testimony. Then it was JT's turn as a witness.

Stanton's attorney asked, "In your statement to the court, you claim you recognized the defendant as one of the murderers of your father ten years ago. Is that correct?

"Yes."

"My client claims he's never met you and has no idea who your father was. Can you explain that?

"Yes, my father was the town drunk in New Braunfels, Texas, for years. If he didn't come home by dark, my mother would send me out to bring him home. In June 1850, at fifteen years old, I went to town to look for him. He wasn't at any of his favorite spots. I returned to the saloon to see if he was begging for drinks. Then, I heard a fight going on down the alley. One lit lamp stood near the chaos at the far end of the alley, but my end lay in darkness. I flattened against the wall and inched my way closer and closer. I hid behind the second-story staircase. Then I saw four drunk strangers beating and kicking my father. My father was drunker than they were and unable to defend himself. I didn't see a way to help him without getting stomped, so I memorized their faces and as much about them as possible." JT paused to swallow. "Look how big Stanton is, and he kicked my father's head in. He wore shotgun chaps, old, square-toed boots, and a blue chambray shirt. The defendant also wore a red bandana with a green jeweled gold-colored clip. He wore a white hat with a horsehair band. Oh, and rock grinder rowels on his spurs. I can see why he doesn't remember me, but I sure do remember him."

The court chuckled. The judge demanded silence.

Stanton's attorney rested his case. The attorney for the prosecution stood up and calmly walked to the jury.

"Gentlemen, you heard Mr. Grant's description of his father's murder from memory. When arrested, I would like you to see those items in the defendant's possession.

The attorney pulled a gold clip featuring a green jewel from his pocket and gave it to the closest jury member. "This gold clip with a green jewel was found in Mr. Stanton's suitcase." Next, the attorney fished around in another pocket and pulled out a horsehair band. "This hat band was found on Mr. Stanton's black hat, not a white one." Then the attorney returned to the prosecution table and pulled a pair of spurs from his briefcase, "And these, gentlemen, are a pair of spurs with rock grinder rowels found on Mr. Stanton's boots."

Stanton said, "You can't tell they are rock grinders from that distance."

The judge admonished Stanton and then asked JT to answer the question.

JT looked Stanton in the eyes, "because they had a long shaft and the rowel marks left on my father's face."

The tension in the courtroom reached its peak as the jury announced their verdict, finding Stanton guilty of his heinous crimes. The sound of cheers and applause filled the space, the sense of justice served palpable in the air. The judge, with a stern voice, sentenced Stanton to life in prison, ensuring he would never harm another innocent person again.

As the commotion settled down and the courtroom began to clear out, JT made his way past Stanton, who was now being handcuffed by the officers. JT's voice was low and menacing as he spoke to the convicted criminal, "You remember now, don't you." His eyes glinted with satisfaction as he watched Stanton growl in frustration.

Back at the doctor's office, JT found Billy in bed.

"Dey gonna toss dat scum in a seventy-five foot well and seal it with hellfire?" Billy asked with enthusiasm.

JT beamed back at him, pleased to hear the old Billy again, "Did they ever? He got life."

Billy smiled; some of the scabs on his face cracked, but he didn't seem to care. "Doc, when's my parole? I wanna go home."

Chapter Twenty

August 20, 1860, New Orleans, Louisiana

New Orleans played tricks on Carrie's mind. It was a rare and exciting culture that allowed liberties you couldn't experience anywhere else. Last night, she ordered gumbo for dinner. The taste of creole spices was a new sensation for her, spicy hot with shrimp.

However, she had to down a glass of milk afterward. She had never seen a shrimp before, let alone eaten it. It was delicious. She planned to order another creole dish that same night because she might never return there again.

As she set foot on the streets of this bustling city, a wave of excitement and curiosity washed over her. The people, with their unique creole accent, spoke in a way that was foreign to her ears, yet strangely charming. Some even spoke in a smooth and elegant French, which added a touch of romanticism to the air.

The atmosphere was alive with the scent of exotic foods and the sounds of lively entertainment. Everywhere she turned, there were musicians playing in the streets, and people dancing and revelling in the festive mood. It was a scene that she had only read about in novels, but now it was all happening right before her eyes.

The architecture of the city was also something to behold. Each building had its own distinctive style, with ornate balconies jutting out from every floor. It was a sight to see, as the people above conversed with the pedestrians below, creating a lively and intimate atmosphere.

The locals were also friendly and welcoming, eager to share their customs and traditions with the curious outsider. She was delighted by the quaint custom of having beaded necklaces hung around her neck, a symbol of their warm hospitality.

It was a stark contrast to the city of Columbus, which she had left behind. Here, she felt alive and free, immersed in a world of new experiences and discoveries. Despite the city's location in the southern part of the country, she was tempted to stay and she might perhaps have stayed had it not been for Ruth or her children who were waiting for her in California.

As she disembarked from the riverboat, two young boys with ebony skin and bright smiles eagerly offered to carry her belongings to the Chateau Le Moyne. With a grateful nod, she watched as the boys deftly lifted her luggage as if it weighed nothing at all. After entering, she tipped them, knowing someone would take it them from them if she did it in public.

Upon entering the chateau, she was met with a stunning sight. The opulent hotel room was a far cry from the modest lodgings she was accustomed to. The drapes, bedspread, and pillows exuded an unmistakable air of luxury, with their smooth and silky texture hinting at the finest satin.

Though the price tag for this lavish accommodation was more than she had initially intended to spend, she rationalized that the safety of her hard-earned money was of utmost importance. After all, she had heard tales of opportunistic thieves lurking in the shadows, ready to pounce on unsuspecting travelers. No, it was much wiser to entrust her funds to the chateau's secure vault, even if it meant a few extra coins spent.

Tomorrow, she would board a steamship headed for Port Lavaca and then take another steamship to San Antonio. JT's ranch was twenty miles further, and she would have to hire someone to take her overland. But right now, all she wanted to do was slide into that opulent bed and enjoy a decent night's sleep, knowing the money was safe.

***

A knock at the door woke her at an ungodly hour. Who could that be? Couldn't they tell by the lack of light under the door that she had gone to bed? The knock came again.

"Wait, for goodness' sake." She pulled a wrapper on and donned socks. Carry placed the Colt in her wrapper pocket to avoid being caught unaware. At the door, she asked, "Who is it?"

"It's Benjamin Stein."

The name sounded familiar, but she couldn't place it. "When and where did we meet before?"

Carrie heard him sigh. "I made the diamond ring your husband commissioned." Her hand closed around the diamond ring as it hung from her neck. She removed it and put it in the wrapper pocket. Did he come all this way to recover a paid-off diamond ring?

Confused but curious, she opened the door, "Did you follow me from Columbus?"

"Yes, of course I did. But I started two weeks after you left Columbus. I want to talk to you about the diamond ring. I've come to purchase it back from you." He replied straightforwardly.

"Why?"

He shifted his weight and sighed again. "I must have it because you said you would sell it. It's the most intricate and beautiful ring I've ever created. My heart sank when you didn't fall in love with it on the spot. So, I want it back. I'll pay you." He explained.

Carrie wondered how she would sell the bauble if she needed the money, but she knew the jeweler would offer half the ring's value, if not one-fourth. She still had the same problem back in Columbus; what was it worth? But, of course, she doesn't need it now that JT has given her enough money to reach the ranch. But there's no way she will dwindle her finances either. And he can't be trusted.

"I'm not interested in selling it. I changed my mind about it."

"But I've come all this way to buy it." His face flushed, and he clamped his jaw shut. He reached past her, pushed the door open, then stepped inside to close the door behind him.

Carrie's heart pounded in her chest as she stood face to face with Mr. Stein, her hand clutching the Colt tightly while the other hand tightly gripped the diamond ring in her pocket. "Who do you think you are, busting in here?" she spat, her voice shaking with anger.

Without warning, Mr. Stein's hand shot out and connected with her cheek in a vicious slap. Carrie stumbled backward, her vision swimming as she tried to regain her balance. Her cheek throbbed with pain, and she tasted blood in her mouth.

Gasping for breath, she struggled to her feet, her hand still tightly wrapped around the Colt and the other gripping her cheek which stung.

"Remember, I said I didn't care for you back in Columbus, and I hated that husband of yours even more. I'll take no slack from you. Give it to me. Where is it?" Mr. Stein snarled, his face contorted with blind rage.

Carrie knew she had to play it smart. There was no way she would hand the ring over to this man. She was done being beaten up by these entitled men. In a split-second decision, she said, "It's in the vault downstairs." Which was where she should have placed the ring in the first place.

But her words only seemed to anger Mr. Stein further. With lightning speed, he drew a pistol from behind him and pointed it at her. Before she could even react, he had grabbed her by the lapels of her wrapper, hauling her roughly to her feet. "Well, now get dressed to liberate my life's work," he growled, his breath hot on her face reeking of cigars and alcohol.

As he slapped her once again, Carrie's rage boiled over. In a sudden burst of both anger and determination, she pulled the Colt out and pulled the trigger. The sound of the gunshot echoed through the room as the crook stumbled backwards, his grip on her loosening as he fell to the floor, his face etched with shock and horror.

Carrie did not react. He tried to get up but in a split second he lost consciousness and thudded to the ground. Carrie leapt over his body and ran down the stairs, her heart pounding with adrenaline. She screamed for help, her voice echoing through the corridors of the hotel as she sprinted towards the lobby.

As she burst through the doors, she was met by the hotel manager, who had been alerted by the noise coming from her room. Breathless and shaken, she recounted the events that had just transpired, her voice trembled with emotion.

"Get the sheriff. I shot an intruder in my room upstairs. Hurry." She said.

The manager dispatched a runner to fetch the sheriff. "Are you all right, madam? It looks like he hit you with something."

"His hand was enough to stiffen my spine, and I plugged him." spat Carrie.

Carrie pulled the fist holding the diamond ring out and, taking the manager's hand, pushed the ring into his palm and closed it for him. "He was after this. Please put it in the vault for me, will you?"

"Of course, madam, as soon as the authorities arrive, I'll take care of it. He slid the ring into his breast pocket. He led her to a couch near the stairs. He called out to another boy, "Bring me a blanket for Mrs. Wagner." She forgot she was in a nightgown and wrapper.

Her heart still raced, feeding heaving lungs. She trembled and wrapped her arms around herself, realizing she still had the pistol, and slid it back into the wrapper pocket.

A doctor entered the hotel doors and asked the manager where the injured man lay. Then the sheriff showed up and walked straight toward her.

Carrie stood, but he motioned for her to sit again. Then, he tipped his hat and said, "Ma'am, what happened?"

"Mr. Benjamin Stein, who broke into my room, came to rob and beat me. He followed me here from Columbus, Ohio." Explained Carrie.

"Why would he do that?" asked the Sheriff, clearly astonished by the bizarre story.

"You won't believe me, but he made a diamond ring for me that my husband commissioned, and I didn't respond to the gift with the right amount of awe as he expected. And he wanted it back." grimaced Carrie.

"Lady, you expect me to fall for that story? I wasn't born yesterday and had been sheriffing since before you were born." asked the Sheriff incredulously.

A guest came dashing down the stairs and informed the sheriff the man who got shot was still alive.

The manager spoke up, taking the ring from his breast pocket to show the sheriff. "This is the ring the man wanted." He flashed it to the sheriff and tucked it in his pocket.

The sheriff said, "Let's go back to that room and sort this all out, ma'am." He motioned for her to proceed with him. The manager offered his arm. She still trembled, and the manager covered her hand with his to steady her.

When they arrived at the room again, the sheriff wasted no time entering the room or questioning the suspect. "What's your story, mister?" He nudged Mr. Stein's arm to gain his attention.

Carrie noticed she had plugged him in his side and felt not one sliver of regret. She's in the wild west now, and a woman must know how to care for herself. She'd do it again in the same circumstance. JT's lectures on safety had sunk in, and she answered the door armed.

"The bitch shot me. I wanted to purchase my ring back. That's all."

The sheriff shook his head, "So you thought roughing her up and trying to rob her made your actions acceptable." The sheriff turned toward Carrie, "Ma'am, do you want to press charges?"

"Of course, I do. I'm not going to let you release the toad. But how long is this going to delay my travel? The good Lord has decided I'm not getting anywhere on time." sighed a frustrated Carrie.

"I guess about a week's delay because this case will go before a judge and jury, but we have a permanent judge." explained the sheriff.

Carrie watched as the helpers arrived to carry Mr. Stein off to jail, her heart still raced with adrenaline. The sheriff and doctor both wished her a good evening before rushing off, leaving her alone with the hotel manager.

He looked at her with concern, his eyes flickering to her trembling hand. "Are you alright?" he asked gently. "That must have been a harrowing experience."

Carrie nodded, her breath still coming in short gasps. "I'll be okay," she said, her voice shaking slightly. "But I could use a drink."

The manager's face softened with understanding. "Of course," he said, his tone sympathetic. "May I offer you a hot cocoa? It's a soothing drink that might help you sleep."

Carrie shook her head, a fierce determination in her eyes. "Thanks, but I need a brandy," she said firmly.

He smiled, "Cognac or schnaps? On the house, of course."

<u>Isaiah 40.29</u> *He giveth power to the faint; and to them that have no might he increaseth strength.*

September 12, 1860, The Plantation

The long journey to JT's ranch in New Braunfels, Texas, took its toll. Exhausted, Carrie felt like she'd been the victim of a five-mile stampede. Texas weather had one setting: fire pit. Her winter trousseau trapped moisture against her skin, causing chafing and thirst only satisfied by downing copious amounts of water daily.

Armadillos, fire ants, and scorpions scampered across her path every chance they got, and she screamed every time one of those green anole lizards ran near or on her. The snake population must outnumber humans in this state. She figured there were more snakes here than in the rest of the country combined. Her skin constantly crawled. Everything in Texas wanted to find something to kill.

About half of the population only spoke Spanish, meaning she was clueless most of the time. And everyone Mexican and American are Texicans, except for yours truly. Does anyone feel welcome here in the lone star state besides the natives?

She looked forward to meeting JT's brothers, or The Boys, as he calls them. One or both of them might look or act just like JT. Maybe that will help keep loneliness at bay.

Down to the last leg of the trip, she arranged passage from San Antonio to New Braunfels. The closer she got to New Braunfels; the crop yields looked downright profitable. There were cattle ranches, too. Next, she saw darkies wearing rags at work picking cotton. Their bodies glistened with sweat. They weren't employees; they were enslaved! Carrie turned away in horror. Oh, dear Lord, grant them strength and mercy.

Upon arrival in New Braunfels, she hired a carriage to complete the last leg to the ranch. So many people spoke German here, which made sense once she stopped and thought about the history JT shared. A German prince donated all this good land to these people and only required ten percent profit annually.

Today, after sixteen years, will Carrie's dream come true, or will the nightmares continue for eternity? Stockpiles of internalized rage tasted rancid on her tongue, held back by clenched teeth. This day would also allow Aunt Tildy, if she were her mother, a chance to reinforce Carrie's invisibility. What if Tildy was ashamed of her for some reason? Or did circumstances control Aunt Tildy's decision-making? Why didn't she return like Carrie dreamed and perform the great rescue?

A little while later, the driver announced their arrival. "Here we are, ma'am--the Grant Plantation.

What does he mean by plantation? But she would not ask a stranger about the grant's business.

Ted, the driver, turned the wagon down the main road toward the house, and Carrie looked out in amazement. This couldn't be right - JT had never mentioned anything about a Southern mansion or how big it was.

The long road led to a grand, white house in the middle distance. The sun glinted off the windows, and a beautiful emerald lawn stretched out in front of the house, bordered by neatly trimmed bushes that lined the entrance road. As they approached, Carrie could see the elegant architecture of the mansion, with its stately columns and grand entrance.

On the right side of the large porch stood a vast shade tree. Its branches stretched out like open arms, providing refuge from the heat of the day. The tree was a magnificent specimen, with a thick trunk and lush green leaves that rustled in the light breeze.

As they drew closer, Carrie could make out the details of the house more clearly - the large windows, the two chimneys rising from the roof, and the intricate mouldings that decorated the eaves. It was a sight to behold, a mansion that beat any shack on the Nebraska plains any day.

As the wagon rolled up to the front of the house, a beautiful middle-aged woman with chestnut hair to match Carrie's exited the opulent wooden entrance to greet the visitors. Carrie spotted the streak of grey hair woven into Aunt Tildy's hairdo covered with a net. Women in the south wore nets in their hair to keep it off their necks in the heat. She was petite, fine-boned, and had the same gray-haired birthmark as Carrie's. She found her long-lost mother and struggled to maintain composure. There are explanations to be shared and perhaps blame that would keep them apart.

"Good afternoon, Ted; it's sweltering. Would you and your guest like to come in for refreshments?"

"No, thanks, Tildy. She isn't my guest; she's yours." Ted jumped down to help Carrie out of the wagon.

Tildy's eyes lept to Carrie's face, and her facial features softened in recognition of the gray streak in Carrie's hair. "Oh my God, is it you, Carrie? My Carrie, my baby." With glistening eyes and extended arms,

Tildy's welcome tempted a complete reconciliation from Carrie, but the betrayal and a broken heart kept her seated in the wagon.

"Yes, I'm Carrie. Could we go inside to talk, please?" Her mother's smile disappeared, replaced by flat eyebrows and a clamped jaw.

Carrie turned toward the driver, "Thank you, sir, for your kindness."

He asked where the luggage should go.

Aunt Tildy spoke up, "Leave them here. The boys can bring them to the house when they come from the fields. Thank you for bringing Carrie out to me."

Carrie headed toward the house and heard steps following close behind. She's finally about to face her nemesis after all these years and experiencing equal measures of nausea and anger.

Nevertheless, she received a warm greeting. Why? Seeing her face, the gray streak and Aunt Tildy's prompt recognition erased all doubt. She had finally found her mother.

Carrie's mother stepped ahead, opened the door, and waited for Carrie to enter. Carrie removed her bonnet and gloves, leaving them on a side table. Then, momentarily stunned, she stared at the face of her betrayer. A face she resembled almost precisely. How dare she call her my baby?

"Carrie, dear, please sit in the parlor, and I'll see about refreshments." Tildy left the room.

She took this opportunity to acquaint herself with the house. It was more like a mansion built not too long ago. JT never mentioned the place. She didn't know why not; anyone would be stunned by the opulence. The rooms were large, wallpapered, with drape-covered windows. The wooden floors sparkled as if a layer of glass covered them. JT said the family existed by modest means. That's why they moved in with Aunt Tildy. She touched the wallpaper because she had never witnessed such perfection. It's not wallpaper at all. It appeared to be material interwoven with golden threads. The furniture that enhanced the grand home surprised her as well. JT never mentioned they were rich. Quite the opposite. She believed JT's father died near his fifteenth birthday if memory serves correctly. Maybe it was Aunt Tildy's money. Could that be why JT wants to marry and stay in Texas? Aunt Tildy's money might someday become Carrie's money.

Tildy returned with a silver tea tray, which she placed on a table before the golden brocade Victorian settee. "Carrie, come sit here and have some tea. Tell me what you've come to say. You came a long way to say it." She poured tea into a cup, then asked Carrie, "Sugar or milk?"

Carrie took a seat and replied, "Milk, please." Tildy handed her the cup and saucer with a spoon. Then she sat back with her cup of tea, waiting for Carrie to speak.

"Very well, I came to find out why you abandoned me?" Carrie's voice sounded rushed and high-pitched. Darn, she shouldn't have blurted it out like a knife to Tildy's throat. She continued. "How could you have decided one child must go and keep the other?" A chill ran down Carrie's spine, and she rubbed her arms to warm up. Amber eyes roamed the room, looking at everything except Tildy. "What did I do wrong?" Are you sure you want to know? Trembling, she added, "Don't lie to me." Her tears flowed as she dug into her purse for a handkerchief. "Why did you hate me so much?" If you love your child, you don't toss them aside. Sobbing, Carrie's handkerchief covered her face. Then she heard Tildy leave her chair and felt the cushions give as she sat beside her on the settee. Close enough to render a sharp slap to the face, she supposed. Maybe she deserved to be slapped for not pausing and letting Tildy get a word in sideways.

Tildy asked, "Is that everything you wanted to say? I want you to have your say before explaining to you what happened. Otherwise, you won't listen." Tildy took a sip of tea and placed the cup and saucer on the tray.

Carrie's hands lowered to her lap, and she gaped at Tildy. "If there's an explanation, I would love to hear it."

"I'll tell you the whole story. Then you can decide how it suits you. Our story begins in Germany. Your father and I qualified to receive a grant for land in America. The poor do not have opportunities to own land in Germany. The same families owned the land there for centuries. So, we were happy to pack up our small family and build a new place. We arrived at the docks two days before the ship would sail. Your father went to the dock to load our property on board. But Jacob got caught under a commercial wagon loaded with goods bound for Texas and died within the hour. I arrived there too late to say goodbye." Now mother's tears threatened. Carrie denied a strong urge to hold onto Tildy's hand.

"You mean that neanderthal sitting in the wagon that day was not my father! Oh, thank God." But Mother didn't smile. Carrie washed a stubborn grin from her insensitive face. When she thought about the story from her mother's point of view, there was a good reason for sorrow. She had lost the man she loved, Carrie's birth father. Giving in, she took Tildy's hand, "I'm sorry for your loss and for interrupting. Please go on."

"They disqualified you children and me from sailing without your father. So, I went to the pub the next day and auctioned myself off. The highest bidder marries me and sails to America to build a new home and raise crops. A woman alone with land usually doesn't stay single for long. And I guessed right. Heir Ackermann did save me from being stranded in Germany where we would have starved."

Carrie suddenly realized her mother had been in a horribly desperate spot. She admired the bravery and courage it took to stick to the family's goal while doubting she would have done the same.

"The winner and I married that day, and we sailed for America the next. I did not tell him beforehand that I had two children. I rushed the two of you onto the ship before boarding with him. He was angry and didn't want someone else's children, especially a girl who couldn't do a hard day's work in the field like a boy. He told you to call him father. Grief-stricken at the loss of your father, picking out a man to replace him within twenty-four hours was nothing but pure desperation."

And Carrie thought she had tough choices to make during the last year.

"On the voyage, Eduard became ill with Scarlet Fever. So, he needed to be isolated from the other passengers. The ship, scheduled to dock in New Orleans, docked in New York instead, and the Captain forced us off. Herr Ackermann became livid. We had already paid for our passage to New Orleans, but now we had to buy a wagon and supplies to finish the trip overland."

"When we got to Cincinnati, he made me leave you behind. He threatened to kill you. I feared he'd make me give up Eduard, too. I knew he would do it because he beat me often. The only solution I could think of was to leave you at an orphanage until I returned and got you. At least you'd have a roof over your head and three meals daily. Oh, Carrie, please forgive me."

"Oh, Mother, of course. But wait a minute. You planned to come back. Why didn't you?"

"I came back, but the orphanage in Cincinnati had burned down, and the children scattered to several orphanages. There were no records showing which child went where. So, I had no way of knowing where to find you."

"I vaguely remember a fire, and we moved once. Ruth and I ended up in Columbus. No one told you that?" Carrie said.

"What took you so long? I prayed you'd find the message in the Bible and come to me. I've been sick with worry." Said Aunt Tildy.

She loved and protected me.

Carrie crumbled inside after all the nasty things she had said to her mother. She saved her life. The years of living with betrayal melted away, and love filled her heart. "Because I never opened that German Bible once. JT saw the message and told me his Aunt Tildy might be my mother."

"JT? Oh, Justice. Do you know Justice?

"Mother, before we go any further, please give me that kiss and hug I foolishly ignored." Tildy wrapped Carrie in hugs and kisses all over her entire face. Whatever she had expected, this wasn't it. Hearing her mother's tears of joy sounded so strange at first, but the fears Carrie had harbored soon melted away. This reaction is not from a person who cruelly deserted their child. Something broke inside Carrie. Her stomach unwound from its familiar knot. After all these years, finding out there was a warm, loving reason for her separation from the family she had loved for the past sixteen years nearly brought Carrie to her knees. But the pain it had caused her mother closely cleaved her in two. Dear Lord, please help my mother in her grief. Amen.

She sensed it, felt it in her bones. The burden of betrayal she had nursed most of her life floated away. She harbored no doubt that her mother's story rang true. Love cures betrayal. Years spent stewing in an angry soup, only to find a rainbow at the end, pointed out there are two sides to every story. Something she taught the children at the orphanage but never personally enforced. She thanked God for the miracle and hugged her mother tightly. "Mother, I'm so sorry I arrived late. Please forgive my rudeness and delay."

"None of that matters now. You're here."

"It's impossible to tell you how much I love you." Said, Carrie. "Mother, where is Eduard? Away at school? I've missed him so."

Her mother clasped hands and lowered watery eyes. "I'm sorry, baby. Eduard died a year after I left you at the orphanage, and we buried him under the cottonwood tree out back. Herr Ackermann complained that Eduard cost him too much money on doctor's bills, and, of course, we were low on money because we had to pay our way to Texas. He forgot everything he had came from me.

Carrie watched as the blood drained from her mother's face. "Ackermann worked him to death, didn't he?" The liquidity of her anger pooled in her stomach, waiting for the answer.

With tears in her eyes, Mother said. "My Eduard was only three years old, but Heir Ackermann thought him old enough to do simple chores. Yes, I went out with Eduard to do the work for him. The doctor said his heart would always be weak and could not do strenuous work. Herr Ackermann would abuse me because the women's work fell behind."

The wick on her temper reached detonation. "No, Mother, I don't understand. Why didn't you save him instead of putting up with Herr Ackermann? He poisoned our family. He was your ticket to America. I understand that, but you didn't have to keep him. You

536

gave me away to save me. So why didn't you save Eduard?"

Her mother's eyes drooped. Then, after a minute—in a dull voice, Mother answered. "This is our first day together in many years. I know we have much to forgive each other for, but I will not tolerate your insolence. Understand?"

Carrie's turn to ponder for a minute thought better of the situation and spoke. "Yes, I understand."

"We got here late in the first year. We needed to send our ten percent of the profit quickly. I couldn't figure out how to get anything done without Herr Ackermann. I would have lost the granted land. We were lucky the prince accepted our reason for a low income the first year. She locked eyes with Carrie. "We could not come up short again. Eduard and I needed him to work the land."

"But Mother, couldn't you find somewhere safe for him?"

Carrie's mother stood and stomped her foot on the floor. "Charlotte Margarete Luisa Johanna Schubert! Do you think I didn't try? Texas, twenty years ago, did not have orphanages. Eduard had a weak heart, and no one else could care for him properly." She waved a finger under Carrie's nose. "I couldn't use one of the horses to take him to a doctor because we needed the horses to work the land. I couldn't ask another family to take him because they were struggling like us. Do you honestly think I don't love and miss my son as much as you do?"

Carrie broke down in tears, "I'm so sorry, Mother. Please forgive me." She hugged her mother.

They dabbed at each other's tears and tried to smile. "That was a long time ago. The man responsible is six feet under, entertaining the devil as he should be."

Carrie nearly choked, then laughed at her mother's dry humor. "Mother, was that my real name you rolled off your tongue a minute ago?"

"Of course, the same your father and I gave you at birth. Charlotte Margarete Luisa Johanna Schubert."

"Shubert? I wish I had known it."

"The caretaker wrote it down. I gave her your full name."

"No wonder you couldn't find me." Another mystery solved after all these years. But, of course,

Carrie wouldn't have been invisible at all if some caretaker hadn't neglected to pass on the information.

"Well, I think we need a change of topic. You mentioned Justice before. How do you know him?"

"I had a husband convicted of bank robbery and murder and hanged this past January. The man he supposedly murdered was a Pinkerton agent who happened to be JT's best friend, Hank Lipton. There were rumors that Philipp, my husband, had a female accomplice. After the hanging, I left Columbus for California, and JT assumed a false personality and followed me, presuming I must be the accomplice, which I wasn't."

"Good heavens, Carrie, how long were you married?"

"Only two weeks when he robbed the bank. The murder came later."

"Wait, you're here. Where is Justice?"

"When you call them by their full names, I laugh. JT said they all hated their names and went by JT, Roy, and Jud."

"JT can say whatever he wants, but his mother called them Justice, Royal, and Judge. So, I call them the same out of respect for their mother."

"Well, where JT is--is a very long story that has my nerves shredded to the snapping point. He's tracking down the man who kidnapped Billy, my adopted son. I'm worried sick about them both."

"Do I correctly sense a romantic relationship between JT and you?"

"Yes, we want to marry, but there's no way it will work."

"Well, young lady, now you have to start at the beginning and tell me everything. Then, maybe I can help."

"I can't tell up from down anymore. I've broken promises, failed as a mother, and can't marry the man I love."

"Tell me already."

After Philipp's conviction, Ruth and I, my best friend from the orphanage, made plans to start over someplace far from Columbus, Ohio, because of the scandal. We chose California and adopted two little girls from the orphanage."

"There are more children? Oh, Carrie, I can't wait to meet them."

"We can talk more about them later. Ruth and the children left for California last January on a wagon train. I had to stay for the hanging and work my way west. I promised Ruth and the children I'd be there by November. I've blown that deadline. Ruth had enough money for a down payment on a mortgage on the land and to build a house, but that's if everything went to plan. What if they go into winter insufficiently prepared? We shouldn't have decided on California. The trail is fraught with danger and hardship, and I sent them out with a hired stranger to guide them. To catch up on lost time, I'd have to take a ship around the horn, and even that is a journey of several months." Carrie paused to sip tea.

"Oh, I have a better idea than that. You can buy passage on the U.S. Mail steamer down on the Gulf coast. It takes you to Panama, where you can board a train to the Pacific coast and buy passage on another U.S. Mail steamer to San Francisco. The whole trip is three weeks, but costly."

Elated at the prospect, Carrie asked, "Mother? How exciting. How much is it?"

"The last time I checked, it was $300 a person."

Crestfallen again, "Good heavens, that is expensive; I can't afford that."

"Don't worry about that now; I have money. JT's got money. The big question is may I go with you?" she asked tentatively.

Carrie blinked at her mother, taken aback, "Yes, of course, you can; I'd love it if you came with me. And come to think of it, I have JT's money. But isn't this ranch yours?"

"It's only half mine. The Grant boys own the other half. Maybe I'll sell my half or give it to them." She sighed.

"You sound eager to leave."

"Your arrival today is the answer to many of my prayers. And I thank the Lord you arrived. I can't wait to leave here."

"Goodness, mother, why?"

"Come with me; I want to show you something."

Walking through a hallway to the back of the house, Tildy pointed outside the window. Carrie's eyes followed. The field lay a fair distance from the home, but a cotton field with enslaved people hard at work was apparent to the naked eye. Like the poor unfortunates she had witnessed on her way to New Braunfels, these people toiled under the hot Texas sun. Their clothes weren't in tatters, but sweat rolled down their bodies. She looked away, ashamed. Cotton picking is why her driver called the ranch a plantation.

"That's why I want to leave. After JT left us for Chicago, things gradually got worse, and we might have lost the ranch. The boys grew cotton instead of ranching and sold what cattle we had left to buy other people to do the work for them. Since then, they have made money on the backs of others. Quite a lot of money. Nowadays, I stay in the house."

"But you own half, and they own a third. JT won't be happy with this turn of events."

"Yes, I know, but they are men, and I am an old woman. I'm glad to hear JT doesn't support slavery."

"But mother, this is not good news for our romance." Sighed Carrie.

"What do you mean?"

"I told him I can't marry him because I previously committed to Ruth and the children."

"Why is that a problem?"

"JT doesn't like children and is a Texican through and through. He's already told me he won't give up his ranch to accompany me. Instead, he wants me to send for my family and live here. But I can't do that because Ruth is a darkie with freedom papers."

Her mother's hand shot to her mouth, "Oh, my, I can't believe Justice said that. And Ruth is watching over the children. We do need to get there as soon as possible."

"I agree JT doesn't believe war is coming and thinks Ruth will be perfectly safe in Texas. He's a hardheaded man and accuses me of the same. When he arrives and discovers the situation, his primary concern will be to save his ranch from his brothers. Romance will be the last thing on his mind. He'll probably need your support to oust them."

"Are you sure the two of you are in love?"

Carrie laughed, "He gave me all his money. I took that to mean he loves and trusts me. Wait until he's in the same room as me; you'll have no doubt. And he's the same man who found your message in the Bible and thought his Aunt Tildy might be my mother."

"Yes, bless him for that."

"And another complication, Billy, the boy I adopted, turned out to be the son of the woman who murdered Hank Lipton, JT's best friend. When JT put all those links together, he figured Hank would want him to raise Billy. He didn't discuss it with me. Instead, he announced it one morning at breakfast like the new Sheriff in town. Billy informed JT that he and I had already made an adoption decision, and whether JT fit into the picture was to be determined.

"Let's return to the parlor for some fresh tea, and maybe we can snack on something.

Carrie followed her mother to the kitchen. Then they returned to the settee in the parlor.

"What happened after Billy said he wanted to go to California with you?"

"Soon after that, a Marshall kidnapped Billy off the riverboat, and JT promised to find him for me, and he won't return until he does. So now I wait until JT and Billy show up. What if they don't come back? What if the Marshall sent Billy to prison? It's my fault; I didn't keep track of him on the riverboat. I'm a horrible mother. I hadn't seen him for hours, but I wasn't worried. Why wasn't I worried about him? Every mother is supposed to protect their children from harm, and my child disappeared from under my nose."

"Shush, my darling, no woman is born a childcare expert. My record is pretty flawed. Why would a Marshall send Billy to prison?"

"His mother was a thief, fancy woman, and murderer and taught him how to be a small-time criminal. And she snuck into my hotel room and sat on my broken wrist. She pulled a gun on me because she thought I had the bank robbery money and wanted it back. Then she bashed Billy on the head with the barrel of her gun. I shot Leticia Brown in the heart."

"Oh, Carrie, stop. My frazzled nerves can't take much more. "Carrie draped an arm around her mother.

"Since I left Columbus in January, my life has consisted of one catastrophe after another. I haven't slept on a peaceful day the entire time. A reckoning is coming, mother; I feel it in my bones. I'm expecting a devastating heartbreak, but which will it be? Maybe JT and Billy won't ever come home. Or if they do, will JT choose his ranch over me? If so, my heart will shatter.

"Carrie, have you learned anything today?"

"What do you mean?"

"Don't prejudge the man. For one thing, he's got a lot on his mind. Marriage is a much more serious decision for men. A mountain of responsibility comes with it—especially marriage to you. You're forcing him to make tough decisions. If he loves you, he must also love your previous life choices."

Carrie! You have three children, and the law may want one of them! Do you know how crazy you sound asking a cattleman to give up his Texas ranch? And there's no time for him to problem-solve his love life while trying to save your son. Sweetheart, in Justice's shoes, I'm afraid I'd walk away if I had to make the same decision." Mother laid her hand over Carrie's and gently squeezed.

Carrie flashed a weak smile. "So, this is what it's like to have a real parent?" Receiving advice that burns a bit while going down but sounds logical. She faded into the gold brocade, reminding herself she had prayed for a mother going on seventeen years. Suddenly tired and overwhelmingly hot, Carrie tried to push up her woolen cuffs.

"My goodness, girl. Now that I notice, what in the world are you wearing? You look done in. Upstairs with you, young lady, get those clothes off and rest. I'll send you lemonade to help you cool off and a bath." Said, Mother. "I think you will fit in something of mine until we can get to town and buy you some decent clothing before you suffocate."

Thank you, Lord, for the gift of undying love from a parent.

Exodus 20:12 *"Honor your father and your mother, that your days may be long upon the land which the Lord your God is giving you."*

Chapter Twenty-One

October 26, 1860, Waiting in Texas

The days seemed to drag by, and still no JT or Billy. It's been two weeks. What's taking so long? Maybe JT can't find Stanton. No, JT will find him. Is one of them injured?

Mother decided to start packing. Whatever Justice agreed to, she still packed, going to California with Carrie. So, mother and Carrie packed clothing, bed linens, blankets, and tablecloths. Then Tildy pulled a box from under the bed and opened it, and tears fell.

"What is it, Mother?" Carrie asked, noticing the sadness etched on Tildy's face as she held the box.

Tildy took a deep breath and reached into the box, pulling out a tiny sailor boy outfit. She clutched it close to her heart. Carrie watched as her mother ran her fingers over the delicate fabric, her eyes filled with tears.

"What's in this box is all I have left of my baby boy," Mother whispered, her voice cracking with emotion.

Carrie gently reached out and spread both palms across the folded clothes in the box, taking in the small size of the outfit. It was clear that Eduard had never had the chance to live his life.

Battling tears herself, Carrie said firmly, "We're not leaving this behind. Eduard's memory goes where we go."

Mother nodded as she refolded the sailor suit and placed it back in the box, her face softening with gratitude for her daughter, "Thank you, Carrie."

"Nonsense, I miss him almost as much as you do," Carrie remembered Little Ed. "Wait, Mother. I have something to show you."

Carrie dashed down the hall to retrieve Little Ed and returned at lightning speed. "Look, Mother. This is Little Ed. Ruth made him for me soon after I arrived at the orphanage. I cried for you and Eduard every night. Ruth made him for me to hug at night and not feel alone. But, of course, she slept with me, too."

"Oh my, Carrie, what a beautiful gift from your friend. She sounds like the perfect friend for you."

"She is." Carrie handed the doll to her mother.

Mother brushed the hair out of his eyes, "Do you mind if I hug him for a while?"

"I'd be insulted if you didn't."

They shared a giggle.

"Would you mind if I dressed Little Ed in Eduard's sailor suit?

"What a great idea. Yes, dress him in Eduard's sailor suit and hug him as much as you want." Carrie said.

After dressing Little Ed, Tildy said, "Let's take a break. We've been at this for a few hours. I think I'll lie down and take a little nap. "Mother climbed in bed with Little Ed in the crook of her arm.

Carrie kissed her mother's cheek and went to write Ruth a letter. It may not get there before she does, but Ruth must be worried by now. She wished everyone good health and advised Ruth they would arrive by U.S. Mail steamboat in San Francisco.

November 15, 1860, At Last

Time had stopped. Carrie no longer counted the days. She helped with the garden and the laundry as time passed to keep herself sane. She retrieved more clothespins and wiped the sweat from her forehead with a sleeve. The laundry will dry in this heat before she can put clothespins on it. Carrie, poised to stab a clothespin onto the sheet, heard hoofbeats and a horse whiny from the front of the house. Stabbing a couple more pins onto the sheet, she turned and ran to the house.

God, please let it be them.

Carrie pulled the back door open and raced to the front of the house. The front door hung open, and she ran out onto the porch. There they were, tying their horses, and mother stood with them.

"Oh my God, you're home. I thought you would never arrive." Carrie said.

JT rushed toward her, and she leaped into his arms, breathing in the aroma of horse, sweat, and manliness. Their lips locked together as if starved. His embrace soothed the worry away. Then she remembered Billy and pulled away from JT's hungry lips. "Thank you for bringing Billy home to me."

Carrie ran to Billy but saw his ravaged face, "What's happened to your face, Billy?" Trembling fingers traced the wound, then wrapped him in a hug.

"Carrie, ya squeezin' my guts too dang hard, cain't breathe."

She let go of him.

Billy asked, "Is Aunt Tildy your mother or not? We've been bustin' at the seams to know."

Carrie pulled her mother into the circle, "Mother, this is my adopted son, Billy. Billy, meet your new grandmother."

Billy hugged Tildy in immediate acceptance.

Mother smiled, "Welcome to the family. Call me grandma. And tell us please what happened to your face."

JT said, "Let's go inside and catch up with each other.

Once inside, JT took in the grandeur of the surroundings. Then, he turned toward Aunt Tildy and asked, "What happened to the house?"

Mother shook her head and said, "Your brothers will have to explain that to you, not me."

JT scratched his head.

Mother asked everyone to gather in the parlor, then she ordered refreshments and joined them.

"Who scarred you like this?" Carrie asked again as she cupped Billy's ravaged cheek.

Billy said, "That Marshall that throwed me off'n the riverboat. Well, he ain't no Marshall. That slut Lettie sank her claws into him two years ago, and he wanted the $20,000 she stole. I told 'em she died and left no money. He didn't believe me and tried to beat the answer out of me. Finally, JT showed up on time to save me. He's a good Pinkerton."

Carrie restrained herself from pinching Billy's earlobe. This new Billy seemed to have grown up in a few months. Dragging on his earlobe isn't appropriate anymore. "Oh, Billy, your sweet face. This is all my fault, and I'm so sorry."

JT pulled Carrie from the settee into a warm embrace, "Don't blame yourself; Stanton, a long-time murderer, and thief, did this to Billy, not you. And he's one of the four men who murdered my father."

"You were there?" Mother asked. "You never said a word about it."

"That's because I'm ashamed to admit I didn't try to help him," JT said. "But I shouldn't have accepted the blame. I'm not the one who killed my father, and Stanton was the one who did this to Billy's face. Not you, Carrie."

Carrie lifted Billy's hand to her lips, "Did you kill him, JT?"

"Didn't have to. The court sentenced him to life. That's why we were so late getting here."

"Yeah, and we waited for a spell for me to heal up," Billy said.

Simultaneously, a servant came from the kitchen carrying a tea tray, and JT's brothers walked into the house.

Carrie claimed a seat next to Billy on the settee and noticed JT staring at the darky woman as she set the tea tray down. The woman was dressed in plain Muslim material like an enslaved person, not like a servant. He looked as shocked as she expected, then looked up and around at his surroundings again. Then, walking up to the woman, he took her gently by the arm and asked her name.

"Ellie, Masser Grant."

JT took Ellie's arm into his as any gentleman would, but Eliie trembled nonetheless. "Hello, my name is JT. Please call me as such, and I'm not your master."

The brothers joined them in the parlor. Roy spoke first. "Well, look here, if it isn't the prodigal son, come home at last."

Jud stepped closer to JT and offered a hand, "Good to see you home again, JT."

JT shook his hand. "Thanks, I 've been looking forward to it."

Carrie's heart jumped to her throat. Oh no, he's happy to be here. Has that dreaded hurricane arrived?

Sizing his brothers up, JT asked, "Would one of you please explain to me what's happened here? At this ranch? With this servant? With this house?"

Roy adopted a nasty sneer, "What do you care what happens here? You got up and left ten years ago and left nothing but silence behind."

I think I like you, Roy.

"I told you when I left that I would earn the money to save the ranch. I had it three years ago, but my ex-wife robbed me blind, and I started over."

"Yet, we never heard a word of it. In ten years, you couldn't drop us a line, tell us you were alive, and inform us of your plans. We were up against the wall and had to think of something."

Gently holding Ellie's arm toward Roy and Jud, he said, "So you resorted to buying fellow human beings and, I suppose, planted cotton. How many slaves did you buy?"

Jud glanced at Roy and stepped out of the way.

"Yes, the ranch is a plantation, and we grow cotton. We have forty-two slaves. And we've become quite wealthy. No thanks to you." Roy scanned the house's interior with a sweep of his arm to indicate the apparent wealth surrounding them."

It's a plantation now. You don't want a plantation, do you, JT?

"I own one-sixth of this plantation. That means I own seven slaves, and I'm freeing them. Ellie, here is one. She will pick out six more for me."

Ellie fell to her knees, crying and thanking Jesus. JT helped her up. "Don't cry, Ellie. You can go now if you wish." She backed out of the room, probably concerned about what the other two Grant boys would do.

There's the man I love.

But JT wasn't finished with them yet, "You knew I went to Chicago to work as a Pinkerton. I said as much when I left. That's where I've been for the last ten years. You'd be surprised how many criminals and lowlifes needed to be brought to justice. So, I've been busy."

Roy grunted in reply.

"Roy, maybe you're right about me. I went to town the night our father was murdered and did nothing to save him. Four drunk cowboys kicked and beat him to death. I felt so guilty that I couldn't get far enough away from this ranch and couldn't bear to look my family in the face. Whenever I picked up paper and pencil to write home, I knew I should tell you all I witnessed, but I couldn't. I needed to forgive myself first."

Watching JT's passionate debate to regain the family ranch proved Carrie had been right. Their relationship was doomed from the start.

He's staying, and I must go.

Silent tears escaped down her cheeks as she decided whether to fight for what she wanted one last time or see the writing on the wall. She'd endured a long demanding journey and was quite tired of obstacles. But, no, the storm was here raging at full strength, demanding its due.

Carrie leaned toward Billy to kiss his unblemished cheek and told him she would finish packing now. Then she quietly left, seeking the privacy of her room. At the head of the stairs, she grabbed the newel post for support. The pattern on the wallpaper wiggled a bit. She made her way, keeping a hand on the wall, denying herself the luxury of fainting. What good is fainting going to do? When you wake, the intolerable issue that caused you to faint is still there to be solved. Besides, she could still hear the howling hurricane winds blow, tearing her dreams apart.

Roy spoke with venom. "So, you left us to struggle along as best we could. I didn't know big brothers did that. I will never forgive you."

He'll stay to patch it up with his brothers.

"Oh, I'm sorry, boys, this is Billy. Billy, my brothers Roy and Jud. And my fiancée is..."

Once inside, Carrie closed the door against the chaos and leaned her forehead against the door panel. But the storm remained. Not the petty fight over some Texas land below. This storm raged within. Part of her wanted to label him a betrayer and start stockpiling his faults. But she loved him, and she'll love him forever. He found her mother and saved her soul. How could she hate him? Bursting into sobs, she slid down the door into a miserable heap. There isn't another man like JT in the world. And she lost him and all their future children for whom she had prayed.

Please, God, give me strength.

Carrie heard a soft knocking at the door, "Carrie, sweetheart, please let us in."

Using the doorknob, she hauled herself up off the floor, "Who's with you, mother?"

"It's me, Carrie," Billy said.

Carrie opened the door just enough to allow them to enter and quickly closed it.

"I'm so sorry, baby," Mother pulled Carrie into her arms. "You're convinced he means to stay?"

"Oh, you"Oh, mother, doesn't it sound like it to you?" Carrie wiped the tears away. "I'm tired and want to leave for California to lick my wounds peacefully. I would like for us to leave tomorrow. As it is, this house will haunt me the rest of my days."

"Don't worry about this house. We both know the northern army will burn it to the ground someday."

Carrie couldn't hold back a laugh at her mother's remark. Having a mother is a blessed gift. No matter what happens, you are her top priority, and she still loves you even if you're wrong. Perhaps she's found the support to work through her heartbreak.

"Carrie, stop yore cryin'. If'n JT is the man for you, go brand him." Billy said.

Surprised, Carrie wiped her nose and turned toward Billy, "What do you mean brand him? In front of his brothers when I know he's staying?"

Billy shook his head, "Ya don't knowd that. Ya decided he's guilty without a trial."

"Carrie, listen to the boy. He knows JT as well as you and spent three or four months with him during a trying time. You can't assume something that affects the rest of your life. You have to find out for sure." Mother said.

"I'll make a fool of myself." Carrie debated.

"You're a fool if you don't fight for your man." Mother said.

Yes, she's exhausted. But Mother and Billy were right. If not for any other reason, she needs to do this for their future children in danger of never being born. Daughters who would wrap him around their little fingers. And sons who would stand shoulder to shoulder with him at work. Mother and Billy are dead right? She's no coward and won't slink away at night without a word. She needs JT's decision first, and then she'll plan.

Carrie enclosed Billy and Mother in a triangular hug and kissed them on the cheek. "Come to think of it, my days of sitting back and waiting for the next betrayal are over."

Carrie left the room smiling for their sake, but as soon as she crossed the threshold, she began planning her approach to JT. The noise from downstairs had diminished, but what was the outcome? Maybe she'll strike gold and find him alone. When she reached the head of the stairs, JT popped up in front of her as he reached the top. Almost treading on him, she stopped and said, "I need to talk to you."

He took her hand, "I'm looking for you, too. Let's go in here." He pulled Carrie through the closest bedroom door and locked them inside. JT's brows were drawn together when he faced her again, and he moved in close, keeping eye contact.

"Carrie, I need you to listen to me for a minute." He sounded worried.

"Alright, go ahead and say it." Here comes the turndown, so she steeled herself.

Gently rubbing her tears away with his thumbs, he said, "I'm sorry I got carried away downstairs. It shocked me when I saw Ellie. But now, it's time to talk about us. I love you." He curled her into his arms.

"I love you, too. But it's time for us to face reality. You love the ranch and want to stay, and I must leave as soon as possible for California. Do you agree?"

"No, it hasn't ended yet, Carrie. I won't let it. I have a proposition for you that I think you will love. Interested?"

Carrie turned away from his attempt at joking around, failing to see the humor. Even when she lost Philipp, her heart never felt this devastated. How will she ever overcome this pain? "Stop joking, JT. I'm not in the mood." He tightened an arm around her waist. She glanced at him only to find matching anguish.

"I didn't mean to joke. I love you, and I can't be parted from you ever. You're under my skin, making yourself all kinds of comfortable. I told Roy and Jud I'm selling my portion of the ranch to them and freeing my share of the enslaved people since I'll be going with my wife and family."

Carrie saw his lips moving but wasn't sure she understood him right. He smiled at her. "What did you say? Did you call me wife and say you're going to California?" Did she dare hope again? Can her wounded heart fly with joy now that her dreams have come true?"

"That's where you'll be, right? So, then that's where I'll be."

With her mouth agape in shock, she searched JT's handsome face for telltale signs of joking. He didn't break eye contact and smiled confidently. She laughed, then kissed him. Dozens of creamy white doves flew from her heart, declaring pure happiness to the world, encouraging her to kiss him how she had always wanted to. She had a reputation to protect but now could safely place her reputation in JT's hands without worry. She traced his lip with her tongue, hungry for his taste. And her empty arms flew around his neck with one hand buried in his hair. She loved those dark curls. One naughty leg curled around his, and familiar hands roamed between her waist and backside as she leaned into him.

He asked, "Will you marry me tomorrow at the courthouse? I can't wait long enough for a church wedding."

Carrie threw her head back, laughing, "Yes, my darling, yes, but we have to get married in a church when we get to California.

"Your neck is beautiful," he rained kisses from ear to shoulder.

"Please do that for the rest of my life."

"I promise, but I have something else we need to talk about."

Her feet found solid ground once more because he said but. There's a disclaimer that's going to break her heart. Nothing ever comes easy. She walked to the bed and sat down.

He sat next to her. "Don't be discouraged. I want to talk about Billy."

"What about him? Oh, you still want to adopt him?"

"Yes, I talked to him about it while we were away. We agreed if I ever made you cry again, all deals were off, and I promised him I wouldn't. Please approve. The two of you are the family of my heart."

Smiling, she asked, "And sir, what about the two little ones waiting for us in California?"

"We're going to need a lot of bedrooms, aren't we?"

Tears of happiness threatened to fall, "Yes, my love." Crawling into JT's lap, she kissed him, and he lifted her into his arms and stood.

"Let's go find your mother and Billy and tell them our good news."

As they approached the door, Carrie turned the knob, and they stepped into the corridor. Mother and Billy were standing outside. But JT hadn't seen them because he kissed her again.

"Ahem, JT, tell us what's happenin' before ya swaller her whole? Grandma and I have a stake in this game, too."

Mother kissed Billy on the cheek.

JT slowly pulled his lips away from hers. "But these lips are so sweet."

flatterer. Please put me down. I want to tell them the good news." Carrie said.

Her mother squealed.

"We're getting married tomorrow at the courthouse, and JT is adopting Billy afterward.

Billy hugged her, but mother asked, "When do we leave for California?"

"Yes, I'm late, and the children are waiting," Carrie said.

"Let's get our family on a solid foundation, then plan the trip west," JT said.

"You promised we're going to California. You're not lying, are you?"

"No, of course not. I have no use for a plantation or enslaved people except the seven I'm freeing. We can start planning the day after tomorrow if you like?"

"You can't free them in Texas. As soon as we leave, someone will sell them back into slavery again, so we need to free them in a non-slaveholding state."

"Justice, I told Carrie about a quick way to California, which might work for freeing the slaves too. The U.S. Mail steamboat accepts a few passengers on the Gulf waterway each trip. We can use that route to San Francisco and will be there in three weeks. And we can free the enslaved people in Mexico on the way."

JT's face lit up, "The railroad across Panama. That's a great idea."

"But JT, it's expensive. We can't afford to pay $300 per slave and set them free in Mexico. That's $2,100." Carrie said.

Her mother said, "The fare is $300 if you go to San Francisco. I don't know what it costs to go to Mexico, but it would be much less. We're not that far from the Mexican border."

"Carrie, don't worry about money. I collected the reward on Stanton's head. Would you believe he was worth $5,000, dead or alive?

Carrie nearly swooned, "We'll have enough money to enlarge the house." She bounced on the balls of her feet like a well-rewarded child.

Another knock sounded at the door. Carrie answered the door.

Jud stood there. "Pardon me, Miss Carrie, but could I speak to my brother briefly?"

"Of course, come in."

"What does he want now?" Asked JT.

"N-Nothing, JT. I wanted to ask if I could go with you. I hadn't cared for Roy's plans for a while but had nowhere else to go. Can I go with you if you plan to leave this place?"

JT offered a hand to his brother, Jud. And he shook it. "We can use another strong back and experienced hands where we're going."

"Where's that?"

"California boy, California. We will start from scratch and build a home for all of us. Carrie and I are getting married tomorrow morning, and I'm adopting Billy. Once my family is legally mine, we'll plan our move."

JT hugged her around the waist. "I hate to say this, but when my woman is right, she's right. After all this time, both the ranch and Roy changed. And you're probably right about a war coming, too. So, you better marry me to keep me on the straight and narrow."

Carrie's smile faded as she glared into her intended's eyes, "Billy, if he ever makes me cry again, shoot him."

Billy said, "First, da chaperone has to learn me to shoot."

Carrie retorted, "Don't worry, I can teach you myself."

"Then shoot me yourself," JT said. His arms closed around her as he planted another passionate kiss. She heard shuffling as the others in the hallway faded away. He's finally all hers and always will be. Her lifelong feeling of invisibility floated away like a dream. And love filled her heart to brimming over.

Deuteronomy 7:9 *"Therefore know that the Lord your God, He is God, the faithful God who keeps covenant and mercy for a thousand generations with those who love Him and keep His commandments.*

Chapter Twenty-Two

November 17, 1860, Wedding Day

The family gathered at the courtroom as morning dawned, their hearts bursting with joy and delight. Carrie looked exquisite, adorned in her mother's stunning German wedding gown, which was embellished with beige lace and beads that shimmered against the early morning light. The soft fabric accentuated her feminine beauty, while the elaborate beading added an aura of elegance and class.

Billy had woven bluebonnets and curls into her hair to form an exquisite floral crown that framed her face. The delicate tendrils cascaded down her back, whispering secrets to the gentle breeze as she glowed with a sense of freedom that arose from her very being.

The 17th of November would be hailed as the happiest day of her life. Her heart's overflowing delight pulled her lips into a wide smile that lit up the world around her. She felt like she walked on air, her steps light and carefree, as if dancing to the beat of her own heart. And she knew right then that she was ready to embark on a new journey filled with nothing but love.

As the carriage came to a halt in front of the courthouse, JT's eyes were fixed on his stunning bride, with his heart pounding in excitement. As soon as the carriage door opened, he rushed to her side, extending his strong arms to help her down. Carrie's heart fluttered with joy as she slid down his body, feeling the warmth of his embrace.

The moment her feet hit the solid ground, JT pulled her close, his lips finding her delicate neck with a gentle kiss. Carrie's skin tingled with pleasure, as she leaned into him, revelling in the sensation of his strong arms wrapped around her.

With his lips still caressing her skin, JT whispered words of love and devotion into her ear, his voice low and husky, sending shivers down her spine. Carrie felt as if she were in a dream, lost in the moment, as the world around them faded away, leaving only the two of them in each other's arms.

For a moment, they remained locked in each other's embrace, lost in the ecstasy of their love, until finally, with a deep sigh, they parted, their eyes still locked in a passionate gaze which was broken only by Billy's remark.

"Sheesh, you two, cain't ya wait long enough to say, "I do"? Billy asked.

"Billy, my darling, someday you'll be as deliriously happy as we are today and won't notice the world around you," Carrie said.

JT and Carrie smiled at each other as they entered the building holding hands and hurried towards the judge's office.

The wedding ceremony seemed to go by in a blur, with the two-minute ceremony feeling like a heartbeat. Despite the brief nature of the occasion, Carrie remembered every little detail from JT's gaze locked onto hers as they stood facing one other, him reaching out to touch the top of her hand with his thumb, a gesture that made her heart skip a beat. The warmth of his touch sent a shockwave through her, making her feel like she was the only person in the world who mattered.

As the words of the ceremony flowed around them, Carrie and JT exchanged vows, their voices soft and full of emotion. Then, with a swift movement, they sealed their union with a kiss, their lips meeting for the first time as husband and wife.

It felt like all she had ever been through had led to this moment, to finding her way to JT and she found herself beyond grateful for both life and God and the mysterious ways in which they both worked. JT's might and desire were evident as he pulled Carrie from the ground and wrapped her in his powerful arms. She felt weightless as if she were floating on a cloud, immersed in the warmth and security of his arms. His lips met hers with such ferocity that it stole her breath away, her heart skipping a beat with each passing second.

Relief flooded through Carrie's body like the released energy of a broken spring in an overwound clock. Fear, anger, vengeance, and heartbreak were dreadful memories relegated to yesterday. There's no room for such negative thoughts in an ecstatic heart. She prayed for this outcome for months but feared God had other plans.

After the judge appointed them husband and wife, JT said the sweetest thing. He said, "My beloved, I gave you a new identity today, Mrs. Grant. Wear it proudly."

Thank you, Lord, for showing me the light and giving me the strength to persevere.

Billy approached, "I want to be the second to kiss the bride." He kissed her cheek and wished them happiness. Bless him. He had tears in his eyes. Then Jud congratulated JT, wished them joy, and kissed Carrie's cheek.

Carrie and Tildy served as witnesses while the judge finalized JT's adoption of Billy.

"Are you happy, child?" Mother whispered in her ear.

"Mother, I can't imagine how I could be any happier. He's the air I breathe." Carrie whispered back.

"I know exactly how you feel, my darling." Mother whispered, taking Carrie's hand.

Back at the plantation, Mother would keep a sharp eye on Billy for the night. No more shenanigans when he should be in bed, and Billy offered no protestations. And the newlyweds retired after dinner.

In Carrie's moonlit bedroom, locked away from the world, JT pulled his bride into his lap and kissed her. "That scent is positively delicious. Roses?"

"At least you have years to learn to tell them apart. It's Jasmin."

While intertwined, JT turned her under him as he pushed them onto the bed. His fingers furiously removed the hairpins, causing bluebonnets to rain down. Then he palmed her skull and trailed a row of kisses from behind her ear down her shoulder. She desperately needed his skin against hers and pulled at the buttons on his shirt. He took over the handling of the shirt, and she unbuttoned her blouse, pushing the shift straps down.

"What? No corset?"

"It's Texas." She blurted out before crushing his lips again.

His hand sought out a breast.

"Wait, I have to tell you something." Carrie hovered her hand over her breast, keeping his hand at bay.

JT exhaled and asked, "It can't wait until tomorrow?"

"I think I better tell you now. Mother said I should tell you before things progress." Carrie twirled a lock of hair and bit her lip.

He slid to her side with his head propped up by his left hand. "How curious? I'm listening."

"Put your head on my shoulder. I can't say this with you staring at me." She scooted closer to him and avoided his eyes.

JT sank into the bed, laying his head closer to her breast than the shoulder.

Carrie fiddled with his wavy hair, "Um, ah, Philipp and I, we never, well, I'm still a...."

JT's head popped up, and they locked eyes. "Are you trying to tell me you're a virgin?"

Carrie blew out a cleansing breath, "Yes, yes, I am."

"Two weeks, and he never..."

"No, I thought he was giving me time to adjust, but we know the real reason now."

"I have never understood that man. What a fool!" growled JT.

"So, my dilemma is fine with you? Carrie smiled in excitement.

"Your dilemma isn't a dilemma, and it's the best gift you could have given me, baby." He paused and then asked, "Is that the whole confession?"

Carrie caressed his hairy chest and said, "I love this hairy chest. I love running my fingers through it."

"Truce is over, baby." They kissed again, but this time his hands were busy doing some exploring of his own.

As the fire built up in Carrie's body, she knew this was the beginning of a new life. Finally, she's free to love her man the way she wants. Only he can be trusted with her precious body and spirit. His chin moved roughly against a silky cheek as he moved to claim tempting lips. She parted her lips, allowing his possession of her.

Carrie deserved to be happy, have more children, and rejoice in her newfound soulmate. Two bodies intertwined, becoming one. She'd never be invisible again.

"I want to kiss you until you're dizzy, touch you all over until you're crazy with desire, and pleasure you for the rest of this night and every night for as long as I live," said JT.

Carrie shuddered as his sensuous words sank in. Trust and commitment forever together. He would never betray her. Starting at his waist, she slid hungry hands along his sides and up his back, pulling herself closer. She permitted her lusty legs to encircle his waist, pleased to demonstrate her affection and desire. Carrie's soul rejoiced at their union.

Carrie couldn't get enough of him, their lips melding —seemingly made for each other and how she fits against his body as no other man would suffice. She had never wanted anything so much in her whole life as much as she wanted this man. One hand and then the other slid up his chest to lock tight around his neck, pressing neglected breasts hard against him. A need buried deep inside flamed to the surface, and she suddenly realized how much she needed his touch.

Nuzzled against her neck, he said, "I want you, need you, and love you from this day forward." Again, her lips parted, allowing him to possess her. This time she made it free to taste him.

Carrie sighed dreamily, "Nothing in this world could be more right," she said, rubbing a curious calf along his lower back. She existed before this night, but now her existence has transcended. Her curse has been vanquished.

Carrie had endured a long, bumpy road, but the good Lord kept her on the right path. Hallelujah!

<u>Matthew 19:6</u> *"So then, they are no longer two but one flesh. Therefore, what God has joined together, let not man separate."*

December 20, 1860, San Francisco At Last

San Francisco at last! Carrie's brood gathered on the deck while the steamboat docked. The crew struggled to rig the gangway. The sun made the mid-fifty's temperature bearable with only a shawl. Happy to be at the end of their trip, she took a moment to familiarize herself. San Francisco has to be five times the size of Columbus, with busy streets and a huge port. Yet, it was infinitely more welcoming because no one here knew her.

A boy ran up the gangway shouting, "Message for Miss Carrie Wagner, please." JT was nearer to him, took the note, and tipped the boy.

Walking to Carrie's side, he handed it to her, "So much for your anonymity, my sweet. Who do you know in San Francisco?"

"No one. I'm shocked." She turned the envelope over and tore it open. Then, pulling out the note, she said, "It's from Ruth."

At least three people asked, "What does she say?"

"Ruth's here in San Francisco with the children and gives us an address. We are to come immediately. Why is she here? Oh dear, what went wrong?" Carrie's heart raced as she imagined a dozen disasters that could have happened to them. Was Ruth ostracized from California because of the two white children? What if no one granted her a loan? Oh no, she could have run out of money. Or something disastrous could have happened on the Oregon Trail. They must hurry.

JT lost no time getting them to the specified address. He helped Carrie down from the wagon and knocked on the door of the dwelling.

Ruth opened the door while holding Michelle. Her eyes disregarded JT as she said, "Carrie, oh my God, Carrie, you're here!" Carrie slid past JT to jump into Ruth's embrace, wrapping her arms around Ruth and Michelle.

"Ruth, I've missed you and am so happy to see your cheerful face again." Carrie rained kisses on Ruth's cheek and Michelle's head. "How did you know we would arrive today?"

"I didn't. I paid a boy to greet all the U.S. Mail steamboats. With instructions, to give you my letter. And it worked." Ruth said.

Curious, Carla rushed to the door and wrapped herself around Carrie's legs. Almost a year later, the children still recognized her.

"Mommy, you're late," Carla said.

Michelle's tears fell. "Why are you so late?"

The tone of Michelle's voice accused Carrie of not caring. Carrie took Michelle from Ruth's arms, "Because I found more people for our family to love. That's how much love I have. Enough for you and everyone else. You will grow to love them, too."

"Carrie, are all these people with you? Step aside and let them in. I don't want the children to get sick. It's near freezing outside." The Headmistress at the orphanage constantly harped on everyone to keep the door closed because the children could catch their death. Ruth had listened.

Carrie shuffled next to Ruth. Everyone surged forward in her wake. "These people are new family members, Ruth. This is JT, my husband."

Ruth shook his hand as suspicion crept into her voice. "A husband? I thought you swore off marrying again?"

"Glad to finally meet you, Ruth," JT said, smiling.

Carrie wrapped an arm around Ruth's waist and beamed with happiness, "I did, but I found the kind of love that binds two hearts together forever, and I trust him." She left it at that since there was more family to introduce.

"I want to introduce you to my mother, Matilda Ackermann. JT found Mother for me. Can you believe it?"

"Your mother?" Ruth's tears fell. Tildy held out welcoming arms, and Ruth walked into them. "I'm mighty glad to meet you. Carrie prayed every night to find her family again."

"I'm aware and felt awful about it. But we talked it out, forgave each other, and put it in the past. God has blessed me again. I have two daughters now, Carrie and you." Mother, beaming ear to ear, embraced Ruth again.

Carrie continued with the introductions, "And this ranch hand over here is JT's little brother, Jud."

Ruth left Tildy's arms to greet Jud. "Mighty glad to meet you, Jud."

They shook hands. "Honored, Ruth. We've heard so much about you. I'm surprised you don't have wings."

The group laughed at Jud's comment. But Carrie's reply drew even more hilarity, "You mean you can't see them? They're obvious to me."

"And this is my third adopted child, Billy." Carrie motioned for him to come forward to meet Ruth.

"What a fine strapping lad you are. Welcome to our family. Welcome everyone to our family." Carrie could have kissed Ruth for not physically reacting in horror nor voicing any concern about Billy's face.

Carrie introduced Billy to Michelle and Carla as their new big brother. Carrie and Billy led the two little girls to the settee. Carla held on to the sleeve of Carrie's blouse. Michelle moved to sit in Billy's lap. Billy tousled her hair, and Michelle smiled. Then, the girls asked about what happened to Billy's face. He launched into a tale of piracy on the open sea, captivating them instantly.

The mother hen in Ruth took over. "Now everyone can put their coats, shawls, or whatever and lay them across the bed in that room over there." Ruth pointed, and everyone trotted off in that direction except Carrie.

Carrie heard one of the drivers ask, "Can we unload the baggage now, ma'am?"

Ruth responded. "Yes, of course, There's a room at the top of the stairs. Please put it all in there, and we can sort it out later. Thanks." She retreated but rebounded to add, "Please keep the door closed between going in and out. I have small children here, and I don't want one of them wandering off or getting sick. Thanks again."

Mother left the back room, calling, "Can I make some tea or hot chocolate?"

"Ruth darling, Mother is addicted to tea."

"It'll be my pleasure to make tea for you, Mrs. Ackermann. We are out of chocolate."

"Don't be silly. I know how to make tea. You come over here and catch up with Carrie. I'll be in with the tea tray momentarily. And don't call me Mrs. Ackermann. It's Mother to you and Carrie. You probably saved my daughter's life more than once, and I was serious about having two daughters now." Mother retreated into the kitchen.

"Thank you, Mother."

"Thank you, Mrs. Mother." Ruth giggled.

Carrie noticed the house had only rudimentary furniture and nothing, but wooden chairs hung on the walls. The raw wooden planks that built the house still had that fresh milled scent. And Ruth looked haggard and thinner than before. Carrie was not the only one who had suffered a dangerous journey; Ruth did it without another adult to consult. They almost arrived here too late. Carrie felt guilty because she never needed to stay for Philipp's hanging. He wasn't worth one minute of her concern. While she lives, Ruth will never know hunger or strife again.

JT and Jud entered the room and found chairs to accommodate two Texicans next to the fireplace.

Ruth turned to JT and asked, "How did you get the mountain to come to you and get married? I'm dying to know."

"Whatever do you mean? My wife took one look at me and forgot all about widowhood." JT said.

Even Carrie laughed. "As my memory serves, husband dear, you fell right into my trap." Maybe her lie trumped his. Landing JT was like breaking a loco mustang while balancing a book on her head. Darn, near impossible, but worth the fight. For a long while, she thought teaching the mustang to read would have been easier. "Ruth, tell us why you're here in San Francisco."

Ruth sighed and dropped her eyes to the floor. "The truth is I ran out of money, plain and simple. We didn't have a budget for costs along the trail. Therefore, we didn't have enough money to buy land and begin building. And we couldn't winter in Oregon without a house. So, we drove the wagon here and rented a house for the winter." Ruth stopped burying her face in Carrie's shoulder, "But I didn't know you would show up with a whole new family."

Carrie, worried about Ruth, noticed her pallor for the first time. She hugged Ruth close around the waist and found her downright skinny. Ruth's experience traveling cross country with two children has taken a mental and physical toll, and Carrie means to set that right. She felt Ruth go limp, and Carrie slid to the floor to lessen the impact.

JT gently lifted Ruth into his arms. "Where should I take her?"

Jud helped Carrie up off the floor.

Carrie pointed, "Into the bedroom with all the coats. Then she addressed Billy. "Please move all the coats to a chair so JT can get Ruth into bed."

Mother placed a palm on Ruth's forehead, "She's got a fever. I'll pull down the bed covers for you, JT." Mother rushed next to JT's side as he carried her to bed. Calling over her shoulder to Carrie, she asked, "Carrie, darling, I set water to boil. Could you finish setting up tea?"

In the kitchen, Carrie started on the left side of the kitchen and opened all the cabinet doors looking for something to cook for dinner. The cupboard stood empty except for crackers, canned sardines, canned peaches, and a large unopened bag of oatmeal. So, for tonight we have oatmeal with peaches. We'll shop tomorrow.

Billy walked in with his new siblings, following close behind. "Can I do something to help?"

"Yes, thank you. Please finish making this cup of tea for Ruth. I want to check on her. "Do you think you can start a pot of oats for dinner? Enough for all of us. The bag is right there." She pointed toward it.

"Sure thing, go."

Carried was delighted to find Ruth awake but not thrilled that she struggled with JT to rise out of bed. She sat on the bedside and corralled both of Ruth's hands. Ruth, my love, you're exhausted. Don't argue with me. You don't have to worry about anything again. We're all here now to relieve you of the stress.

Tears rolled down Ruth's face, "I don't blame you for being angry with me. I'm sorry I ran out of money. We didn't consider that one of the oxen would die or that--"

"Shhhh, I'm not angry, and there are no more money problems. My husband and mother are wealthy, and Jud has a nest egg. I have a couple of hundred dollars left myself. So don't worry about money. Are you listening to me?" She rubbed her hand up and down Ruth's arm consoling her. Ruth's hands and arms felt cold despite the fever.

Not entirely convinced, Ruth next said, "And there's nothing in the house for everyone to eat."

"Billy's in the kitchen. He's starting a big pot of oatmeal, and we can have some peaches. We'll shop tomorrow. Stop worrying. You've done a great job, my dear. Now we need to get you healthy again."

"JT, we need a doctor for Ruth. Mother says she has a fever. And she's lost a lot of weight and doesn't look like her old self. She needs pampering.

Jud spoke up, "I'll fetch the doctor. JT, you stay here. I'll be back as soon as I can."

Carrie blessed him.

JT inserted, "Don't worry about anything anymore, Ruth. You've done an excellent job getting this far with the children in tow. We have the money to buy land and build a house whenever ready."

Ruth sighed, "Bless you. I need a rest from decision-making and worrying, which has worn me plumb down to a stick. But I saw some beautiful land between here and the Oregon border,"

Billy walked in, balancing the cup of tea. He handed it to Carrie.

Carrie smiled at him, 'Thank you, son." Then, she placed the cup and saucer on the bedside table and began fluffing the pillows and stuffing them behind Ruth so she could sip tea.

Mother followed Billy back to the kitchen.

Carrie lifted the teacup to Ruth's lips. "What's the story with this house?" Carrie asked.

"Oh, that's so good. I'm renting it, and rent money runs out in January."

JT begged, "Carrie, sweetheart, would you please tell Ruth to quit worrying? Everything is covered."

"JT's right, Ruth. They all, including Mother, sold their ranch shares to their remaining brother and moved on with me, and JT brought in a murderer worth $5000. He's a retired Pinkerton man. What do you think, JT? Should we stay here for the winter and look for our place in the spring?"

JT worried his chin stubble, "I like half of your idea, dear. How about we stay for the winter? But in the meantime, I go find our homestead and purchase it before spring. And Ruth, I'll also check out the land between here and Oregon. That way, all of us can relax knowing we own our land. What do you all think?"

"Oh, no, Mr. Grant, you buy whatever you think is suitable for this family. Don't pay me no mind."

"See, Ruth. I told you he was a keeper."

"Yes, of course, but I don't think this place is big enough for all of us to winter over here."

"No problem," JT said, "We'll rent an additional house if we have to."

Ruth looked slightly perplexed, "Carrie, can we talk alone?"

"Yes." Everyone except Carrie quietly left the room.

Once behind the closed bedroom door, Ruth asked, "Carrie, I realize all those people are your family, but how do they feel about darkies? I need to be safe, and none of them wants to sell me south or kill me." Ruth clutched the neckline of her dress tightly and stared at Carrie with big round eyes.

Like they used to, they laid their heads on each other's shoulders and hugged snuggly. "Oh, what was I thinking? Of course, you're frightened. I can assure you none of them want to harm you," Carrie thought of a way to intrigue Ruth, "But the new family members have a story to tell you about how they decided to come with me that will take away all your fears. I wouldn't have brought them with me if I thought they would harm a hair on your head."

"What's the story?"

"How about we invite them back in, have tea, and become one family? After hearing them out, if you're still not convinced, I'll listen to your concerns."

"If I'm still scared, you'll tell them to go?"

To Carrie, she sounded on the verge of hysterics. "Hopefully, it won't come to that, but I promise to do anything to keep you safe." Carrie smiled and patted Ruth's shoulder. "You're safe; I'm here now."

Ruth sunk back into the pillows as relief flowed over her. Carrie saw the muscles in her face relax.

"All right, Carrie, I'd like you to stay next to me while I hear this story if you don't mind."

"Anything for you, my friend." Carrie opened the bedroom door and invited the entire family to come in.

As they gathered, bringing a bench, Carrie said, "All right, my Texas family. I need you to tell Ruth your story about your decision to come with me to California. Ruth is overwhelmed with so many new people in the family. How do I put this delicately? Put yourself in Ruth's shoes. She needs to trust you all not to harm her in any way. I think your stories will calm her."

Mother suggested JT should start the story because it all begins with a murderer he was tracking down."

"And a broken-hearted woman ladened with anger, hate, and betrayals," Carrie added for humor.

Mother harumphed, not finding it funny, "Honestly, Carrie, this is our story, not yours. You can cry in your soup some other day." Ruth giggled.

Mother was right, even though they disagreed at times. Everything isn't about Carrie all the time. Mothers soon prevail. It's not because she wants to nitpick you every hour of the day. She's the only person in the world who loves you no matter what you do. It's her job. And Carrie needs to learn how to be more like her mother. Carrie's children would grow up to be better citizens, with Tildy as their grandmother—no more misplaced children. Once was enough. And what if Mother hadn't left five-year-old Carrie at that orphanage sixteen years ago? She would have never met Ruth, JT, or Billy. The thought sent shivers down her spine. Never question the road God has set for you.

JT said, "Actually, Ruth, it begins with you and the years you spent teaching English to Carrie. She developed a habit of reading any newspaper she could put her hands on, and wouldn't you know it, war is coming."

JT's audience was soon entranced by his story, their hungry ears hanging on his every word. He was perfect at everything he did, his voice carrying the rhythm of the tale with effortless grace. As the story unfolded, Carrie watched in awe as the expressions on his handsome face changed, each emotion bringing the characters to life in a vivid and captivating way.

As she listened, her heart swelled with love and admiration for her husband, who was not only a gifted storyteller but also the perfect father for their future children. And now, she suspected that another child might be on the way, as she had been feeling nauseous lately whenever cooking food. She decided to keep the news to herself for the time being, allowing everyone to get settled and used to each other.

It had only been four weeks since they were married, but Carrie knew that JT was the one she had been waiting for all her life. She thought back to the words of the Headmistress, who had preached to the girls at the orphanage years ago, reminding them that it only takes once. And now, as she looked at her husband, she knew that those words had been prophetic.

This time last year, Carrie could not have imagined that she would be experiencing such glorious happiness. It was as if fate had finally smiled upon her, bringing her the one person who would love her unconditionally and share her dreams and desires. And as she watched JT, lost in his storytelling, she knew that their love was strong enough to withstand any obstacle that may come their way. For in each other's arms, they had found a love that was pure, true, and everlasting.

She finally had the family she had dreamed of: her husband, mother, children, and Ruth.

She was complete.

My life is blessed, and I thank God every day.

<u>1 Corinthians 15:57</u> *But, thanks be to God who gives us the victory through our Lord Jesus Christ.*

Made in the USA
Las Vegas, NV
19 January 2024